The critics love Liz Ryan

LIZ RYAN

One More Chance

CORONET BOOKS
Hodder & Stoughton

Copyright © 2003 by Liz Ryan

First published in Great Britain in 2003 by Hodder and Stoughton
A division of Hodder Headline
This paperback edition first published in 2004 by Hodder and Stoughton
A Coronet paperback

The right of Liz Ryan to be identified as the Author
of the Work has been asserted by her in accordance with the
Copyright, Designs and Patents Act 1988.

1 3 5 7 9 10 8 6 4 2

A CIP catalogue record for this title is available from the British Library

ISBN 0 340 82921 4

Typeset in Plantin Light by
Phoenix Typesetting, Auldgirth, Dumfriesshire

Printed and bound in Great Britain by
Mackays of Chatham Ltd, Chatham, Kent

Hodder & Stoughton
A division of Hodder Headline
338 Euston Road
London NW1 3BH

ACKNOWLEDGEMENTS

Very special thanks to Mary Davin-Power, who made it fun in the sun when it might have been a gun in the sun! Mille mercis to Rita Degrave for all the Barry's tea and G & T, to Sheila Desamais for those deep-breath days out, to Sharon Plunkett for that voice of sweet reason, and to Philip Nolan for not killing me when he had the chance.

Vous êtes formidables mes braves et je vous embrasse très fort.

I

There are days in all our lives we wish we could undo. Days destined to change the shape of everything, in ways we fear will annihilate all we love, all we value, all that makes us who we are.

Shona Fitzpatrick's day was Friday, November 16, 2001. After a long lunch, her boss returned to the tourism office, spent half an hour in it and then, sauntering over to her, affably asked her to work late.

On Monday, her life would be lying in fragments at her feet, like a heap of building bricks knocked over by a careless child. But she didn't know that yet. Even if she had known, she'd still have done what she did.

Pleasantly – because Terry O'Hagan wielded power – she nodded up at him from her desk, his hand resting paternally on her shoulder as he stood over her – or was it his paw? Terry O'Hagan was a large creature, tall, bearded and big-boned with shaggy fair hair and curiously sharp teeth; when she thought of him she always visualised a bespectacled, yellowing old polar bear.

'Sure' she ageed evenly, 'what's the story?'

'Hotel grants' he replied, 'while the meeting on Monday is about grading criteria, the budget issue is bound to come up. You're not busy or anything this evening, are you?'

Of course you're not, his tone conveyed, a thirty-six-year-old worker bee like you couldn't have anything more important than your career to think about. And you do want that promotion, don't you? Let's not play footsie here, Shona, you're after my job and I know it. Well then, go get it. If you can. I've got the upper hand, because I'm the one who recommends you for it. Or not.

'Actually' she smiled, not letting him bait her, 'I'm meeting Brendan for dinner tonight. But I'll call him and let him know you need me until – what? – let's say eight?'

'Let's say nine' he countered as she knew he would, which was why she hadn't said nine herself, in which case it would have been ten. 'You don't mind, do you?'

Mind? Oh, no, why should I mind? Another late date, another evening ruined, our table gone, Brendan giving me grief again – why would I mind?

I hate you, Terry O'Hagan. Everyone in this office absolutely loathes you with seething passion, and I personally would like to club you senseless with some prehistoric implement, you shambling, sexist old dinosaur.

'Ah, anything for you, Terry. I know the grants report is a bit behind.'

He frowned briefly but sharply at her, reading her meaning: *you've got* behind with it, haven't you? Innocently, she spooled him out another smile. He loved women staff to smile at him, the more playfully the better. Everyone reckoned his marriage was in tatters.

'Good, then I'll leave you to get on with what you're doing now, and see you later.'

Hoisting his tweed jacket off its peg, he slung it over his shoulder, and she glanced at her watch: four thirty. Terry O'Hagan always went to the pub at four thirty on Friday evenings, where he knocked back six or seven pints before returning to the office around seven to collect his briefcase, which would undoubtedly be stolen if he took it with him to

2

the rowdy, crowded pub. How he could embark on pints now, after a lunch which had certainly encompassed claret and probably brandy as well, was beyond her, but that wasn't her problem.

For the moment, her only concern was to get through this grading report and make sure Mrs O'Brien's B & B out in Connemara got into next year's *Charming Country Houses* guide.

Poor, valiant old Emily O'Brien! She'd run her Georgian mansion as a B & B for over thirty years, gamely slogging on even after her husband fell off his ladder while shearing some ivy that had got entangled in the gutters. Fell off and, as she put it, 'went and died'. It was now seven months since Séan had gone and died, and Shona was determined that, come January, Emily's rambly old mansion would have its coveted listing in the new edition of *Charming Country Houses*. American tourists, in particular, toted their copies like bibles, quoting 'log fires' and 'home-made porridge' and 'rose gardens' as if from the gospel. Emily's house had all that stuff, but – more importantly – it had Emily herself, a sixty-year-old bundle of genuine Galway charm.

First, though, better call Brendan. Picking up her mobile, tucking her hair behind her ear, Shona dialled his number, which rang twice. 'Bren? Hi, Shona here—'

'Let me guess.' Even now when it didn't sound quite so flip as usual – why? – his Aussie accent did what it always did to her, something tingly, sensual. She could see him raking back his rusty-red fringe, flicking his eyes over his watch. 'Old Slobberchops wants you to work late again? Ring the restaurant, tell them to try and hold our—?'

She groaned. 'Oh, God, Bren, I'm sorry. I really am.'

'Yeah. I know. You always are.' Untypically, his tone was flat as a tomb.

'It's only an hour . . . I'll go straight from the office and be there by nine fifteen.'

'Right. Or nine thirty. Ten at the latest.' Did he actually sound a little bitter?

'No! I said nine fifteen and I mean it! Come on, don't start me on a guilt trip. I have to humour Terry until I get moved into hotels, you know I've had nine years of B & Bs and there are only so many cooked Oirish breakfasts a girl can eat.'

She was relieved when he laughed reluctantly, 'Oh . . . okay. I'll see if they'll keep the table. But Jaysus, Shona, I've had it with this stuff. I really have. And then when you get your ruddy promotion it'll be dinners, won't it, pub crawls with Italian delegations and Bunratty banquets with Herr Honcho from Hamburg, champagne with François from France, anything and everything to get their tourists into your hotels . . . when am I ever going to get a look-in? Huh?'

Fair question, Bren. Fair question, and I can't blame you for asking it.

'Tonight! Later! I promise!' Resolutely, she injected a girly laugh into her voice. Girly and, she hoped, alluring. Brendan was a good guy and she was getting very fond him . . . plus, he'd lasted way longer than any of the others. Nearly a year, now. She'd begun to feel they might actually be getting some-where, had the sensation of an angler on a riverbank, playing a golden, gleaming salmon. With just a little more patience, she was sure she could land him.

'All right. See you later – not a minute later than nine fifteen.'

'Yessir.' Grateful for his tolerance – it was the third time in five weeks – she hung up and went back to her paperwork. She wouldn't have time, now, to go home to change into the red dress he particularly liked, but she knew he wouldn't mind that. God bless Brendan Wright; blast and bugger Terry O'Hagan.

Everyone else had long gone home, it was well dark and Shona was alone in the office when, shortly after seven, Terry returned from the pub. Not that his shambling steps deceived her when she heard them in the lobby; he wasn't head of the hotel division for nothing, his genial mode could switch to sharp-as-tacks when need arose. As her friend Crys had more than once remarked, he was a guy who 'wanted watching', even in his fatherly fifties.

Oh, God! Just occasionally, Shona wondered how on earth she kept on smiling at everybody in this business. Smiling non-stop, even on rainy winter nights like this one, even when you were shattered after an eleven-hour day of phone calls from Kimberly in Kansas wanting to know whether Mrs Murphy's B & B had *really* once accommodated James Joyce – oh, *wow!* – of documents from Dublin containing news of yet more budget cuts, of journalists enquiring whether the food-poisoning rumour was for real . . . but that was the tourism industry for you. Even when she hated it, she loved it: how could you not, with so many weird and wonderful people parading through it?

But it certainly was hard work. Although she was only in charge of the welfare, promotion and supervision of two hundred B & Bs in one small westerly chunk of small westerly Ireland, Shona sometimes felt responsible for the entire country, entire planet, entire galaxy. 'Hello, you must be the aliens, welcome to Shannon airport, here's your coach, we'll be stopping off for Irish coffees at Durty Nelly's en route . . . here are your press packs . . . oh, Jim's luggage is missing, oh dear, well let me just see what I can do to *fix* that . . .' Smile, smile, smile. And now, one for old Slobberchops as well, because she wanted to manage hotel marketing, forsake poor old Emily O'Brien for more money, more status, more perks?

But I'm thirty-six, she reminded herself briskly. I can't wet-nurse the old dears in their country cottages for ever. If I don't get promoted – soon –I'll be an old dear myself, plumping up my cushions, flopping down on the butt that never did get itself in gear. In top gear: Shona Fitzpatrick, Head of Hotels Divison, see, it says here on my embossed card, let me give you one! Much as I love my dear ladies, tourism is showbiz, sooner or later you want top billing. I do, anyway. A company car and an expense account, a detached house on a full acre, three foreign holidays a year when *someone else will have to smile at me*. Okay, Terry, you got that? I want my promotion and I want it bad, that's why I am about to be sweet and kind to you when I could cheerfully embed a hatchet in your head.

Swivelling on her chair, she beamed at him, smelling the alcohol fumes as they wafted across to her. 'Hi. Hope the hospitality went well?'

That was what they always called his absences in the pub: 'hospitality', the pretence that he'd been entertaining some crucial 'clients' or 'contacts' who might direct seventy zillion tourists his way if he poured enough Guinness into them. Curtly, he nodded, but didn't answer as he removed his jacket and loosened his tie. Watching him, Shona swiftly divined the reason for his silence: with half a dozen pints under his belt, on top of whatever he'd had at lunch, he was literally too drunk to speak.

Good. He wouldn't be able to do much work, so, on the hotel budgets, she could get away and meet Brendan earlier after all. Still smiling, she faced him with perky enthusiasm.

'Right then, let's get started then, shall we? I have the file ready right here.'

She indicated it on the computer, and he frowned at her, as if trying to recollect who she was and why they were both here at this hour on a wet November night. And then, suddenly, he lurched back to the door without the remotest warning or reason, shut it and clicked down the snip on the lock.

Ping! That tiny sound had her on her feet immediately, every nerve in her body and every wit in her head abruptly bristling with anticipation, intuition, the utter certainty that Terry O'Hagan was about to do something nasty, dangerous or possibly even lethal. Languidly, her friend Crys's voice rose from the sofa where she'd first said it while idly polishing her nails: 'That fella wants watching, Shona. Just wants watching, is all.'

Oh Christ, not now, not with the entire building empty and Dave, the security man, gone home! Clenching her fists, distantly noting that they were sweaty, she forced herself to face the drunken, ominously belligerent-looking bear in front of her, his beard damp with raindrops.

'Terry? What's the matter? Why are you locking the door?'

'Am . . .' he mumbled. 'Am . . . ambitious little bitch, aren't you, Shona Fitzpatrick?'

Only he couldn't enunciate it clearly; what she heard was 'ambish' little bish, aren'tch, Shona Fishparrick?' Feigning fearlessness, she stood her ground.

'What do you mean?'

His eyes narrowed as he moved closer to her, forcing her to back up against her desk. 'You know whash I mean, misshy, you want my job, don'tch? Well, maybe shome day you'll get it, but not before you pay for it. There'sh a price for everything, y'know.'

Menacingly, he leered at her, and then suddenly his hand shot out, grabbing the front of her shirt as he hauled her into his alcoholic orbit, eyeball-to-eyeball, up against his huge hefty body.

She didn't even think. There wasn't time. Instead she yanked back her arm, steadied it and propelled it forward, hitting him such a resounding wallop across the face that he yelped, reeled backwards up against the wall with a slam. Then, in slow motion, he slid down it like a hurled ice-cream, melting into a messy puddle on the floor.

Grabbing her coat and briefcase, she unlocked the door and ran, resisting the temptation to kick his ribs for good measure as she went.

She hadn't driven much more than a mile when her pulse began to slow, her breathing come down from its Olympic high. After all, nothing had actually *happened*, Terry had not got to do whatever it was he'd had in mind. It wasn't the first time he'd come on to her – twice on 'familiarisation' trips abroad, he'd followed her down hotel corridors to her room, which she'd had to hastily lock – and although she was shaken she was physically intact.

The damage, it horrifically began to dawn on her, was not to her at all; it was to him. His king-size ego would be badly dented, when he examined it tomorrow morning in the cold light of sobriety. And he was, notoriously, a man who knew how to hold a grudge. He would make her pay for his attempted misdeed, twist it to look as if she were the one who'd assaulted him.

Well, she had hit him. But what choice did you have, with a six-foot drunken lech? Experience had taught virtually every woman in the office that there was no point in trying to reason with him, all you could do was save your skin, fast, and leg it out of his space. The only one who thought otherwise was Brendan, who when he'd heard about the chase down the Edinburgh hotel corridor had had to be restrained from tackling Terry 'in a way he'd remember, permanently'. For precisely that reason, Shona began to decide against telling Bren what had happened tonight. This time, she reckoned, he wouldn't listen to any amount of reason; he'd stalk into the office first thing on Monday, seize Terry and lay him out cold. Which would definitely be the end of her promotion hopes, if they weren't toasted already.

Were they? Could it actually be that, because of this alcoholic old oaf, she was doomed to babysit her B & B ladies for the rest of her life, never get an inch beyond where she was now? Until she was forty, fifty, for ever and ever, amen? Oh, sweet *God*! Rage and frustration, coupled with residual fright, made her swerve sharply into a parking space outside the restaurant where she was to meet Bren, whereupon she remembered that he wouldn't be here yet; instead of being late she was an hour early. Cutting the engine, she pulled her mobile from her bag and called him again.

'Bren?' She could hear her own breathlessness. 'I – something's happened – I mean, changed – I got away early after all, I'm here at Kyver's and I – I'm just dying to see you . . .'

She actually was. Without telling him why, she wanted him with her here and now, scooping her up into a hug, putting everything right in that cheery, comforting way of his, grinning as he pushed her nose with his forefinger and told her what 'an ace sheila' she was.

But his voice, when it came after a short silence, didn't sound cheery at all. It sounded irritated and exasperated. 'You're at Kyver's? Now? But you said nine fifteen, so I've dropped in to visit Dad, we're here having a chat and a coffee – for God's sake, Shona, I've only just got here, I can't up and leave right away!'

Oh. No. Of course not. Drawing a deep breath, she forced herself to see his point. His dad was a widower who worshipped his son, the only one not in Australia, and he was perfectly entitled to enjoy Bren's visit without interruption. As Bren was equally entitled to enjoy it. She couldn't expect him to keep changing his plans every hour on the hour, to suit her volatile requirements.

'Oh. Sorry. I didn't realise. It doesn't matter. I'll go in and wait for you in the bar, read the newspaper. Take your time and say hi to your dad for me.'

'Right.' He sounded calmer, but she sensed she'd made a tactical error. He'd rush things now with his poor father, abandon him earlier than planned and arrive here out of breath and out of sorts. She wished she hadn't called him at all.

'See you later, then.'

They hung up, and she sat bleakly in the car, feeling the evening changing in tone, in mood, in everything a night out with your lovely, adorable boyfriend was supposed to be.

Shona had read all of the news pages and was into features before she registered Brendan's car swinging into a space outside the restaurant, and smiled as she glanced at her watch: nine fifteen. Neither punishing her by being late nor indulging her by arriving early, he was being his inimitable rugby-playing self; fair. 'Fair do's, mate' was one of his habitual expressions, one of the traits that drew her to him. In an often unfair world, he was rock-reliable, and for this as well as much else she was slowly, oh so sweetly, falling in love with him. She'd fallen *for* him immediately they'd met, last Easter over porcelain teacups at Emily O'Brien's house, of all the ridiculous settings, where his arrival had caused her cup to clatter audibly in its saucer. Introducing him, Emily had beamed.

'My artificial insemination advisor' she announced glee-fully, and Shona had gaped at the grinning little sixty-year-old. 'Your *what*?!?'

But that, it turned out, was exactly what Brendan was. Trained in Australia as some kind of cattle cross-breeding expert (the technicalities were more than she cared to explore) he'd packed up his widowed father five years before and swept them both back to Ireland, 'the land of our ancestors' as he explained with a grin, where now he worked for the Department of Agriculture. On this particular day, he'd been visiting the prize bull with which Emily supplemented her income, and been invited to partake of tea afterwards along with Shona, clutching her clipboard on her annual B & B inspection visit. After forty-five minutes of Barry's tea and Mr Kipling's 'exceedingly good cakes', he'd asked her out on a date, within full earshot of the delighted Emily. Sometimes Shona wondered whether Emily had hatched the whole thing, and was very grateful to her if she had. After eight months with Bren, she sometimes still couldn't believe she'd found an eligible man of her own age – not just eligible, but fun, articulate, interesting and chunkily attractive into the bargain. Although they still didn't live together, because that was the one point on which Brendan was curiously old-fashioned, she felt now that their relationship was gradually reaching some kind of pivotal stage, one that was causing her to lose an increasing amount of sleep.

Am I, she wondered now as she looked at him walking towards her, ready for this man? Really ready, on every count? Could I make a commitment to him, if he asked me? If he wanted permanence, and children, a home and all that goes with it? Could I tailor my life around him, cut down on my workload, on my travels, my time with Crys and the girls, adjust my life to give him the priority he'd be entitled to expect?

Could I, if the chips were down? Am I ready?

At thirty-six, I certainly should be. But if I am, what about my promotion? What about that extra income and company car and three holidays a year . . . would they be compatible with marriage, kids, running a home? Everyone says marriage is all about compromise, and everyone also says I'm not the compromising kind . . . yet sometimes I think I'd do anything for Brendan Wright. Anything at all, because I adore him and, at this precise moment, am devoutly glad to see him. He's everything the likes of that lout Terry O'Hagan never was and never will be. He is that rarity, a good man.

'Hi, sweetie.' She raised her cheek to meet his lips as he swept up and kissed her, his vivid green eyes surveying her in their candid way. 'Bit hassled, are we?'

'Oh . . .' She thought she'd done a good job in the ladies with lipstick and hairbrush. Evidently she hadn't. Or else he was even more closely attuned to her than she thought. 'I'm fine. They have our table ready for us . . . are you hungry?'

He usually was, because he spent so much time out on farms, had a rugby-player's build and been brought up, as he said, 'on a red-blooded Oz diet' by his father, Fred. His mother, Amy, had died when he was twelve, leaving Fred to raise three small sons alone, of which Brendan was the eldest. It was surely this, Shona speculated, that had formed Bren's firm views on what he called 'the value of family life'. Not that she disagreed with 'family life', she simply didn't know how to go about such a project, when there was so much else to be done. She loved her career, she'd invested heavily in it and it mattered fundamentally to her. Just as fundamentally as any man's mattered to him. How did you fit it all *in*, these days? Germaine Greer had created a monster.

'Yeah. Ish.' He smiled a shade ruefully, she thought, as she handed him a menu, but only had time to briefly scan it before a waiter arrived to take them to their table. It was a nice round one in a corner, with a white linen cloth and a vase of pale yellow flowers, near Lee the pianist who was playing something by Carly Simon. Usually Bren winked at Lee when they arrived, whereupon Lee segued into one of Shona's favourite songs, 'Blue Bayou' or 'Summer Breeze' or 'Smoke Gets in

Your Eyes'; but tonight he seemed vaguely distracted. Shona felt Lee noting the omission, and smiled a little awkwardly.

A waiter appeared, flourishing pad and pen. Shona ordered prawn mousse and brill, Bren settled on some kind of piquant tomato followed by rare steak, and the waiter recommended a light Beaujolais as a compromise between their diverse tastes.

Compromise. See, Shona told herself, it's easy. I'd prefer a Chablis but for Bren's sake I'm perfectly happy to share a Beaujolais.

She realised he was looking at her, his chin propped on his knuckles, his expression speculative. God, she loved those freckles of his, that wayward fringe, that permanently hovering smile! Feeling Terry O'Hagan melt away, she reached across the table to him with her mind and heart.

'How's your Dad? How was your day?'

Over the first part of their meal he told her about Fred, who was fired up about his recent discovery that you could play chess on the internet, and about his day, which had involved a lot of laboratory work. Shona smiled: Bren preferred the field-work side of his job, but had to juggle both.

'Well, it was pouring all day, you were better off indoors!'

'M'mm. I guess so. How was your day? I couldn't make out what was going on.'

She hesitated. 'I could hardly make it out myself. Terry wanted me to work late. But then he – we – had a bit of a – disagreement. I think I – I may have blown a hole in my pro-motion prospects.'

He frowned into his empty plate. 'Is that why you're looking so hassled? Terry chasing you down corridors again? If he is, Shona, then I've had enough. I'm going to sort him out for you. It's time a stop was put to all this.'

She loved him for saying that. But devoutly did not want

13

him to do it. She could fight her own battles . . . and besides, Terry O'Hagan had already been hit a resounding wallop. The last thing she needed was her boyfriend marching in like a Victorian father to 'sort him out'.

'No – it was just a disagreement about something.'

'About what?'

Oh, God. 'About my future. He's trying to use his power as a weapon over me, knows I won't get his job when he moves to Dublin unless he recommends me for it. That was why he asked me to work late, just because he could. I – I hate him, Bren! He's making my life a misery!'

Ooops. She'd already said too much. But, surprisingly, he didn't immediately answer. Instead he took his napkin from his lap and started screwing it into tight, weird shapes, gazing alternately at her and into the log fire burning in the wall to his left.

'I see.'

He *saw*? Nonplussed, Shona didn't know what to say next. Usually, Brendan was good at sensing things, but tonight there seemed to be some awkwardness in the air, something not falling into shape. Had he woes of his own, was that it, that he wasn't telling her about? She was relieved when, after a pause, he reached for her hand and took it, examining it slowly before kissing it, very lightly, on the fingertips.

'Shona . . . you know . . . I've got very fond of you these past few months.' As if to confirm it, he surveyed her appreciatively, his gaze taking in the face that was not unlike his own, fresh and freckled, only her eyes were heather blue and her hair was a deeper shade of copper, smooth almost down to her shoulders. Leaning forward, she tightened her hand in his, murmuring over the candle between them.

'And I of you, Bren. I feel . . .' What did she feel? Pausing to get it exactly right, she weighed her words: happy with you?

Safe? Loved? Yes. All of those things. But before she could utter any of them, he put his finger to her lips.

'Shh. I don't want you to say anything, Shona. I want you to listen.'

Oh? Blinking slightly, she sat back in her chair, wondering what he wanted to say, what was making him look so suddenly serious. It dawned on her that he looked like a man who had made some kind of decision, and her stomach somersaulted – surely – not – he wasn't going to *propose* to her, was he? Here and now, on this wet winter's night out of the blue . . . could it be . . . here it comes? Crunch, Shona!

'I'm listening, Bren.' Her voice hung like a little puff on the air, her body tensed in a collision of terror, anticipation and rapidly rising euphoria. This was one of those moments every woman remembered all her life, and already she was savouring it, sealing the flowers and fire and candle into her mind, catching Lee's eye across the piano and trying to ignore his wicked wink, trying to look demure when she wanted to—

'Well . . . I don't quite know how to put this . . . but I've been thinking . . . about us . . .'

'Yes' she murmured, 'so have I. More and more . . .'

Twisting her hand in his, he didn't appear to hear her as he shifted on his chair, looking into her eyes in that frank way of his, that aura of fairness somehow mantling his shoulders.

'And I've come to the conclusion that . . .'

Yes! Something inside her made the decision for her, her heart outstripping her mind, her every concern about the job which, at this moment, might have been on Mars. He was going to ask her to marry him, and she was going to say yes. Yes, Brendan, I love you, I am suddenly sure of it, I want to be your wife and have your children and that, now, is all that matters to me. I will compromise if need arises, as it surely will, I will give you total priority and arrange the rest of my life around—

'That we're not . . . really . . . suited, Shona.'

From somewhere above the room, or outside the restaurant, or possibly a hundred miles away, she heard Lee starting to play it, undoubtedly inspired by the visible intimacy between them: 'Smoke Gets in Your Eyes'. Never again, she knew, would she hear it without remembering the day her life detonated. The day it all blew up in her face, her career, her stillborn marriage, her lovely, lovely Bren. Her whole future, her whole being.

She knew the colour was emptying from her face, without the faintest inkling how pale she was turning. All she registered was the sudden concern in his face, the music slowing and wavering, uncertainly, before changing into something else. He was gazing at her, pouring a glass of water.

'Oh, God, Shona – I'm sorry. I am so, so sorry. I didn't mean to do it this way, I've been too brusque, a pig . . . come on, let's go outside and get you a breath of air.' As he spoke he was standing up, coming round to her side of the table, his arms around her shoulders as he lifted her to her feet. Tottering out of the room in his embrace, she heard some aside to the waiter about 'not feeling well'. The understatement of it was like a stalagmite alone in Alaska.

Outside, she collapsed onto a low wall, and he sat beside her, dismally chafing her hand until finally she turned to him, chilled to the bone, scarcely able to speak.

'Are you going to give me a reason?'

'Yes. Of course.' With a sigh, he stared bleakly across the car park. 'It's . . . it's your *drive*, Shona.'

'My what?'

'Your job. Your commitment to it. You hate your boss but you love your work, you are already married to it and I am selfishly afraid that I would always come a very poor second to it. As would any children we might have.'

Children. She'd never yearned to have them, but now it hit her that she was thirty-six. Children were not going to be an option open to her for very much longer. Brendan was taking more away with him than his love; he was taking her life, their family, children and grandchildren and . . . with absolute certainty, she knew she was about to howl as if she were a child herself, hurl herself down on the ground and scream her heart out.

'I see. Well, in that case, there's no point in prolonging this – this – is there?'

Dizzily she stood up, located her car and, gathering the remains of her dignity, made her way to it. Sitting on the wall behind her, Brendan made no attempt to dissuade her. As she got into it, she knew she would always wonder what might have happened if she had attempted to dissuade *him*, reason him round, assure him that he was, by far, the most important element in her life.

But she did not, could not, do it. He did not look like a man who wanted to be an 'element' in anybody's life.

Personally, Aileen Hegarty blamed it all on *The Irish Times*. Until it started analysing everything, the Leaving Certificate had simply been the exam everyone sat at age eighteen. Either you passed or you failed, or if you were brainy and stayed out of the pub for long enough, you got honours that whirled you off to university. But then the *Times*'s ongoing analysis of the whole thing had turned it into more than just an exam; gradually it had become every teenager's passport to life, the vital document without which every door would slam in their faces and they would turn, overnight, into social pariahs. You might as well go out stark naked, these days, as emerge without your seven-A Leaving Certificate.

Finn, her son, was now perilously close to twenty. And he

had failed his 'Leaving'. Not once, but twice. Twice was definitive, twice was officially the end. Neither she nor his father Joe knew what to do with him next, and worse, he didn't know what to do with himself. Admittedly it had been his own fault first time round, the only thing he'd studied was girls, but the second time he'd worked a bit. And still failed. Reacting as if the word 'failure' was tattooed on his forehead, Finn was now living up to what he felt society predicted for him, hanging out in pubs, playing snooker all day, wandering the streets of Ennis and Lahinch in menacing black leather studded with spikes, his skull shaved bald except for a purple coxcomb down the middle, which made him look not cool, as he thought, but somehow pathetic. Aileen felt profoundly sorry for him, even while wanting to shake him by the ears: why wouldn't he do some kind of apprenticeship in one of the options still open to him – plumbing, for God's sake, or carpentry or anything manual? After all, plumbers, carpenters, electricians and such people made fortunes nowadays, couldn't keep up with demand.

He wouldn't do it, Finn said firmly, because he'd only fail that too, wouldn't he? He was thick, he was hopeless, and that was that. Let's not discuss it any further, Ma, I'm sick of the whole thing.

Aileen thought he was deeply depressed. And that any kind of job would occupy his seethingly unhappy mind.

'What about McDonald's, then? You can't hang round the streets for the rest of your life, Finn.'

'Wanna bet?' That was all he would say, and she was at her wits' end.

But the Leaving Cert wasn't the only thing *The Irish Times* had to answer for. Its other crime was almost worse. A year or two ago, it had come up with what was undoubtedly a brilliant wheeze in its property pages, a Thursday feature called 'Take

Five'. The idea of this – in the midst of a property boom that had propelled Irish house prices sky-high – was to illustrate five houses for sale, one in Ireland and the other four abroad, usually in Spain, France, America, Italy or Greece. Overnight, the nation had become hypnotised by this, agog to see what beautiful villas could be had in Majorca or Florida for the price of a two-up-two-down in Raheen or Ringsend. And the awful thing about it was that she, Aileen, had become hypnotised like a magician's rabbit; every time she looked at one of those gorgeous foreign houses she pictured herself sitting on its balcony or patio, sunning herself over cocktails, sauntering to its pool for a swim. Her *Irish Times* had had to be put on special order at the newsagent's, because if you didn't get there by ten on Thursday mornings they were all gone. She could never get there by ten, because her B & B guests were barely finishing their breakfasts by then, poring over their maps while she explained how to get to Galway, Westport or the Cliffs of Moher. Sometimes, when she heard Finn still snoring upstairs, she longed to jump off the Cliffs of Moher.

Meanwhile, her addiction was worsening, she needed ever stronger fixes of her drug, and she had found several ways of getting them. One was a magazine called *Homes Overseas,* which in turn had driven her to ask Finn to teach her how to use his computer, because the internet contained addresses she surfed for hours, gazingly longingly into the depths of ski chalets, beach villas, country mansions, Roman townhouses, Miami apartments and Canadian log cabins. And then – oh joy, oh bliss! – Channel 4 had started a programme called *A Place in the Sun.* Multiple and devious were the ways by which she contrived to tuck herself away in front of the television at five o'clock when it screened, fascinated to see whether the featured buyers would bid for the converted water mill in Tuscany, or the old rectory in Provence, or the loft in Madrid . . . there was no question about it. She was hooked, she was a drug addict, foreign houses were her fix.

Could you, she sometimes wondered, get help for this? Could you go to a therapist and say, 'Erm, excuse me, but I seem to have a little problem, my son is a disaster and I've taken refuge in daydreaming all my waking hours about houses in foreign countries? I'm frying bacon and eggs when I want to be arranging my freshly cut, dewdropped roses in my beamed sitting room with a glass wall overlooking Lake Garda'? Probably you could. Therapists would treat anyone for anything these days, there was a bucket of money to be had out of Ireland's growing army of nutters, all convinced that theirs was the weirdest neurosis on the planet.

If only, she thought as she loaded the dishwasher on this wretched winter's evening, I could talk to Joe about it. I shouldn't need to be thinking of any therapist. But Joe . . . Joe isn't the answer, is he? Joe is part of the problem.

Not that there's anything *wrong* with him, as such. As husbands go, there's a lot worse. He doesn't gamble or womanise, he's not violent or mean or lazy. He's just . . . so . . . so damn *dull*. Reliable, and steady, and all those other things I once saw as virtues, and so predictable there are times I want to set fire to the chair under him. Off to work at eight every morning, home at six, pub four nights a week from nine to eleven, the same conversation with the same people in the same pub night after night after night . . . and he wonders why I won't go with him any more. I won't go, Joe, because I got bored *rigid* with it! I told you that, but I might as well have been talking to the wall, because you still enjoyed it, and you still do. Okay, sitting in a pub isn't a crime, but it's not exactly inspiring either, is it? Not romantic, not very flattering that you'd rather discuss Man U for the nine hundredth time with Dave Damn Doherty than – surprise! – take your wife out to dinner or the cinema or even for a walk after work. After all, I work too you know, I run this B & B, have run it year in and year out for – what? – fifteen years now. I pull my weight in this marriage, and I do my best to be an attractive wife as well. All right, maybe I could lose a pound or two, but I'm not in bad shape for forty-two, and my mind is alive, alert; we're not talking a vegetable here. I certainly read *The Irish Times* every Thursday, that's for sure! So what is the attraction of Laffy's pub, what is so wonderful about working in that hardware store that virtually the only thing you can talk about is rivets and sanders and non-drip emulsion, huh? I have had sanders up to here, and in case you haven't noticed, you're not actually married to a can of non-drip emulsion. I am a hale and hearty woman, and I am your wife!

I am going barmy. I am, aren't I? Barmy at forty-two, babbling at fifty, locked up at sixty . . . my poor goon of a son coming to spoon-feed me my mashed carrots. That's where it'll all end, with me in a paper gown laced up the back, gibbering about a two-bed duplex in Gibraltar. What's more, the end might be nearer than we think, if business doesn't pick up.

Well, I can't blame *The Irish Times* for that. I blame Osama Bin Laden. All those cancellations since September, Americans dropping out in their droves . . . and then this boom economy isn't helping, the tourists can't afford to come here the way they used to. As for the Irish themselves – well, who can blame them for wanting their holidays somewhere sunny, after last summer? Especially when it's cheaper to go to Greece or Spain than stay at home. When the politicians start banging on about our wonderful prosperity, they're certainly not talking about me, or anyone else who runs a B & B. I'll have to start putting ads all over the place, and soon, if I want any bookings this year.

Do I? No. Right now, at this minute, I don't. After fifteen years I am sick and tired of doing the same thing over and over, living with a man who says and does the same things over and over, in this same house that I've long outgrown. Funny, it seemed so perfect when we bought it! But we were poor then, youngsters who didn't care what kind of a roof we put over our heads. I'd never seen a single episode of *A Place in the Sun*, I had no idea that houses could be anything other than semi-detached boxes in straight lines with net curtains and three-piece suites. I thought number 16 Glen Heath, when we bought it, was the absolute ultimate.

Now, it's like ourselves: frayed, clapped out, badly in need of revamping. Only we won't be able to afford revamping, will we, if business is going to be down this summer? I'm going to have to get my head out of the clouds, stop reading 'Take Five' and start thinking of ways to drum up custom . . . God be with the days when Shona Fitzpatrick used to send me droves of guests, more than I had room for sometimes, we used to have to send the overflow round to Noreen Foley! But then of course Shona got promoted, taken off the front desk at the tourism office to work behind the scenes . . . she was such a nice girl, Shona, and now I scarcely ever see her. I wonder what she's up to, these days, I wonder how she is?

Crys Sheehan had never seen her friend Shona Fitzpatrick cry before. Of course she had her odd down day like anyone else, but normally she was so cheery, confident, there was something almost invincible about her as she zipped through life – something that Brendan Wright had managed, last night, to puncture. Now, Shona was spouting like a sieve, and Crys's warm heart went out to her as they sat in her kitchen, where sympathy did not restrain her from polishing her nails in flamboyant shades of cherry and gold. Like worry beads, her nails were her resort in a crisis, she could fiddle with them as she reflected on the problem.

'But Shona, you told me you weren't sure about him. I mean, you were keen and all that, but you did feel ambivalent about marriage and especially kids, what domesticity might do to your career.'

Shona embarked on another Kleenex. 'Yes, well, I needn't worry about any of that any more, need I?'

'But it's important. Just because you want to live with a man on your terms doesn't necessarily mean he'll feel the same way. It seems to me that Bren simply called your bluff, and you didn't have an ace up your sleeve. Otherwise you'd have told him he was mistaken, that your "drive" wasn't more important to you than him, or marriage, or a family. You'd have discussed the whole thing like two grown adults – instead, you just flounced off in a flurry of wounded pride.'

'I didn't! I simply – simply . . .'

Shona stalled. Crys, blast her, had a way of putting her manicured finger on things. Huh. It was all very well for her to talk, at twenty-nine years of age with a lovely husband and all the time in the world to think about having children. Not that she had any yet, after five years of marriage, but she simply didn't understand anyone who wasn't sure about having them, because she longed for them herself and adored the offspring of others. Nor did she understand the career aspect of yesterday's disaster, because the whole concept of a 'career' sailed over her head like a fighter jet. When Shona first met Crys she'd been an air hostess; in the seven years since she'd been a hotel receptionist, a dental receptionist, an opinion pollster and a boutique assistant. The minute she got bored she moved on, and had so far lasted six months as a school bus driver.

Crys didn't want to get 'bogged down', as she put it, she wanted to be flexible to fit her work around the real love of her life, an international aid agency for which she slaved voluntarily, tirelessly and enthusiastically. Shona supposed it was in her genes: her dad Dick Dooley had met her mother, Njanga Diahssu, on a Red Cross field project in Lesotho in 1970. Dick was a doctor and Njanga was a supplies co-ordinator, and the exotic fruit of their Irish-African marriage was the lovely, lively Crys, who'd weathered her childhood in an Ireland which did not, at the time, unreservedly welcome little black girls. Crys was not pure black, but she was smoky and willowy, with tight beaded braids, and she was realistic in the way you probably had to be after twelve years as the only 'darkie' in your class. Shona cherished her friendship, which was sassy, compassionate, crisp and warm as buttered toast.

She sniffled, and sighed. 'Okay. Maybe I did chicken out—'

'Yes. You did. Why?'

Languid as a sleek, leggy cat, Crys polished another nail and held it out for admiration. But Shona wasn't deceived. Crys expected a sensible reason, wrapped in a well-balanced argument.

'Because I – I don't know why, is why!'

Crys arched an eyebrow. 'I see. Then let me reiterate my previous point, which is that you are not ready for, arguably not suited to, the holy wedded state of matrimony. You want Bren but you want your career too . . . you want jam on both sides of your bread, lady.'

'Is that a crime?'

'Did I say it was?'

'No, but . . . anyway, there's no point in discussing either one, because they're *both* up in smoke.' Wretchedly, Shona began to wail again, and Crys got up to make more tea with a reflective air.

'H'mm. Well, I have to tell you up front, Shona, hitting your boss was not a smart thing to do.'

'No, I can see that, but what else was I supposed to do? He was d-drunk and if you ask me he was d-d-dangerous.'

'M'mm. And now he's probably planning to sue you for assault. As well as spending his weekend stabbing pins into your career doll. You'll be lucky not to get the sack.'

Shona gasped. 'What? But – but it was his fault, not mine! He'd have to explain why I slapped him, for a start—'

'You slapped him for having the cheek to ask you to work late. That's what he'll say. No witnesses, are there?'

Oh, no. Even as Crys said it, Shona saw it; that was exactly what Terry O'Hagan would say. Furthermore, he would probably spread lies about her all over the gossipy tourism industry, so that when she got fired for assault she wouldn't even be able to get work anywhere else. In one fell swoop, she had gone from promotion candidate to dole candidate . . . oh, sweet Jesus. This was such a nightmare it was nearly distracting her from the other nightmare, the prospect of life without Brendan, just when she'd decided she loved him to bits and was prepared to have all his blessed babies.

'I was, you know, Crys. I really was prepared to do it. I'd decided just that very minute that I would make a commitment to him and have his children.'

Wryly, Crys grinned as she poured the tea. 'Whose, Terry O'Hagan's?'

'Brendan's! God, don't give me grief!'

Putting down the teapot with innate grace, Crys reseated herself at the kitchen table which, as always, was strewn with paperwork from Save the Children, Amnesty, APSO and numerous international agencies. With slight shame, Shona was forced to concede that there were people worse off than she currently was herself. Much worse, cold comfort as it was.

'But Shona, *chérie*, marriage and motherhood are not things you *decide* to do. They're things you *want* to do.'

'I wanted to do them.'

'Did you? Are you sure? For what reason?'

'Well, the normal reasons, Crys, obviously!'

'There are many "normal" reasons for such projects, Shona. Some are vocational. Others stem from fear . . . fear of loneliness, of old age, of social insecurity. While I don't doubt your love for Brendan, and won't even mention your no less passionate love of all his predecessors, can you honestly tell me that you'd *love* to be a mother? Love to have kids, even as they were smushing strawberry jam into your Paul Costelloe suit?'

Uhhh. Instinctively, Shona recoiled, and Crys smiled. 'If you ask me, Shona – as appears to be the case – you are not exactly the world's most maternal woman. Not everybody can be, you know, it isn't a presidential edict or anything. What would be stupid would be to force it, or pretend. That would also be unfair to the kids, and probably cause friction with their father.'

Reluctantly, Shona conceded the point, albeit not aloud. Brendan was indeed the kind of man who'd expect the mother of his children to adore them, pamper and cosset them and put them at the pinnacle of her world. His avowed 'family values' were precisely that, and – and maybe there had been just a hint of panic in her decision to indulge him? He was a great guy, and she wasn't getting any younger.

'Well, I . . . oh, dammit, Crys, why do you always have to be so bloody perceptive! All right, I admit it, maybe I don't long for children the same way you do, but—'

'But then, Shona, the good Lord has saved you from a dreadful fate. Saved poor Bren, too. You'd have made each other quite miserable, eventually. You mustn't marry, you know, just because everyone else is doing it. It's neither measles nor mandatory.'

'Huh. That's all very well for you to say, with Gavin Sheehan safely under your belt—'

Crys exploded laughing. '*Under my belt?!* I must say, Shona, you have a winning way with metaphor. Gavin would be fascinated to know he's under my, uh, belt.'

Torn between anguish and reluctant laughter, Shona frowned into her mug of tea. 'Well, you know what I mean. You have a lovely husband and I'm entitled to want one too. I'm thirty-six and I don't want to be single for ever.'

'Why not? Some people are extremely happy being single. It frees them up.'

'Well, it isn't freeing me up. It's starting to – to chafe at me. I want to share my life with someone, like everyone else.'

'Yes. Naturally. You're a generous, giving person. But maybe you should consider a widower, or a divorcé, someone who already has a family and won't want another.'

'But men don't come made to measure, Crys! I was so lucky to meet Bren, and now . . . now I've lost him and you're not even being sympathetic about it.'

'I would be, if I thought you two were compatible, because I liked him. But don't fake it, Shona . . . you wanted him, I reckon, on your terms. One kid, max, if any.'

'That is not true. Totally not true. I loved him – still love him – and I am absolutely devastated that he doesn't seem to want me any more. My heart is *broken*, I tell you.'

'Uh-huh. And your heart was also broken, as I recall, by what happened with Trevor, and Colm, and Aidan . . . sorry, Sho, but your track record isn't great here, is it? The best that can be said for it is that it's consistent. You always adore your men and they always dump you and you're always devastated. There's a pattern, which in my opinion is based on their suspicion that you will never put them on the pedestal they aspire to be on, in your busy life. Men don't like being fitted in around other things, they don't like the idea that a woman's career might matter as much to her as they do – maybe, God forbid, even more. It doesn't flatter their notorious pride.'

'But lots of married women have great careers!'

'Then find yourself a man who's willing to accommodate yours. A widower, like I said, or a divorcé, or a house-husband type. If, that is, you still have a career to worry about after Monday. You'll probably just be handed your P45 and waved goodbye.'

Distraught with worry at the prospect of it, grieving deeply and genuinely over Brendan, Shona couldn't understand how she could possibly laugh at such a remark. But somehow she did, choking on her tea, eyes watering. Crys was so stoically pragmatic, never let anyone wallow in misery because, as she infuriatingly said, 'there's always someone worse off, honey.' Even as she spoke she was nonchalantly polishing her last nail, long legs propped up on the table in painted-on jeans, eyeing the biscuit tin as if crisis and food were not wholly incompatible. Shona shook her head as Crys nudged it over to her.

'Crys, be serious, please.'

'I'm afraid I'm being perfectly serious, Sho. That guy O'Hagan will be out to get you, but good.'

'Probably. So what am I going to do?'

'Ah. Now there's a question. Attack, or defend? We're going to have to put our minds to this . . . wouldja like to stay to lunch? An army marches on its stomach, you know – God, where is Napoleon anyway, when we need a strategist?'

Looking around, she said it as if Napoleon were a missing cat who might wander in at any minute, and for the second time Shona laughed in spite of herself. In spite of Terry O'Hagan, whose wrath would indeed be ferocious, and in spite of Brendan Wright, whom she was already missing like an amputated arm. Whatever about wanting children, she had so badly wanted *him*.

Joe Hegarty was, in his own estimation and that of all who knew him, a good guy. A nice, decent, hardworking husband who couldn't see why God had inflicted him with such a useless dosser of a son and an increasingly restless wife, who had developed the most peculiar habit of devouring property pages, property programmes and property websites as if they were caviar. As he put his key in the front door and let himself in, he wondered what he was going to find this evening. Saturdays were the busiest days at the hardware store, he was entitled to hope for a hot delicious dinner, Aileen with a welcoming smile on her face, Finn maybe even at home doing something useful for a change . . .

Finn wasn't there. Joe could tell immediately that he wasn't, because when Finn was there the house reverberated to the sound of music. Now it was silent, apart from the rustling of newspaper pages in the kitchen, which smelled of something burning.

'Aileen? Is there something in that oven –?'

With a gasp of guilt his wife leaped up, flew to it and extracted a cremated chicken. 'Oh, God! I'm sorry, Joe, I was roasting you a nice chicken for your dinner but I must have forgotten to set the timer . . . I got distracted . . .'

Dismally, Joe stared at the smouldering chicken. Was Aileen going through an early menopause, was that it? She was only forty-two, same as himself, still his sweet pretty wife to look at, but there had to be some reason why she kept burning things these days, or forgetting them, or both.

He wasn't the kind of man to mention words like 'menopause' – in fact he would rather put his arm in the blender – but suddenly, this evening in late November, it dawned on him that he was going to have to say, or maybe even do, something. At this rate, Aileen would soon be a domestic danger.

'Distracted by what?'

Despairingly, she swept her hand in the direction of the table, on which lay a thick stack of papers and magazines. Joe scarcely had to glance at them to know what kind they were – the new porn that she'd got hooked on, the porn that was turning his lovely wife into a mess and a menace. And yet . . . even as she looked at him with that mixture of guilt and desperation, something about her hit him square in the solar plexus. Even if she was a mystery to him these days, her brown eyes were still so big and beseeching, their lashes still so lush and long, her rosy cheeks blushing just as they had the day he'd asked her to marry him.

God, was that a long time ago, or what! Twenty-two years . . . they'd only been children, their parents aghast, everyone whispering about how it would never last. But it had lasted. Through the proverbial thick and thin, ups and downs, even their anguish when Finn's baby sister had died in infancy, and never been followed by any other child. That had tested their marriage almost to breaking point . . . but they'd held in together somehow, and survived. Until now. Now, as he gazed at the charred chicken and the property supplements, Joe wondered whether his beloved wife might not be going just very slightly round the bend.

'Jesus!' he snapped with a sudden surge of rage, under which he could feel swirling frustration. 'This is out of hand! You're losing it, Aileen! You're dreaming of castles in Spain all day long, day in and day out! What in God's name is the *matter* with you?'

It worried him when, instead of briskly retorting that she was perfectly all right, she sank down on a chair and surveyed him with a long, somehow speculative look. Her silence was unnerving.

'Well? Are you going to tell me, or not? What does a man

have to do these days to get a decent dinner and a warm welcome in his own home – jump up on the table and dance a fandango? Strip naked and swing from the chandelier? Hey?'

Dreamily, she continued to look at him, and despite himself he sucked in his stomach . . . was it him that might be the matter, was that it? Admittedly his once abundant hair was losing both quantity and quality, admittedly he'd gained a bit of a paunch – and yes, his snoring was a problem. He knew that, but what in hell could he do about it? Besides, other guys snored. Nearly all of them. She'd be a long time finding one that didn't . . . sweet, suffering Jesus. She hadn't actually found one, had she? Some other man, a fling, an affair, a toy boy, whatever you called them these days . . . oh, no. Surely not. She couldn't have. Not his Aileen. Besides – who? When? Why? Suddenly, he felt as if someone had swung an ice-pick into his spine.

His voice, when it emerged, sounded saw-toothed. 'Aileen? Are you listening to me? I'm asking you a question.'

'Yes, Joe. I know you are.'

Her dreamy look was so detached, it frightened him. 'Then answer me! Tell me what it is that's turning you from my wife into a woman I scarcely recognise! Tell me why in hell you can't stop guzzling all this property stuff! It's unhealthy, you know, at this stage, it's abnormal, it's getting to be an obsession.'

Slowly, still looking at him as if from a distance, she smiled. Smiled the oddest, most enigmatic smile he had ever seen on her face in their entire life together.

'Joe. I've been thinking. Have you any idea what this house is worth?'

He froze. She was losing her marbles. She was planning to sell their home. Their perfectly good, comfortable, nearly paid-for home that he had worked his *nuts* off for! Shock scorched through him, zipped through his whole stocky, weary body.

It had been a long week at work – and now, this. He knew that unless he steeled himself he would lose it, go ballistic.

'Yes, dear. I know exactly what it's worth.'

Surprised, almost eagerly, she blinked at him. 'Do you?'

'Yes. It's worth an arm and a leg, and every other bit of me that I've slogged to a stump for the past fifteen years to pay for it. It's worth blood, sweat and tears. Not only my work, but yours as well, has kept its roof over our heads, provided a home for our son, a shelter from all storms, a meeting place for friends and family . . . what it's worth financially I neither know nor care, but I tell you what it's worth to me: it's worth a bit of respect.'

Very carefully, he kept his tone low, as if talking to an over-wrought child. Initially, it seemed to work. Aileen nodded agreeably, her honey-blonde hair bobbing round her face.

'Yes. I suppose it is. But Joe – it's also – I reckon – it's worth at least four hundred thousand euros.'

That was when it hit him. Hit him like a hammer: our marriage is in trouble here. We, Aileen and I, Mr and Mrs Joseph Hegarty, are in some kind of awful trouble. The kind that women just suddenly spring on you, when you haven't a bull's notion why or how.

'Is it? Have you been having it valued, while I've been out at work?' His hands clenched round the top of a chair. Steady, he thought, steady on, don't panic.

'No. I just know. That's the going rate round here. That's what these houses are selling for, near Galway, plenty of parking, solidly built, big garden, handy for Shannon airport, the university, the hospital, shopping centre, cinemas, restaurants . . .'

Even in the midst of his shock, he was surprised. Four hundred thousand? He never read the property pages the way she did, couldn't image that a semi-dee for which they'd paid a mere thirty-five thousand pounds could possibly be worth such an enormous, ludicrous sum. She must be hallucinating. Gingerly, sinking down on a chair alongside her, he took her hand and looked searchingly into her face.

'Aileen. Tell me something . . . is it – er – um – is it – ah – women's troubles? Is that it?'

His tone was gentle, his expression understanding. But hers went blank.

'What?'

'You know . . .' Oh, God, this was excruciating! Surely she knew he hated these delicate feminine subjects, they were a mystery to him, a minefield, yet he was raising this one now, doing his best, could she not even meet him halfway? Help him *out* here, before he choked? Apparently not; she simply looked baffled. Maybe he wasn't making himself clear. Bracing himself, he started again.

'Well . . . you're over forty . . . maybe you're reaching a point in your life . . . where . . . ?'

His tone was pleading, and abruptly she burst out laughing. 'Yes! I am! That's exactly it, Joe, you've got it in one!'

Phew. Hugely relieved that the worst was over, he beamed at her. And then it was as if she turned the garden hose on him, full blast, connected to an icy waterfall.

'I have reached the middle of my life, Joe, and I am bored stiff! I am sick of looking at Finn hanging round like a lost ghost, I am sick of waving you off to the pub four nights a week, I am sick of the same old thing, over and over and over! I want something new, something fresh – I want to sell this house, and move!'

Move? Move, she said, *move*? But – 'But why? For what? To where?' Had she been speaking Serbo-Croat, he could not have been more bewildered.

'I don't know where, Joe. I'm not even entirely sure why. All

I know is that I need a change – we all need one – and I would very much like you to start considering the possibility of selling this house, on which we can make an absolutely huge profit.'

He felt like crying. He might very well cry, after he'd strangled her. Moving house was, notoriously, sky-high on the stress list. Stress they didn't need, superfluous stress, to absolutely no purpose that he could see. Letting go of her hand, he drew back from her, caution replacing concern.

'But the profit would be eaten up by the next house we'd have to buy. I mean, Aileen, we've got to live somewhere—'

Triumphantly, she nodded. 'Yes. We do. But not necessarily here.'

'What's wrong with here?'

'Well, the weather's awful, and bookings are down, and—'

'Aileen, the weather's awful all over Ireland, bookings are down all the way from Kerry to Donegal! What difference does it make if we swop houses ten miles down the road – ?'

Thoughtfully, she sat back, contemplating the burnt chicken for a moment before speaking. 'None, if we move ten miles. But I'm thinking . . . maybe a thousand miles would be good. Maybe that would be far enough to make a difference.'

A thousand miles. Joe felt sweat beading up on his forehead. A thousand *miles*, she said . . . from his hardware store, from his pub, his mates, his garden that he liked to dig over and grow veggies in . . . and what about Finn? Where did their son fit into this lunacy?

'Aileen – I – I have to say, I think you're having some kind of brainstorm here. We can't just up sticks and move a thousand miles! We don't speak any foreign languages – bar the one you're speaking now – I have my job and you have your B & B business, we have a son—'

Her eyes flared. 'Yes! A son who badly, urgently needs a kick in the pants! Either Finn can move with us, make himself

34

useful helping us abroad, or he'll have to get a job and a flat of his own here, because we can't have him moping around us for the rest of his days. It's not doing him any good, and it's driving me nuts. He's filling this house with negative vibes and he's hanging out with a bunch of losers on the streets.' Gathering momentum, she gulped a breath, and ploughed on. 'As for my B & B business, I could run that anywhere – maybe some places are less dependent on the American trade than Ireland is. And as for you – you're over forty, there's probably some kind of redundancy deal available, the store could hire someone half your age at half your salary – maybe even Finn! Oh, Joe . . . think about it? Please, at least say you'll do that much?'

Her look was imploring. His was that of a man hit by a truck. He'd thought those property pages were a hobby, an odd but harmless amusement – he, apparently, had been an utter fool. With resentment born of shock, resistance born of pride, he mulled it over in mutinous silence. Had she been hatching all this for weeks, for months? Or was it some kind of spontaneous combustion? One way or the other, it was a fine thing for a man to come home expecting his dinner, and get his house sold over his head instead. You just never knew where you were with women, the whole species was completely impossible.

And worse, a dissatisfied woman was a dangerous woman, or so his mate Dave Doherty had led him to believe. Aileen had never seemed dissatisfied before, but clearly she was now – with what, exactly? With her life in general, or with her . . . her marriage? Their marriage? Somehow the whole situation felt as if it had a subtext to it. A subtext he was going to have to read, carefully, small print and all.

Abruptly, frostily, he stood up. 'I'll go down to the takeaway' he announced, 'and get us some chicken and chips for our dinner. Unless you'd rather have paella, perhaps, or frogs' legs?'

Aileen smiled, but she didn't laugh, and that was when Joe Hegarty knew that he'd been right. His marriage, out of a clear blue sky, was in trouble for some completely unfathomable reason. And might be in even deeper trouble, if he didn't figure out what was wrong and what he was going to do about it. Maybe, en route to the takeaway, he'd just drop in at the pub and see if Dave Doherty was there, have a word with him about this extraordinary domestic development.

After all, Dave Doherty should know about marriage in crisis. His wife had left him years ago, and that was why he would almost certainly be in the pub, ready and willing to offer advice. Putting his jacket back on, decamping with a grunt, Joe felt as if his wife's wildly gleaming eyes were following him down the hall and out to the car, all the way to the bar stool onto which he could hardly wait to collapse.

2

It was a weekend made in hell. Ten times – twenty, thirty? – Shona reached for the phone, rehearsing all her reasons for calling Brendan, refusing to hear anything and everything Crys had said about his maybe not being the right man for her.

Of course he was the right man! Okay, admittedly she'd made mistakes before, but Brendan was different. He was honest and decent and fair, handsome and solvent and delicious. He wasn't gay, wasn't married, wasn't divorced or bereaved, wasn't toting a clatter of children urgently in need of a mother. He had no baggage, no ties bar his delightful dad, he was the ultimately eligible bachelor. He was *perfect*!

Perfect, except for this one incomprehensible drawback: he'd dumped her. She thought they were ideal for each other, but he didn't. He, apparently, thought she was a workaholic who'd never give him the attention he deserved.

All right. So maybe she did have other interests besides him. Was that a crime? Punishable by banishment? If she *didn't* have other pursuits, he probably wouldn't have been interested in her in the first place, because then she'd have been the clingy, clutchy kind of woman who gave men claustrophobia. It was totally unfair, and in between crying jags she kicked a lot of doors, thumped a lot of walls and ate an entire sack of Tayto cheese 'n' onion. When the crisps were all gone she found a box of chocolates he'd given her and started in on those, savaging them systematically until the box was empty. Empty as her entire life, lying reproachfully at her feet . . . should she go out and buy another?

Ha! If only you could do that, just buy another! If only it weren't raining, if only she didn't feel so sick, if only she could swallow her pride instead of sweets, and ring him. But the phone kept rebelling; every time she picked it up it put itself back down, refusing to let her reason with him, argue, plead, do whatever it would take to get him back. Meanwhile, Crys's words kept ringing in her head like the bells of some blasted cathedral: 'Maybe you're just not marriage material . . . you're not maternal . . . you don't decide you love someone, love decides for you . . .'

What the hell did that mean? Over and over she replayed the restaurant scene in her head, but got no further to under-standing it, to figuring out why an imminent proposal had turned into sudden rejection, a train she'd never seen hurtling through the tunnel. Not to mention public humiliation, she would never forget the scene, or set foot in Kyver's restaurant again. Brendan, at the very least, could have had the sensitivity to boot her out of his life somewhere private, here in her own apartment for instance.

With a sigh, she sank down on a sofa, clutched a cushion to her and looked around the apartment. At least it, unlike him, had been a good investment. Spectacularly good actually, who would ever have thought that a two-bedroomed Galway flat, bought for fifty-five thousand pounds would be worth four times its price nine years later? Not that its value mattered, since she'd no intention of selling it – not until she could afford that lovely detached house somewhere scenic, anyway, and besides that was supposed to come with a husband built in. The husband who . . . my God, she thought in sudden panic, I'm thirty-*six*, this is a *nightmare*. Soon, people will stop saying

I'm single and start saying 'Ah, no, she never married . . .' I'll be a write-off.

And meanwhile, what about my job? There's no way I can turn up tomorrow morning and simply face Terry O'Hagan as if nothing had happened. Crys is right about that, if nothing else. I'm going to have to see the personnel director and lodge a complaint about him, because he'll certainly be lodging one about me. Maybe it'll even go to court, he'll have a sexual harassment case on his hands and I'll have an assault case on mine? The worst-case scenario is inquiries and tribunals and the whole thing dragging on for months, for years . . . oh, no, please don't let it come to that. Terry O'Hagan is a drunken slob, a sexist menace, but I shouldn't have hit him. I had no choice only to hit him. But it was a tactical error. It gives him ammunition to fight back.

Damn, damn, damn!

Getting up, Shona ran her hands distractedly through her hair, glimpsed her reflection in the mirror and decided to have a bath. A long, warm, scented bath, after which she'd phone her mother. Susie was a great mother, the kind who dispensed sympathy and then asked 'So what are you planning to do?', listened with interest to the answer – if, in this case, there was one. Susie wouldn't nag or reproach in that maddening way that made daughters feel like dimwits. If she were here, she'd be all hugs and reassuring smiles, but unfortunately Susie lived in Athlone, where she owned a boutique and her husband Tom ran a fleet of charter cruisers on the Shannon. Both Mum and Dad were smashing parents, but they were busy people, and at thirty-six Shona knew she was a bit old to go crying on their shoulders. At this stage, she should have children of her own, be the one dishing out sympathy and common sense!

Well – whatever about Brendan – common sense would start in the office tomorrow morning, with a crisp visit to Kevin

Cassidy, the personnel director, to officially shop Terry O'Hagan.

Shop him, Shona thought fuming, when what I'd like to do is fry him alive! He's been making my life a misery for years, and I'm not putting up with any more of it. That office isn't big enough for the both of us, and one of us is going to have to go.

I'm hanged if it'll be me.

'So there I'm afraid you have it, Ms Fitzpatrick. You accuse Mr O'Hagan of sexual harassment. Mr O'Hagan accuses you of physical assault. We appear to have a stalemate here.'

Kevin Cassidy leaned back in his swivel chair with the detached look of a man not about to take sides. In turn Shona sat back in hers, knowing he would have to take some kind of action.

'Yes. We do. So what do you propose to do about it, Mr Cassidy? Obviously, two antagonists can't continue to work together under these conditions. I've already explained to you that there's been a problem for quite some time. Mr O'Hagan frequently gets drunk, has followed me down hotel corridors on trips abroad, leches at all the women in the office—'

'Yes. So you say. These are serious allegations that will have to be investigated.'

'Indeed they will. And in the meantime?'

Twirling his biro, Kevin sighed. Sometimes he privately yearned for the good old days when women had never been let anywhere near the workplace, such hassles had they brought in their wake. That said, Shona Fitzpatrick was an excellent worker, popular and dynamic. He'd never known her to imagine problems where none existed. Besides, this wasn't the first time that rumour had reached his ears about Terry O'Hagan; it was merely the first time anyone had made a formal complaint. Now, a chain of events would have to be set in motion.

'In the meantime, I'm going to have to suspend you both.'

Steeled as she was, Shona gasped. 'Suspend – us both – what! But he's the one who—'

'That's what you say. He says you're the one who – look, this is the last thing I want to do. It's going to cost our budget big-time, since you'll both be on full pay, and it's going to be extremely inconvenient since someone else will have to do your work as well as his. But I have no choice. There are procedures in these situations and this is the procedure in this one. I'll be putting it in writing and giving a copy to your union representative, who'll attend all further meetings on the matter. We're probably going to end up at the Employment Tribunal in Dublin, if and when we can get a date fixed. As a rule, there's a three-month waiting list.'

Three months? Horrified, Shona absorbed it. For the next three months – before the case even got started – she was going to be effectively unemployed? Paid to do nothing, mope around at home, without even Brendan to cheer her, a wedding to distract her . . . but she'd go mad! And what was going to happen to her promotion, after this? Even if she won the case, if Terry O'Hagan got fired and was gone, might she be labelled 'Trouble', be perceived as a liability to work with?

Well, she had anticipated a possible court case. But only as a last resort, without any idea that it might take so long to even schedule. Suspension had never crossed her mind. It had seemed much more likely that Kevin Cassidy would simply summon both parties into his office to slug it out, referee the row and then make some decision. Like demoting Terry for instance, moving him out of circulation.

'But – but surely it's possible to sort this out in-house? Ask any of my female colleagues, they'll all tell you what goes on.'

Kevin frowned. Probably she was right, but his hands were tied. Problems weren't sorted 'in-house' any more, they were 'processed' through 'appropriate' bureaucratic channels. He wasn't a director as such these days, he was just a mediator. Everything wended its way through lawyers and courts and tribunals, munching mountains of money, consuming centuries of time. No point in telling Ms Fitzpatrick his personal opinion, which was that this very messy confrontation was probably going to take months, even after it reached Dublin, to resolve. Then, even if she defeated the notoriously devious Terry O'Hagan, it would cost her dearly. No financial award or personal satisfaction had ever, in his experience, compensated anyone for the heartache, the suspense, the paperwork, the sheer slog and the bitterness engendered by court cases. They were emotionally exhausting.

'Ms Fitzpatrick, I'm sorry, but you've initiated this and now you're going to have to patiently see it through. Mr O'Hagan, ditto. All I can do is facilitate you both on your way to what I hope will be eventual justice. Now, you'd better see the secretary about the paperwork.' Fractionally, ruefully, he smiled. 'I must say I wouldn't mind a little holiday myself, on full pay. Why don't you just enjoy yours, make the most of it?'

Stung, Shona sat upright. 'Because I love my work! Because it shouldn't be mucked up by some sex-starved creep who should never have reached a position of power to abuse! I've been in the B & B sector for nine years, I want to move into hotel marketing, not waste my time doing nothing!'

Kevin stood up. 'I know. I know. But there we are. If you find time hanging heavy on your hands, why not try a bit of free-lancing, approach one or two hotels on a short-term project basis? You're a marketing natural, and' – unexpectedly, he winked at her – 'if you don't tell me anything about it, then I won't know, will I? I'll just get head office to go on paying your salary until your problem gets sorted out.'

Taken aback, Shona considered. What was he saying to her? Go out and keep busy, make some contacts – in case you might lose your job and need them? Make a bit of extra money, I'm on your side here? That was certainly what it sounded like – in which case, she'd better look grateful. And sound grateful. Standing up in turn, she reached across the desk to shake his hand.

'Well, Mr Cassidy, I'm sorry you can't personally sort it out. But if I'm to be a free agent for the next few months, then I will try to use the time constructively. Thank you for your – your – intervention.'

Wretchedly, they looked at each other, silently, mutually acknowledging the absurdity and injustice of the situation. It was infuriating, but that was the system; the good old days of pistols at dawn were long gone.

Unlike Bob Geldof, Aileen loved Mondays. They were her day off, the day on which she had lunch with her mother and sister in Galway city, after which they would all go to the cinema or shopping or whatever interesting event might be happening. Today, it was her master plan to haul both Tessie and Dympna along to the Foreign Property Exhibition at a hotel in Salthill. Of course they both thought she was bonkers, had told her so several times since she'd first started reading 'Take Five', but she was determined to get them used to the idea that soon she would be moving abroad.

Would definitely be moving abroad, whether Joe Hegarty liked it or not, whether Finn Hegarty chose to come or not. All weekend she'd been discussing it with Joe, even in bed late at night where once they would have been catching up on the sex life for which, these days, they seemed to have so little time or energy. How could she have time, with so much cleaning and laundry to do, her four guests all wanting breakfast at the crack of dawn? How could he have energy, when he came back from the pub at midnight with six pints swilling round in him, was snoring twenty minutes into the conversation? 'Baloney' he called it; she was talking 'complete baloney' and there was no point in pursuing it because, eventually, she would grow out of this crazy phase. Dave Doherty had assured him that she would. Wives took notions sometimes, Dave said, but they weren't to be taken seriously, it was all just harmless fantasy.

Fantasy. Is that a fact, Aileen fumed as she parked her little Ka near Haydon's restaurant where Tessie and Dymps would be simultaneously converging. I'll give him fantasy. As for Dave Doherty, is it any wonder his wife left him, the man knows less than zero about anything. What Joe sees in that boozing moron is beyond me . . . thank God I at least don't go to the pub any more, don't have to listen to the pair of them spouting rubbish!

Tessie and Dymps were already waiting when she went into the restaurant, studying the menu as if they weren't going to have the shepherd's pie same as usual. Both were looking well, she thought, Dymps a rosy, happy housewife in her mid-thirties, looking very pretty today in a new cherry-red coat; Tessie the widowed but cheery matron she'd been for ever, her grey hair dyed blonde, her smart teal-blue suit taking a good ten years off her sixty-four. Sometimes her slight deafness led to daffy conversations, but she had a heart of gold. Aileen felt a little punch of affection for both mother and sister, with whom Monday lunch was always fun.

'Hey, sis!' Dymps greeted her with a grin. 'How's it going!' Even as Aileen grinned in turn, bent to kiss them both, a waitress arrived with the bottle of white wine they always shared, whisking away Aileen's coat as she seated herself.

How was it going? Not great, if the truth be told, it couldn't be great with business so bad, Finn so chronically unemployed and Joe so – so not *listening*! But she wasn't going to talk about any of that now, she'd come here to put it all out of her mind, and so she beamed brightly at Dymps.

'It's going! How are you, how are the kids?'

'Bold as brass.' This was totally untrue; Dymps's two children were lovely, bright youngsters who gave as much affection as they received, not only doing well at school but actually enjoying it, popular with their pals, such a credit to their mother that she had hardly any choice only to pretend they were scourges. You didn't brag about your brats when they weren't brats at all – especially not to their aunt, the mother of a notorious disaster. Conspiratorially, Dymps winked. 'You'll never guess.'

Aileen grinned; Dymps was great for gossip, always had some new story about neighbours or parish politics or impending revelations that 'would make your hair curl'. Eagerly, she and Tessie leaned forward in unison to hear the latest – about Father McDonagh's girlfriend, as it turned out – while food arrived and the restaurant began to buzz busily. Tucking into a hot plate of lasagne, Aileen was vaguely conscious of some knot loosening in the back of her neck, the feeling of being somehow massaged, ironed out. God, it was good to get away from it all, good to have these weekly girls' get-togethers!

Airily, Dymps nattered on, Father McDonagh had been thoroughly dissected, a brown-envelope councillor had been comprehensively trashed and they were into the question of stretch limos by the time their plates were eventually empty, with the pleasant prospect of apple pie, or possibly tiramisu, beckoning next. Stretch limos were currently in vogue for teenagers' parties, and Dymps had been astounded to see one wending its way up the backwater boreen where she went walking every weekend in remotest Connemara.

'I mean, Connemara for God's sake, there I was in my wellies out in the wild west, the absolute arse end of nowhere, nothing to be seen for miles only the heather and lakes and mountains, and next thing there's this white *yoke* with pink *lights* flashing up beside me, twenty foot long, with a driver in a peaked *cap* and music blaring loud enough to wake the dead . . . I dunno, I think Ireland's gone mad. Barking mad, if you ask me.'

Looking intrigued, Tessie laughed. 'Well, it was far from stretch limos I was reared, in my day we walked everywhere or cadged a lift on a cross-bar, everyone nowadays seems to think the past was romantic, but we were bloody frozen, I'd have given my right arm for a ride in a stretch limo . . . where d'you get a stretch limo, anyway? Are they expensive?'

Simultaneously, Aileen and Dymps caught the eagerly wistful note in their mother's voice, and thought the same thing: that's what we'll do for her sixty-fifth birthday next August. A big family party somewhere fun, to which she'll be driven in a white stretch limo. It's vulgar as hell, but she'd love it. Tessie grew up poor, and now it's her turn to be pampered.

Only then, Aileen remembered, I might not be here. I might, with any luck, be in Italy or Portugal or . . . or wherever I am, I'll come home for Mam's birthday party. Nowhere in Europe is more than a few hours away by plane, I'll put a few bob in the bank and make sure I get back from wherever it might be. Which reminds me, we'd better get moving if we're going to this property exhibition. Another one! They'll scream. But they'll humour me, and come. Let's get the bill, and get going.

Looking up for the waitress – they took turns to pay and it was her turn – she scanned the room, and her swivelling gaze was suddenly arrested by a back she recognised. Not that she'd normally recognise people from the back, but she'd recognise Shona Fitzpatrick instantly, because she wore her shoulder-length hair in such a distinctive style, cut in a V-shape that was both attractive and unusual. Delighted to see her – it had been at least a couple of months – she pointed her out to Tessie and Dymps.

'Look, that's Shona Fitzpatrick over there, you know, the girl from the tourist office who used to send me buckets of business before they moved her off the front desk? She's a sweetie, I must just run over and say hello to her.'

Paying the bill, leaving Dymps to escort their mother to 'the ladies' where she never went unaccompanied, Aileen went to get her coat off the rack and approach Shona, who was finishing lunch at a corner table with a sinuous, vibrant-looking young black woman. As she neared their table the younger woman looked up and gave her a friendly smile, whereupon Shona turned curiously around.

But – dear heavens! – what was wrong with Shona? Never before had Aileen seen her looking anything other than perky and peppy; today she looked as if someone had hit her with a hurley, her beautiful blue eyes puffy as if she'd been crying. Taken aback, Aileen hesitated; but then Shona smiled and jumped up.

'Aileen! Aileen Hegarty, how are you! C'mere, let me see you, say hello to Crys – this is my friend Crys Sheehan – Crys, this is Aileen, one of my favourite B & B ladies, she lives out near Oranmore. We used to be in cahoots, once upon a time, she does the best Irish breakfasts in the business and I'd send her lots of tourists—'

'Yes' Aileen rejoined ruefully, 'in the days when there were lots!'

She shook hands with the tall, sparkly Crys, and Shona nodded. 'Tell me about it. Down to a trickle now . . . but still, there are some, and who knows, maybe there'll be more when the Americans get their nerve back.'

'And prices go down! But how have you been, Shona, what are you up to in that back office they locked you away in?'

Expecting a chatty rundown on what was happening in the tourism office, she was taken aback when, instead of babbling enthusiastically on as she usually did, Shona bit her lip with a look that said she didn't, for some unexpected reason today, want to talk business.

'Oh, this and that – it's managing without me for the moment while I have a long lunch with Crys here.'

Indeed, the pair had looked engrossed in conversation. But now Crys glanced at her watch, startling Aileen with a flash of vivid tangerine nails, and reached for the jacket on the chair behind her.

'Whoo whoo, lunch was longer than I realised, I'm gonna be late! Sorry Sho, gotta fly – good to meet you Aileen, sit down here and take over for me.' Across Shona's shoulder, she winked a woman-to-woman kind of wink, one that said that Shona was not in great form today, needed cheering up. And then, in a flurry of bags and scarves, she hugged Shona and was gone, leaving a somehow breathless vortex in her wake. Aileen peered into it at Shona's unusually pale, frazzled-looking face.

'Shona? I – I'm not one to snoop or anything, but – are you – okay?'

She asked hesitantly, because although she'd long liked Shona she'd never known her intimately, and was surprised when Shona shook her head as if to say no, she wasn't okay actually.

'I – I'm all right. Just a bit bothered at the moment. But how are *you*?'

Visibly making an effort, she smiled her welcome-to-

Galway smile, and Aileen warmed to her valiance. 'I'm fine, right as this rain that never stops! I'm with my mother and sister, we're going to the Foreign Property Exhibition out in Salthill.' With a wave, she gestured to Tessie and Dymps as they wended their way back across the room, making for the coat rack. Curiously, Shona raised an eyebrow.

'Oh? Off to buy a château or a parador? New shoes aren't enough any more?'

She grinned archly, and it crossed Aileen's mind that Shona would be a great asset to take along to a property exhibition, because she had such an eye for what could be done with a premises. But presumably Shona had her work to get back to.

'No, not shoes, a house! I'm moving into the big league! Thinking of maybe moving abroad, it's a pity you've got your work to go to because otherwise I'd invite you to join us—'

'Moving abroad? Aileen, you're joking!' She looked amazed, and Aileen felt her spine stiffen. 'No, everyone thinks I am but actually I'm not. I'm perfectly serious.'

'But – well, I must say this is all a bit mysterious, but if you are serious then I'd love to come with you. I don't have to go back to the office at all today, as it happens.'

'No? Don't you really? Why not? You were always the busiest little bee I ever knew.'

Seizing her jacket, Shona was already shrugging herself into it. 'Well, I'm not now. Long story. But first, why don't you introduce me to your mum and sister? We could walk to the exhibition, if you like, Salthill is so near?'

'Good idea, we could all use a bit of exercise after that lunch! Come on then, let's go, I'm delighted you're free.'

Off they sailed, all four of them in stately procession, making introductions as they went and Aileen made a mental note: I must have a drink with Shona afterwards, and find out what's wrong with her. Why has she no work to be doing on a Monday afternoon? It's so unlike her, she looks as if some rug has been suddenly pulled out from under her.

The property exhibition was jammed, chock-full of estate agents and people coming in out of the rain, shucking off rain-coats and folding umbrellas in a way that gave the place a steamy, vaguely conspiratorial air. While Tessie gazed amazed at grandiose Italian palazzi – 'But you'd never be done dusting that' – and Dymps peered into turquoise swimming pools – 'Oh, the kids would kill for that' – Shona interrogated Aileen sotto voce as they made their way from stand to stand.

'You really are serious? A B & B, in some country you've maybe never even visited, whose language you don't speak – but why, Aileen? What's come over you?'

Pen and pad in hand, jotting details of houses that caught her eye, Aileen paused en route from the Algarve to Marbella. 'Itchy feet have come over me, Shona. A restlessness under my skin that's driving me mad. A life set in stone, a boring little house and, if you want the truth, a boring little husband. Oh, not that he's a bad man, but he – he's – so – so predictable! Work, drink and dig the garden, that's all Joe ever does. That's his idea *of living*. Meanwhile I'm stuck at home with our son Finn, who has failed his Leaving Cert for the second time and is now hanging round the house like peeling wallpaper, drooping and grizzling and giving off this aura of – of complete despair. He looks like the last of the Mohicans and he sounds like moaning minnie, spends his time on the streets and his dole money on drink, he'll soon be putting away more than his father . . . meanwhile it's pissing rain and I barely have a dozen bookings a week . . . sorry. I don't mean to bang on, only you asked.'

'Yes, I did. And I'm really sorry to hear all this. You were always one of my favourite B & B ladies, seemed such a happy camper.'

'Yes. Well. We all have to seem happy, don't we, in the tourism business? Maybe I even was happy, or content at any rate, until a year or two ago. Until I started wising up to what a big wide world is out there, what a lovely lifestyle, not to mention what great value at the moment – look at that hacienda there for instance, only two hundred thousand euros! I'd sell my plain, ordinary house for at least twice that – and I am going to sell it, as soon as I find somewhere suitable in the sun.'

'But what about Joe, and Finn?' Shona was bemused; Aileen looked so resolute.

'Joe is going to have to accept it, and come with me if he wants to stay wedded to his wife. Finn can either stay here, get a job and shape up, or he can come with us and make himself useful. I'm sure I'll need plenty of help – oh, look!'

Aileen grabbed her arm and, following her suddenly rapt gaze, Shona looked: pinned to a felt board on the French stand was a picture of a large, creamy-looking house with turrets at either end – no, not a house, this was more of a château, positively palatial. Aileen was staring at it with the suddenly hungry look of a chocaholic at a sweetshop window, breathing deeply as if trying to inhale its very essence.

'Isn't that bliss? Isn't that just divine? Come on, let's go take a closer look.'

'But Aileen, that's not a house. That's a Disney castle.'

Overhearing her, the estate agent purred. 'No, not a castle. A *manoir*. Seventeenth century, eight bedrooms, five hectares of land, plus pool, naturally. Two outbuildings, a wine cellar, a forty-metre salon and . . .'

And you two certainly aren't going to buy it! That was what

his grin said, widening as Tessie and Dymps hove up behind, peering at the picture in turn.

'Ooh' Tessie breathed rapturously, 'that's lovely. I wouldn't mind spending my summer holidays there, Aileen love, I'd give you a bit of a hand with the laundry and all if I could sit out in that rose garden!'

Somehow touched, Aileen swung round to her. 'Would you, Mum? Would you really?'

'Yes' Tessie insisted loyally, 'I would. If you – if you really wanted to buy it. But – but it's huge!'

'Mmm.' Falling silent, Aileen moved forward to study the picture more closely. The '*manoir*', as the man called it, certainly was huge. And old, which according to all the magazines probably meant dry rot, or termites, or lethal wiring, or the whole works. Five hectares was over ten acres, which meant work, work, work. Keen on gardening as Joe was, this would certainly put his back out. And keep him out of the pub, if there was a pub . . .

'Tell me' she said squinting at it, 'where is it exactly?'

The man's smile widened. This lady appeared to be completely for the birds. You didn't choose a house and then find out where it was; you chose an area after extensive research and then found a suitable premises in it. But there you go, that was the Irish for you, mad as hatters. Thank heavens the exhibition was moving on to Manchester tomorrow, and he'd be moving with it.

'It's in the Languedoc, madam. In France.' She looked like the kind who wouldn't know the Languedoc from Las Palmas.

'H'mm.' Again Aileen squinted at it, and behind her Shona, Tessie and Dymps squinted in turn. Until now Tessie and Dymps had indulged her peculiar preoccupation, but now a kind of shiver ran from mother to sister, as if sensing some kind of impending cataclysm. But it was a ridiculous house, a manor for crying out loud, with turrets like something out of *Cinderella*! They'd better watch Aileen here, at this apparently vulnerable moment, keep her from saying or doing anything rash. Maybe it was the wrong time of the month for her to be attending property exhibitions, because if she was her normal sensible self she shouldn't have glanced at this ludicrous house for more than five seconds.

After a long, pregnant pause, Aileen turned to the man. 'Do you have a map?'

Oh, yes. He had a map. Wearily he produced and unfolded it, with a look that suggested he was utterly, utterly wasting his time. Barely camouflaging impatience, he stabbed his finger into it. 'This is the Languedoc, madam.'

'Yes. I've heard of it. Languedoc-Roussillon. What I want to see is exactly which part of it this house is in.'

He pointed a manicured finger east of Toulouse. *Languedoc-Roussillon*? Maybe she wasn't quite as far off the wall as he'd thought. You never could tell, these days.

'It's just here, madam, near the village of Mézalas.'

'How near?'

Ah. He had it now. She was one of the ones who watched *A Place in the Sun*, who did know the questions, after all. Not that she'd asked the main one yet: how much is it?

'Quite near. Approximately one kilometre. Toulouse is two hours away—'

'Two hours? But it's barely an inch on this map!'

Patiently, he nodded. You had to remember that Ireland was tiny. 'Yes, well, France is a very large country . . . anyway, Mézalas is a charming little village, with a grocery shop, bakery, petrol station, pharmacy, two restaurants and a church.' Like the French themselves, the Irish were reputedly fond of churches.

'I see. And pubs? Does it have a pub, or a bar?'

Oh, Christ. Trust the Irish. 'It has two small cafés which – ah – which close at eight in the evenings, sometimes earlier in winter.'

Aileen beamed. 'Perfect. So. Tell me more about it. What kind of condition is the house in, why are the owners selling, what are the main activities in the area, does it get many tourists?'

Almost reverently, Shona, Tessie and Dymps stood behind her, collectively holding their breath, incredulous that this conversation was happening. Aileen couldn't be interested in such a property, not unless she really was going bats. Looking trapped, the estate agent cleared his throat.

'The owners are selling due to old age, the place is too big for them. Wine is the main local industry, by far, although there is some tourism . . .'

Poor man's Provence. That's what the Languedoc was called in the trade, not that he was going to tell her that; people went there when they couldn't afford Nice or Antibes or snazzy St Tropez. Some optimists even touted the Languedoc as the next Provence, though personally he wasn't amongst them, not with all those feuding vignerons and dozy villages resolutely resisting the twenty-first century, those petrifying flash floods that swept entire hillsides down into raging torrents, those twisting narrow streets where you got wedged between somebody's kitchen and somebody's grape truck, and dented your beautiful BMW. He wouldn't live in the Languedoc if it were to beg him on its bended knees.

But apparently there were lots of masochists who would. Taking a card from his pocket, he handed it to Aileen. 'Please give me a call at any time, madam, if you wish to visit this property.'

There. That was calling her bluff. And sure enough she

merely put it in her pocket, thanked him and sailed off to visit the next stand, where a stone cottage in Brittany snared her attention. Clearly the woman had absolutely no idea what she wanted, and with a sigh the agent turned his attention to other, more serious punters.

Night had fallen by the time they finished touring the exhibition, and Shona and Aileen were dying to sit down somewhere for a drink and a chat. With flying kisses, Dymps went scooting home to cook her kids their dinner, but Tessie hesitated, looking anxiously at her daughter.

'What does Joe think about all this, love?'

Aileen grinned cheerfully. 'He thinks I'm off my rocker.'

Tessie frowned. 'He thinks you're after a docker?'

'No! He thinks I'm *off* my *rocker*!'

'Oh. Well, frankly, dear, so do I. I must admit, so do I. Even if that rose garden was very nice, you'd need a fleet of gardeners to mind it.'

Aileen embraced her as she fumbled for her car keys. 'Don't worry, Mam. It'll all work out, you'll see.'

Looking dubious, Tessie located her keys and nodded. 'Well, if you say so. I just hope you're not going to do anything rash, that's all.'

That, Aileen thought, is exactly what I'm going to do. For the first time in my life I am going to abandon common sense, I am going to do something absolutely wild and wonderful. Won-der-ful!

'No, Mam. Of course not.'

Looking both unconvinced and vaguely pleading, Tessie set off to find her car, and when she was safely out of sight Aileen turned to Shona.

'Jar in Cavanagh's?'

The pub was barely two minutes away, with a log fire blazing and a cosy winter atmosphere. Ordering hot port for them both, Shona inspected Aileen with naked interest.

'So – tell me! Are you really moving abroad, actually serious about this?'

'Yes. Totally. Nobody believes me, but I am. I've been a good person all my life, solid and reliable, and where has it got me? Into a rut, that's where. My son and my husband are in a rut too – so, I'm going to blow the rut sky-high. Run for cover, lads, Mum's gone mad!'

Shona laughed. 'Well, good luck with it so! Are you going to sell your house, or rent it out or what?'

Aileen reflected. 'Sell it . . . if I can persuade Joe. It's worth a fortune these days, we'd make enough to buy a place abroad and have enough to live on for a year or two while I got a new B & B going in Spain or Italy or . . . tell me, what did you think of that castle in France?'

'I thought it was gorgeous – and insane! That's not a B & B, Aileen. That's a hotel. A five-star job. Huge overheads. For God's sake don't bite off more than you can chew.'

'H'mm . . . maybe you have a point there. Still, I'd like to see it, if I could only convince Joe to come with me – but never mind all that for now, tell me what you're doing swanning round on a Monday when you should be working.'

Briefly, Shona hesitated, staring into her warm glass. And then it all poured out in a torrent.

'I've been suspended from work. I'm caught up in a sexual harassment case which is going to the Labour Court. Full pay until it does, but meanwhile I'm at a loose end – stay out of the office, Ms Fitzpatrick, until further notice. Plus, my boyfriend ditched me last Friday night.'

Aileen gaped. 'What? That nice fella – Brendan? – but I thought—'

Dipping her head, Shona let her hair screen her face. 'Yeah.

I thought, too. Thought he was about to propose, actually. How wrong can you be, huh?'

Looking up, she smiled a bright, brittle smile, her lavender-blue eyes abruptly glazing with tears. Horrified, Aileen gazed at her. But – surely not Shona Fitzpatrick, of all people! Lovely, bright Shona, whose life always seemed so sussed, so – so under *control?* How could any man not want this gorgeous woman, this achiever, this talented, energetic – oh. *Oh.*

Was that it? Too talented, too energetic, too much to take on, if all you wanted was a nice wife at home safely making meals and babies? Aileen had heard of that syndrome, of insecure men who felt threatened by dynamic women. She wouldn't have thought that Shona would even date such a person, but then . . . Galway wasn't exactly exploding, by all accounts, with eligible bachelors.

Twenty-two years ago, she'd settled for safe, steady Joe herself, with a kind of mild affection coupled with relief. Love, her mother had assured her, would grow with the years. And, in its way, it had grown. She and Joe turned into a team, working well together, respecting and trusting each other, with even a few laughs along the way. Which maybe was as much as you could hope for when you were just an ordinary person, not gorgeous, college-educated, sophisticated and shiny like Shona Fitzpatrick.

Curiously, she surveyed Shona, who was looking like a beautiful piece of Waterford crystal with a crack splicing clear down its centre.

'God, Shona, I'm so sorry to hear this . . . were you . . . were you madly in love with him?'

Shona, she thought, was the kind of woman who'd never settle for anything less than love, the dramatic, full-blown, passionate kind of love people like her could aim for. And sure enough, with unexpected vehemence, Shona sat bolt upright and nodded furiously. 'Of course I was! For nearly a year! The longest I've ever been in love with anyone!'

Crikey. What was this? Why did she suddenly look so rattled, sound so – so defensive? Baffled, Aileen backed hastily off. Never having met Brendan nor seen the couple together, she didn't know anything about their relationship. All she knew was that, over the years, Shona had famously got through a lot of men. In fact it had even been funny at one stage, her colleagues in the tourist office used to joke about 'the current Kleenex' who, like his predecessors, would soon be history.

Was this the first time that Shona herself had ever been 'binned'? Was that it? Wounded pride, damaged ego? Oooh . . . ouch. But they were not close enough friends to discuss that, so warily Aileen changed the subject.

'And – uh – this harassment case? What happened?'

Composing herself, Shona told her. '. . . So that's why, on a Monday afternoon, I have nothing else to do only lunch with Crys and inspect French castles with you. Thanks for inviting me, Aileen. Your project took my mind off my own problems for a few hours.'

Thoughtfully, Aileen sat back, draining the last of her port. How outrageously unfair, that someone like Shona should be getting such grief from both her boyfriend and her boss! She was usually so great with people, so good at her work, should have long since got not only married but got that promotion too . . . and then, in what Joe would call 'a blinding flash of the bloody obvious' it hit her. Here was what she could do, to cheer Shona up, distract her and work with her again, in that mutually productive way they'd once worked!

Sitting back, she nursed the idea for a moment, wondering what would happen if Joe said no.

If Joe said no, she wouldn't listen. She would go ahead and do it anyway. Resolutely, she plunged ahead.

'So . . . tell me, Shona . . . does this mean you have . . . you have a bit of time on your hands at the moment?'

A hollow laugh. 'Yeah, you could put it that way! What on earth I'm supposed to do for the next three months – not to mention the rest of my life – is beyond me.'

Leaning forward, Aileen put her work-worn hand on Shona's slim, elegant arm. An arm that felt fragile as the wing of a bird. 'Here's what you're going to do. You're going to come to France with me, and look at that castle. Several castles, possibly. Dozens. Not to mention cottages and mansions and farmhouses and water mills and . . . you speak French, don't you?'

Yes. Shona did, had au-paired for a French family as a teenager and later done a course at the Alliance Française, because the west of Ireland lured so many fishing-mad French tourists, who mobbed her office in summer.

'*Oui*. I do. But—'

'And you've driven on the continent, with the road on the wrong side?'

Bleakly, Shona smiled. 'Yes, I have. With the road on the wrong side.'

'Then that's settled. I'll tell Joe tonight and we'll book ferry tickets tomorrow.'

'What? But Aileen – whoa! What about your business, what about your son?'

'Shona, it's November. Two months after September 11. Business is hardly booming. As for my son – he can come with us, if he likes. As can my husband, we can fit four in the car. Alternatively, Finn can cook his father's meals and his own while I'm away, do the laundry for the pair of them, wash sheets and fry eggs for any unlucky tourist who might arrive in my absence. They are two grown *men*, two *adults*, if they won't come with me then they can cope without me.'

Her voice was suddenly firm, and Shona stiffened in turn, infected by Aileen's visibly gathering resolution. Although they were not friends as such, in the way she was friends with Crys, she'd always liked Aileen. Always liked anyone who could make up their mind to do something, and make it happen.

Besides . . . besides it would show Brendan Wright that she wasn't sitting round moping over him, wouldn't it? She could let him know, through mutual friends, that she'd gone to France on – on whatever business he cared to imagine. The very word 'France' made most people visualise champagne and romance and . . .

'Aileen, do you know what. I would love to go to France with you. Absolutely love to! You get a list of houses off the web, I'll drive and translate and give you my professional opinion of where would be a good place to set up a B & B – we'll run away together, do a Thelma and Louise!'

In a flash, in the mere minute it took, they were laughing over it, and shaking hands on it. And then, with a kind of grim grin, Aileen stood up.

'Give me your home number and I'll call you tomorrow. Right now, I'm going home to break the news to Joe – who will no doubt be delighted, raring to go.'

Shona arched an eyebrow. 'D'you think he will?'

'The hell he will. But what is it they call this in French? A fate accomplee? You and I are hitting the road, Shona, and that is that. Partners in crime, AWOL, whatever they call people who run away together.'

'I believe' Shona rejoined as she shucked on her jacket, 'they call them all kinds of unflattering things, and tell them to get their butts back to base pronto.'

Rehearsing her speech in the car as she drove home, Aileen toted it into the house as carefully as if it were a live grenade, and went to find Joe. He was sitting in his favourite armchair, reading the sports section of his favourite newspaper. As she came in, he lowered it cautiously, as if ringing down the curtain on some baffling play which might or might not actually be finished.

'So how's the mother? And sister? Nice lunch?' Pointedly, he glanced at the quietly ticking clock on the wall, as if to suggest it had certainly been a long one. Aileen peeled off her coat and seated herself on the sofa opposite him.

'Yes, lovely lunch, thanks, with Mam and Dymps. I met Shona from the tourist office in the restaurant, and then we all went to the Foreign Property Exhibition together . . . Joe, I need to talk to you.'

Immediately he sat up in alarm, as if she had pulled the pin on the grenade and was aiming it at him. 'Oh? About what?'

'About France. I saw a gorgeous castle and lots of other lovely houses . . . I want to go there to look at them.'

Ah. So she was serious. Was actually about to push the button that would blow their entire life sky-high. Frantically, his mind flitted to doctors, counsellors, therapists, and when he finally spoke it was in the genial tone of one humouring the dangerously unpredictable.

'I – ah – I see. France, eh? Where they make all that wine and cheese?'

'Yes. It looks lovely. And we've never been there. I'd like us all to go – you, me and Finn. Shona says she'll come with us to drive and translate.'

'Shona? The one who used to send us all those tourists?' Desperately, he tried to stall for time.

'That's right. She – she's taking a bit of a career break at the moment. And this is just the right moment, Joe – winter, off season, you could easily get a bit of leave from work and God knows Finn has little else to do. If we went there now, we might even find a property and be in business in time for next summer.'

His newspaper slid to the ground, and he looked at his wife; his hitherto wonderful wife whom he loved dearly, even if he was sometimes at a loss how to express it. Like an inexorably receding tide, she was slipping away from him, for absolutely no reason that he could identify. They hadn't had a row, had they? He didn't treat her badly, did he? She wasn't abused or starving or short of anything, was she? Certainly nothing that he could see. Apart from the ongoing problem of Finn, and the now distant loss of their infant daughter, they were a relatively lucky, normal, often happy couple.

Yet here she was, trying to hurl him head-first out of his home and into France, a country about which he knew nothing and cared less. For over twenty years they had lived together, pulled together and built a life which seemed to him entirely satisfactory; now she was throwing it back in his face. Try as he did to suppress it, resentment began to simmer somewhere deep inside him, and he groped frantically for a way out of this unnerving, incendiary terrain.

What was it Dave Doherty had said? 'You've got to show them who wears the trousers, mate, when the chips are down'? In retrospect that sounded a bit muddled, but he grasped the essence of it. There were times when a man had to stand up for himself, assert his authority.

If he went along with this nonsensical plan she was trying to spring on him, she'd have their house sold and the whole lot of them installed in France by the end of the week. Stoutly, he steeled himself.

'Aileen. Love. Listen to me.'

Agreeably, she nodded. 'I'm listening.'

'Have you any idea how many power drills we sell in the six weeks before Christmas? How many trees and fairy lights and boxed gift sets of tools? There's no way I can take a holiday at this time of year. So why don't you just leave it for now, if you still want to go to France later on maybe we could manage a little trip in February after the January sales are over . . . you could read up a bit on it in the meantime . . .'

It didn't work. Wasn't going to work. He could see it in her face, the adamant way she looked at him.

'Joe, I want to go now. Shona is free now. She'd be a huge help. If you can't come, then I'm going to go anyway. I'll take Finn with us, since he has nothing else to do, and if we find a suitable place you can come over in February to see it – Joe, I am giving you fair warning, I am *serious* about this. The Irish tourism industry is heading for recession, knee-deep in it already, and I want us up and running somewhere else before it's too late.'

Icicles speared his skin. 'But Aileen – what on earth would I do in a place like France? What would Finn do? For God's sake—'

'Joe, Finn could hardly do less than he does here. As for you – you're so handy, so good at plumbing and woodwork and all sorts of DIY, you'd get work in a flash. Maybe not a steady job in a store, but *work*, for sure, repairmen are in demand everywhere. You could apply for voluntary redundancy, we could sell this house and have plenty to live on until we got sorted! Please, Joe, come on, don't think negative – I can make this work for us, I promise you I can, if only you'll pull with me.'

Oh, God, how he hated that imploring look of hers, that made him feel like a bastard when he was only trying to be reasonable! No man in his right mind would go along with such lunacy, dive headlong into a vat full of frogs' legs, a notoriously nancy country where he didn't even speak the lingo, where they didn't even have pubs by all accounts . . . sweet suffering Jesus. No pubs. You'd lose your mind in a place like that.

63

Time, Joe. Play for time. It's your only hope here.

'All right. I tell you what. I can't go with you now, but you go ahead. Take Finn with you. I'll hold the fort here. See what happens and we'll talk it over when you get back.'

For a moment, silence stood between them, that pivotal silence of compromise. And then, having won half the battle, she smiled placidly at him. 'Okay. Let's do that so. Where is Finn, anyway?'

'Upstairs in his room, on his computer.' Even as he said it he wished he hadn't mentioned the computer, on which they both suspected Finn of visiting some very dodgy websites. Apparently there was some way to lock it, but neither of them knew how, and besides you could hardly child-proof a computer against a man of nearly twenty.

Aileen stood up, surprising him by placing a hand briefly but affectionately on his shoulder, reassuring him in that body language couples exchanged after two decades together. 'Don't panic' her touch told him, 'trust me on this one, it will work out.' What she actually said was 'Right. Then let me go have a word with Finn.'

She was out of the room and halfway up the stairs before it dawned on Joe that she had not even mentioned cooking dinner, at nearly seven o'clock with two hungry men in the house. If she didn't do it soon, he'd have to go to the takeaway yet again, with its compensating advantage of being so near the pub.

For nearly a year now, Aileen had felt some unidentified but distinct frisson of dread whenever she went upstairs to the bedroom in which her son, when not out roaming the streets, shut himself for hours on end. It was always dark in there, always pumping with music except when pulsating with silence, the silence that meant Finn was 'researching' something – what? – on his computer. It was silent now, and she knocked loudly, politely as parents were expected to do these days.

'Finn? Finn, I want to talk to you.'

No answer. After an interlude, she knocked again. 'Finn! Let me in, please! Urgent business!'

She heard his sigh as he shut down his computer, his heavily reluctant footsteps as he got up and went to admit her. What had he been doing, that he couldn't leave the computer switched on? It had been a serious mistake to let him install his own phone line. He paid for it out of his dole money, but it meant they were unable to study the bill, track what sites he was visiting.

The door swung open, and framed in it stood her tall, thin, pale son, sporting a residual case of adolescent acne, a black T-shirt spelling FCUK and a purple hedge down the centre of his skull. Despite his youth, there was a weariness in his hazel eyes, a been-there-done-that shrug in his slouch.

'Hiya Ma. What's up? Any sign of dinner?'

Walking past him into the dim room, she snapped on the light. 'Finn, any time you're hungry, you don't have to wait for me to cook. There is food in the fridge. There are recipe books. You can read. We are not talking the third secret of Fatima.'

Warily, he grinned a fraction. 'Yeah, but yours tastes better!'

Sweeping a stack of magazines off the bed, she sat down on it. 'Flattery will get you nowhere. However, I've come to discuss something else. To invite you somewhere.'

Warily, he raised one studded eyebrow a fraction. 'Oh? Yeah? Where's that? Not the FAS centre again, I hope?'

'No. I've given up hope of ever persuading you to do a FAS course. Of ever seeing you studying or working at anything. I've decided that, since you're free as a bird, you might as well come to France with me.'

Both eyebrows rose this time, and he exhaled a kind of bemused whistle. 'France?! You're not actually going to look at these houses on the continent? Dad says you're barking . . . but you'll get over it if we just play along till it wears off.'

The patronising tone in which he said it stung even more than the information itself, but she kept her voice steady. 'Well, Dad is wrong. I am going to look at houses in France, with a view to selling this one, so I am giving you the option of coming to see your new home before I buy it. Unless you have anything more urgent on hand?'

Stung in turn, he laughed without humour. 'Ma, get real. We live here. Galway, Ireland. You know bog all about France.'

Unblinkingly, she nodded. 'True. Not a lot. That's why I'm going to see it. And that's why I'd like you to come with me. Unless you find a job and a home of your own soon, it's where you may well be living this time next year. If not sooner.'

'Ha! Fat chance! Why d'you want me to come with you, anyway? I don't even speak the lingo—'

'No. But you could share the driving. Shona Fitzpatrick is coming with me – you remember Shona, from the tourist office?'

He scratched his skull. 'Yeah. Vaguely. Where's she in all this?'

'I just told you. Coming with me. For moral support. I'd like yours, too.'

'Ma, you're bats! There's no way I'm going off on some girl fest to France! Yak yak yak, oh look, let's buy that hat – Jesus, over my dead body!'

She recognised his tone. It was the same one in which he said 'No, I can't get a job' and 'No, I'm not doing any course' and 'No, I dunno how to cook' and 'No, it wasn't a porn site.' If he were not her son, if she had not personally given birth to him and did not therefore love this monster she had created,

66

Aileen thought she would very much like to hit Finn over the head with a steel mallet.

'I see. Well, don't say you weren't given the choice. Since you choose to stay here, you can practise cooking while I'm away and learn to use the washing machine. Your father will need feeding when he gets home from work and, in the unlikely event of any guests checking in—'

'Oh, no!' Electrified, he stalled her with an upturned palm. 'No way! I'll cook for Dad and me, if I have to, but if any guests want rooms I'll send them over to Mrs Foley.'

Wearily, she sighed. Talking to Finn – or trying to talk to him – was like talking to the carpet. 'I was going to say that, if any guests arrived and you looked after them in my absence, you could keep the money.' Pointedly, she glanced at the computer. 'Your phone bills must be hefty.'

'Not hefty enough that I need to earn it the hard way.'

What? What *did he say*? Even as alarm scorched through her veins, it scorched across his face too, and she saw that he had said something he fervently wished he could retract. It was all she could do to remain vertical, struggle to sound impassive.

'Is there an easy way to earn money, Finn? If there is, I wish you'd share it with me.'

But a steel shutter had slammed down over his suddenly bland countenance. 'Nah. Not that I know of – not unless you're a politician, ha!'

Again his laugh was mirthless, leaving her groping in horror at the possible reasons why he didn't want to go to France. Indifference? Secret fear? Or some other agenda? It was the latter that sealed her determination, her sudden absolute resolve to do all in her power to get him out of this room, this house, this lethargy and this mysterious sub-world he inhabited. As she stood stiffly up, her spine felt like a length of freshly forged, rapidly cooling steel.

'Right. You run the house while I'm away, Finn, if only for yourself and your father. Otherwise I'm turning you out of it when I get back. Got that?'

His surprise segued into an easy smile. Her threats were regular and harmless. 'Ah, sure, where would I go, ma?'

'I don't know and I don't care. Now, I am going downstairs to cook dinner for us all and you are going with me to peel the potatoes for it.'

It was his swift agreement that sealed her suspicions. 'Sure. Let me at 'em!'

Grinning, with mock chivalry, he swept the door open for her, and as they made their way downstairs together she knew for certain that she would come back from France carrying the keys to a new life for her family. A new life in which both husband and son would have to join her, because otherwise their old one would crumble and disintegrate.

Was going to disintegrate one way or the other, if she had to dismantle it nut-by-bolt with her bare hands.

3

'We'll take my car' Shona announced, 'on the ferry to
Cherbourg. Then we'll drive all the way down to the
Languedoc.'

Gazing at the map between them, Aileen was mystified. 'But
why not just fly to Toulouse and rent a car there? It looks like
an awful long drive from Cherbourg—'

'It is an awful long drive. That's the idea. Since you've never
even been to France before, you need to see as much of it as
possible. This route will take us right down through
Normandy, the Loire, Charente-Maritime, the Dordogne, the
Midi-Pyrénées and finally into your castle country around
Carcassonne. Two days from Cherbourg if we average 500
kilometres a day. Three, I suppose, realistically.'

'What?! Plus the ferry trip? But Shona, we'll never drive that
far that fast, it'll take us till Christmas . . . it's *miles*!'

'Yep. France is huge, Aileen. You'd put Ireland in its pocket!
The drive will help you to get your bearings, adjust to the
language and climate and to driving, as you so quaintly put it,
on the wrong side. You can do some of the driving yourself
once you get used to it.'

Aileen quailed. Carried away on a tide of excitement, only
now was she beginning to glimpse the practicalities of her
project, wonder nervously if she might, after all, be biting off
more than she could chew. Suppose they got a puncture! She
didn't even know how to change a tyre. Suppose someone had

an accident, what was the French for 'call an ambulance'? What if . . . if Joe would only come with them, show some interest and support!

But Joe, apart from refusing to have 'any truck' with the whole scheme, was more determined than ever to stay at home since Aileen had confided to him her worries about Finn's invisible activities. Nothing that she could exactly put her finger on, only . . . only . . . she could barely bring herself to articulate what she suspected.

'Drugs' she finally whispered, and Joe nodded as if not entirely surprised.

'H'mm. Well, I didn't want to worry you, with no hard evidence to go on, but I've sometimes wondered the same thing myself. If he's using them, I'll lather the daylights out of him. If he's dealing them, I'll crucify him. Only in order to catch him, Aileen, I'm going to have to watch him. Watch him closely, and try to get proof.'

Wretchedly, Aileen nodded, feeling guilty that she should be leaving both husband and son at such a sensitive moment. But it was for their good that she was going . . . while Joe would never acknowledge it, alcohol was a drug too. He was in denial, and if challenged Finn would probably go into denial also. Like father, like son? The sooner she got the pair of them out of here, the better.

But first, find somewhere to take them. 'Right then' she said briskly to Shona, 'let's get going. I'll phone that estate agent and get him to set up some viewings. Plus as many other agents as I can find in the area – ones who speak English, I hear most of them do.'

Shona smiled, and made a mental note to pack a dictionary. Aileen was like someone who, having only ever swum in the shallow end before, was now blithely striking out across the Atlantic.

Tessie was 'not one bit sure about all this, love'.

'Well, try to get your head around it, Mam. I am determined to come back from France with a house.'

'A mouse?'

'A *house*! A lovely house for you to spend lovely holidays in, down south where it's sunny, Dymps can visit too, we'll all have a great time next summer, wait and see.'

'I don't know what's come over you at all.'

Nobody, apparently, knew what had come over Aileen Hegarty. Most of her friends laughed when they heard she was leaving on Saturday, while Dymps's amusement turned to sudden panic.

'But Aileen, you can't really be thinking of – of emigrating!'

She'd never thought of it as such before. And wasn't going to think of it as such now. France wasn't Australia, for God's sake. 'Dymps, you can fly to France in less time than it takes to drive to Dublin. Don't be so dramatic.'

'But – but what about our lunches in Heyden's? What about Mam? She'll have a fit, you know, if you go – we all will! We'll *miss* you!'

Aileen winced. But she could not afford to get emotional about this. 'You won't have time to miss me, you'll be visiting so often, I'll visit you too, plus there's such a thing as a phone you know, and post and e-mail . . . anyway, I'm only going to have a look around. Our own house isn't even on the market yet.'

'Well . . . have a good time, then, if you're only looking . . . maybe you'll hate it and change your mind.'

'Maybe I will.'

That was, Aileen silently acknowledged, a possibility. Maybe she would loathe France on sight and that would be that. Maybe she'd find a house in Spain or Portugal instead, maybe the whole thing would take years . . . but as Saturday approached she felt her spirits rising, her sense of purpose crystallising, and was seized with enthusiasm. At last, she was going to be like all those people she'd seen on tv, visiting villas, pondering swimming pools, decorating guest bedrooms in gorgeous sunny colours! Well, in her head, anyway, until Joe came round to the idea, came to visit the house she'd selected and fell in love with it.

He would love it, wouldn't he? He'd have to, because for all his faults he loved her, didn't he? He wasn't the romantic type but he was the predictable type . . . wasn't he?

Yes. Of course he was. That was one of the virtues for which she'd married him. Stop worrying, Aileen, and start packing.

Crys was a colourful, inventive cook, and Shona was looking forward to the 'last supper' to which she'd been invited tonight. 'Gavin will be here too' Crys promised, 'to pour wine into you. French wine, naturally, to get you into the spirit of your odyssey.'

'We're only going for a fortnight!'

'Whatever. See you round seven.'

So now it was seven fifteen, and here was chunky, cheery Gavin filling her glass with Chablis, here was Crys passing a big bowl of Dippas and a dish of spicy salsa. One of the things Shona loved about Crys was that she always saw the bright side of things, and she was seeing it now.

'France! Just the job. Take your mind off Brendan Wright and Terry O'Hagan. You'll have great craic – wish I could go with you.'

'Excellent idea! Why don't you?' Shona beamed, and abruptly sensed some fleeting vibe, a kind of electric frisson, pass between husband and wife. Exchanging glances, they seemed to hesitate just fractionally before Crys answered.

'Because we have our jobs, for one thing. And because . . . for another thing . . . we . . . um . . . we're trying for a baby. We are trying like blazes for a baby, Sho. This is the wrong time for us to spend even one night apart, never mind two weeks.'

Oh. Oops. She hadn't meant to pry, and now all three of them were faintly blushing. Of course Shona had long known of their problem conceiving, but this was the first time it had been openly aired. Awkwardly, Gavin edged out of the room, muttering something about checking the casserole, and Crys twirled the stem of her glass contemplatively between starry blue fingernails.

'It – uh – it's just a bit sensitive at the moment, Sho. I mean, we've been married five years, we're starting to get a bit . . . a bit . . . concerned.' She bit her lip, and in horror Shona glimpsed a liquid gleam in her eyes. Until now, Crys had always made light of her devout desire for children, joking that 'the world has plenty to go round', immersing herself in the voluntary work 'that'll make it a better world for them – and for mine, when they come'. Only now did it dawn on Shona that maybe this was why Crys had chosen the job she had, driving a school bus . . . to be near the children?

Feeling impotent, she leaned across the coffee table to her friend and touched her hand. 'It'll happen, Crys. You'll see. One of these days you'll simply wake up and – bingo! Triplets! There's no medical reason why not, is there?'

'No. None, according to the doc. Gavin and I are both fertile as rabbits. In theory, at any rate.' She sighed a rare sigh, and Shona smiled supportively, resolving to look on the bright side as Crys usually did herself.

'At least you've got each other!'

Crys smiled back, but it was not her usual exuberant smile. 'Yeah. We have. Long may it last.'

'What?'

73

'Oh, nothing. I'm just being a pain in the ass. Let's put on some music.' In a flash she was on her feet and the room was filling with Bonnie Tyler, belting out 'Lost in France'. Invitingly, Crys curled a beckoning forefinger. 'C'mon, up, dance!'

Raising her arms over her head she started to sway sinuously, and Shona got up laughing: probably she would soon be very lost in France, with Aileen Hegarty navigating. 'Plus' she shouted over the music, 'you're young! Buckets of time!'

She'd said it often before, and it struck her that maybe it was time to stop, the line was wearing thin. At that moment Gavin came back into the room, and they looked at him in unison; five years older than Crys, he was thirty-four. Not as young as all that, to start a family . . . mortified, Shona saw that he had heard her. But Crys grabbed his hand and pulled him to her. 'C'mere, white man, and dance with me!'

Obligingly he did, and the mood changed, the tension melted. Crys was a wonderful dancer, lithe as liquorice, and Gavin was one of those rare Irishmen who liked to dance, sliding with casual ease around the room, hand in outstretched hand with his wife. Although they could hardly have looked more different – he was freckled and sandy, she was black velvet – there was something in tune between them, something that made Shona think she must have imagined it, that Crys couldn't have made that wry comment about 'long may it last'. They looked like the kind of couple who'd last into eternity and beyond. The kind who not only adored but understood each other, were almost psychically attuned. You could see it in their eyes, their bodies, their very footsteps as they weaved in and out around each other, communicating without a word.

Jesus, Shona thought, they are so lucky. They are great together, and so very, very lucky. I only hope they know it.

The music ended, and minutes later they were seated around the table, Crys ladling out her shellfish casserole, laced with lime juice and coconut cream. 'So, tell us about Aileen, Sho?'

'H'mm . . .' Considering, Shona sat back to reflect for a second. Now that she thought about it, there was a lot she didn't actually know about Aileen. Nice lady, nice B & B, nice husband in a stocky, gruff kind of way . . . problem son, friendly sister, slightly daffy widowed mother.

'D'you know, I don't actually know all that much about her. I mean, I know *about* her, but I don't actually *know* her, in herself. We just seem to like each other for some reason, always got on well when we had business with each other . . . she still runs her guesthouse, but something tells me she's outgrown it. I'm not entirely sure why she wants to move abroad – maybe she's not even sure – but I get the feeling she's reached a kind of crossroads, wants to test herself in some way. Maybe even test her family?'

'That's for sure' Gavin remarked, 'if she plans to uproot the whole lot of them – how many children did you say she has?'

'Just the one. A boy of nearly twenty. Failed his Leaving twice. Unemployed. She's worried about him.'

'Well, you would be' Crys mused, 'about a hale and hearty young fella who can't find anything to do. We can always use more volunteers at APSO or the Red Cross, if he's got time on his hands.'

'Crys' Shona said wryly, 'I don't think he'd be a whole lot of help to you, God love him.'

'And why has she picked the south of France, in particular?' Gavin looked curious, and Shona grinned. 'I think it picked her! She saw some crazy castle at the property exhibition that caught her fancy – my mission will be to steer her well clear of castles and try to help her find somewhere manageable. Six or eight guests is as much as anyone can manage solo, in my considerable experience of the B & B business.'

'But the son is unemployed, you say . . . . could he not pitch in and help? Earn his keep?'

'Gavin, the son is a punk with studs in every orifice and a purple coxcomb down the middle of his shaved skull. I don't think he's the pitching-in kind.'

'H'mm. I'd pitch him out, so. She won't do him any favours keeping him at home at twenty years of age. Layabout.' Indignantly, Gavin helped everyone to more wine, and then without warning changed tack. 'South of France, you say?'

'Yes. Not the ritzy side, though. We're heading for the Languedoc.'

'Would that be anywhere near Lourdes?'

Quizzically, Shona tried to place Lourdes on her mental map. 'Not a million miles – why?'

'Because if your pal Aileen should set up a B & B anywhere near Lourdes, Crys and I will come down to be her very first customers. In case you haven't heard, we're in search of a miracle.'

The words bounced amidst them like marbles, rolling into a glassy silence, and suddenly Shona felt very, very *de trop*. Much as she loved her friends, this was clearly not the ideal night to be with them. The atmosphere was that of a steaming, botanical hothouse, one frantically trying to propagate a baby, one in which there was no place for a single woman whose attitude to babies had always been privately, secretly ambivalent. Oh, of course, she would have had some if she'd been asked to . . . but she hadn't been asked, had she? The creatures remained a mystery to her, and she had never fully understood Crys's fascination with the subject. Besides, look at Finn Hegarty, surely a living lesson in the folly of the project! As an investment, she'd sooner put her money on a three-legged greyhound.

'Okay, let's go!'

Shona sat revving her sky-blue Citroën Picasso, and in a flurry Aileen chucked her bag into its boot, hurled the requested wallet of CDs into the front passenger seat, and ran back to give Joe a last kiss, Finn a last hug.

'Be good, the pair of you, behave yourselves while I'm away! There are steaks and chicken and curries in the freezer, plenty of clean clothes in the—'

Lolling up against the front wall, Finn waved languidly. 'Yeah, ma. You told us already. In the coal bunker.'

Aileen laughed. Joe turned with unexpected asperity to his son. 'Shut your mouth' he snapped. And on that happy note, Shona backed out of the drive while Aileen was still settling in beside her, looking flustered.

'Check out the music. I brought Dire Straits, Andrea Bocelli, Queen, U2, Elton John, Stones, Nirvana and Charlotte Church . . . what'd you bring?'

Half expecting Aileen to turn back for a last look at her family, Shona was surprised when she didn't. Instead she picked up the music wallet and flipped through it. 'Dean Martin, Robbie Williams, Joe Dolan, the Corrs—'

'*Waahhh!* Not the Corrs!'

'Yes. Sorry. And the Chieftains. In case we get homesick. And Daniel O'Donnell'

'Daniel O'Donnell?! Chuck him out the window. Right now.'

'But I like him!'

'Aileen, you can't like him. Not unless you're a ninety-seven-year-old nun or a four-year-old altar boy.'

'Huh?' She blinked, but Shona was laughing as they drove away. 'So we're getting to know each other already! If you dare put Daniel O'Donnell or the Corrs on that deck, I'll post you home in a jamjar.'

'Well, actually I'm not crazy about your Andrea Whatsit or that Church girl . . . you don't by any chance snore, do you?'

'I beg your pardon? What a weird question.'

'Well, you see, the thing is, Joe snores. Snores his head off. It's been driving me nuts for years and I cannot tell you how much I'm looking forward to getting a good night's sleep at last. Fourteen of them. I'm nearly looking forward to that more than anything else.'

'Oh? Really? Well, I can relate to that. I once broke up with a boyfriend because he snored. Made me yearn to put a pillow over his face and hold it there until the noise stopped. In the end I had to choose between him and jail. Mind you, I would have pleaded insanity.'

With a kind of gratitude, Aileen nodded. 'It would drive you insane, wouldn't it? You have to really love someone to put up with it.'

'Well, I guess I didn't love Aidan Belton, then! Whereas you must love Joe Hegarty – well, of course you love him. He's your husband.'

'Yes. Mind you, I think they should mention snoring in those marriage preparation courses they make you do. Joe and I have had more rows over it than anything else.'

'But he can't help it, can he?'

Unexpectedly, Aileen's face darkened. 'He could try. He could stop drinking six pints four nights a week. The booze makes it worse – he doesn't believe me, but some day I'm going to make a tape and play it back to him.'

Oh? Shona hadn't known Joe drank. But then they all drank, didn't they? Half the men in Ireland spent at least that much time in their pub, if not more; Joe's consumption was hardly excessive by Irish standards. Twenty-four pints a week? – hah, kids' stuff!

'Well, don't worry, I don't snore. You'll get your beauty sleep.'

'Thank God for that. We can share rooms so, along the way . . . will we stay in hotels or guesthouses or what?'

'Depends where we are and what's available. I'd like to try a bit of everything – except camping which should be illegal for anyone over the age of ten.'

'Why? Is it awful? I've never done it.'

'I have. With a bunch of friends on Greek beaches the summer I was twenty. I can't tell you how thrilled I was when the police cleared us off to youth hostels.'

'Greece? I've never been there. Never been anywhere much, really . . . I got married the summer I was twenty. Of course Joe and I have been on holidays since then, but only on package trips to Majorca and the Canaries, since Finn's been old enough to go to sunny places. When he was small we used to go to Kerry or Cork – Joe's parents live in Cork, and we were broke in those days. Besides, you can't go anywhere too hot with a small child.'

Nooo . . . Shona couldn't imagine not going anywhere hot, she lived for the sun and had travelled avidly ever since her teens. She couldn't imagine being broke, either, didn't see anything romantic in it at all. Unless a man earned at least as much as she did herself, what was the *point* of him?

What was the point of husbands who snored or layabout sons who looked like savages? You'd have to be literally madly in love to put up with the likes of what Aileen appeared to put up with.

And yet, Aileen was the married one, the securely 'settled' one whom society respectfully called 'Mrs', while she, Shona

Fitzpatrick, was the problem. She was the one who'd never yet married anyone, good, bad or indifferent. The one who'd been dumped only last week and cried herself to sleep every night since. Where was the logic in that? Frowning, she tried to work out the logic until Aileen's voice cut across her reverie.

'Shona – do you always drive this fast?'

She glanced down, and the speedometer said eighty mph. 'Only on decent roads! This one to Rosslare's not bad.'

It was not bad at all, but still Aileen looked faintly anxious, clutching surreptitiously at the edge of her seat, stifling gasps as they zipped along; Shona guessed she must be a steady forty mph driver herself, who would take years to reach the south of France if allowed behind the wheel. So I won't let her behind it, she thought, until we get there.

Rosslare appeared well ahead of schedule, where they had time for lunch before driving onto the ferry, parking in its innards and taking their luggage up to their extremely snug cabin. Looking at it, Aileen was relieved: if Shona snored in a space this tight, I surely would smother her. Thank God Joe isn't here!

Without bothering to unpack, Shona threw her luggage on the upper bunk, pinned up her hair and threw a sweater over her shoulders. 'Come on, let's go up on deck and stretch our legs.'

Following her, Aileen grasped an essential point of information; Shona somehow seemed to be the boss on this trip, was taking charge in some invisible way. Aileen didn't object in the least – on the contrary, it was a pleasure not to have to do all the thinking and organising for a change. Yet she was the older one, it was her house they were going to find . . . so how come Shona was the one with the air of authority?

Because she'd travelled before, probably; because she knew France and it would hold no surprises for her. Because she was brisk and organised by nature, the kind of travelling companion who wouldn't be fazed by anything. Cheerful, too; so far she hadn't even mentioned her broken heart, although her eyes were puffy when she briefly removed her sunglasses. When she put them back on she looked lovely, much younger than thirty-six in white trainers, blue denims and white linen shirt, with her hair pinned up and barely any make-up. In the tourism office she'd always worn a jade-green uniform, tights, lipstick and heels, which while appropriate had been formal. Now, she seemed fresh and relaxed.

Up on deck it was a mellow afternoon, warm for November, and they stood looking down into a calm, emerald-green Irish Sea as the ship prepared to depart.

'My God' Aileen murmured, half to herself, 'I can't believe I'm doing this. I'm on my way to buy my house in the sun, at last.'

To her surprise, Shona draped an arm around her shoulder and squeezed it. 'Yes, you are! Don't expect too much, Aileen, we might not find the right one in a mere two weeks – but we'll have fun whether we do or not, have a lovely holiday at least. And I have a mobile phone if you want to call Joe to let him know how you're getting on . . . here, why not give him a shout now, let him know the ship is sailing?'

Rummaging in her pocket, she held it out, but Aileen shook her head. Later, she would talk to Joe, of course, and Finn as well; right now she wanted this moment to herself.

This is *my* moment, she thought. I own it, it belongs to me. I don't want to share it with anyone. This is a perfect moment, full of hope and promise. How many of those does anyone get, to call her own?

Over the course of the trip, Shona and Aileen discovered many things they had not known about each other. During dinner, accompanied by a bottle of wine to which Shona insisted on treating them, they talked about their childhoods, their schools, their friends, their families and their interests, which in Shona's case included 'swimming, travel, tennis and soccer'.

'Soccer? You go to soccer matches?'

'Yes – and I play it! Love it. I'm goalie on a women's team.'

Really? How odd. Aileen didn't know any other women who played soccer. The news made her feel a bit frumpy; as Joe often remarked, her idea of exercise was raiding the fridge. Well, she did walk a bit – usually guiltily, after she'd raided it – but that was hardly what you'd call sporty. No wonder Shona was so slim. A little enviously, she said so.

'Oh, that's not just the soccer! I work out at a gym as well, and watch my diet like a hawk.'

Aileen gaped. She certainly didn't seem to be watching it at this moment, was in fact hoovering up a beef stroganoff. 'Do you?'

'Yep. Have to look good in the tourism industry – especially if you want promotion – and besides my kind of guy goes for well-toned women.'

'Does he? And what's your kind of guy, Shona?' Aileen asked a trifle gingerly, not wanting to unleash a torrent of tears for Brendan Wright.

'My kind of guy – mmm, this is delicious – my kind of guy is well-toned himself, in mind and body. Fit, successful, good-looking, articulate. The kind I can take anywhere in complete confidence, knowing he'll never say the wrong thing or make a show of me.'

'I see.' Fleetingly, Aileen thought of Joe, who'd once famously told a woman in a department store that the outfit she was trying on was 'criminal, madam, criminally hideous on you or any woman'. Which cringe-inducing candour had been a surprise, because he never noticed anything she wore herself. If he had, if he'd ever commented on any new outfit or hairdo or any effort she made, she might not have raided the fridge quite so often.

'But – but what about his personality? I mean, don't you want someone kind and supportive and caring? Someone who'd ... er ... um ... love you? I'd have thought you were a romantic kind of girl, Shona.'

'Oh – let's have some dessert – I am. I mean, I was, once. Years ago. But then I got sense. Romance is wasted on the young. Once you hit thirty, you get sense. I did, anyway.'

Aileen was intrigued. 'Did you? How? Why?'

'I grew up. I realised that I could furnish myself with most of the things men provide in – uh – some marriages. Nice home, clothes, car, holidays, all that. Of course, sex and friendship are important too, but you can have those without getting married. The only thing marriage really offers is joint parenting for children, and social status for adults. It's important to have that ring on your finger – d'you think that chocolate pie might be as good as it looks?'

Baffled, Aileen turned to inspect the dessert trolley. What happened to this diet Shona claimed to scrupulously follow?

'Why don't we share a slice? If your diet permits?'

'Oh, it permits now – I'm going to take a break from it while we're in France! We're only halfway there yet, but never mind.' With that she got up to fetch a plate of the pie and two spoons, leaving Aileen wondering, sipping the last of the wine that emboldened her to ask the next question.

'And – and what about children? What about ... er ... Brendan?'

Seizing her spoon, Shona held it aloft a moment before plunging it into the pie. 'Yes. Brendan wanted children.'

Curiously, Aileen waited. But nothing further came. When the pie was despatched, Shona sat back looking strangely satisfied, not at all the tragic figure she'd cut in Heyden's of Galway barely a week before. Even her puffy eyes seemed to be calming down, clearing up. 'And what about you, Aileen?'

'Me? What about me?'

'You, and Joe, and Finn! You're a wife, a mother . . . do you recommend it as a career option?'

Spluttering, Aileen laughed. She certainly hadn't married Joe as a 'career option'. She'd married him because . . . well, because you simply did, didn't you, when a man said he loved you and asked nicely and didn't have a prison record? When you were fond of him and he seemed the kind who'd call the doctor if you were ill, paint the house if it needed painting, take out the bin without having to be reminded every Wednesday night?

Joe, God love him, even endured Tessie's visits with good grace, teasing her since her hearing had gone wonky: 'Did that money fall out of your handbag, Tess, or mine?' If he wasn't a prize he wasn't a handicap either – unless you counted the snoring – their marriage certainly wasn't a mistake or anything. The mistake, if mistake there was, had come after-wards. Two years, to be precise, after the wedding. Its name was Finn.

'It doesn't exactly work like that, Shona. You can't give a marriage marks the way a teacher would give an exam marks. All I can say is that mine, on balance, is pretty good. Joe may not be sophisticated or handsome or very successful, but I could have done worse.'

It was only a tiny rebuke, and Shona accepted it with a wry smile. 'Sorry, I didn't mean that the way it sounded! So you're happy, then?'

'Yes. Of course. Why wouldn't I be?' Why, indeed? Suddenly Aileen wanted a cup of tea, and an end to this rather personal conversation.

'No reason! I'm just always interested to know whether marriage is as great as it's cracked up to be, that's all. Since everyone thinks it's high time I got married myself.'

Aileen peered over her shoulder in the direction of a tea dispenser. In this self-service restaurant you had to get up and get everything. 'Do you think it's time you did?'

'Well . . . yes, if I want to have children.'

'And do you want to?'

Chin on knuckles, Shona reflected. 'That's the question. The one question I can never honestly answer. Children devour so much time and attention and . . . I love my work . . . and . . . I've just never been a hundred per cent sure.'

Standing up, Aileen went to get a pot of tea. 'In that case' she advised over her shoulder as she went, 'I'd strongly advise you against it.'

Startled, Shona stared after her. What was that candid, yet enigmatic, remark supposed to mean? Aileen Hegarty was the first woman she'd ever met who didn't instantly, automatically say 'oh yes, motherhood is the most wonderful thing in the world, the best day's work I ever did.'

Aileen refused to be drawn as they finished their meal, changed the subject and then suggested a visit to the ship's cinema. Baulked, because she'd been enjoying getting to know her, Shona gave in; after all, they would be spending many more evenings together. Meanwhile, it could certainly be said in Aileen's favour that she wasn't a nosy woman, didn't have to know every blessed thing about you before she had any right to know. Like Shona, she seemed to feel that friendship evolved gradually, could not be brewed in two minutes like a cup of Maxwell House. After the cinema they went to their cabin, fell instantly and deeply asleep and awoke nine hours later to find the French coast already in view.

Chirpily, Shona waved at it: she hadn't seen France for two or three years, and suddenly realised she'd been missing it. Her last visit had been to a tourism conference in Lyon, where she'd had an absolutely wonderful time. The kind of carefree time you couldn't have, could you, if you were fretting whether your husband had made the kids their ReadyBrek and whether everyone had found a clean shirt for work or school?

Was that what Aileen was, in fact, fretting about now? It must be, she supposed, because she was quiet as they dressed and went up on deck, looking not exultant but thoughtful, plucking absently at a strand of maple-blonde hair whipped loose by the wind.

'Penny for them?'

'Oh . . . oh, I'm just drinking it in! My first sight of France . . . imagine, Shona, this could be my new home some day. Maybe even by Christmas.'

'No, Aileen, sorry! Definitely not by then, Christmas is only six weeks off, buying a house takes months even after you've found one.'

'Oh, you're so – so realistic! So businesslike! Let me dream, just for a minute . . . will it all be completely exotic, when we drive off? Immediately, totally French?'

'Totally. Virtually your first sight will be a splendid historic landmark with big golden arches. The French call it McDo, short for McDonald's.'

'Oh, no!? There was never any McDonald's on *A Place in the Sun* or in the magazines.'

'I'll bet there wasn't. Bet all the houses were thatched and timbered, or slate and stone? Covered in vines, surrounded by lavender with a white lunch table out front, right? Knee-deep in grass and butterflies, tablecloth floating on the breeze, baguette, home-made apricot jam? Black bicycle, wicker basket, pink roses, terracotta pots?'

'Yes! Exactly!' Aileen's face filled with such a mixture of bliss and indignation that Shona was forced to smile contritely; maybe this dream was too delicate, too fragile to make fun of. Even if you couldn't work very long in tourism without developing a sense of humour.

'All right! Then we'll find you the last lovingly restored, authentically charming old house in France . . . cheer up, I was only joking!'

Aileen smiled, but Shona saw that she'd been right: this project was important to her. Very important, for reasons that would no doubt unfold as the trip progressed. Leading the way down to the car deck, she located a map in the Picasso when they reached it, and handed it to Aileen as she started the engine.

'*Voilà, chérie.* Your future begins here. Start plotting the way to it.'

Cherbourg was not France's finest city, but Aileen nodded sympathetically as Shona explained why: the entire coast of Normandy had been bombed virtually to powder during the war, rebuilt in a hurry afterwards. Housing homeless people had been more urgent than architectural niceties.

'That's sad. I've often thought about the millions of people who died, but the loss of all those lovely old buildings never crossed my mind.'

'Happily, there are plenty left inland. The further south we go, the more you'll see.'

Sitting back with the map on her lap, Aileen was instantly distracted from her job of navigator by brief glimpses of the occasional old building that had survived – ones like those she had seen on television, with thatched roofs and ancient timbers.

'That one looks as if it was designed by Hansel & Gretel plc!'

Adjusting to driving on the right, Shona smiled without replying. Later, she could unwind and enjoy herself, after she'd found her way out of this town, teeming with traffic, which appeared to have been designed by Global Chaos plc.

Speculatively, Aileen sniffed the air. 'Something smells different . . . what is it I smell?'

Shona couldn't say. France was no longer redolent, as it had once been, of garlic and Gitanes cigarettes. 'I dunno – what?'

'Bread! Baking bread, that's what it is! My God, look, they're queueing for it!'

Sure enough people were, chatting in groups outside one bakery after another, and Shona smiled. 'Sunday morning is gourmet morning in France. Sociable, too. Everyone goes to the shops for bread and cakes, then to the florist to get flowers for whoever's cooking lunch . . . they don't mind queueing because it gives them a chance to gossip like blazes.'

'Are they gossipy?'

'Ha! Aren't people everywhere?'

'I suppose. God, Shona, I'm going to have to do something about learning a bit of French, I can't even read the names or signs.'

Shona considered. 'I'll teach you a bit, if you like, while we're driving along.'

Looking delighted, Aileen beamed at her. 'Would you? Would you really?'

'Sure. I'm a bit rusty, but it always comes back after a day or two.'

'How did you learn it – at college?'

'No, my degree is in commerce. I learned French as an au pair the summer I left school. I worked for a family in the Dordogne and damn near killed their child.'

Electrified, Aileen froze. '*What?*'

'Mmm. Not deliberately, but very nearly. She was barely a

year old. Her mother told me she was allergic to eggs and never to give her any. What I understood was that I was to give her an egg for lunch. So I boiled one, mashed it up with milk and spoon-fed it to her. An hour later, she was in hospital on a life support machine.'

Silence. Complete silence, while Aileen absorbed this, looking as horrified as if she'd been the child's mother herself. Reflectively, Shona sighed. 'Young Sandrine survived, was none the worse in the end, but talk about a fright. I resolved to learn French properly after that. And I did.'

No response. Shona swivelled her head a fraction to glance at her. 'Aileen? What's the matter? You look aghast – but it was eighteen years ago! I'm sure baby Sandrine is hale and hearty these days, probably has her mother's heart broken like every other teenager.'

More silence. A long, long silence, one in which Shona regretted having told the tale, which seemed to be affecting Aileen in the way, she supposed, only mothers could be affected when they heard scary baby stories. At the time, it had taken the unlucky infant's mother a good week to recover, a week Shona still recalled as the most excruciatingly embarrassing of her life.

They had travelled several miles out of Cherbourg and into the countryside before the colour began to creep back into Aileen's face and she spoke at last in a low, strained voice. 'I'm glad the child survived, Shona. Very glad. Your life would have been ruined you know, you'd never have forgiven yourself even though it wasn't your fault.'

'Tell me about it! I was coming out in cold sweats for months afterwards. Still do, if I think about it . . . hey, wouldn't it be fun to see if I can find the family while we're here? Look them up in the phone book and maybe even visit them, the Dordogne is kinda on our route? I'd love to see Sandrine and her little brat of a brother, he was only two then but he must be a strapping chap by now. '

Aileen gripped the map as it ballooned across her knees. 'I – I'd really rather not. We're going to be busy house-hunting, we only have two weeks.'

'True. Oh well. Maybe some other time. Don't panic, Aileen, it was only a thought! I wasn't suggesting jumping off a cliff.'

'Sorry. I – I'm just a bit disorientated. Besides I don't speak any French, I wouldn't be able to talk to them. Let's put on some music.' Taking a CD at random from the wallet Shona had brought, she slipped it into the deck without even looking to see what it was. Charlotte Church wafted up: the 'voice of an angel'.

'But I thought you didn't like Charlotte Church?'

In one swift motion, Aileen ripped it out and slammed Queen into its slot. 'No. I don't. I – Shona, d'you think we could find a pit stop some time soon? I'd really like to splash my face and have a coffee.'

Bemused, Shona nodded. Aileen was looking pale and edgy, as if something about France, or the music or the drive or something, was unsettling her. 'Sure. We'll pull in at the next village – are you okay?'

Breathing deeply, Aileen leaned forward and dropped her head between her knees. 'Yes. I'm fine. Just a little dizzy spell – bit car-sick or something. All I need is a glass of water and a breath of air.'

So they pulled in, and fifteen minutes later Aileen was perfectly revived, having had both and even survived a visit to an old-style French loo, which she pronounced 'the most unspeakable horror' she had ever encountered. Shona laughed, but she agreed with her.

'That's the first thing I'd do if I was running the tourism

show in a wealthy, modern country like France. Dynamite all this dreadful plumbing. Some of it's a real nightmare – as bad as the Irish public transport service!'

'Or health service' – Aileen shuddered with feeling – 'it could leave you lying on a trolley in a hospital corridor for days.'

Shona mused on it as they got back into the car. 'I have to warn you, hygiene is not France's strongest point. But so much else is so beautiful . . . this isn't the kind of country you can take or leave, Aileen. You'll either love it or loathe it.'

'I see. Well, right now that could quite honestly go either way.'

The countryside gradually mutated from urban to rustic as they drove along, and Aileen sat quietly inspecting it, absorbing Shona's steady flow of information.

'Colleville-sur-Mer – there's an American war cemetery there that gets as many tourists in a year as Ireland gets.'

'You're kidding.'

'I swear. Millions. Maybe not so many this year though, after September 11 . . . that road goes to Villedieu-les-Poêles, which means God's Town of the Frying Pans. The French never stop thinking about food. Normandy is big into cider, cream, cheese, potatoes, beetroot and shellfish. Agricultural turf.'

'Really? And what's the Languedoc into?'

'Wine! It's quite different down there, equally cute to look at but in a completely different way. They drink pastis and play boules and take long naps . . . you'd be hard pushed to find a phone booth open in the afternoons. Too warm for work.'

'Even in November?'

'Can be. Let's turn on the radio and get the weather forecast.'

Shona snapped it on, and after a little while the forecast duly came up. Aileen saw with astonishment that Shona actually understood it.

'Yep, sunny down there, twenty-five degrees, the mistral is blowing a bit on the coast.'

'Well. Imagine that. The man might have said Mars has just exploded for all I understood.'

Serenely, Shona drove on, dispensing bits of news along the way. 'The population of Normandy is about the same as Ireland's, three and a half million, le Mont-St Michel is the most popular site in France after Versailles . . .' Really she was a mine of information, and Aileen thought how lucky she was to have the company of someone so – so useful! Not just chatty and cheery, but fluent and knowledgeable. Shona would be able to negotiate with estate agents and all kinds of people she'd never even thought about until now . . . solicitors, builders, the gas company, phone company, water and electrical companies. Repair men, delivery men, those aggravating men who always said no, they couldn't come before Thursday fortnight and when they did it would cost five zillion euros. There would, now that she thought about it, be quite a lot of people involved in the acquisition, furnishing and decorating of a house. Dozens. In fact it was daunting, actually. What if Shona couldn't see the whole thing through? What if it took months and she won her court case and had to go back to work? It dawned on Aileen with hideous clarity that she would be high and dry without Shona. Yet she couldn't possibly ask her to stick with the project, which would surely take until Easter to complete at the earliest.

Oh, God. Oh, well. She'd just have to hope for the best and make maximum use of Shona's skills while they were available. Sitting back, she admired the scenery some more and began to secretly plot ways of seducing Shona into staying for as long as she possibly could.

'Okay. Enough driving. Let's find somewhere to stay.'

Agreeably, privately relieved, Aileen nodded. Shona drove very fast, they'd clocked up a long distance and – and dear God, France had some awfully high bridges, hills and dramatic villages clinging to cliffs by their fingernails. Going over one particularly terrifying bridge, with a view down into a swirling river miles below, she had nearly passed out, had to shut her eyes until a wave of dizziness receded. She'd never known she suffered from vertigo, but . . . uhhh. Please don't let there be many more high bits like today's. Please let the rest of it be gentle, like Galway.

They were coming into the outskirts of a town, with hoardings advertising several hotels which, she was pleased to see, boasted very reasonable prices.

'Formule . . . Campanile . . . Ibis . . . Kyriad . . . ?'

Shona shook her head. 'God, no. Little prison cells. Computerised, no staff, you check in and out by automated credit card. Get out the guidebook and let's see if there's anything run by human beings.'

Hoping that human wouldn't equal expensive, Aileen fished it out and Shona pulled into a lay-by, where she ran her finger down the page and swiftly picked a promising-sounding inn. 'L'Auberge de l'Etang. Forty euros, that all right?'

Aileen quailed. 'Each?'

'No, for a twin room. With bath and option of eating *en famille*.'

'Eating with the family? But – but how would I *talk* to them?'

Shona laughed aloud. 'Aileen, if you plan to live in France you're going to have to muddle along! Come on, let's find this place.'

Without much difficulty they soon did find it; an adorable little inn swathed in coppery autumnal leaves, with a tiny duck pond and a genial man who said yes, certainly he could give the ladies a room. Tonight, Madame would be cooking her famous marmite, if they would they care to dine on the premises?

Decisively, Shona said they would. An hour later, after a nap on deliciously soft cottony beds and a hot shower, they came down to join the family, which consisted of papa who was stoking a log fire, maman who was chef 'of both cuisine and family', an adult daughter and a chubby, gurgling baby. While Shona began to talk amiably to them, Aileen was struck dumb. Not one single sentence was she able to understand, nothing whatever beyond 'bonsoir'.

I never bargained for this, she thought with some small degree of mutiny. I never thought about the wall of French to be climbed over. Never realised, either, how well Shona speaks it.

Good job too. At least tonight she won't have any excuse for trying to poison the baby.

Heaven. Sheer heaven, that was what it was to sleep all night without Joe Hegarty snoring alongside. Waking profoundly refreshed, Aileen rose early, bathed and went down to breakfast before Shona, where she was dismayed to find nothing on the table only two bowls, a baguette and a pot of jam. Despite last night's 'marmite', which had turned out to be a fragrant fish stew, she was hungry again now. When Madame came bustling in to ask what she'd like – tea, coffee, hot chocolate? – she wondered how you said 'mixed grill with brown toast, strawberry yogurt and some fruit, please'?

'You don't,' Shona informed her when she eventually appeared. 'The French don't do that kind of breakfast.'

'Don't they?' Shocked, she reflected on this. In her B & B, no guest ever left the house without a good hot breakfast under their belt; it was a point of pride, almost competitive. Shona's chum Emily O'Brien was the acknowledged champ in their area, famous for home-made porridge, sausages, bread, fresh juice and fresh flowers every morning. Whereas this family, friendly as they were, didn't seem to know breakfast from – from these blue bowls! What were bowls for – cereal?

No. Drinking out of Shona said, pouring hot chocolate into hers and dunking a chunk of baguette; there wasn't even any butter, or plates! Not impressed, Aileen made up her mind: when she got her French B & B off the ground, she'd do proper breakfasts. With proper cups. And plates. And everything. So there.

It was after ten by the time they left, setting out into country-side that was changing rapidly, the dairy pastures of the north giving way to first crops and then fields of frosted silvery sunflowers. On the plus side, it was a beautiful sunny day; on the minus side, there were several more bridges, canyons and ravines. Queasily, Aileen shuddered, but said nothing.

'We're coming into Cathar country' Shona announced. 'Knights Templar, Simon de Montfort and all that.'

Oh. Feeling on uncertain ground – who the hell was Simon de Montfort? – Aileen gulped as she spotted a fortress high up on a hill. 'We – uh – we're not going up there, are we?'

Yes. Evidently they were. The road wound higher and higher, narrowing and twisting horribly, until it was just a steep track into the sky. Clenching her fists, sweating, she fell silent while, with much inching along edges, unnerving crunching of gears, they wended their way to the towering top. Up left was the fortress; down right was a plunge to perdition, into infinity. I never could have driven this, she thought, never in a million years. Finally, nonchalantly, Shona pulled in, jumped out and whistled admiringly at the surly-looking fortress.

'Wow! Cool castle, huh?'

'Yes – er – Shona, d'you think I could borrow your phone?'

'Sure.' She handed it over and, shaking, Aileen seized it. Out of the blue, she felt an urgent longing to talk to Joe, to hear his familiar voice. Punching the numbers she waited while the phone rang in Galway, thinking how odd it was to be calling from this remote, spectacular outpost.

But Joe had left for work, and Aileen felt a flash of irritation zip through her: wake up, Finn, get up and answer the phone! If my husband's not there I want my son, I want to talk to my family!

No response. Giving up, she handed the mobile back to Shona. 'Goddammit, I know he's there. Fast asleep, the lazy bastard.'

Shona grinned. 'Your lovely little boy, you mean?'

'Yes. Only he's neither little nor lovely. He's . . . oh, I just don't know what he is. Unemployed, is what. A worry, is what.'

H'mm. Shona thought for a moment on that. Aileen looked both annoyed and anxious. But really it was a pity, in this lovely place on this lovely day! Her own spirits were high as a kite, she was enjoying the trip, the sun, the adventure and change of air.

'Oh well, don't worry. You can call again later. Look – down there, see?'

Aileen looked, and nearly fainted. 'Down there' was the other side of the steep hill they had just climbed, a vast, distant expanse of reddish land punctuated by villages, churches and a narrow, weaving, treacherous road back down. It looked barely wide enough to accommodate a skateboard, never mind a car.

'Uh – Shona, I don't think I'm very good on heights. Or those roads like S-bends. They're making me nauseous.'

Oh? Oh, dear. Knowing what was coming next, Shona

thought maybe she'd better say nothing. The Languedoc, when they reached it, would be full of ups and downs and – um. Airily, she smiled. 'Shut your eyes then, until we're down on the flat and we'll take the autoroute to Albi.'

Autoroute. Thank God. Gratefully Aileen smiled back. Nice wide comfy road with lots of lanes, that could hardly climb up into the clouds, could it? Trustingly, like a child, she got back into the car and they set off. How come nobody on *A Place in the Sun* had ever mentioned that France was a series of sheer cliffs and soaring bridges, with raging rivers a million miles below? How come nobody had ever mentioned that the language was completely impenetrable, or that you couldn't get a decent breakfast? Not that it mattered at this moment, because she only would have lost it anyway, on that last bend where there had been birds swooping way *under* her line of vision. With gathering momentum, a wave of apprehension started to coil and loom, poise itself somewhere over Aileen's spinning head: apparently there were aspects of this project nobody warned you about. It was going to be more than simply a question of choosing a new house and planting fistfuls of geraniums. Had Shona not been with her, she might well have just tottered to the nearest airport, and gone home.

Albi was a beautiful, graceful old town and after a very long haul they arrived in time to visit its cathedral, to stretch their legs in its winding medieval streets before selecting a hotel where, as night fell, comedy ensued: the light in the corridor cut off every twenty seconds. Twice they were plunged into darkness and, when they finally stumbled to their room, they couldn't see the keyhole to open the door.

'We'd better tell reception there's something wrong with the lighting' Aileen said, but Shona shook her head. 'No, there's nothing wrong with it. It's just on one of these bloody timers

French hotels use to save electricity. Run down the corridor and push that little button, that'll bring the light back on.'

Well! Honestly! Feeling her way, Aileen edged to where the button was glowing, unable to believe that management would risk people breaking their necks in the dark in order to save pennies. What if you were old or handicapped or tripped over your suitcase in this miserable gloom? Snapping on the light, she made another resolution: her B & B, like the one in Galway, would be *bright*. Bright and cheerful with none of this penny-pinching that only annoyed people and put them off the whole place. Although this was an otherwise pleasant hotel, she was resenting it already; it seemed to have what the Americans would call an 'attitude problem'.

'Then say so' Shona suggested. 'Management won't fix it if they don't know about it.'

'Well, yes. True. 'But I can't speak French.'

'Okay, then I'll do it. Later, on our way out to eat.'

And so she did, nonchalantly but firmly, at the reception desk an hour later. Impressed, Aileen watched and listened, realising there was a professional way of complaining, a technique for getting the message across without conflict. Shona never raised her voice, smiled charmingly in fact, whereupon the woman at the desk smiled back, noted her comments and said something conciliatory.

'There we are' Shona said airily as they sailed out, 'she's going to tell the manager that we love the hotel but consider the lighting dangerous. The rest is up to him.'

Good. Aileen felt a surge of satisfaction; it really was much better to say something than seethe in silence. Only fair, too; management could hardly solve problems that nobody ever mentioned. On her own modest premises, she'd been baffled and enraged one day last year by a Swiss guest who'd loudly complained at the end of his four-day stay that he couldn't read in bed because the bedside lamp was broken: the bulb was merely blown and she'd have replaced it immediately if he'd only told her.

As they made their way on foot from the hotel into the centre, Albi was glowing in the dusk, a mellow little city to which they both warmed as they wandered round inspecting menus. How delicious, Aileen thought, to be able to go out on a November evening wearing just a light woolly, to saunter round without feeling at all chilly. Mind you, Shona looks a bit tired, but then she must be. I'm bog all help to her as far as driving is concerned.

But it was Shona who did most of the talking during dinner, keeping up lively and animated conversation until they got to the coffee stage when, finally, she began to flag. Feeling guilty, Aileen wondered whether maybe she'd like a liqueur? She certainly deserved some little treat. Shona smiled – how pretty she was, with that wide mouth and those mauve eyes! 'Mmm, maybe a Benedictine? It's from Normandy, where we drove through yesterday. But only if you'll have one too – go on, try it.'

Obediently Aileen tried it, and liked it, and there was a lull while they gazed into it, gradually absorbing the fact that they had covered a huge chunk of their journey today, and would reach their destination tomorrow. Carcassonne, at last, and that castle to visit! Plus three other premises the estate agent had selected, assuming they arrived at noon on schedule. Thoughtfully, Aileen surveyed Shona, who seemed to be lapsing into some kind of nostalgic reverie.

'Thanks for doing all this driving, Shona. I really appreciate it. I'll start doing my bit soon, I promise – just short trips to begin with, but enough to give you a break.'

'Mmm . . . it's easy really, you know. You'll get used to it in no time.'

But her mind seemed to be drifting, her glass tilting in her hand as it rested on the table, her eyes following people down the street as the Albigensians began to wend their way home to bed. Sympathetically, Aileen smiled. 'You are tired, aren't you? You're saying nothing but I can see you are.'

Shona thought about it. 'No. It's not that. I'm just a bit . . . distracted.'

'Oh? By what – this lovely city?'

'No. By Brendan Wright. I'm wondering where he is at this moment, what he's doing, who he's with.'

Speculatively, her eyes widened, and Aileen saw veiled emotion in them; a kind of hurt, a kind of ache. Swiftly, Shona changed the subject.

'And my job. I'm wondering about that too. I can't believe I've really been suspended, am going to court . . . I must have been in shock or something, because it's only starting to hit me now, to sink in just how fragile my future is looking.'

'Well, two huge shocks one on top of the other would knock anyone sideways. But Shona, I can't imagine anyone whose future could look less fragile – you're so qualified and capable, you'll never be short of work. And you're so sweet, so attractive and extrovert and good-humoured, the next man will be very lucky to get you.'

'H'mm . . . and the next, and the next. Until I'm forty and suddenly they're all dating dolly birds and I'm history. I don't know what or why it is, Aileen, but men just seem to – to slide off me, somehow! I don't know what I did to send Brendan running, but I wish I knew . . . wish I knew how this court case is going to pan out, too. Suppose I lose it, lose my job?'

'But how could you? It sounds quite clear-cut to me. He assaulted you, had been harassing you for ages.'

'Yes. And I hit him. That's assault in turn. The union rep says he can't be totally sure things will go my way . . . even if I don't lose my job I'll almost certainly lose my promotion. I'll be stuck in a dead end. They might even decide to shunt me out of the way to some backwater. Some hellhole I'll absolutely hate. Oh, Jesus, why did I ever wallop Terry blasted O'Hagan!?'

'Because he provoked it and he deserved it. Come on, Shona, cheer up. It's probably just exhaustion. Things will look brighter in the morning.'

Consolingly, Aileen patted her hand. Draining her drink, Shona nodded, but didn't look convinced. In fact, Aileen thought as they stood up to leave the restaurant, she looks like someone who could use a hug, she's really worried about her job, and upset about that boyfriend. A fat lot of use I am to her, dragging her down the length of France on this – this madness!

That's what it is, really, isn't it? Now that we're actually here I can see it. Joe was right. I know nothing about this country or any other for that matter, France feels so – so very foreign! I don't speak the language or have a clue about anything, and the thought of reaching Carcassonne tomorrow, of going to see that château, is beginning to be more terrifying than exciting.

I'm way out of my depth. If it wasn't for having hauled Shona such a huge distance, if she weren't going to so much trouble to help me – in the midst of her own problems – I'd chicken out. I'd ring Joe right now and admit it – yes, you were right. Yes, dear, I'm off my rocker. Yes, I'm on the next plane home, and normal service will be resumed shortly.

When they returned to their hotel, feeling torn, she did ring Joe. But in vain. 'He's down the pub with Dave Doherty' Finn said shortly, in a tone that told her he didn't appreciate being interrupted in the midst of his computer studies.

4

'Ooo' Aileen gasped desperately, 'oooh – ooohh – ooohhh.'

'No' corrected Shona, 'euh. Euh – euh – euh.'

Aileen fizzed with laughter. 'Shona, I can't! I sound like a mating owl!'

Sighing, Shona swung the car onto a roundabout. 'All right. Let's forget the French lesson for now. At least you can count up to twelve. We'll do the alphabet tomorrow.' And with that she unexpectedly burst into song, an old school lullaby that even Aileen remembered, 'Sur le pont d'Avignon'. Delighted not to be thrown out of the car, because Shona must surely be fed up trying to teach such a duffer, Aileen hummed along, and suddenly they were both laughing, loving their ridiculous adventure as the Languedoc-Roussillon unrolled before them, gleaming in the morning sunlight. Hazy in the distance, cresting a hill, an enormous castle hove into view.

'Good God, what's that?'

'That's Carcassonne Cité. Famous landmark. Built to last, centuries ago. We could have lunch there if we hurry, before we meet the estate agent.'

So they drove up to the sprawling castle, Aileen peering at it agog. 'It makes the Rock of Cashel look like a sandcastle!' Inside was an entire fortified town, where they snacked in haste, at an outdoor café under a plane tree. Awestruck, Aileen peered around her, feeling some gear shifting inside her, as if she had arrived at some turning point. 'This is so beautiful . . .

and it's so bright, so warm . . . the sun feels like a beauty treatment, a massage!'

'Yeah, well, shake a leg, we have to find the estate agent's, I assume it's down in the lower town.' Speedily, Shona despatched the last of her coffee and gathered her things, Aileen trailing behind her, reluctant to leave this lovely environment.

But if I find a house, I can come back, can't I? Come back and visit this fairytale properly? If I find a house I'll be *living* here. We all will, Joe and Finn and myself.

If. If, if . . . imagine if.

Back in the car Shona consulted the agency's phone number, rang for directions and, barely ten minutes later, pulled into a parking spot in the business sector of Carcassonne. 'Well, here we are!'

Beaming, Aileen leaned across to impulsively hug her. 'Thank you! Oh, thank you so much, Shona, I'd never have done all this on my own – you've been fantastic. Simply fantastic.'

Blushing, Shona shrugged. 'Don't mention it. And don't – *do not* – say or do anything rash this afternoon. Got that? If the agent shows us any property you're interested in, don't start jumping up and down shrieking that it's gorgeous, it's perfect . . . just play it cool, okay? We'll visit everywhere he's lined up for us and talk about them all later. The main thing is to pretend you're merely interested, that you might or might not buy, depending on numerous factors. You won't get any bargains if he thinks you're mad keen.'

No. Aileen supposed not. But she was mad keen, today! Suddenly it all made sense, her plan was taking shape and she was raring to go, dying to see the château of her dreams, or manor or whatever it might be . . . oh, this whole place was delicious! Look at that blue sky, those rosy flowers, those silvery trees, those yummy shops, those people drinking something pink under that parasol . . .

Shona yanked her by the arm. 'Come on, stop gawping.' Briskly, she led her down the street to the agency, and it seemed to Aileen that even its name was lovely: Les Volets Verts. In the window was an illustration of an old, crumbly house, with faded, pistachio-green shutters.

Inside, all was crisply white, chrome and glass. A chic blonde secretary looked up over a pair of red spectacles. '*Bonjour, mesdames.*'

'*Bonjour,*' Shona replied, taking charge, 'I'm Mme Fitzpatrick and this is Mme Hegarty. We have an appointment with your M Delatre for two o'clock.'

Before the secretary could even reply there was a surge of energy from some inner office and a beaming man of around forty came striding out, hand outstretched. 'Ah, yes, the Irish ladies! Sit down, sit down!'

Down they sat, while he rummaged eagerly in a cabinet and produced a file with the triumphant air of a conjuror. 'The Manoir du Vent' – he glanced at his watch – 'at two thirty, yes? And then Les Oliviers at four, Les Rosiers at five, Mme Tesseron's house at six. We have a busy afternoon – I hope you are not too tired after your journey?'

Although he spoke excellent English, it was still Shona who answered. 'Oh no, not at all, we drove down slowly from Cherbourg.'

Slowly! Aileen gasped. She felt as if she'd been whizzed through a spin-dryer. She also felt invisible, as if Shona were the one buying a house. But it's me, she thought incredulously; it is actually me, you know, even if Shona looks far more likely.

M Delatre threw on his jacket, bundled his paperwork into a briefcase and produced his car keys. 'So, let's go. We'll take my car and we can talk on the way.' Leading them out, he led the way at a trot to a white Citroen and ushered them in: somehow Aileen ended up in the back, with Shona alongside him in front. As they set off, he began to interrogate them curiously.

'So, you wish to buy a guesthouse!? And why have you chosen this particular part of France?'

A perfectly logical question, to which Aileen could think of no answer. Because I'm mad, she thought. That's what my husband says anyway. My husband drinks, you know. He's a good guy, but he drinks. And I hardly dare think what my son does.

'Because it's beautiful' Shona replied, 'because it's in a good tourism area, it's near the coast, it has an airport and the climate is wonderful.'

M Delatre nodded. A chubby chap with chestnut-brown eyes, he seemed delighted to be involved – indeed instrumental – in their project. 'Yes, quite so. It's served by the TGV too – you know, the high-speed train – from Paris. Plus access from Spain is excellent, it's barely an hour to the border. Tourism is one of our premier industries and good accommodation is in great demand. Apart from Spaniards, we get a lot of Germans, Dutch . . . and of course Britons like yourselves.'

Britons? Since when is Ireland in Britain, Aileen wondered? Is he mixed up, because we speak English? Oh, well – this is hardly the moment to get into politics, or geography. Especially since I hardly know where I am myself.

On they drove, out into golden countryside serried with small, stark, knubbly little trees. Miniature trees, barely three feet tall. M Delatre waved an enthusiastic hand. 'The vines. Bare now, of course, after the vendanges . . . the quality of the wine in this area has improved enormously . . . tell me, will you be serving meals in your bed-and-breakfast?'

'Just breakfast' Aileen piped up, and he turned round to

glance at her. 'Really? Well, maybe when you see the Manoir du Vent you will change your mind! It has a splendid dining room.'

'Has it? How far away are we from it?' Impatience was beginning to build in her, with every minute the manor was getting clearer and clearer in her mind, she could hardly wait to see the reality of the photograph she had seen that rainy day in Galway – God, was it really only last week? It felt like years ago. Years, as if she had crossed a threshold from one life, one world into another.

'Oh, not far – fifteen minutes? I have allowed a full hour for our visit, since it is quite a large property. Needs a little work, the owners are elderly and it has become too much for them . . . but a beautiful manor, as you will shortly see.'

Oh, God! Butterflies began to dance in Aileen's stomach, to waltz and jive and tango and – what am I doing?!? Am I able for this, could Aileen Hegarty seriously buy a French house and make a go of it, turn it into a thriving business?

Yes! Of course I could! I did it already, didn't I, in Galway? What's the difference? I ran my B & B there for fifteen years and the only difference is that this one might be bigger – and less dependent on American tourists. This man says they get mostly Europeans here, which might well be a good thing. Americans are so fickle, cancel their holidays if the slightest thing happens to put them off. Not that September 11 was slight . . . still. It's not good to have all your eggs in one basket. Oh, I can't wait to see this mansion!

Leaving Shona to chat to M Delatre, which she did with sunny ease, Aileen sat back, revelling in the rainbow that suddenly rose before her eyes, radiant with colour, with light and hope and every sort of alluring promise. It's a big step, she conceded, but I can take it, I can do it. I can reach right over this rainbow, if I just keep a steady nerve. That's all I need: a rock-steady nerve. And Shona Fitzpatrick. With her help, I know I can do this.

Without warning, they slewed off the main road and up a dirt track that seemed to lead into the parched, dusty middle of nowhere. As the car began to bounce and M Delatre began to beam ever more merrily, Aileen absurdly felt a prick of panic: they were way out in the countryside, with no other people or houses visible at all. What if he was not the nice man he seemed, but a serial axe murderer intent on – on serving them up for supper with bechamel sauce?

Well. Hardly. Her imagination was overheating. After all she had just been in his office, met his secretary, theirs was a perfectly reputable agency, but – but still. This seemed to be a very isolated area. Very lovely, but very remote. Apart from olive trees, nothing seemed to live in it. You couldn't imagine popping out to catch a bus or buy a pint of milk. Tessie would shriek if she could see it, positively swoon with horror.

Slightly hysterically, she giggled to herself, envisaging Tessie clapping her hand to her mouth: 'What? But – what kind of *amadán* of a daughter have I raised? Aileen, love, you can't possibly be thinking of living out here in this – this wilderness!'

With a squeal of brakes, M Delatre's car shot round a bend in the track and there, out of nowhere, appeared the Manoir du Vent, rising majestically out of the red earth. Enclosed by what looked like miles of railings, backed by trees, it was the most imposing house imaginable, built of pale yellow stone, turreted at either end with rows of arched windows in between; completely stately in a haughty, don't-mess-with-me kind of way. Immediately Aileen could imagine ghosts flitting through its baronial halls, dinner-jacketed, cigar-smoking, ball-gowned ghosts, speaking impeccable French as they . . .

'*Et voilà!*' Throwing out one arm, M Delatre opened the door of his car with the other and ran round to open Shona's, then Aileen's, usher them out even though the house was way off at the end of the drive, which looked about half a mile long.

'I thought you might like to walk up, get a sense of perspective . . . it dates from the eighteenth century . . . richly historic . . . tennis court . . . swimming pool . . . nine bedrooms . . .'

Standing back, they surveyed it in unison; it was so big it took quite some drinking in. And then, defying the sheer seriousness of the place, Shona exploded in laughter.

'Jesus! It – it's *ludicrous*!'

'*Ah bon*? Well, I must say, that is not quite the word I would have used. It is a fine house, a truly magnificent *manoir* – no?'

M Delatre looked not entirely amused, but Aileen was grinning too. This house was way, way too much for her. For anyone, unless they planned to set up a refugee camp or some kind of home for the bewildered.

Resolutely, M Delatre ploughed on, up the gravelled drive, up the circular stone steps, and knocked on a weighty iron knocker. Tiny footsteps shuffled within, a bolt creaked back, and a wizened, green-vested little gnome stood blinking in the doorway.

'*Bonjour* Monsieur Dhalluin, Jérôme Delatre here from Les Volets Verts, with the two Irish ladies, you are expecting us, *oui*?'

Looking as if he was expecting the Angel of Death, M Dhalluin stood back, nodded silently and let them in. The hall was the size of a rugby pitch. 'And how is Madame Dhalluin . . . oh, her knees? . . . oh dear . . . I see . . .' There followed some conversation too rapid for even Shona to catch, much nodding and mumbling, and then the gnome's wife came shuffling out, a tiny white-bunned wraith clasping a hand to her black-upholstered, genuine-antique bosom. Handshakes were exchanged, followed by a long, detailed bulletin on Madame's state of health. Surreptitiously, Shona glanced at her watch:

how long would it take to see and hear all this? They'd waste their entire afternoon on this crazy place, and never get to see anywhere suitable. Did she dare nudge M Delatre, very gently, in the ribs?

But to his credit he seemed aware of the problem. 'Sadly, the ladies are pressed for time . . . no need to accompany us, I will show them around for you . . . let us start in the salon.' Leaving Madame to lament the uselessness of her medication, the deafness of her doctor and the folly of living in general, he strode forth and flung open the double doors of *le grand salon*.

Cherubs. That was all Aileen could see, as she stared open-mouthed up at the garlanded ceiling, round the walls at the swagged cornices, down at the acres of polished marble floor; there seemed to be cherubs on every surface, it was a veritable cherubs' convention, cherubs were even flitting on the flaming fireplace. When she tried to speak, her voice snagged on a squeak.

'I – I –' I don't think so, M Delatre, stop right here! We are wasting our time!

But M Delatre pressed blithely on, relating the family history as he threw open windows onto pastoral vistas, punching the fireplace to illustrate its solidity, running his finger the length of the mahogany dado rail. 'And now, the dining room . . .'

Its mahogany table could have accommodated the Venice-Orient Express. Its decor had, apparently, been designed by Louis XIV in collaboration with Doris Day. The kitchen – a mere two or three miles away – could have fed France, possibly Belgium as well. The winter sitting room was ideally suited to an international armaments conference. Shona was smirking almost uncontrollably as M Delatre waltzed around; Aileen felt like screaming. Was this man mad, what on earth could he be thinking of? Finally, firmly, she stopped in her tracks.

'No. No, thank you very much, but there really isn't any point in going any further. This is much too big.'

He blinked. 'Do you think so?'

'Yes. Definitely. I only want to run a B & B, not a Hilton hotel.'

'But do come – just take a look at one of the bedrooms –'

Inexorably he raced up the swirling staircase, leaving them no choice but to follow, wondering how long it took the elderly couple to get up this lot. They'd need to start thinking about going to bed weeks in advance.

Upstairs a long, long corridor ran the entire width of the house, and M Delatre flung open the first of many bedrooms off it. Over his shoulder, Shona and Aileen peered in in unison. Draped, swagged and canopied, it was a veritable presidential suite, big enough for several presidents no matter how vast their egos.

'No. That's enough. Thank you very much, but this house is out of the question.'

Looking deflated, perplexed in a way that suggested France had been insulted for no good reason, M Delatre led the way back downstairs, not so much leaping this time as plodding, to embark on his tortuously prolonged adieux to the château's tragic owners. Clearly, it was going to take them years to sell this pile, should they survive the suspense.

More handshakes, and eventually, finally, they were out. 'Over there' he said in a last defiant effort, waving an arm, 'you have the tennis court.'

In unison, they turned to look. Its sagging net was threadbare, and it was ankle-deep in what looked like cornflakes. Apparently, the unfortunate proprietors could no longer afford a gardener.

As they got back into the car, Aileen reflected that all that glittered was not necessarily gold.

The next property, Les Oliviers, was much better. Still isolated, still large, but manageable with six bedrooms. Their visit went swimmingly until Aileen paused to gaze out the window. 'And those fields . . . all those trees over there . . . who owns them?'

M Delatre lit up. 'Why, you do, if you buy this property! They go with it.'

'What? But they can't. There are *acres* of them.'

M Delatre consulted his paperwork. 'Yes. Ten hectares. Twenty-two acres I believe, in your terms. The owners grow top-quality olives which are pressed locally into the most excellent oil. You will make as much profit on the olives as on your B & B business.'

Aileen had a fleeting vision of Joe, up a ladder plucking olives off trees, driving lorryfuls of them to the local co-op, haggling his prices in French.

'Uh . . . I'm really not looking for quite so much land.'

M Delatre was unfazed. 'You could rent it out. Any of the local growers would be happy to work and harvest it.'

Shona coughed. Aileen got the message: no. Complications. Rows over rents. Vendettas. Shotguns. 'Well, let me think about it. Meanwhile, we'd better hurry, two more houses still to see!'

As they drove on to Les Rosiers she reflected, astonished, on the extraordinary value to be had in France. You could buy a huge manor for a song if you could afford to run a huge manor – and liked cherubs – you could buy a six-bedroom guesthouse if you didn't mind accepting twenty-two acres of olive trees with it.

How would Finn feel about becoming an olive farmer? After all, he wasn't exactly rocketing up any corporate ladder, was he?

The next house, Les Rosiers, was gorgeous. Just as its name suggested, it was swathed in roses, huge yellow ones even this late in the year, and to Aileen's relief it stood on a mere acre or so. Despite the lady who came bustling out to meet them with her litany of medical ailments – was this a French hobby or something? – Aileen's hopes rose. Why the owners of all these places couldn't go out for the afternoon, as was the custom in Ireland when selling, she didn't know; but she was prepared to endure Madame to see this beautiful house. Such a garden! Such a patio, or terrace as they called it! Such lovely views! Bubbling with ill-concealed enthusiasm, she toured the garden with Shona at her heels, feeling vibes in the back of her neck: don't say anything! Don't say boo! It was all she could do to stop herself from making an offer on the spot, before she'd even seen the inside.

Inside, when at last they reached it, she gasped. At least a dozen cats were roaming the hall, the sitting room, the kitchen and every available surface; the whole place reeked of cat. Slamming to a standstill, she could barely keep her hand from flying to her mouth. And then the rest of it swam into focus: peeling wallpaper, mildewed brickwork, cracks in the ceiling, electrical cables hanging loose. Behind her, Shona froze.

M Delatre attempted to sweep the cats away. Madame looked shocked. Shona and Aileen clutched each other. Consternation prevailed. And then Shona recovered her powers of speech, muttering something swift but decisive as she stalked out. Frantically, M Delatre raced after her.

'Please, madame, do not be hasty . . .'

'I am not being hasty. I am allergic to cats. And that house is swarming with them. Absolutely teeming. Plus it is damp and it needs at least two thousand euros' worth of rewiring. If my friend wishes to buy it, that is up to her. I will wait for you here out in the fresh air.'

On strike, she sat down on a bench, arms grimly folded for the ten minutes it took Aileen to go through the charade of viewing. When she emerged she was pale.

'Right. I've seen that. Let's go.'

Off they set yet again, the atmosphere in the car slightly less cordial than before. Evening was falling as they retraced their path in the direction of Carcassonne, where one Mme Tesseron was expecting them, no doubt with her medical report at the ready.

But no. Mme Tesseron did not mention her health. Instead she insisted on sitting everyone down in her way-too-small dining room in a narrow townhouse on the outskirts of town, serving orange juice while she explained her problem. It was her daughter. Her poor daughter had recently been divorced. Her poor daughter lived in Toulouse. Her poor daughter was now all alone, apart from her two poor semi-fatherless children. So now *alors* she, Madame, must move to Toulouse to help her in her hour of need. She did not want to sell her townhouse – *ah non*, certainly not! – but what could a mother do when . . . ?

A mother, Aileen thought, could for chrissakes sake *stop talking*! We're not social workers, we're here to buy a house and this doll's house is not going to be the one. So please, please stop, we don't know your daughter and there's nothing we could do about her even if we did. 'So you see, my poor Myriam, she must take the children to school every morning before she goes to work, she must work because her good-for-nothing ex-husband is unreliable with the alimony . . . Myriam, I said, you must be firm . . . !'

On it went, on and on and on, until even M Delatre was beginning to look frantic, Shona was glassy-eyed and Aileen, who understood nothing bar a divorced daughter, was starting to wonder how exactly France defined a crime of passion. That was what it would be, wouldn't it, if she ripped that cast-iron frying pan off its hook and bludgeoned Madame to pulp with it?

Finally, M Delatre raised a weary hand. '*Oui* . . . it is terrible . . . but now perhaps if we could just tour the house . . . ?' Grudgingly, Madame gave her permission, whereupon it took them precisely five minutes. Barely a tenth of what the monologue had taken.

Dazed, they reeled out into the street. 'I think' Shona said with icy politeness, 'perhaps that's enough for one day.' Yes, M Delatre concurred, it was indeed, he was very sorry about – um – but if the ladies would be patient perhaps he might find them something yet. All was not lost, do not despair . . . did they have a contact number? Exhausted by Mme Tesseron, suddenly shattered, Shona gave him her mobile number as they drove back to the agency. It had been a long, long day.

'And nothing to show for it' Aileen wailed as they waved him adieu, heading for where the Picasso was parked. 'Those houses all looked so lovely in the photographs, I was sure at least one would be suitable.'

'I get the feeling' Shona remarked, 'that this may not be quite the bargain it seemed. You're going to have to kiss a lot of frogs, Aileen, before you find your prince.'

Their only consolation, that sorry evening, was the adorable gîte Shona had found for them to stay in. Booked through one of her contacts in the French tourism office, it was a converted barn beside the owners' farmhouse, big, beamed, warm and comfortable. It would make a perfect base for the next ten days, and cost very little off-season for such a high standard. Dropping her suitcase on its flagged floor, Aileen all but wept with joy.

'Oh, yes! Shona, this is smashing, you're a treasure!'

'It is nice, isn't it? I only wish it were for sale. I'm not sure how many more Mme Tesserons I can take.'

'Me neither. I was going to invite you out to a nice restaurant in Carcassonne tonight, but I think we're both too tired . . . is it too late to find a shop and buy some food I could cook here?'

'I'm not sure. Let's ask at the farmhouse, they could surely tell us.'

So they asked, and were sadly informed that yes, it was too late. But if they liked, their helpful hostess would happily supply them with a chicken, some vegetables, cheese and wine?

Great. With alacrity they accepted, were given milk and eggs as well, plus fruit, coffee and yogurt for the morning. While Shona made some calls to Ireland, Aileen set about making dinner, comforted to have a kitchen to call her own. For this long a trip, you needed a base to relax in. In the morning, they'd stock up at a supermarket.

By the time Shona got off her phone dinner was nearly ready, and they sank down at the table clutching glasses of wine. 'Who were you talking to?' Aileen wondered. She didn't know any of Shona's friends or family.

'My parents. And my pal Fintan in Limerick. And my other pal Crys, who's black in the face, you might say, trying to make a baby! She and her husband Gavin have been trying for five years, but no go. They're getting panicky.'

Aileen remembered Crys, whom she'd met that day in Heyden's. 'Poor things. But who knows, it could happen yet.'

'Mm . . . I hope so, because I think it's starting to put a bit of strain on their marriage.'

And so they settled in for a cosy evening, talking girl talk over their lazy, amiable meal, which visibly impressed Shona. 'You're such a good cook. All I can do is snip packets.'

'Oh, I enjoy it . . . but my mother's much better at it. Nothing fancy, but tasty traditional dishes, stew and colcannon and stuff. Jesus, if she could have seen the places we saw today! I think she's petrified that this is all going to turn out to be a huge mistake.'

Shona frowned into her glass. 'Well, it could be, if you get it wrong. We need to explore the area tomorrow, get our bearings, visit more agents and refine our criteria. I think M Delatre just showed us everything he had, willy-nilly. Let's draw up a list tonight of what you want – top ten priorities – and refuse to visit anywhere that doesn't match up. Time's short enough without wasting any more of it.'

Good idea. So after dinner they sat round the table, narrowing down things like condition of property, number of bathrooms, size of garden, distance from airport, town, coast and other amenities . . . surprisingly, it took two hours. But the result was a masterpiece, and Aileen collapsed into bed wishing she'd thought of it in the first place. Smart Shona strikes again – I'd nearly strangle her, if she wasn't worth her weight in gold! Now there's a thought. A piece of gold jewellery, to thank her for all this – and free B & B for life, if she can ever face France again.

'Well' sighed Shona five days later, 'God loves a trier.'

Truly, they were trying. They were visiting every agency in every town and village they could find, searching further and further afield. Aileen had tackled a few brief drives, memorably including a nightmare episode on a roundabout, and she had learned an extraordinary amount of French. Her vocabulary now included such essentials as 'septic tank, ordnance survey, conveyancing, dry rot, supporting wall, freehold, cockroach . . .' even if ordering a coffee was still beyond her. Shona had issued all agents with an ultimatum: 'Get rid of the owners. We want them out.'

'Out?' they blinked. 'But madame, that is not common practice—'

'Out. Out of sight and, especially, out of earshot. Get them to leave the keys with you, with neighbours, with anyone they like just so long as we don't have to hear about their lumbago, their knees, their divorces or their entire life stories. If they have animals, lock them up. The animals, I mean.'

'Well . . . this will not be easy.'

'If they don't go, we don't go. Got it?'

Yes. Most of them did get it in the end, and it saved a great deal of time, almost doubled the number of houses visited each day. But nothing was right. Still too big, too small, too near, too far, too old, too new . . . one house was perfect apart from its DIY spiral staircase, which Shona declared 'lethal'. Another was perfect except that its garden was separately located down the road. Another would have been ideal if only you didn't have to go through one bedroom to reach the next. And so forth. By day six, Aileen was beginning to panic. Most evenings she rang Joe, and thought she sensed smugness in his sympathy: oh well then, be back soon, eh, to home and hearth?

Yes. It was beginning to look as if that might be the case. Which was a shame, because the more she saw of the Languedoc the more she was liking it, with its twisty old villages, tolling church bells, shady plane trees and men in berets, playing bowls on strips of sand . . . in Ireland it'd be raining and they'd all be in the pub. The food was excellent, too, the air was warm and the light was quite extraordinary, clearer than she'd ever seen it anywhere except once on a summer visit to Donegal, at Malin Head one June evening. She and Joe had been on their honeymoon.

On day six, after visiting a record nine houses, she and Shona had a row. A stupid row that brought them almost to blows, all because Aileen wanted to top up Shona's mobile phone credit. Shona refused; Aileen blew a fuse.

'But I'm using it as much as you! Don't be ridiculous!'

'You're being ridiculous. It's my phone.'

'Then I'll make all my calls from booths from now on.'

'Oh, for God's sake!'

After a huffy few hours they got over it. But it made Aileen feel vulnerable, guilty, and anxious. Time was running out, patience was wearing thin, Shona was starting to look as if she might have had enough. Had she? Then maybe they'd better take a break, on Sunday when the agents didn't work anyway, and do something else. Something colourful, some local activity . . . 'I know!' she shouted on Saturday, spotting a poster on a wall. 'Let's go see a bullfight!'

Had she suggested seeing open-heart surgery, Shona could scarcely have looked more horrified. 'Are you mad? Bullfights are cruel, horrible, poor dumb animals goaded and tortured for fun . . . uhhh.'

'Some people say that's not so. A Spanish man who once stayed with me said they're poetic and balletic.'

'Bullshit.'

'Then I'll go on my own, so. You take the day off and relax.'

'Right. There's a flea market in Marseillan I'd like to visit . . . where's your bullfight?'

'Uh – I think the poster said in Biz – Boz – ?'

'Béziers? Okay. They're both east of here, then. You can drive as far as Béziers and I'll take the car on to Marseillan, pick you up on the way back.'

So that was what they did, Shona privately pleased to have an afternoon to herself, Aileen apprehensive as she got caught up in the throng surging towards the bullfight. At first it was fun, ablaze with colour and pageantry, but as it progressed her enthusiasm gradually waned. The outcome was inevitable, the bull stood no chance, and once the toreadors started hurling their spears into the creature's neck she knew she'd had enough. Woozily, she left at the first opportunity, wondering how long it might be before Shona came to get her. Feeling like a child at its school gates, she sat down on a wall to wait . . . and wait and wait, as it turned out, for fully two hours. By the time she finally spotted the pale blue Picasso drawing up to where they'd agreed to meet, she was extremely glad to see Shona, who looked as if she'd had a much better time. With alacrity, she jumped into the car.

'You were right! It was awful. How was the flea market?'

'Wonderful. Look in the back.'

Turning, Aileen looked, and was astonished to see a complete garden set: a white circular wrought-iron table with four slatted chairs to match, the kind you saw in magazine features about French country life. There were two large terracotta planters as well, plus a long white wooden box with a tiny window curtained in blue check gingham.

'God! You've been busy . . . have you room at your apartment for all this stuff? And what's that box?'

Shona smirked with the satisfaction of a woman who'd done a good day's shopping. 'The box is for baguettes. French version of a bread bin – pretty, huh? As for the rest of the stuff, no, there isn't room at my apartment for any of these things . . . they're for you.'

'What?!?'

'For your new house, when you get it. I couldn't resist them. House-warming present, just a bit premature! Maybe they'll be good-luck charms, if we have a bit of furniture then we have to find somewhere to put it, huh?'

'Oh, Shona . . . you can't possibly have bought these things for me.'

'Why not?'

'Because – are you out of your mind? If I don't find a house we'll have to take them all the way back to Galway with us, there won't be room for those cases of wine you said you wanted to buy.'

'True. Very true. Which means we'd better find you a house, fast! We only have three days left.'

Yes. Touched as she was by Shona's generosity – not to mention optimism – Aileen shivered as she acknowledged the awful prospect of maybe, after all, having to leave the lovely Languedoc empty-handed.

I so wanted this to work, she thought. I love this place, I want to live here and I want my family to live here. It's so pretty, it's peaceful, it's sunny and . . . and slow. So slow; a different pace of life entirely, a different quality of life. It would do us all so much good, in so many ways.

So why, oh why, can I not find a house?

With mounting desperation, they crammed visits to twenty houses into the next three days, and on two occasions Aileen was very nearly prepared to make a bid for a property that wasn't quite right. But Shona wouldn't let her.

'It's nearly right' she pleaded, 'that wall just needs knocking down . . . the kitchen could be extended . . .'

'No' Shona said firmly. 'Don't do it, Aileen. It's not what you need and you'll only regret it for years, for ever . . . trust me.'

For some reason Aileen did trust her. In the time they'd been together she'd come to like Shona more and more, could feel the confidence of friendship evolving – rather lopsided friendship admittedly, for the moment, because in France Shona was simply able to *do* so much more than she was. The give-and-take balance was impossible to get quite right, here, but it would settle when they got home, when Shona's court case came up and she was the one in need of support, a helping hand.

Meanwhile, they were running out of road. Had run out. There was no point in denying it any longer: their mission had been a failure. Aileen wanted to weep as she sank down at a café in Carcassonne on their last evening, could barely speak to the waiter when he asked her what she wanted.

'I want to stay here!' she felt like howling. Even Shona couldn't disguise it; they were very, very disappointed. Silently, they stared into their drinks for a long, ponderous interval, twirling swizzle sticks morosely. Eventually, Shona lifted her head.

'We don't have to go. We could stay on a bit longer. Maybe another week—'

'No. I wish we could, Sho, but it just isn't possible. I've spent nearly every penny of the money I'd saved up. Plus I can't leave Joe and Finn on their own any longer. It's so good of you to offer, but – well, all I can say is, you've been great. And I hope you've enjoyed yourself. It's been fun, hasn't it?'

'Yes' Shona conceded wistfully, 'but it'd have been a lot more fun if you'd found your pad. What am I going to do with all that stuff I bought for it?'

'I'll put it in our garden shed. It'll give me hope. And then I'll start searching all over again, in magazines, on the internet, saving up until I can afford to go on another recce trip – maybe I'm not meant for France, after all! Maybe it'll be Italy or Spain in the end . . . would you come with me again next year if I organised it a bit better then?'

Even as she asked the question Aileen regretted it; Shona had more to be doing with her life than accompanying her on these wild-goose chases. By this time next year she would be long back at work, with no time to spare, and probably a new man claiming her attention too. Maybe – if things really went well – Finn might have found a job by then, business might have picked up and Joe might be . . . well . . . their marriage might have moved beyond this itchy, restless phase.

'I would come' Shona responded loyally but realistically, 'if I were free to. I just haven't a clue where my life is going at the moment. Which is why I was so delighted when you asked me to come here with you, it's given me something useful to do, some sense of purpose . . . I wish we didn't have to head back tomorrow. Especially with nothing to show for ourselves. You really wanted this, didn't you?'

'Yes' Aileen admitted frankly, trying not to sound as crushed as she felt. 'I did. But there we are. That's the luck of the draw. Now, let me buy you a delicious dinner in some lovely restaurant, and even if we have nothing to celebrate we'll still have champagne. This is our last night in the Languedoc and we are going to enjoy it if it kills us.'

They did enjoy it, and it did nearly kill them. Next morning, as they packed the Picasso, they both had thundering hangovers. Shona was looking particularly pale, and Aileen wondered if she was dreading the thousand-kilometre drive back to Cherbourg. Bravely, she made a bid to cheer her up.

'I'll drive. Even if I didn't get a house, at least I learned how to do that much. You get in the other side.'

Shona complied without argument, and as Aileen started the engine she was touched to see the farmer and his wife in the rear mirror, waving goodbye from the main house behind the gîte. Sadly, she lifted her hand and waved back.

'Right, got everything? Off we go, then.'

The sun was still shining, as it had for the entire ten days they had been in the Languedoc, but it was less warm now, and after an hour or two Aileen turned on the heater, making a warm cocoon of the car as Shona dozed off beside her. A sleeping Shona meant no navigator, but Aileen didn't mind, because she didn't feel like talking. She would simply follow the signposts and drive as far as she could before evening fell.

But it was a tear that fell first, a fat silent tear that caught her by surprise as it plopped onto her lap. Impatiently she brushed her eyes with her hand, refusing to let herself be swamped with disappointment. After all, much worse things happened to people than this: failing to fulfil a dream was nothing compared to some terrible accident, for instance, injury or bankruptcy or divorce, losing someone you loved.

She had lost someone she loved, once. She had lost her two-year-old daughter, Hazel. She had learned, then, to put things in perspective, had known immediately that little else would ever matter very much again. If Hazel were alive today she would be seventeen, might even be sitting in that seat beside her. Hazel Hegarty instead of Shona Fitzpatrick, helping Mum to find a house in France . . . only then, houses in France might not be necessary. The Hegarty family might be perfectly happy where it was, a wholly different family to the one it had become after her death; scarcely a family at all, sometimes, only a collection of fragments.

Only fragments. Suddenly Aileen thought of Finn, and badly, urgently wanted to get home to him. Poor Finn . . . and poor Joe, who'd done his best then, and still did his best today. Since Hazel died they had tried, tried and tried again to rearrange themselves, to put themselves back into some kind of working order. Sometimes it very nearly worked; other times it seemed almost hopeless.

Their family had been perfectly balanced, it had had four people in it until suddenly, one day without warning, it only had three. It was skewed, it was scarred and it would never, ever be the same again.

Never. That was why she was trying to take it away, take it out of itself, and turn it into something else. Not a new family, which was impossible; but a different family, one that might learn to live at last without Hazel.

At least, she thought, I still have my dream. I can still hope. Whereas I will never have Hazel again, for whom there was never any hope.

That night they stayed in a hotel in Nontron, had an early night and hit the road soon after eight next morning, with Aileen still at the wheel. Ironically, she was getting used now to driving in France. Beside her, Shona was awake and alert, much fresher today. On the long stretches of autoroute they listened to music on and off, lapsing into occasional patches of reverie in between.

It was in one such patch that Shona turned to Aileen, looking speculative.

'Why? That's what I still haven't quite got my head around, Aileen . . . why do you so much want to come here? Why do you want to uproot your family and . . . I know business hasn't been great lately in Ireland and Finn hasn't found a job yet, but . . . is that enough? Enough to make such a major move? Is this project just a result of circumstance, or is it something in you – in your head, in your heart?'

Pausing, Aileen thought before replying. She felt far less cautious now with Shona, able to talk to her almost as she did to her sister Dymps, freely and honestly.

'Well . . . no. If you want the truth, Sho, it's not just Finn, or business being bad. There are all kinds of other reasons . . . some of them, as you say, in my head. Or in my heart.'

'Oh?' Shona sat up, looked attentive, even sympathetic in some way, without seeming snoopy. She was, Aileen knew, simply taking an interest, bonding in the way women did bond at a certain point in budding friendships.

'I suppose one reason would be lack of adventure in my youth. I married so young, I missed out on so much . . . not that Joe was any mistake or anything, he's a good man and I love him still. But I've never *done* anything, other than be a daughter, wife and mother, running a little B & B. I've never taken a risk, stretched my horizons, seen anything or even travelled anywhere much. So there you have a first factor – call it curiosity if you like. I want to see new places and challenge myself, find out just how far I can go and what my capacities are.

'For another thing, I'm forty-two! I think at that age something happens in your head – in mine, anyway. You suddenly realise that life isn't infinite. What you don't do now you never will do, unless you give yourself a real push. You're comfortable and you're ticking over and it just gets harder and harder to get up out of that old armchair. On the plus side, being forty-two gives you confidence. You can say to yourself, hey, I've got this far, haven't messed up too badly, there's a reasonable chance of succeeding with the rest of it. And even if you don't succeed, you don't have so much to lose, because you've already used up at least half of your time on this planet. At worst, you can only make a bags of the downhill half!

'And then, last but not least, there's the . . . oh, I don't know . . . the kind of spiritual element to it. The voice in your heart that simply directs you to where you know you should be, without rhyme or reason. I'm not particularly religious, but I often wonder what adventures sleep in our souls . . . we're all pilgrims, really, are we not? Moving, growing, seeking, learning . . . I didn't want my dreams, my instincts, to lie dormant inside me until I die. I wanted to let them out to – to *party*!'

Shona laughed. 'Uh oh. Midlife crisis, huh?'

'Yes. I guess. And why not? I'm entitled to go bonkers if I want, so long as I don't harm anyone.'

'Mmm. But might you harm Joe, or Finn, by hauling them out of their home? Do they actually share this ambition with you, do they want to move?'

'No. They don't. But whether they want to or not, they need to. Joe is stuck in a rut at every level, while Finn . . .' Uncertainly, her voice trailed off, leaving Shona looking at her, wondering, waiting.

'While Finn . . . Shona, if I tell you something, something very private and secret, will you promise me never to let it slip to anyone? I know you wouldn't tell them deliberately, but this is something that I never want known around Galway, or anywhere else for that matter. Something to consign to a locked box in your mind.'

Not immediately replying, Shona weighed it first. 'Yes. I've got the picture. I can do that, if you're sure you want to tell me.'

'I do want to tell you. The only people who've ever known are my mother and sister, plus Joe's family. There was no reason or need to let it go any further . . . but it seems to get harder and harder to keep it bottled up. Sometimes I think I'll explode with the – the sheer secrecy of it.'

Patiently, Shona waited. Clearly Aileen needed to rev herself up for this, whatever it might be – Jesus, Finn hadn't done anything awful, had he, stolen something or mugged someone, become a burglar or started drug dealing?

After a pause, Aileen took a deep breath, and ploughed on. 'When – when Finn was very little, only four, he had a baby sister. He was only two when she was born, and now she was two in turn. Her name was Hazel. We named her after that beautiful woman who used to be on the old pound notes, Lady

Hazel Lavery. She was dark and she had those same huge eyes. She – she was the sweetest little thing imaginable.'

Stunned, Shona scarcely dared breathe. She'd never known, remotely suspected, that Aileen had any other child than Finn.

'We adored her. She completed our family, she was the source of such happiness. And then . . . one day, when I was at home with the children, somebody knocked at the door. Two young, neat and very determined Mormons. I couldn't get rid of them. Not that I was worried about the children, because they were in the living room near me, sprawled on the carpet playing with a puzzle. A big chunky toddlers' puzzle, too big that they could possibly swallow any pieces, made of rounded wood that they couldn't cut themselves or hurt themselves in any way. So I must have been at the door for at least ten minutes before . . . before I went back to them.'

Pausing, Aileen swallowed. Silently, Shona waited, feeling something crawling slowly up her spine,

'When I got back to them, Hazel was lying on her back on the floor. Her eyes were wide open and her face was blue. I knew instantly – snatched her up, turned her upside down, slapped her on the back, over and over and over, harder and harder . . . shaking her, shouting at her. I would have hurt her had she been able to feel pain . . . but she wasn't. She – she had swallowed a sweet. A big hard sweet that . . . that Finn had given her. He . . . he loved his little sister, he was only trying to be kind to her. But he – it – killed her.'

Exhaling, Shona felt as if her skin was crumbling, prickles of icy horror darting from every nerve in all directions.

'I didn't know he had any sweets. There were none in the room. When we asked him later, he said it had been in his pocket. Someone had given it to him and he'd sucked it and it had been too much for him, so he'd put it in his pocket and forgotten it. And then he found it while – while I wasn't there.

While I was trying to get rid of those Mormons. He thought he was helping me by giving it to Hazel, he thought she'd like it and it would keep her quiet. It lodged in her throat and she – she asphyxiated.'

Shona didn't speak.

'Of course I rushed her to hospital, the doctors tried everything. But it was far too late. I knew it was even before we got there. Finn never said a word on the way, never spoke when we got there, didn't speak for four days afterwards. Four days is a very long time for a little boy. We were afraid he might never speak again.'

Abruptly, Shona thought of Joe. Oh, sweet Jesus. How on earth had Aileen told Joe? How on earth did you tell your husband that your daughter . . . how did you ever, ever break such a thing? How did you explain it, and live with it? Every day thereafter, for the rest of your life, the rest of your marriage?

Some marriages would not survive. Could not. Joe's and Aileen's must have been strong as steel, gone through hell and fire, to carry them through to wherever they were now. Must have been much, much deeper than what she'd had with Brendan, because they, she was sure, would have split up within months of such a tragedy. He to whom having children was so important; she to whom it wasn't. Their relationship, she saw with belated insight, had been romantic and fun and fitted all her specifications . . . but it hadn't had texture. It hadn't had what it would take to get through something like this.

She barely dared ask a question. Not about Joe's reaction, because that was too painful, she could hardly bear to think about it. But about Finn.

'Did – did Finn understand? Did he remember for long afterwards, did it – did it affect him?'

'Yes. Oh, yes. It affected him profoundly. In my view, it still affects him to this day. We did everything in our power to reassure him, to let him know it wasn't his fault and that nobody blamed him. Which was true because, naturally, I blamed myself.'

'But—'

Without turning to look at Shona, Aileen held up her hand. 'I just did, okay? Let's not go into all that because that's just the way things were. The far more important point was Finn . . . when he finally started speaking again, we simply said that Hazel had gone to play with God and that she was happy . . . I remember the way he looked at us when we said that, so serious, trying to understand. And then he just nodded, and picked up a toy and started playing with it. He never mentioned Hazel again. Not once, not ever, not to this day. The whole subject of Hazel Hegarty, her very name, became taboo in our home. Especially whenever Finn is around. Whenever he's even in the house.'

'Do you – do you think he remembers?' Shona felt as if she were walking barefoot on glass.

'Yes. I'm sure he does. I know he does. Maybe not clearly, maybe not even consciously. He was only four. But it – it's *in* him. It's part of him. It has shaped his life and made him who he is today – an edgy, defensive young man with no confidence or self-esteem whatsoever. A man who thinks, at nineteen, that he's worthless and his life is worthless – who thinks God only knows what, way down in his heart. I wish I could talk to him about it, but I'm afraid to . . . if I'm wrong, if he has in fact forgotten, I could do terrible damage. The situation is too fragile to risk taking a scalpel to it.'

'And Joe . . . what does Joe . . . ?' Shona couldn't articulate.

'Joe thinks Finn may have long forgotten. I think that's what Joe wants to believe, for whatever reasons of his own. He says Finn probably just distantly remembers the day his sister died, but none of the details. Maybe he's even right. I wish I could believe that he is. That's one of the reasons I love Joe . . . because he never blamed Finn, and he never blamed me. He was distraught, in fact he was very nearly destroyed, but somehow he pulled together some huge surge of strength that steered us all through the next days, weeks, months . . . it's been fifteen years, now.'

That was when it hit Shona. She could almost guess the answer to the next question before she asked it, framing it very carefully. 'And – and has Joe recovered, do you think? As far as he could?'

'Yes. As far as any father could, I think he has. I think he reached ultimate recovery point about five years ago – thus far, and no further, could he go. That was when he started to drink . . . not heavily, by some standards, but steadily. When the pressure had finally eased off him to get us all through, when he got time and space to think about his own pain. He was never able to think about that until he felt Finn and I were relatively safe, that I'd started to put the memories behind me and Finn had . . . forgotten.'

As if an ice-cube was stuck in her throat, Shona sat struggling with her voice, her shock, her numerous questions that were too dangerous, too intimate and too agonising to ask. Many women, she knew, would simply snap in Aileen's position; pills, hospitals, nervous breakdowns, their lives, their minds irreparably ruined. But not Aileen. Aileen Hegarty could tell this story, actually drive this car while she told it, without weeping, only barely flinching. While she, Shona Fitzpatrick, wanted to cry like the rain, and began to realise, with shame, that she was crying. Tears rolled down her face and she struggled vainly to stop them, while Aileen, incredibly, mustered a wan smile, patted her hand as if Shona were the one to be comforted.

'Don't, Sho. It's contagious and it'll be your fault if I put us into the back of that lorry.'

With enormous effort, Shona reached for a tissue, dried her face and sat up, breathing heavily, staring fixedly at the lorry until she mastered herself. What, in Christ's name, could she possibly say?

'So' Aileen said at length, 'there you have all the answers to your question. There you have the many reasons why I want to move my family to France, or wherever it may be . . . we moved house at the time, of course, just a few months after it happened. We thought a different house might help Finn to forget. So we settled near Oranmore and I started my B & B business . . . Joe thought some kind of work might be therapeutic for me. Keep me too busy to think. And he was right, up to a point. It did help.'

'But now . . . now you think maybe Joe's the one who needs help?'

'Yes. If he can ever be made to acknowledge it. I don't think he realises that he's the more fragile, now, of the two of us.'

'Have you – ever – tried counselling? Either of you, or both?'

'No. I felt I had to deal with my own feelings in my own way, I didn't want to hear how other people cope, what the "normal" responses are in such a situation. I wanted to make it on my own and I knew I could make it on my own, if I was let, if I was simply given the time and space. The only people I talked to were Dymps and Tess, my sister and mother – they were enough for me. They were wonderful.

'As for Joe – he's a sturdy, old-fashioned Irish man, Shona. He would never have any truck with any of that "American palaver" as he calls therapy. Plus, he has a lot of inner strength . . . even if he's used up an awful lot of it. I would dearly love to see him, at this stage of his life, moving to the sun and doing something more – more fulfilling than selling hardware. He likes his job, but he's been in it for years, there's no further scope for him – plus, the company is offering a voluntary redundancy scheme at the moment. If I could persuade him to avail of it, he'd be entitled to three weeks' pay for each of the twenty years he's worked. It would be enough to get us on our feet somewhere new, especially with the profit we'd make on selling the house.'

Yes. No doubt it would. But Shona couldn't think about any of that at this moment; all she could think about was baby Hazel, and how incredibly strong Aileen had been, and how very much it would have meant to her to find a new home, here in France, to make her own. How much more it would have meant than she ever could have guessed.

Thinking about it, she turned it over and over in her mind, sensing that Aileen did not mind the silence that settled between them. Without speaking, they both knew that they would talk about it later, talk much more, when they were feeling less raw, when the moment was right.

'I think' Aileen said suddenly, 'if I step on the gas I can get us to Cherbourg by tonight, in time to catch the next ferry. D'you trust me to pick up a bit of speed?'

'Yes' Shona replied simply, 'I trust you, Aileen.'

The rest of the day went by in a blur, the kind of lull that follows a storm. Aileen's tale had sliced into Shona: stormed her, shocked her to the core. Anything she might say seemed superfluous, maybe even hurtful if she didn't get a grip on the whole thing first, and so they drove along the hypnotic motorway with the radio tuned at low volume to Classic FM, on which Mozart was wafting soporifically. The car was warm and quiet, oddly peaceful as they gradually passed one milestone after another: Poitiers, Angers, Laval. Then Avranches, and at last, as night fell, the first signs for Cherbourg began to appear.

When Shona's mobile rang, they both jumped, gasped with the shrill unexpected shock of it. It sat in its car socket, on speaker mode, and Shona's finger shook as she clicked it on. Without preliminary, barely giving her time to say hello, a male French voice filled the car.

'Mme Fitzpatrick, *bonsoir*! It is I, Jérôme Delatre!'

Neither of them could instantly think who Jérôme Delatre might be, but the voice sang out in the evident assumption that they knew, was almost shouting with intrusive joy, violently at odds with their pensive mood.

'I have found it! I have here on my books, fresh in this evening, the house of your dreams! Is Mme Hegarty with you – please tell her – you must come immediately – where are you at this moment?'

Oh, God. Oh, no, no, *no*. Aghast, they gazed sidelong at each other, and Aileen put on the indicator, slid the car off the road into a lay-by. Appalled by what she was hearing, she was abruptly incapable of driving another inch.

'M Delatre' Shona groaned, 'we are in Normandy. About thirty kilometres short of Cherbourg, where we are about to catch the ferry home.'

'What?' There was an astonished silence. 'But – oh, this cannot be! I assumed you were still here in the Languedoc, still house-hunting . . . have you found a property, is that why you are leaving?'

'No. We're leaving because – because we only had two weeks at our disposal, there are family commitments in Ireland and financial considerations . . . I'm sorry, but you're too late. We've spent two days driving up here, we're as far away as we possibly could be, the ferry is sailing tonight and we have to be on it.'

Another silence. Less strangled, more thoughtful. 'I see . . . Mme Fitzpatrick, may I ask you, does your mobile telephone have internet facility?'

'Uh – yes, it does, but –'

'Then please, I ask of you just one small thing. Stop for one minute. Wait, wherever you are, for just the one minute it will take me to e-mail you the photographs of this house. I assure you I would not waste your time, after the last – um – somewhat embarrassing episode, if I did not think this house is absolutely perfect for you. For Mme Hegarty, I mean.'

In the gathering dusk, Aileen and Shona stared at each other.

'Mme Fitzpatrick? Are you there?'

'Yes – yes, I'm here, we both are. But M Delatre, it's not possible! We're too far away! We can't—'

'Totally perfect. It's near Mézalas. No cats, no cherubs, no vast estate, no repairs, none of the previous problems whatsoever. Six bedrooms, four bathrooms, one hectare – plus a small gîte, separate, on the same site. It is a joy, I promise you, and it will sell very quickly. But I wanted to contact you before any of my other buyers, to compensate for wasting your time before. Please allow me to send these pictures, at least.'

Shona looked at Aileen. Her face was frozen.

'All right. Send them.'

He clicked off immediately, and Aileen gripped the steering wheel. 'No. You shouldn't have said that, Shona. I don't want to see them. We're too far away, we're going home, it's too late, and that's that.'

'Aileen, a little while ago you asked me to trust you. I did. Now I'm asking you to trust me. Just for one minute, until these pictures arrive. Okay?'

'Okay.' Her voice was toneless. Sitting back, folding her arms, she leaned into her seat, and Shona leaned in turn, waiting, holding her breath. If M Delatre was wrong in any detail of what he had said, she would kill him. If he was right, she would also kill him. The Languedoc, at this point, felt further away than Mars.

Beep. Beep beep beep. One by one, over they came, eight photographs flying through cyberspace. Aileen shut her eyes. 'I refuse. I won't look.'

'Then I will.' Gripping the phone, Shona stared at the screen, and there it was: the loveliest house she had ever seen in all her life. Long, broad, washed in grey-blue, flanked by soaring cypress trees, engulfed in pink roses, its door and shutters painted in ash-lavender, the whole edifice flooded with the blazing sun of the south. Inside were a long beamed lounge, state-of-the-art kitchen, vast timbered bedrooms and tiled, immaculate bathrooms. Every detail bespoke a house that was nurtured and burnished, cared for by someone who adored it. At a stroke, Shona was slashed by sheer, utter love. Smitten, stricken, breathless.

'Aileen.'

'What?' Arms akimbo, Aileen was staring rigidly down the motorway.

'Look.'

'No.'

'Aileen.' Her voice was a whisper. 'You've got to have it.'

'Why? Has it got the cherubs of my dreams?' Her tone was acid with resistance.

'Aileen, it – it *is* the cherub of your dreams! It is *gorgeous*! Beautiful, exquisite, perfect . . . please, please look.'

As if on a swivel, Aileen's head snapped round, and she looked. One-two-three-four, there, are-you-satisfied!? – and then, on the fifth photograph, she paused. Paused for a long, long moment. Temporarily, she seemed suspended; and then she burst into tears.

'Oh, Jesus! Jesus flaming Christ! How could he do this to me – it – it's so beautiful – the bastard! That man is an absolute bastard and I will never forgive him for this!'

Sobs wrenched from her, harsh anguished rasps that horrified Shona; she could remain dry-eyed while telling the terrible tale of her daughter, yet she was demolished now? But—?

And then, in one swift flash, she saw it. Saw everything that was engulfing Aileen, and saw what she must do. Now, instantly.

'Out. Get out of the car.'

Aileen lifted her face, streaming with tears, and gaped. 'What?'

'Out. You've driven enough. I'm doing the driving back. Change places and be quick about it.'

'Shona! Stop it! Stop this, I can't stand it! You know I have to get home to my family and I haven't any more money, it's another thousand bloody kilometres back down there, I can't afford petrol never mind accommodation or the – the *fortune* it would cost!'

'Aileen. You can't afford *not* to go back. Joe and Finn are two grown men, they can cope without you for a – another few days. Here, ring them and tell them, right now, what's happening. As for the money, you can pay me back out of your first year's takings.'

'No! Shona, nobody makes a penny their first year in business! I can't afford—'

'Aileen. Listen to me. You – we – have to do this. If you want everything I think you want, not only for yourself but also for your husband and your son, then we are turning this car around this minute and going back down to the fucking Languedoc. Do I make myself clear?'

Immobilised, wild-eyed, Aileen stared back at her, apparently assessing the extent of her insanity. Grasping the phone, Shona punched it vehemently.

'Monsieur Delatre? Shona Fitzpatrick here. Yes. Sit tight. We're on our way. We will be in your office first thing on Monday morning. If you sell that house to anyone else in the meantime, if you breathe mention of it to a living soul, if it is not everything you say it is and more, I will personally serve you up for supper on Monday evening, sliced on a silver tray, with an apple in your mouth. Got that?'

Without waiting to hear whether he had or not, she hung up, unbuckled her seat belt, leaned across Aileen and opened her door.

'Right. Out. Move it. If you're not in the passenger seat by the time I'm in the driving seat, I'm leaving without you.'

5

Aileen was having trouble breathing. Having trouble standing, too. Gingerly, lest it vanish from under her, she sank onto a garden bench to stare, in silence, at Le Mas des Cigales.

There she remained, rooted to the spot, as if viewing a newly excavated masterpiece by Monet.

Shona, too, was hypnotised. Enthralled. Le Mas des Cigales was the most exquisite, delicious house she could ever have dared to hope for, better even than its photographs, because it was not only beautiful, it was . . . it was . . . what on earth was it, that was luring her into love? Something about its atmosphere, its peaceful aura, its light-filled garden, its book-filled rooms . . . its age, its quietude, its dignity?

They'd seen bigger. They'd seen grander. They'd seen cheaper. They'd seen nearly a hundred previous houses but not one of them could hold a candle to what they were seeing now, this low-roofed, two-storey, cypress-cradled building with its louvred lavender shutters, its thick faded walls and sloping garden, serenely standing on a hill overlooking the village half a mile below. If I lived here, Shona thought, I'd walk down there every morning for coffee on the square, I'd potter round the market filling a wicker basket with fruit and flowers and vegetables, and then I'd walk back up again, soaking up this sunshine into every bone in my body. This is absolute bliss.

We've got to have it. We've simply got to.

I mean, Aileen has to. What on earth is she dithering over?

I know I told her not to say anything rash, but all she has to say now is yes. Yes, please, wrap it up, I'll take it. She can't go on sitting there all morning . . . we've been here two hours already, it's nearly lunchtime. Not that we're going to be able to eat. This is too exciting – so thrilling I'd shriek aloud and turn cart-wheels, if we weren't supposed to act cool and composed. I'd do *jail* for this house. Not just the house, which is perfect for her, but for that adorable little gîte as well, that looks like a doll's house. I can't believe it's included in the price. Okay, it's only got one bedroom, but it has a lounge as well, a bathroom and a kitchen, it's big enough to live in. If you weren't living in the main house, which I would give my eye teeth for, with those beams and ancient tiles, that huge kitchen and sunny living room, those big bathrooms with their white porcelain . . . oh, God. This is just too gorgeous, I can't stand it. What in hell is she waiting for?

Calm. That's what this house has, in spades. It knows what it's about, it doesn't have to prove a thing. It's not chintzy or fussy, not stark or minimal, it's simply a home: warm, comfort-able, with the happiest vibes in creation. It's a shame the owners aren't here, because for once I'd love to meet them. Whoever planted and worked this garden, whoever fished out those old sleigh beds from some market, whoever put those green check cushions with those blue striped ones . . . whoever polished that floor to that leathery sheen, filled that vase with so many yellow roses, piled that basket to bursting with tom-atoes and courgettes . . . they must have loved living here, whoever they were. And I feel sorry for them, because it must be breaking their hearts to leave Le Mas des Cigales. It'll break mine, if we leave without the keys and deeds to it. Aileen, would you ever for pity's sake come *on*!

But Aileen sat dreamily, chin on knuckles, elbows on knees, leaning forward, gazing so thirstily at Le Mas she looked as if she were guzzling, couldn't get enough of it. Encouraged but somewhat bemused, M Delatre strolled patiently on the sidelines, idly dead-heading roses in the borders, waiting for them to think and talk, make up their minds in peace. Shona was glad he wasn't putting any pressure on them, but she couldn't stand much more suspense, herself.

Finally her patience snapped and she went over to Aileen, sat down beside her on the white-painted wooden bench, looking at her sidelong.

'So? Is there a reason not to buy this house?'

No answer.

'What? Somebody left the cap off the toothpaste?'

A vague smile, but still no reply. Perplexed, Shona persisted, obscurely noting the fine network of lines the sun was tracing in Aileen's face. It was a lived-in face and, at this moment, poignantly radiant. A weary face, lit today with dreams.

'You are going to buy it, aren't you? It is perfect, isn't it? Everything you need to live in comfort, to run your B & B successfully? Lots of light, lots of space, lots of garden? Neighbours within shouting distance, but plenty of privacy? Gorgeous view over the valley and village? The only thing I can see wrong with it is that it's unique, which means I can't have one as well.'

Turning her head, Aileen squinted across the grass at the gîte, and spoke at last.

'What would I do with that little wendy house? Put Finn in it, maybe, so he could have his own—?'

'Are you mad?! Rent it out, of course! Anyone would give their right arm to stay in that!'

'But it's tiny. Only big enough for two at a squeeze.'

'Well, admittedly, but . . .' Slowly, Shona's voice trailed off as she, too, studied the gîte. It was small. Barely as big as her apartment back home. Small and snug and . . .

'Aileen, sign something quick before the owners change their minds. Unless you don't want this place. If you don't, after we've driven all this way for the second time, then you will never find anything else. Not only because there is nothing else that could compare with this, but because I am going to take that pitchfork out of that shed over there and run you through with it.'

Laughing, Aileen sat up as if a spell had been broken, as if she were rejoining reality. 'Yes! I do want it, Shona! I love it, I adore it to bits! I am in house heaven!'

'Then let's break the glad tidings to M Delatre. I'm sure that briefcase of his contains every single one of the nine thousand, seven hundred and eighty-five papers you'll need to sign. In triplicate. You do know about French paperwork, don't you?'

'Yes. I've heard it can be a bit—'

'They'll want to know where your granny's cousin's budgie was born, what it was doing on the seventeenth of August 1936 at four pm, its blood group, its social security number and the registration of the car it was driving on the day Madame-next-door bottled that new batch of beetroot. Aileen, let's get moving! We have work to do!'

'But—'

'But what?' Impatiently, Shona blinked, already standing up.

'I – I can't! Can't just buy a new house, snap, as if it were a pair of shoes! I'm going to have to call Joe!'

Oh. Yes. Well. Naturally. Shona had forgotten him. 'Okay. Call him. Tell him. Whoopee, gorgeous new house! Lucky Joe, lucky Finn, look lively, lads!'

'And – and then there's the money. I'd have to put down a deposit. Ten per cent, M Delatre says.'

'Yes. Of course you would. That's normal . . . though we'll haggle the price as much as we can, might get it down a few thou.'

'Maybe . . . but it's still a lot of money. The kind of money I don't have in my handbag.'

Oh. 'Well, no, of course not. You'll have to set up a bank transfer . . . Aileen, you do have the funds, don't you? Enough for a deposit? I mean, you've been planning this, you must have been saving?'

Aileen nodded. 'Yes. Sort of.'

'Sort of? What do you mean, *sort* of?'

Almost guiltily, Aileen flinched. 'I mean that – that Joe and I were saving together for years, for – for Finn to go to college. We thought there'd be all kinds of expense, we thought – thought he would go to college. When he didn't – well, we just left the money in the bank, in case . . . it's still there. That's my deposit money. I'll have to talk to Joe about it.'

Irresolute, Shona considered. 'I see. You mean you can only get at it if he agrees?'

'Yes. It's in a joint account. And then he'll have to agree to sell our house in Ireland, too, to pay the balance when this sale completes.'

Shona pursed her lips, held out her mobile. 'Here. Then you'd better talk to him pronto. I'll go haggle with M Delatre while you're doing it, see if I can shave anything off the asking price.'

Reaching out to take the phone as Shona spun away, Aileen looked at it and quailed, feeling like a schoolgirl bracing herself to confess to teacher that yes, it was she who set fire to the science lab.

'Oh, Joe . . . oh, please! Please-please-please! It's gorgeous, I promise you! You're going to absolutely love it – take a few days off work and get the next plane down. You have to see this house. Put the bank on standby, tell them to be ready with the money – if you hurry we can pick you up at Carcassonne airport tonight.'

Standing in the manager's office which was the only place to take a private call, Joe Hegarty stared out through its glass wall, up on a gantry from which the entire hardware store was visible. Down below, pre-Christmas customers swarmed like ants. In his brown overall with its red logo emblazoned on the back, he felt extremely warm. Felt a need to go outside for fresh air, after what Aileen had just shouted to him from a thousand miles away. His wife – there was no further denying it – was experiencing some problems with her sanity. Just when her crazy project had seemed to be fizzling out, when she'd been ready to return empty-handed – this.

'I will do no such thing. We are up to our eyes here and there's no way I could take an hour off, much less "a few days", even if I wanted to. Which I don't.'

'But it's *beau*tiful, Joe! It's perfect!'

'Aileen. It's in France. We live here. In Ireland.'

'That's another thing. Get out the Yellow Pages and look up a couple of estate agents, call them, put our house on the market.'

'Aileen. Please.' He heard his sigh, infuriated and exasperated. 'Listen to me—'

'Joe, if we're not quick we'll lose it! This house will sell in a flash! You should see it – you will see it, when—'

Down on the shop floor below, Joe could see his colleague Larry beckoning to him, stabbing at his watch. The cordless drill delivery was late, someone was going to have to call the suppliers urgently to find out where it was.

'Aileen, I have to go. So let me be brief. I am not flying to France. I am not selling our house. I am not taking our savings out of the bank or sending them anywhere. Have you got that?'

'But Joe – oh God, you don't understand—'

'No. I don't understand. At all. But I hope you understand. No. As in no way.'

'Joe –'

'No! Goodbye!'

Crushed, feeling almost as if Joe had punched her, Aileen clicked off, stood irresolute for a moment and then, hunching into her jacket, set slowly off across the garden to tell Shona, who stood talking and gesturing at M Delatre. Something about the pair of them – their tone, their gestures – suggested the house was already sold, that it was only a matter of refining the details. Briefly, Aileen paused to look at them, wondering how Shona was going to react to this fatal blow. She'd been so immersed in the whole thing, put so much into it, that now it was almost as if she were part of it.

Not, she thought, that anyone could be as devastated as I am. I really thought . . . I was so sure . . . maybe Joe will come round yet, if I go home and plug away at him, but by then Le Mas des Cigales will almost certainly be sold. After all we've gone through to get it, I can't bear to lose it. I just cannot bear it.

But I know Joe. I know that voice, that tone you can't argue with. He rarely says no, but when he does say it, he means it. He's digging his heels in, it'll be like trying to reason with a mule.

If only I could get at the money, I'd go ahead regardless. I'd put down the deposit and worry about the consequences later. I'd drag him over here and make him look, make him see . . . make him agree, in the end. But the money is his as much as mine, I just can't get at it without him. Christ, I could cry! I could scream, lie down on this lawn and weep. Only it wouldn't do any good, wouldn't change anything, would it? I am stuck.

At this very last minute, just when I've found what I've so long wanted, I am bogged down, thwarted, stuck.

Enquiringly, M Delatre looked round as she walked slowly towards him, as did Shona, taking in the wretched spectacle: hands in pockets, head bowed, Aileen scarcely needed to speak. Her body language communicated defeat from every pore.

Almost as if she were trying to stave off the bad news, Shona spoke first. 'Great news. M Delatre thinks the owners might negotiate a bit – not a lot, but maybe five thou less than they're asking. Of course, I've told him that the whole deal is subject to a surveyor's report. Nobody in their right mind would buy a two-hundred-year-old house without checking for damp, dry rot, termites in this part of the world.'

Aileen could barely whisper. 'Shona. Could I – could we have a word in private, please?'

Politely, M Delatre nodded, moving out of earshot to tactfully inspect the window frames. Aileen took a deep breath. 'Shona, Joe – Joe won't do it. Won't hear of it. I got him at a really bad moment, he was busy and he – he just refused point blank. I – I can't get at the money.'

'Oh, Jesus.' Sounding somehow shot, Shona exhaled as if a bullet were whistling through her.

'I'm sorry. I am so sorry. I was sure . . . sure he'd fly down to see it at least, with a bank draft in his pocket on the off-chance that I might be right and he might actually like it. But he won't even come to look at it. After dragging you all this way . . . not just once but twice . . . I can't tell you how awful I feel.'

'Yes.' Surveying her, seeing how the light had dimmed in her eyes, Shona could see exactly how Aileen felt. Joe's refusal was more than merely frustrating; it was symbolic. It said 'No, we're not in this together. No, I don't want any part of your

plan to move our family, change our family, help our family.'
It was a sad, and serious, marker in the Hegarty marriage.
Digesting all its implications, Shona stood silent for some time,
digging a divot in the lawn with the toe of her shoe.

Eventually, Aileen grimaced, dredging up her voice from the
depths. 'So . . . after coming all this way . . . I can't go any
further. I can't buy Le Mas des Cigales. We may as well go and
break it to M Delatre, get it over with.'

'No.' Shona held up her hand in that traffic-stopping way·
she had. 'Not yet. Bear with me, Aileen, give me a few minutes
. . . I'm thinking like mad here.'

Aileen couldn't see what there was to think about. Short of
flying to Ireland, kidnapping Joe and forcibly flying him over
here, there was no way to make him see Le Mas, make him see
sense. She was a married woman. Unlike Shona, she was not
free to do what she liked, make her own independent decisions.
Other people had rights, had claims on her life, on her time
and on her money. She couldn't act alone.

Floaty as she had felt only a few minutes ago, she felt heavy
as lead now, sinking back down on the garden bench while
Shona paced round in a circle, looked up at the house, walked
back from it, walked right round it, came back muttering to
herself and, finally, stopped halfway between the gîte and the
house, looking out over the valley, down to the church-spired
village. Neither of them spoke. And then Shona spun round.

'I tell you what. I'll buy the gîte.'

Eagerly, she beamed, and Aileen looked totally blank.
Looked as if she hadn't heard, as if the whole thing had sailed
right over her head. Impatiently, Shona took a step towards
her. 'Did you hear me? Are you listening? I said, I'll buy the
gîte. If you're agreeable.'

Aileen's mouth opened. Nothing emerged. Shona revved
up. 'Aileen! Do you or do you not want me to do this? Wake

up and think about it, fast, we haven't got all day to dither.'

'You . . . you want to buy the gîte?' Dazed, Aileen stared at her, with a distinct lack of alacrity, Shona thought.

'Yes! It's a sweet little gîte, I love it and I could live in it! Come here on my holidays, without taking up any of your rooms. This is a master plan, I'm a genius! So say yes!'

'But – but Shona – any time you wanted to come here, you'd stay with me anyway, for nothing – I can never thank you enough for all you've done—'

'Aileen, you can't afford to give me a room in the main house. That's your B & B, it has to pay its way, you won't have room for friends. So I'll buy this separate apartment from you for ten per cent of the total price. Twenty-two thousand. I have that much in my savings account, I can call my bank right now. Is ten per cent fair, d'you reckon?'

'But—'

'Whenever I'm not using it, I can rent it out. Off-season, your mother or sister can use it for nothing. Then they can stay with you too, without being in your way, without taking up space you need for paying guests.'

'But—'

'Aileen, if you say that once more I will be forced to slap you. First, I am going for a short walk. Down to that village and back. Half an hour. When I return, you will tell me your decision. Okay?'

And with that she was marching across the grass, over to M Delatre, singing out to him like an insouciant blackbird. 'M Delatre, let's go for a coffee!'

Alone on her bench, Aileen sat lost in thought, communing with the house because, she felt, it had a soul. It was speaking to her. It was telling her that God had sent his personal emissary, in the guise of Shona Fitzpatrick, to save her, and she should be very, very grateful. She should gather her wits, dash after Shona, scream 'Yes!' before either of them had time to change their minds. She should be on her knees, prostrate with gratitude.

She was prostrate with it. She was, when she allowed herself to consider Shona's 'master plan', delirious with delight, dizzy with it. If it were her decision alone, she'd be running down the hill right now, yelling, grabbing, signing and sealing on the spot.

But . . . Joe. Oh, dear God. What on earth would Joe say, if she came back with this awful deed done, with the deposit paid by Shona, who would henceforth own part of the property? Would he rally, would he allow himself to be reasoned round, or – or would he simply divorce her? She wouldn't blame him in the least, if he did. This was an absolutely outrageous thing even to consider, much less do, without his consent. When she got back to Galway, it would be what Dymps called a 'make-or-breaker', it would put their marriage on the line.

And, if he didn't relent, what in hell would she do then? With a house on which Shona Fitzpatrick had paid the deposit? She couldn't complete the purchase, neither could she refund twenty-two thousand; they'd have to drop the whole thing and Shona would lose her money. Which she, Aileen, would then spend the rest of her life trying to reimburse. While living in Galway with a husband she would resent for ever more – or without any husband at all, after Joe walked out.

That's what I'm risking, she thought. I am risking losing not only Shona's money, but my husband. That's what it boils down to: the wrecking of lives right, left and centre. I can never thank Shona enough for her offer, but the answer is no. I can't accept, can't even think any more about this. Sweet Jesus, what if she lost her court case, lost her job, and had no money just when she needed it! I can't imagine what's come over her.

Would she actually like to spend her holidays here? Or is she just being businesslike, does she think the gîte could be a good little investment?

But Joe would throw a raving fit. Foam at the mouth, leave me! Which is not the idea at all. Admittedly, our relationship is not exactly blooming at the moment, but it's just a rocky patch, one we're going to have to work our way through. At the end of the day he's a good man, we have been together for more than twenty years and – and I love him. He's Hazel's father, and Finn's. I can't do this to him.

Ah, no. It is heartbreaking, I am gutted to have to abandon Le Mas des Cigales, but the answer, as Joe said himself, is no. As in no way.

Shona did not return in half an hour. A full hour and more passed, during which Aileen continued to sit on the garden bench, looking at the house with her eyes full of tears. M Delatre had not yet locked it up, she could have gone back inside if she wanted to, toured its rooms again, on her own, savouring one last sight of them, inhaling the scent of the yellow roses which, for the rest of her life, would always remind her of this bittersweet day. The day she lost hold of her dream, but gained a friend who would endure for ever. Never, when she set out with Shona Fitzpatrick, had she suspected her capable of doing any of the things she had since done. Things that seared her heart, and sealed their friendship.

If nothing else, she thought, I've got that much out of this first – and only? – visit to France. I've got a real friend. Maybe that was how things were meant to work out, after all. For that alone, I'm glad I came here. I am very glad we did this.

But where is she? What's she doing? Checking out the village, I suppose, maybe having lunch with M Delatre, tactfully leaving me alone for a while to pull myself together. Well, then, that's what I'd better do. She doesn't need me moaning in the car beside her all the way back to Cherbourg – oh, God, back to Cherbourg *again*!

Dreading the thought of it, Aileen stood up, walked around the entire perimeter of the two-acre garden, taking photos of trees and flowers, village and valley, house and gîte on a disposable camera she had bought. I'll pin them up in the kitchen, she thought, and Joe will have to look at them every day until . . . no. Don't kid yourself, Aileen. It is not going to happen.

Finally, after nearly two hours, she heard footsteps. Shona, returning alone on foot, waving cheerily as she crested the hill. 'Hi, I'm back!'

'Where's M Delatre? You were gone so long, I thought you'd eloped with him.'

'Ha! He should be so lucky! We were just talking, had a couple of coffees, then he had to scoot because he had an appointment at two. But he's coming back to pick us up at three. So – did you consider my proposal?'

Nodding, Aileen tried not to look as grim as she felt. Tried to look everything Shona had a right to expect of her. 'Yes. I did. It was a wonderful idea and I'd have given anything to take you up on it . . . but I can't. Apart from not being quite sure why you wanted to do it, Sho, I can't risk it. If Joe didn't give in, what would we do? You'd have paid the deposit on a house I couldn't go ahead and buy. The whole thing would be a terrible mess.'

Unexpectedly, quite airily, Shona nodded. 'Yes. It would. I thought it out a bit more, talked it through with M Delatre . . . and now I've come up with another plan. Much better.'

Aileen froze. 'No. Shona, whatever it is, I don't even want to hear it. Let's leave well enough alone, forget the whole thing.'

Looking around her, Shona grinned. 'Sorry. You're

marooned here with me. You're going to have to hear it. Brace yourself, missus!'

Aileen clapped her hands over her ears. Shona yanked them off and sat her back down on the bench. 'Okay. Listen and don't interrupt till I've finished. What I'm thinking is this. *I'll buy Le Mas des Cigales. Not only the gîte, but the whole place.*'

Aileen clamped her hand to her mouth. Shona continued. 'It's a great investment, Aileen. I've seriously thought it out. I already have enough for the deposit and I'll borrow the rest from the bank, get a mortgage, or venture capital. Which I'll pay off by running the place as a B & B, just as intended. Now – here's where you come into it – I'm going to give you a choice. Either you can run a mile from the whole idea, in which case I'll employ someone else to run it – or you can do it for me. If Joe won't sell the house in Ireland, or quit his job, persuade him to compromise. Rent out your Irish house for a year, get him to take leave of absence and come down here. Run my B & B for me, see how it goes and then decide whether you – both – want to stay on. How does that sound?'

Aileen's throat felt as if it were on fire. 'Shona' she croaked, 'you can't. You cannot buy Le Mas des Cigales just because Aileen Hegarty wants it.'

'I'm not buying it because you want it. I'm buying it because I love it, and because it is a terrific opportunity to make money. If it's well run – and I know how well you run your Irish B & B – then it should at least break even the first year. I don't expect instant profit. Just enough to pay the mortgage and cover expenses. Including you.'

'M – me?'

'Yes. You and Joe. You'll need something to live on! If you can make that much out of it, I'll be a very happy camper. Then, at the end of a year, you can let me know whether you want to stay on. If you do, I'll give you the option of buying me out, on condition I keep the gîte – which Dymps and Tess can use whenever they want. If you don't, I'll bring in someone else to run the place at that stage . . . maybe someone Irish who'd love to live here for a while. Does that sound fair?'

Aileen was speechless. Speculatively, Shona looked at her, and looked at the house. Between them, she knew, they could do this. Aileen would have her opportunity, while she, Shona, would have an eminently resaleable property, should she ever need to sell it. But right now there was nothing she wanted less, because she, too, had fallen in love with Le Mas des Cigales. If it merely paid its way, held its value, and permitted her to keep that gorgeous little gîte . . . well. Wow! Property, as her mother never tired of saying, was an excellent investment. And tourists, as M Delatre had said barely an hour ago, were discovering the Languedoc. A cheaper, less crowded alternative to Provence, it was moving up. Aileen would be well able to fill the four double guest rooms of Le Mas.

Provided, of course, she didn't have the coronary she looked as if she might be about to have.

'Aileen? You're allowed to speak now, I've finished my spiel . . . so is it brilliant or what?'

A strangled nod. Groping in pocket for hanky. Muddled mumblings.

'Is that a yes?'

A flood of tears. Mortified, Aileen just couldn't help it; she was overwhelmed. She felt exactly the same way she'd once felt when a doctor had told her a cyst was benign: it was like being handed her whole life back, brand new, to do with as she wished.

And Joe . . . Joe, she knew in an instinctive flash, would do it. This much he would do, for her. He'd refuse to sell their house, but he wouldn't refuse to rent it out. He'd refuse to chuck his job, but he'd agree to take a year's sabbatical. That was what marriage was all about: as Shona said, a compromise.

Warily, she still didn't speak. Not for a few minutes, not until she got her mind in gear and frantically tried to think of possible problems. But only mundane, minor things came to mind – furniture? A car? Taxes, overheads? They'd need to work out that stuff between them, get everything straight from the start. But Shona, she knew, would be as fair and honest as she would be herself.

Eventually, mopping her eyes, she lifted her face. 'You – you're sure, Shona? You can swear to me on a stack of bibles that you really do love this house, for its own sake? That you genuinely consider it a good investment, on which at the bare minimum you will not lose one cent?'

Yes. Thoughtfully, Shona sat down on the bench beside her, her gaze drifting past the pale, barely blue walls of the old house.

'D'you know, Aileen . . . look at those trees down the hill there . . . they're not in bloom, but I'm nearly sure they're citrus. Orange. You'll be able to serve your guests freshly squeezed juice in the summer.'

Next day, holding her breath, Aileen stood immobile in the appropriately named *immobilier* agency while Shona signed the preliminary purchase papers for Le Mas des Cigales. It would take three months to complete the deal, and already Shona's Irish bank was holding her to ransom, charging a fortune to transfer the deposit funds to France. Bandits, Aileen thought furiously, bloody bandits! And then: this had better work. Work out really well, for all of us . . . it's happening so fast, it's terrifying.

Calmly, Shona stood up, shook hands with M Delatre and established what was to happen next: in February, there would be a final, formal signing of approximately ten billion papers, in the presence of the owners and assorted solicitors. 'And then' she grinned mischievously, 'we pop the champagne? Wild celebrations?'

Looking as if he had never heard of wild anything, M Delatre smiled cautiously. People didn't normally joke at such a serious moment. Privately wondering whether the Irish might be a bit odd, he volunteered the name of a solicitor Shona might care to use. 'Great' she chirped, 'I'll take your word for it that he's a trusty chap?'

M Delatre looked aghast. 'Oh, but of course, madame, I assure you . . . most respected . . . many years . . .'

Shona laughed. 'Yeah. Right. Show me a solicitor who's not out to turn a fast buck, Jérôme, and I'll show you the Promised Land.'

Jérôme? She was calling him by his first name? And worse was to come.

'You wouldn't by any chance know of anywhere we could store some garden furniture? A table, four chairs and two planters?' She smiled her most charming smile, and to his astonishment M Delatre found himself considering the problem.

'Umm . . . well, this is most unusual . . .'

'We've bought them, Jérôme. For our French residence. Any old shed will do, a garage, a barn, whatever.'

'I . . . uh . . . very well. Leave them here with me, in the yard at the back, and I will . . . er . . . see what I can do.' Looking flustered, he ushered them out with the air of a man in need of a little lie-down. Hastily, Aileen followed Shona to the car, heaved the stuff out with her, carted it round to the back of the agency and plonked it in the yard, where M Delatre stacked it with an air of incredulity.

'Thanks a mill, Jérôme. Very kind of you. We'll pick it up in February.'

Amazed by Shona's cheek, suppressing hilarity, Aileen grabbed her sleeve, dragged her down the street and then, safely out of sight, they both exploded laughing. 'Oh, was that fun!' Shona cackled. 'The French are so formal, I love winding them up! Now, let's explore this village a bit more – after all, it's our local now.'

Yes. With newly proprietary interest, they returned to Mézalas and embarked on a tour of its cobbled streets: a soaring old stone church, tiny grocery, fairytale bakeries, pristine butcher's shop. Two restaurants, three medical centres, a cemetery, a hardware store, a mairie, a school and two cafes, all smugly snoozing in the mellow sunlight. Over the central square, in which a fountain trickled, massed rows of plane trees shaded a sandy area where a group of men stood slowly, stalwartly playing *boules*. Aileen smiled.

'I'll have to get Joe a navy beret.'

'You sure will. He's going to love it here . . . when you tell him.'

After much agonised debate, Aileen had decided against telling Joe until she got home. This kind of thing just didn't work on the phone; she needed to sit down and break her news at a moment when Joe would be neither rushed nor tired. Desperately she took photos of everything she saw, thankful that it was a sunny day; the village of Mézalas looked extremely enticing.

As did that café over there, because her blood seemed to be tingling for some reason, she was feeling faintly light-headed.

'Shona, let's have a – what do you call it again? Milky coffee?'

'*Un café crème.* You'll be able to say it perfectly, and a whole lot of other things too, by the time we get home.'

Home. Unexpectedly Aileen thought of it with affection, was almost looking forward to setting off on the long voyage back. Fascinating and fruitful as France had been, she was suddenly eager to see her family, sleep in her own bed, eat in her own kitchen, settle in by the fire to tell Joe the whole extraordinary tale. Tessie, too, and Dymps . . . they'd be mystified to hear that Shona Fitzpatrick was buying a house, and relieved that Aileen Hegarty was not. Not yet, anyway, not for the moment. They would look on it as a stay of execution.

Shona made her order the coffee, and she made a total hash of it, wincing as she heard herself mangling the simple phrase.

'But I'll learn' she pleaded, 'I promise I will . . . I'll learn everything I need to know about living here.'

Shona sipped and smiled. 'Yes – probably the hard way! I felt like I was on another planet that summer I was an au pair. Everything seemed so different, so stiff . . . the French have hearts of gold when you get to know them, but it takes ages, because they're not exactly exuberant. Don't expect the neighbours rushing round with cakes and plants, you'll have to reach out to them, join a few clubs or something if you want to get to know people. The first ten years are probably the hardest! At night, except in summer, it's lights out and early to bed.'

Early to bed . . . that would be a novelty, all right, for Joe. In fact it would be a novelty for the Hegarty marriage, quite a healthy one Aileen thought – not that she would tell Joe about this aspect of living in France. Let him come here first, and search in vain for his pub, his drinking buddies. When they failed to materialise, well . . . he'd have a lovely new home to go to, wouldn't he, his lovely if slightly neglected wife to turn to? Even if the project didn't work out, if they returned to Ireland at the end of a year, at least Mr and Mrs Hegarty might have crumpled a few sheets by then. Joe would have no choice but to turn to her in the absence of Dave Doherty – who, she decided resolutely, would not be welcome to visit.

Dave Doherty was what her mother called A Bad Influence.

Finishing their drinks, they set off to retrieve the car and embark, at last, on the drive back to Ireland. As they got into it Aileen turned to look around again at this village that would soon be hers, and Shona started the engine. 'Let's go take one quick last peep at Le Mas . . . Jesus, I can't believe I've bought it, am buying it! Did I really sign those papers?'

'Yes' Aileen said firmly, 'you did. You're soft in the head, and I – I'm delirious!'

All the way back to Ireland they talked, talked and talked over and over, about what they had done, were doing, would do. While Shona drove, Aileen did sums on bits of paper, working out who would pay what and contribute what. By renting out their house, she figured, she and Joe would have nearly enough to live on, need to keep only a small portion of the B & B income, while the rest would pay Shona's mortgage on Le Mas.

'Assuming I can fill it, that is, from early May to late October, and half fill it the other months.'

'You will. I have every confidence in you. I didn't spend all these years inspecting B & Bs for nothing – that was why I used to send you so many tourists. You set high standards and you kept them. All you have to do is exactly the same here.'

'You make it sound so simple!'

'It is simple. Trust me.'

'I do trust you. I've learned a lot about you, Sho, since we set out together, and I have to tell you that you've rocketed in my esteem. Not that you weren't high in it to begin with! Not just because you're buying this house, either, and giving me this wonderful opportunity. But because – because I had no idea you could be so spontaneous, so optimistic – even if I'm still not entirely sure why you're doing it.'

Shifting gear, Shona smiled, a little wryly. 'I'm doing it, Aileen, for many reasons. Some are financial, pragmatic. Others are to do with this beautiful country which, ever since I first saw it eighteen years ago, has always enchanted me. Henceforth, I will have a little part of it to call my own, to hold in my hands. But maybe the most important reason of all is – is Brendan.'

Brendan? Bewildered, Aileen paused, pen in hand, to search Shona's face. 'But – what's he got to do with it? You hardly seemed to be thinking about him at all, haven't mentioned him for days—'

'No.' Slowly, serenely, Shona moved up the gears, not taking her eyes from the road. 'I haven't. That's the point, Aileen. I've hardly thought of him at all, for days. He's got competition for my attention. I've fallen in love with Le Mas, which is the beautiful house of my dreams, and more. If it doesn't come complete with the man of my dreams, well . . . half a loaf is better than no bread. I've even found myself wondering whether Brendan might even have been – um – right. Because when I fell asleep last night, I didn't dream about him. I dreamt about my lovely, lovely Mas.'

6

'Over my dead body.'

Grimly, Joe heaved logs onto the fire, somehow conveying that Aileen's plan was consigned to it too. He was looking weary, she thought, after his three-week vigil over Finn, which had in the end yielded no results, no proof that Finn was involved in drugs at all. But the suspicion persisted, visibly taking its toll. Even in the relatively short time she had been away, Joe's hairline seemed to have receded another inch, his neck sunk a fraction into his shoulders.

And now, his wife was trying to yank him up by the roots, dig him out of his home, a home which at this moment was warm, cosy and appealing. She knew she wasn't going to win quickly or easily; she simply knew she was going to win. But not without a lot of chest-thumping and face-saving, because like any man Joe Hegarty had his pride. This evening's attempt was her third.

'A year. It's not long enough, Joe, but it's the most I could get Shona to agree to. Maybe, if we want to stay on longer, you could talk her round . . . she likes you, you know.'

'Does she, now?' Straightening up, he dusted off his hands. He scarcely even knew Shona – only as that attractive brunette from the tourism office, who'd taken his temporarily insane wife to France. And then snapped up that house from under her nose. Even though he hadn't wanted Aileen to buy it, it was annoying that Shona had.

'Mmm! She thinks you'd look good with a tan . . . anyway, as I say, it's only for a year. Just long enough to get some sun, have some fun and get Finn away from his – his friends, whoever they are.'

His contacts. That was what she meant. Whether he was peddling drugs or using them – if he was – Finn would find it much harder to operate in a new environment where he didn't even speak the language. Which was another thing.

'Aileen, for chrissakes, I don't speak a word of French. Neither do you, for that matter.'

'No. But we will, by February. Enough to get by on.'

'Hmph. Enough to buy a loaf of bread, maybe, but not enough to talk to anyone. We wouldn't know a sinner. Wouldn't even be able to watch telly.'

'We can get cable. Sky Sports. I saw it on a television in a café, so you must be able to get it.'

Damn. Another argument shot down. But he had plenty more. 'I'd be a menace on the roads, driving on the right.'

'Well, if I managed it, love, I'm sure you would too.'

Blast. No answer to that. 'I hear the food is very peculiar – frogs, snails, huh! We'd starve.'

'We'll bring over all your favourite things. Rashers and sausages, for the freezer . . . no need to bring tea though, or beans or even Guinness, because they have all those things in the supermarkets. I saw them. They even have marmalade.'

Bloody hell. 'What about paperwork? They probably wouldn't even let us in.'

'You just fill in a form and get a resident's permit. Once you're from an EU country, it's only a formality, Shona says.'

Sinking into an armchair, Joe glimpsed defeat looming. Barely a handful of bullets remained.

'You'd go mad. You'd miss your mother and Dymps, the neighbours, your pals.'

'Actually, they'll probably all come to visit so often we'll see more of them than we do here, we'll be sick of them! Shona says they can stay in the gîte when she's not using it herself.'

'Is that so? Well, I hope her generosity extends to my friends too, because I'd want to invite Dave Doherty.'

Amiably, Aileen nodded. She'd deal with the Dave question later. When they got there. 'Oh, I'm sure that wouldn't be a problem.'

Desperately, Joe ransacked his mind for further ammunition. 'I don't know what they'd have to say about all this at work. A year is a helluva lot of leave to ask for.'

'Well, we'll just have to find out! Probably they'll be delighted to have someone off the payroll, get in a much cheaper temp.'

'Yeah. Or promote someone into my position and demote me into his when I came back.'

'Oh, Joe . . . you're great at your work, they'll be delighted to have you back. Anyway, get it all settled in advance, on paper. Then you'll know exactly where you stand.'

Gloomily, Joe gazed into the fire. He still couldn't grasp what this was all about. Only the bit about shifting Finn made any sense. If Finn could be shifted.

'I don't know, Aileen . . . suppose Finn doesn't want to go? Refuses to go?'

Yes. That was what she was dreading, herself. That Finn might stay here, move in with one of his vague, invisible friends in Galway or Limerick. The friends she'd never met, because although he mentioned them he never brought them home.

'If he won't come, he'll be high and dry. No home comforts, nobody to cook his meals or do his laundry, no phone line, nowhere to put his computer, no use of car, none of that pocket money I know you slip to him . . . Joe, I want you to talk to him. I want you to paint a really attractive picture of life in the sun and persuade him to come. I – I want him out of here, away from every influence. If you can't get him to agree to a whole year then tell him we need him to help us move at least, we'll pay him to shunt furniture and do handyman stuff for – for the first month, anyway. Once he gets there, we'll work out some way to make him stay.'

H'mm. Looking at his wife, Joe assessed the extent of her need, her ardent wish to do this. Clearly, Finn was a pivotal point in this mad scheme . . . and Finn was her only child. Their only one, since Hazel died. Sometimes, he could still see the scar in her eyes, the sadness in her face. She had lost so much, that dreadful day. As did we all, he thought; as did we all. Fifteen years later, and it still hurts so much. Not that she ever admits it, because she knows she should be over it by now. But she's not over it. I'm not over it. As for Finn . . .

Lapsing into reverie, he sat in silence, and Aileen sat with him, patiently, quietly, leaving him to his thoughts, whatever they might be. Evidently some kind of battle was going on in his head, she could see conflict in his face – as was only natural, in the circumstances. She knew she was asking a lot of him.

Eventually, he stirred, reached over to her with a kind of grunt. 'Show me those pictures again.'

In a flash they were hot in her hand, which she was surprised to find was trembling. 'Here – look – oh, Joe, isn't it beautiful?'

One by one she handed them to him, and with melting reluctance he studied them, grudgingly conceding that yes, this house did look beautiful. Not as beautiful as she did, though, when she smiled that radiant smile, so full of eager hope. The one he hadn't seen for months lately, not since that looper in Afghanistan blew up the Twin Towers and her business, overnight, had dwindled to half nothing. The business she had worked so hard to build up.

'All right. If we don't have to spend Finn's college money, if

Shona's buying the damn place . . . we'll do it. We'll go.'
Exhaling the last of his resistance, he sat back, with a sigh that
said 'What can you do, women always win, don't blame me if
this all goes up in smoke.' In one bound she was beside him,
hugging him, beaming in a way that made it all worthwhile.

'Yes! I knew you'd say yes! Oh, Joe . . . thank you.' Dropping
a kiss on his forehead, she hugged him again. 'And – and you'll
talk to Finn?'

Yes. Actually, yes, he would. He would talk to Finn this very
moment, right now while his mother's face was alight with joy.
Getting up, he went to the door, opened it and called up the
stairs. 'Finn! Finn, come down here, do you hear me?'

A silence. And then some shunting, grunting. 'Yeah, yeah, I
hear you, what is it?'

'Come down here. Now. Your mother and I want a word with
you.'

Noting his suddenly firm tone, Aileen was agreeably surprised. Somehow over the years she and Joe had got into the
habit of being . . . well . . . gentle with Finn. Not exactly indul-
gent, but patient, humouring him whenever possible. Neither
of them had any idea how much he might remember about
Hazel; it was liking walking on eggshells. Gradually, imperceptibly, some kind of mantle had gathered around him, as if he
were a trauma victim needing care and shelter. For all his
aggressive attitude, Aileen sensed fragility underneath. But
had they, maybe, been too cautious? Too easy on him? If they'd
pushed him that bit harder, he might have got his exams, might
have a job today, might not be hanging out with . . . whoever
he was hanging out with.

Footsteps thundered down the stairs, and he came into the
room. While Aileen was away he had got two more rings, one
in each eyebrow, and tonight he was wearing a white T-shirt
with a scarlet slogan slashed on it: Sod God. Pale and lanky,

he looked as if his bones were too big for his body, angular and awkward. But more than anything it was the expression in his eyes that struck her, the same one that had greeted her return from France: utter vacancy. Everything in his studded face, his slouched stance, bespoke indifference. For one split second, she felt a flicker of fear. Had Joe caught it? She wondered if he had, because he glanced very briefly at her just as she shivered, just as he was about to speak. And then he did speak.

'Finn, sit down.'

Without argument, Finn sat. He had never been argumentative, or confrontational, with either parent. He simply heard them out and then went his own sweet way. Draping himself on the sofa, he waited for whatever Joe might be going to say.

'We're going to France. In February. All of us. The whole family.'

That did get a reaction, as much as anything ever did. Finn scratched his arm, scratched the back of his neck, and exhaled a long sigh. 'Jaysus.'

'We're going for a year. To this house.' Handing him the photos, Joe remained stolidly planted in front of the fire. 'Your mother is going to run her B & B business in it, and you and I are going with her, to help. There'll be a lot of stuff to be moved, things to be fixed up in the house and so on. So start planning around it.'

Silently, Finn shuffled through the first two or three photos. Then, appearing to lose interest, he put them down and stared, not at his parents, but through them. Clear through them, as if focusing on something or someone else further away.

'Yeah. Well. Okay.'

The indifference in his tone was maddening, and Joe bristled. 'Don't you even want to know where in France, or anything else about it?'

Finn considered. And then he shook his head. 'I know all I need to know. That I haven't any choice.'

Oh, no. Aileen wasn't having that. 'Yes, Finn. You do have a choice. We want you to come, but you don't have to. If need be, you can stay here. By February you might have a job, a flat, maybe even a girlfriend to keep you company while we're away—'

Languidly, he grinned at her, a kind of spectral grin. 'Me? But sure who the fuck would have me? Face it, Ma. You'd want to be out of your mind to want the likes of me.'

He was up and out of the room before either of them could articulate what was in both their hearts: how much, in spite of everything, they loved this lost, sad son of theirs. And how close, at this moment, they were to the brink of hating him.

Like a popped bubble, Shona's high spirits began to dissipate almost from the moment she got back to Ireland. It was winter, damp and grey, and Christmas was coming, which meant not only insatiable commercialism with its grating jingles, but parties. Invitations to lots of parties; it was as if word had got round and people pitied her – poor Shona, suspended from work, broken up with Brendan.

This time last year, she'd only just met him. Vividly she remembered how she'd left Emily O'Brien's house feeling that her feet were scarcely touching the ground, all the euphoria of starstruck joy. He had been so nice, so friendly, attractive, ideal in every way. Now, she would have to tell Emily that her match-making had come to nothing, that she had inexplicably let this lovely man slip through her fingers. Alone in her apartment, not only bored but lonely, she felt like a failure. Was, arguably, a failure. There couldn't be many women who, on being presented with a crystal trophy, immediately let it crash to the ground. Every day she resolved to go and see Emily, and every day she put it off, adding guilt to her other shortcomings.

Even Crys . . . for no good reason she'd been relieved when Crys twice postponed get-togethers to discuss Shona's new house and 'the baby situation', as she called it. Crys would want to know who she was taking to all these parties, urge her to invite Fintan up from Limerick or one of her other male friends . . . but she didn't want to. If she couldn't have Brendan Wright on her arm, what was the point of anyone else? It would only be camouflage, flimsy dressing on a basically bare Christmas tree.

Her parents, delighted to hear of her pending new purchase, began to phone more anxiously as Christmas approached. It didn't sound as if she was getting out much? She mustn't mope at home, what about joining a chess or tennis club? Irrationally, she convinced herself that clubs were code for 'a dating agency', whereupon her mother bluntly retorted that yes, actually, maybe that would be a good idea. The conversation terminated on a strained note, which made things yet worse, because she and her parents were normally the best of pals.

Each day, time hung more heavily on her hands. She hated not working. She missed her colleagues, her B & B ladies, the cheery office banter. Waking up one particularly grim morning, under a blanket of cloud so heavy she wanted to punch a hole in it, she forced herself to do something – anything – constructive today. Over breakfast she made a list, and then she sat down with the phone. The French tourism office in Dublin: its counterpart in Paris, the Languedoc branch, the one nearest to Le Mas, in Carcassonne or wherever it might be . . . she was going to call them all, research Aileen's new business, find out everything about the area from A to Z. At least Aileen's husband had agreed to go – her son too, apparently – so that was something to be grateful for. Resolutely, pen poised, she began to ring the numbers.

All right. Maybe Brendan had a point. Maybe I am a workaholic. But I still miss him. Miss him much more here in Ireland
than I did in France . . . is he never going to call me, never
change his mind?

At last, Crys was free. Arriving one night at Shona's apartment
for supper, glumly toting a bottle of wine, she handed it over
looking somehow stripped, and Shona blinked. For the first
time in living memory, Crys's fingernails were bare. No
scarlet, no emerald, no silver – nothing, only plain buffed nails.
It was as alarming as if the Queen of England had ventured
out without her handbag.

'So' Shona supposed in the shorthand of friends, 'still
nothing?'

Sitting down, folding her hands in her lap, Crys grimaced.
'No. Still nothing . . . Sho, I'm heading for suicidal here.'

Hanging up Crys's jacket, Shona stiffened. Crys Sheehan
was normally the cheeriest person she knew. Crys loved her
husband, loved her work both paid and voluntary, loved –
loved life! If she didn't have a child, would that be the end of
the world? They could adopt, couldn't they?

But, even if she didn't see the magnitude of the problem,
sensitivity restrained her from saying so. Clearly, Crys was
distraught. Shona went to fetch a corkscrew.

'Crys, you are no such thing. I won't hear of such nonsense.
You – you can't see the wood for the trees, is all. This whole
thing is getting obsessional.'

Accepting a glass of wine, Crys didn't drink from it. 'Yes. It
is. You're telling me. It is taking over our entire lives, ruling
everything. Charts, temperatures, thermometers, phases of the
moon . . . it'll be witch doctors next, clinics, fertility treatment
and then, probably, sextuplets.'

Shona laughed. Crys didn't. 'It's not just me, Sho. It's Gavin, too. He's nearly worse than I am, spends hours calculating, speculating . . . it – it's absolutely wrecking our marriage.'

'Can you not – both – just forget about it now and again? Have a night out, go to the cinema or a concert or something? Anything, to take your minds off it?'

'No! Everything has to be timed to the day, the hour, almost the minute. Our sex life is in shreds. Love just doesn't come into the picture any more, it's all to do with planning, anticipating . . . anything and everything except spontaneity. I'm starting to feel like a robot. And what's more, starting to go off sex altogether. It's just miserable when it's so loaded with meaning, when you're waiting for results that never come. You lose sight of everything else, tenderness, desire, fun – it all becomes so deathly serious. I honestly don't know how much more I can take of this.'

Crys looked so wretched, Shona could not but feel wretched for her. And then she thought of Aileen, who'd given birth to a little girl only to lose her two years later. Was that, in a way, even worse? Yet Aileen had battled through, was battling to this day. Crys was going to have to battle too, needed some kind of pep talk . . . abruptly, Shona felt a sense of purpose. Something of that same missionary zip she'd felt when setting off for France with Aileen, as if it were falling to her to care for all these fractured friends.

Well, she thought, I haven't anyone else to care for, have I? Not even my B & B ladies, at the moment. I can surely spare some emotional energy for Crys Sheehan, my favourite friend, when she needs it. And does she ever look as if she needs it.

'Sorry' Crys apologised, 'I don't mean to moan. But if I don't get it off my chest I'll *explode*, Shona!'

'No. You won't explode until after you've had a second helping of the lasagne I've made for you, of which you are going to eat every bite.'

Crys shrugged a kind of rueful smile. 'Yes, Mummy. Or should that be *oui, Maman*? Tell me about this French house you've bought, or nearly bought.'

As they sat down to eat Shona produced the copied photographs Aileen had given her, and told Crys all about it. 'Crazy, of course. Don't ask me what came over me. All I can tell you is that the minute I saw it, I had to have it. And then, Aileen couldn't have it, because at the last minute her husband wouldn't play ball. It was like – like it was simply meant to be mine, I was in the agency signing papers before we knew what hit us. So now, Aileen's going to run it as a B & B for a year – we take possession in February. And' – it suddenly hit her – 'you're coming down then, with me. There'll be room for you in the gîte, if you don't mind a sofa bed.'

Crys studied her lasagne. 'Sho, I can't. I'm not allowed go anywhere. I have to be – available – to Gavin at all times. Round the goddamn clock. Plus, I work you know.'

Shona thought about it. 'Aren't the half-term holidays in February?'

'Yes . . . school closes for a week, but—'

'Then that's that. Give me the exact dates and I'll call M Delatre, make that the week we go. You will tell Gavin you need a – a break! And you do – Crys, you'll snap like a twig if you don't get away from this endless baby problem! You'll have a nervous breakdown and that will hardly help, will it? So please, do this. Shift your focus, just for a week, get some sun and some – some sense of perspective. Gavin will understand, if you put it to him the right way, if he's half the decent husband he seems to be.'

Crys picked up her fork, twirled it, put it down and took hold instead of the plait in which she wore her hair, began to pluck agitatedly at it. 'He – he is, you know. He's a great husband and I – I—'

Suddenly, she was in tears. Dissolving in tears, burying her face in her hands, sobbing so heartbrokenly that Shona jumped up, ran round the table and seized her by her shaking shoulders. 'Oh, my God . . . Crys, is it as bad as all that?'

'Y – yes! Yes, it is! I love him and I know he loves me and I – we – we – just can't understand what's going wrong between us! Why we're not communicating any more, why there are all these silences, it's like some kind of Berlin Wall going up between us! It – it is *horrible*! If this goes on we're going to end up hating each other!'

Never had Shona seen Crys in such a state, so despondent, almost desperate, weeping as if drowning. Was Gavin, behind his normally no less cheerful persona, feeling the same way? Were these two close, cherished friends actually in danger of . . . of drifting apart, separating, splitting up? From where she stood looking at it, holding Crys's shuddering shoulders, that possibility seemed infinitely worse to Shona than not having a baby. The marriage, she suddenly saw, was changing places with the baby, mutating into the core problem.

'Crys, listen to me. You're exhausted. Mentally worn to a thread. You're coming away for a week in February whether you like it or not. If you won't tell Gavin, then I will.'

Expecting resistance, she was taken aback when, after a pause, Crys lifted her head to look at her with gleaming, tear-filled eyes. 'Would you, Sho? Would you do that, for me? Because he'll go ballistic if I tell him I'm going anywhere. He'll say I'm being selfish, say I'm chickening out.'

What? Gavin would say all that? Shona was astounded. Truly, nobody ever could tell what went on behind the closed doors of even the most apparently happy partnership.

'Yes, Crys. Of course I will. I will tell him, in no uncertain terms, that you are having a week away with me in France in

February, and that what's good for his wife will ultimately be good for him.'

French classes. Furniture – bring or buy? A car – ditto? Paperwork? As winter approached its nadir Aileen was overtaken by a kind of frenzied determination to get everything organised for France. Once the structures were in place, she felt, it would actually happen, nobody would be able to back out – besides, business was so bad she had time to fill, time she didn't want to dwell on or in. Not that she was the only one; everyone in every aspect of the tourism industry was hit, with a knock-on effect that meant a lean Christmas all round. No spending sprees this year, no high-tech toys, shiny new cars, expensive outfits or sun-kissed winter breaks. Aileen didn't mind that – what you'd never had you couldn't miss – but it bothered her that so many lives could be altered by the will of one fanatical man five thousand miles away. If it was going to be a meagre Christmas in Ireland, it was going to be far worse for the thousands of families who had lost people they loved on September 11, and she felt very sorry for them.

But in both good years and bad, the Hegarty house was always full for Christmas. On alternate years Aileen and Joe invited either his family or hers to share it with them, and this year it was her turn, and so she invited her mother, her sister, brother-in-law, niece and nephew to join herself, Joe and Finn around the festive table. The more she filled it up, the less time she would have to think about Hazel, the only member of the family who had never sat amongst them on Christmas day. Tiny Hazel, who'd never got beyond her high-chair, chubby arms flailing, flinging food from her spoon at her father. And at Finn. Finn who, since hearing about Le Mas, was spending more time than ever on his computer, sunk in a sub-world of his own. As was Joe, in a different way: after two French classes he abandoned the course for which Aileen had signed them both up, saying it was just too damn difficult, and decamped back to the more alluring joys of Dave Doherty who was keeping his seat warm for him in the pub.

'What about your sabbatical?' Aileen persisted, trying to keep him focused on France. 'Have you talked to your boss yet?'

'No' he said shortly, 'haven't been able to pin him down yet. I'll try and get a quiet moment with him after Christmas.'

Was he evading it? Even though he'd agreed to go? Aileen suspected that he was, might even be hoping that something would yet go wrong. If it did, the plan would collapse and he'd get a reprieve. Saying nothing, she set about making everything watertight, ensuring that nothing whatsoever could or would go wrong. Watching Joe, she could all but see cogs turning in his mind, some kind of war waging in his head.

On Christmas day they all gathered around the oval dining table, herself and Joe, Dymps with her husband and children, Tessie in festive finery and Finn, silent unless spoken to.

And Shona. Shona was with them also, because her parents were spending Christmas with friends in Donegal and she did not, she said, feel like 'playing gooseberry' with them. Uneasily, Aileen wondered whether money might be another reason, after Shona had unexpectedly spent so much more than anticipated in France. Their delayed departure, all the extra driving, had dented both their budgets. Smiling invincibly, she handed Joe the carving fork, and sat down presidentially over the turkey.

'What about your friends, Sho?' she enquired with genuine interest. After all, Shona was becoming, in a way, almost one of the family. 'What are Crys and Gavin doing today?'

Shona smiled. 'They're down at the St Vincent de Paul

centre, dishing up dinner to people who can't afford it or have nowhere to go. They're atheists, don't believe in Christmas as such at all, but they live the most socially valuable lives of anyone I know. They just can't help helping! Crys's father was a medical volunteer in Lesotho you know, that's where he met her mother . . . it runs in the family.'

'I had one too' Tessie piped up, 'it was yellow.'

Aileen suppressed a grin. Tessie's hearing was living a life of its own these days. 'So, Mam' she enunciated clearly, serving potatoes, 'will you and Dymps be coming to France for Easter, now that – uh – we've got a place?'

Tessie looked at her quizzically. 'What's wrong with your face?'

'*A place,* Mam, in France!'

'Oh yes, France . . . I must say, Aileen, I'm glad you're only going for a year. It looks like a lovely house, but it's so far away.'

'Barely two hours by plane.'

'These things wear off, you know. People take notions. Joe, just a wing is plenty for me . . . so have you got tenants yet, to rent this house while you're away?'

'We have a rental agency working on it. They have to check references and so on. But everything should be ready in time, they say.'

'Well, I'm looking forward to it' Dymps beamed, 'you can certainly count me in for Easter. If Shona's not using this gîte of hers?'

And that was when it hit Shona like a brick: *What will I do if I lose my court case? If I actually lose it, and lose my job?*

'Oh no' she said casually, 'I'll be back at work by then. After February, I won't be able to go down to Le Mas again until maybe September.'

'Well' Tessie said, 'I think you're very brave to buy it. And I think Joe and Finn are very brave lads to go and live there for a whole year. I don't know if I could ever do such a thing, I might go mad without my gardening club and my friends . . . are you looking forward to going, Joe?'

All eyes swivelled to Joe, seating himself after carving the turkey. But it was Aileen's gaze he felt on him. 'Yes' he blurted, 'I – it – it'll be a – a change.'

He sounded as if some invisible dentist were poised to extract all his teeth, and a thoughtful, speculative pause settled around the table. Then, inexorably, not hearing the silence, Tessie turned to her grandson. 'And what about you, Finn?'

Finn did not immediately reply. Clutching his cutlery like a child, knuckles up, elbows out, he thoughtfully inspected his plate, as if he had not previously considered it. Impatiently, Joe nudged him. 'Finn, your grandmother is asking you a question.'

His head jerked up. Abruptly, darkly, his whole face flooded with resentment. And his tone, when he finally spoke, was lightly, ironically laced with acid.

'Yeah. Yeah, sure I am. I'm looking forward to France about as much as France is looking forward to me. We'll be great for each other. Right, Ma?'

Everything in his eyes, his voice, his bearing shouted accusation at her, shouted that she was wrecking his life, the life which in reality he did not have.

Oh, God, she thought, I do not know how much more of this I can stand. How much longer I can bear this – this *presence,* in our home, in our life! This – this man, lurking, hovering, seething under every inch of his skin, and ours! I am ready to jump up, overturn this table and shout it aloud for all the world to hear: yes, Finn, you killed Hazel! Not intentionally, but you did! There's the truth of it, if truth you want! *What* do you want? What are we going to do, all three of us? Have it out, lay it bare, dig right down to the bottom of this barrel of bitterness that is corroding our family, eating into our hearts, our minds, our souls?

I'm ready to have it out. Ready, at this moment, to tell you the truth, regardless of what it might do to you. Because nothing could be worse than this – this charade, this never-ending tension. You didn't mean it, we don't blame you for it, but yes, you *did* it! And no, I wasn't there, no, I didn't stop you!

Picking up a glass dish, she passed it down the table with icy calm. 'Try this broccoli, Shona, Dymps . . . I cooked it in white wine stock, it should be delicious.'

As if it were a ticking bomb, Dymps's husband took it from her, and they all smiled at it, at her, gingerly, collectively. As if the table were metamorphosing into a minefield, as if she, not Finn, were the one who needed watching this day of Christmas goodwill.

Two days later, in the lull between Christmas and New Year, Shona rang Gavin Sheehan and arranged to meet him at Moran's of the Weir, a hostelry well out of the way of prying eyes. If a single woman met a married man for a drink in town, it would be all over the place by nightfall that she was having an affair with him. As she drove out to Moran's, Shona wondered: was it the same in France? Did people there, too, add two and two together and come up with five? Or, in that blissful sun, were they too content to care? Maybe the sun had a soporific effect, or maybe it sent them spinning off on torrid affairs of their own?

Here in Ireland, it was a damp, murky afternoon. The kind on which you'd rather be curled up at home by the fire with your husband, if you had a husband . . . Jesus wept, she thought, what am I going to do on New Year's eve? I can't stay home alone, and I can't go to a party alone, because when they all start singing 'Auld Lang Syne' I'd miss Brendan so much I'd slash my wrists.

Gavin was already in the pub when she reached it, looking up at her with naked curiosity as she came in, took off her coat and ordered a hot whiskey. 'Hi' he said with a friendly smile, pulling out a chair for her.

She bent to kiss his cheek. 'Hi, Gav. Thanks for coming.'

'Well, I had to, to find out what this is all about!' Grinning, he waited for her to get settled, looking warm and attractive in a red sweater some adoring aunt had, probably, knitted him for Christmas.

'It's about Crys.'

Reaching for his pint, he looked up from it to blink at her. 'Crys? You've dragged me out here to discuss my wife?'

'Yes.' Her drink arrived and she took it gratefully, wrapping her hands around its warmth. 'She . . . um . . . she wants to ask you a favour. Just a little one. Only she thinks you might get mad, so I said I'd ask you for her.'

He looked bewildered. 'Get mad? Why, what does she want – a diamond-encrusted suite at the Bali Hilton?'

Shona grinned. He seemed to be in a perfectly relaxed frame of mind. Crys must be exaggerating, even imagining the tension between them, as was her dramatic wont. 'No, nothing that's going to cost an arm or a leg! She just wants to take a little holiday . . . a break . . . she wants to come with me to see my new house in the Languedoc when I get it in February.'

He didn't immediately reply. Instead he put down his glass, sat back, and seemed to think about it. 'Your house? In the Languedoc? In February?'

'Yes. Just for a week. She wants to go, because she's been feeling a bit – tired – lately, and I'd love her to come because –

well – these things are more fun with a friend. Of course Aileen Hegarty will be there, but she'll have her husband and son, whereas I – well, it would be great if Crys could be there. For both of us.'

'I see.'

Inexplicably, there was an awkward pause. Uncomfortably, Shona plunged on, sensing that more detail seemed to be required. 'You know, Gav! Girl's stuff, shopping for sheets and towels, deciding what colour to paint the kitchen, visits to markets, all that kind of thing. I've already told the estate agent I want to sign the papers on February 25, because that's when Crys has her mid-term break, she'll be free to come.'

He remained sitting back, pint untouched, looking at her. 'Did she tell you that? That she'd be free to go?'

'Yes – provided it's okay with you. I know you're trying hard for a baby, and you want her – around – as much as she can be, but I think she's a bit under the weather. A week in France would really freshen her up.'

'A week without me, you mean?'

His tone sounded suddenly almost as dark as his Guinness, throwing her off what had seemed to be a straightforward trajectory. 'No, I don't mean that, in the way you make it sound! It's just that the gîte is small, barely big enough for two, and the main house won't be furnished in time for Aileen to put you up. Besides, you don't have a week off work in February, do you?'

'No' he conceded, 'I don't. But Crys does. I was looking forward to having her at home that week, actually, to spoiling her a bit, making her sleep late and . . . take it easy.'

Something in his tone was hardening in some way, some-thing in his face too, and for the first time, astonished, Shona glimpsed a different Gavin. Still a hunky husband, yes, but one who had other plans for his wife, plans that would keep her in bed busily making a baby. He didn't sound at all pleased to find them thwarted. Or even challenged.

'But Gavin . . . don't you think a change of scenery would be better for her? She's getting bogged down, trying too hard – come on, loosen up! It's only one week!'

With a kind of snort, he picked up his glass and drained it, abruptly, in a gulp. 'Shona, Crys is a grown woman. She can do whatever she wants. And I have no doubt that she will do it.'

Uneasily, she eyed him. 'Is that a yes or a no? She won't do it unless—'

Standing up, exuding annoyance, he reached for his jacket. 'Oh, yes, she will. She'll do whatever she likes and the only thing that surprises me about all this is that she dragged you into it, didn't see fit to inform me herself. But then, as they say, the husband is always the last to know.'

He was wrapping his scarf around his neck, and she was amazed by the anger in his tone, by the fact that he was apparently leaving.

'Gavin – for God's sake—'

With a smile that was pure irony, he raised a hand in parting salute. 'Have a ball in France, Shona. Have a really great girls' gig.'

Dismally, Shona sat pondering after Gavin had gone, feeling she'd made an awful hash of things. Clearly he was on his way home to pick a row with Crys, and maybe he even had a point, maybe Crys should have told him herself. But she hadn't felt able to, because he was as wound up as she was, there was a pair of them in it. Oh, God! Maybe now Crys would change her mind, not come after all – which would be a pity in more ways than one.

Cut short, not knowing what to do, Shona nursed her drink

and then decided to go to see Emily O'Brien, in her country manor out in the sticks. Emily always had a soothing way about her, and besides it was time to bite the bullet, let her know that she needn't rush out, after all, to buy a hat for the Wright-Fitzpatrick wedding. Calling Emily on her mobile, Shona proposed a visit, and Emily replied that yes, she was at home, would love to see her and hear all the news.

It was a long drive from Moran's out to Emily's house in Connemara, through fields and bogs dripping with damp, the slate-blue daylight dimming already into dark emerald evening, silhouetting the Twelve Pins where, at this time of winter, you could imagine ancient armies huddling into their folds, plotting, stalking the twilight. Here and there a tiny lake gleamed and was gone, a cottage window winked and vanished, a curlew's cry wound through the wisps of mist . . . turning up both heater and radio, Shona peered out at the narrow road, thinking that this was no terrain in which to be alone. How on earth did Emily stand it, since Séan died!?

But Emily's house, when Shona eventually turned into its neatly raked gravel drive, was glowing warmly, Christmas candles shining in every downstairs window, a red-berried holly wreath jauntily adorning the glossy front door. Around the side, slung blithely across the lawn, the ancient O'Brien Mercedes sat freshly washed, with a tartan ribbon merrily tied to its aerial. For a sixty-year-old widow, it had to be admitted, Emily was putting on a pretty good show.

'Hello!' Pushing open the door as she rang the bell, Shona found it unlocked as usual; Emily took the serenely irrational view that nobody would be bothered coming all the way out here to burgle or otherwise bother 'the likes of' her. Refusing all entreaties, she wouldn't even get an alarm.

'Shona! Come on in, I'm warming some wine, d'you like it mulled?'

'Mmm, yes please!' Embracing, they laughed as they looked at each other, Shona in a plum wool suit, lipstick to match, snugly scarved and shod; Emily small, wispy, white-haired, burrowing into a capacious angora cardi that made her look, Shona thought, like a matriarchal bunny.

The wine was brought into the sitting room in a punch bowl, placed beside the fire to keep warm as they sank into squashy armchairs, each delighted to see the other. Catching sight of a photo of Séan on the sideboard, Shona hesitated.

'How was your Christmas, Emily?'

Unexpectedly, Emily nodded, even smiled with a hint of satisfaction. 'Much better than it might have been. The house party went off really well, it was a great idea to take that grouse shooting-party, they cheered things up no end and I even made a profit. I'm taking another group for New Year.'

'Where do you get them? They must be the only tourists in the country at the moment!'

'Oh, there are always a few, and I have my contacts. But I must say, I'd love to get listed in that *Country Houses* guide – do you know yet whether I have?'

'No – but I can find out. I'll call the office and get someone to check.'

Emily looked puzzled. 'Call the office? But can't you check yourself?'

Shona grimaced. 'No. I'm afraid I can't. I've been suspended from work.'

Emily looked aghast. 'What?! But – you – Shona, I don't understand?'

'It's a long story.' With a sigh, she related it, and then took a deep breath. 'You might as well have all the bad news in one fell swoop. The other bit is that I've broken up with Brendan – or should I say, he's broken up with me.'

There was a pause. But mercifully, Emily didn't hit the roof, even managed to camouflage the disappointment Shona assumed she must feel. 'Yes. I know. He was here a week or so ago, to see about the bull. He told me.'

Eagerly, Shona tensed. 'Was he? Did he?'

'Yes. I can't pretend I'm not very sorry, Shona. But . . . well, maybe it just wasn't meant to be. Maybe he wasn't right for you, after all.'

What? But Emily was the one who'd introduced them, how could she sit here now sounding so – so philosophical? Stung, Shona leaned forward, grasping her glass. 'But he *was* right for me! That's what makes it so terrible! He was the only single, solvent, intelligent, eligible man from here to Tasmania!'

Emily laughed. 'Well, I hear there's a shortage right enough. But that still doesn't necessarily make him the man for you.'

Good grief. Emily was beginning to sound nearly as bad as Crys, any minute now she'd be rationalising the break-up, putting Brendan's side of it. Which he must surely have told her. Shona couldn't contain her curiosity. 'What did he say?'

'He said you were a lovely lady and that the two of you had had a wonderful year together and that he was very sorry things hadn't worked out between you.'

'Did he tell you why they didn't?'

Sitting back, cupping her glass in her hands, Emily considered. 'He seemed to feel there was a – what did he call it? A clash of agendas?'

'Agendas? Hah! Is that what he called it? Emily, I'll have you know he ditched me on the very day I got suspended from work. If he'd only waited, I would have had no *other* agenda only him.'

Faintly, wryly, Emily smiled. 'That's not what I hear.'

'I beg your pardon?'

'I ran into Aileen Hegarty at the market in Galway last week. She tells me she's moving to France to run a guesthouse you're in the process of buying.'

Oh. Gossip. I should have guessed, Shona thought, you can't do anything round here without everyone – but at least it was Aileen herself who told Emily. 'Well, yes. That's true. I am.'

'Tell me about it.'

Shona snatched up her handbag. 'Oh, Emily, wait till you see it! I have the photos here with me, it's divine, sort of a French version of your own house here, you'll love it!' Breathlessly she rummaged, found them and passed them over, a little anxiously; for some reason she wanted Emily to like Le Mas, wanted her approval.

And it was forthcoming. As she riffled through the pictures, Emily's smile spread like melting honey. 'Oh, yes. Oh, Shona, this is exquisite . . . if I were twenty years younger I'd want to go over there and run it for you myself!'

'Well, I hope you'll come visit. Soon, before it gets busy!'

Curiously, Emily looked up, looked at her. 'Will it, do you think? The very first season?'

Firmly, Shona nodded. 'Oh yes. It's in a terrific area, lots of amenties, great access, plenty of local demand, cheaper than Provence. I've been boning up on every aspect. Plus Aileen is so experienced, she'll do a great job of running it. I've already sorted everything with the bank, got the loan, the surveyor's report is watertight – we're raring to go!'

'I see.' Thoughtfully, Emily stacked the photos and handed them back to her. 'Then I wish you the very best of luck, Shona. Who'd have thought our B & B inspector would go into the business one day herself?'

'Huh? Oh, no, Emily, not me! Aileen will be the boss! I'm only buying Le Mas as an investment, I won't even be there very often. Much as I love the place, my career is here. If I win my court case – which I'd bloody well better – I want to get into the hotel sector.'

Do you, Emily wondered, silently. Do you now, Ms Fitzpatrick? And do you want that as much as you wanted Brendan Wright – about whom you have yet to say another word? Any other woman, if I'd seen her ex, would be plying me with questions about him. But it's this house that's making your face light up, this house that's taking hold of your heart. Just as it seems to be taking hold of Aileen Hegarty's, too. I hope you both know what you're getting into, here. There's nothing like business partnerships for wrecking friendships.

'So tell me, Shona, what are you doing for New Year?'

'I'm staying home with the duvet over my head, cursing Brendan Wright, who I hope will be even more miserable than I will myself.'

Oh, no! Even as she said it Shona stretched mentally to swipe it back; but too late. She'd forgotten that Emily had lost Séan only last April, that she would surely miss him even more than she would miss Brendan, after thirty-five years of marriage. A deeply happy marriage, by all accounts. Wretchedly, she groped to apologise. 'Emily, I'm so sorry – I'm a clumsy fool—'

'Don't worry, Shona. I'll be too busy with my shooting party to have much time for moping.'

'I hope so. You're great to take them, Emily. Great to carry on so bravely without Séan.'

'He'd want me to. In fact he'd be furious if I didn't. And I would be furious with myself, if I let everything go to pot. Much as I miss him, he was not the be-all and end-all of my entire life.'

Surprised, Shona surveyed her. 'Really? But I thought . . .'

'What? That we were blissfully happy? Yes, we were. For precisely that reason. He was my partner, my other half – not

183

my whole self. He had other interests and so did I, that's what kept things lively.'

Other interests? What did that mean, exactly? Surely . . . no. Definitely not. Not little Emily O'Brien, who looked as if butter wouldn't melt in her rosebud mouth. Still . . . Shona was intrigued. 'Is there – um – room for other interests, in a marriage?'

'There is if you're talking the same language, both on the same wavelength.' Saying no more, Emily let that lie on the air between them. And then, while Shona was still pondering it, she stood up. 'More wine, while it's still warm?'

Standing up, Shona waved her away. 'No, thanks, I have the car, I'd better go before it's pitch dark. I just wanted to see how you were and – and say sorry for messing up with Brendan. I know you got us together deliberately.'

'Ah well, can't win them all! I'm sorry too, but you'll get over it.'

Grimly, Shona shook her head. 'No. Not this time, I won't. There have been too many disasters with men, and this one was the worst.' So saying, embracing Emily, she headed off to her car, and waved when she got to it. 'Happy New Year, Emily, may it be better than the last one.'

Yes, Emily thought, waving back, it will be better. Not for me, maybe, but for you. What would I give to be your age again, with so much time in hand, time to explore and grow, to find out who you really are and what you really want.

Whatever the hell it is, it's not Brendan Wright, and that's for sure. You may miss his company, miss having a handsome escort to show off socially, miss being admired and flattered and part of a couple – but I can see now that you didn't really love him. Not passionately, not desperately, not in the profound way you have to love a man to spend your whole life

is in her stride, feel none of the plummeting disappoint-
he acutely felt? Instinctively, strongly, she suspected
was stalling. But how to prove it? She could hardly ring
ployers and suggest that her husband was lying to her,
ey please corroborate his story? And, if it were untrue,
tell him she'd found out? He'd go ballistic, accuse her
ing and prying and distrusting . . . none of which she'd
e before, because he was not a devious man. What you
e Hegarty was what you got. More likely he was telling
 – and, when requesting leave, hadn't pushed the
of his case. To him, it was anything but urgent.

e really so hostile to this expedition, that he would
 to cope alone for two months? Alone, apart from
t Finn would hardly be much help, and less comfort.
r husband and partner, and she wanted him. Wanted
this whole thing, right from the start, not just physi-
motionally. She felt as if they were arm-wrestling,
s somehow struggling to hold this whole project at
nted Finn to go, would let her go, but did not want
elf. Try as she might, she couldn't speak.

ined silence was, she thought, almost challenging,
ntment washed through every bone in her body.
was committed to the February date now, he
ldn't be changed at this stage. Not without major
he kind which in turn would cause endless further
g, she clenched her fists, struggling not to let him
s was doing to her.

're sure? There's absolutely nothing you can do?'
t all. I did explain the situation, but they – er –
ould have told them earlier, given more notice.'
didn't you, Joe?'
 before, Aileen! Because things were busy, it
ht moment.'

with him. I loved Séan in that way, I see real devastation when I look in the mirror every morning – but I don't see it in you, Shona Fitzpatrick.

Trust me. You have no idea what love *does* to a woman, nor the loss of it either.

7

With a mixture of thrilled trepidation, Aileen zoomed through the new year tying up loose ends before, at last, leaving for France. Tenants were found for the Irish house, possessions were packed away, Tessie was placated that the venture would be wonderful and, by mid-February, she was within a whisper of realising her dream, of going to live in the beckoning house on the hill. Sometimes when she thought of it something gripped her stomach; some spasm of terror mingling with wild elation, curiosity dancing with delight. To actually do it, to become one of those people skipping off to a place in the sun! But suddenly she found she couldn't watch the programme on television any more – because it didn't follow them up, did it? The cameras never returned a year later, to find out how people were getting on in their new houses and countries. Were they euphorically happy? Or were they lonely, disillusioned, violently homesick? Knee-deep in debt, or blissed out on home-grown tomatoes? Had any of those gorgeous villas been swallowed by a landslide, had anyone been ripped off by rogue builders, had anyone found life impossible, thrown in the towel and gone home? Or was it all meadow picnics, rippling rivers, the glowing picture of all those glossy magazines?

Meanwhile, one even more crucial question remained: Joe.

She knew he was playing for time, putting off his request for leave from work in the hope that some angel of mercy would save him, snatch the whole thing from her and finally she was forced to confront him off, or not?

'Uh' he mumbled, evading her eye, 'ye Something sliced through her. 'What

Scratching his head, evading her gaz of the few remaining chairs in the kitche or felt like home. 'Well . . . I thought i until . . . in case things changed . . .'

She forced herself to fight off panic me. Now. In full.'

'Okay. I've got the leave. I can hav and rubber-stamped.'

Oh, thank God.

'But . . . the only problem is . . . The guy who's going to replace me i and won't be back until – er –'

What!? No! 'Until when?'

'April' he muttered guiltily. 'The you, Aileen – not immediately. Yo over without me and manage th own.'

What? But – this was a family point! If Joe were left alone in G moment down in the pub with what about the tenants, due to

'But Joe – apart from the fa alone! – where on earth would

'I know, I know. But what c mother or yours or someone. I have to make the best of it.'

She felt stabbed. Breathle such essential information

take th
ment
that he
his em
could t
how to
of snoo
ever dor
saw in Jo
the trut
urgency
Was h
leave her
Finn – bu
Joe was he
him in on
cally but
that Joe w
bay. He wa
to go hims
The stra
as disappo
Everyone
knew it cou
upheaval –
delay. Reeli
see what thi
'I see. You
'Nothing
they said I sl
'And why
'I told you
wasn't the rig

'No, well, the moment you picked doesn't seem to have been the right one either, does it?'

A guilty shrug. Howling inwardly, she faced him frankly. 'Why don't you want to do this, Joe? Why don't you want to come with me?'

He flushed. 'I do! Of course I do, and I will! It's just . . . temporary. I'll be on the first plane as fast as I can.'

'Joe' she said stonily, 'you'd better be. Meanwhile, I want it on record that I am very, very upset about this. I am angry and – and do you really expect me to face all the moving, all the unpacking, all the uncertainty of the first few weeks on my own? Apart from Finn who – well. We're not going for ever, it's not the long-haul you thought it would be, so what exactly *is* your problem? Huh?'

Fumbling at the kettle, he looked over her head out the kitchen window. 'Nothing' he mumbled. 'I don't have a problem.'

Right, she thought. You don't have a problem with France. And you don't have a problem with the drink, either, do you?

I am going to cure you of both, Joe Hegarty. Whether you like it or not, you're going, and that is that. We are all going to Le Mas and we are all, somehow, going to exorcise the real problem: the ghost of Hazel Hegarty.

Disconcerted, Shona swallowed the news as discreetly as she could, privately alarmed. Already Aileen's husband was wangling his way out of the first few months . . . ? What if he found further tactics, what if he never came at all, in the end? It sounded to her as if the Hegartys were diverging down different paths, and she found herself wondering about them. Were things okay, between the two partners in this marriage? Not that it was any of her business, only – well, apart from the difficulty Aileen would face in moving without Joe, she had grown so fond of her. They were good friends now, they were in this together, and she really wanted Le Mas to work, to be a source of joy, not friction. It was such a happy house, so full of sunny vibes which Joe would surely feel. Wouldn't he?

'Well' she said consolingly, 'don't worry. Crys and I will be there. Crys can only stay one week but I'll be staying for two. And then you'll have Finn. You'll be fine.'

Yes, Aileen replied, of course she would. Let's not give Joe Hegarty the illusion of being indispensable! Now, had Shona been on to the French electricity people, seen about the switch-over? Was everyone's passport up to date, was everyone present, correct and lined up for take-off? She and Finn would be driving down, did Shona want to put any stuff in the car, had she booked her flight, did she want picking up at the airport?

'That'd be great' Shona said, looking at the list Aileen waved in front of her, as if it were a shield. A list itemising absolutely everything the Hegartys would need in France – except, perhaps, a marriage counsellor?

Well, if that were the sorry case, they might well save on expenses by sharing one with Crys and Gavin Sheehan. Shuddering silently, Shona took her leave of Aileen, making arrangements to meet her at Carcassonne airport, and went home wondering whether sometimes there might not actually be something to be said for being single, for going where you wanted when you wanted without a by-your-leave from anyone.

Listening to the *Gerry Ryan Show* on radio ten days before leaving for France, Aileen found herself standing rooted, stricken, her hand glued to the iron as if it were melting. This morning's subject – sex, for a change – was hardly novel in itself. Ireland had sex for breakfast, lunch and dinner these days, on radio, on TV, in the papers. But it wasn't the subject that brought her to a standstill. It was the awful clarity of the moment, the realisation of how much she liked Gerry, how she listened to him nearly every day, how he had been a constant, disembodied friend for years and years of her life. Sometimes they laughed together, sometimes they quarrelled, sometimes she told him to 'get a grip, for God's sakes' as if he were there in the room having a real conversation with her. He was part of the fabric of her life, of Ireland's life . . . a life which was now, on a reckless whim, about to be traded in for a new one. For at least a year, nothing would be familiar any more, or comforting, or even recognisable. France would be distant and alien and Gerry wouldn't be around to cheer her up, Dymps would no longer be dropping in for tea and gossip, there would be no more lunches with Mam in Heyden's . . . there wouldn't even be a neighbour to turn to in an emergency. Not an Irish neighbour anyway, who would understand what you were saying, haul you in for tea and sympathy, craic and chat.

Oh, God, she thought, what am I doing? What on earth am I doing? Is Joe right, have I lost my mind?

As if on cue, the doorbell rang, and she opened it to find Marion O'Shea on the doorstep, beaming. Marion, her next door neighbour, was a perpetually smiley, busy, breathless little cherub. 'Aileen! How are ya! Can't stop, in a hurry, but I just wondered if you'd be free tomorrow night – few drinks before you head off on your travels?'

Touched, almost to the point of tears, Aileen assured her that yes, she would be free, whereupon Marian grinned, gratified. 'Great. It won't be just me and himself . . . a few of the others will be there too. My place, nine o'clock, okay?'

A party. That was what Marion meant: she and the other neighbours were throwing a send-off party for her. Virtually everyone on the street would be at it, she'd better dress up and make sure Joe did too, because this would be more than just a beer-and-crisps hooley. This would be all the people who formed a kind of second skin around her, the social unit to which she had belonged for fifteen years, and she knew with certainty that they would all behave as if she were emigrating to Australia. There would be gallons of tears and it would be a poignant, painful, memorably bittersweet night.

I must be mad, she thought. Joe's right. I must be going soft in the head. Only someone losing her marbles would chuck her perfectly comfortable life here, amongst nice people in a cheerful country, to go off to God knows what in the middle of nowhere. If it weren't too late I – I might back out, at this moment. Change my mind and just pretend the whole thing never happened. If it weren't for Shona, I . . .

But it *is* too late. I am committed. This is simply a panic attack. I'll calm down and get on with my ironing and be perfectly fine in a minute.

Steeling herself, she made a cup of tea, wondering whether tea would even taste the same in France, and then she did get on with her ironing, for at least ten full minutes, until the door-bell rang again.

This time it was a little man standing on the doorstep, almost entirely obliterated behind a massive bouquet of flowers. 'Morning, ma'am' floated his voice from behind a cloud of gypsophilia, 'would you be Mrs Hegarty?'

Yes, she said bewildered, she was Mrs Hegarty – who on earth could be sending her flowers?

'Your secret admirer' he grinned, handing them over with a wink, 'card in with them. Have a nice Valentine's day, now.'

Oh – so it was. February 14. But – surely Joe –? No. Surely not. In the early years of their marriage he had occasionally come home with chocolates on Valentine's day, almost furtive, crimson with embarrassment, but in recent years he more often forgot. Certainly there had never been anything like this vast, stunning display. Toting it into the kitchen, Aileen was utterly bemused.

It was from Dymps. 'With lots of love' read the card, 'and hugs and good wishes for your new life in France.'

Fighting tears, Aileen fumbled for a vase, feeling suddenly swamped by a tidal wave of emotion. Her vision blurred, her hand slipped, and nearly half an hour passed before she was able to pick up the phone, and call her sister.

Dymps, for the first time in her life, sounded as if she too were having trouble talking. 'I wanted you to have your flowers early' she stammered, 'a whole week to enjoy them before you go.'

'But – but Dymps, won't I see you before then –?'

A tortured pause. And then: 'No. No you won't . . . I can't bear goodbyes. If I came over I'd only howl . . . we'd both be too upset . . . just enjoy your flowers now and ring me the minute you get to France, okay?'

Abruptly, she hung up. Demolished, Aileen put down the phone and burst into tears.

And finally the day dawned, cold and bright as a blade. At least Joe took the morning off work. At least he had the grace to do that much, to keep apologising about not going as he helped his wife and son to pack the car and then, red-faced, hug them awkwardly as they got into it. Alongside him, Tessie trotted back and forth with sandwiches for the journey, warm woollies, a magazine cutting about Paris – that was near where they were going, wasn't it? Wrenched, Aileen assured her that it was, and when the car was finally full Tessie stood twisting her handkerchief, stalwartly resolved not to use it. But her face was anxious and puckered as she clutched her daughter to her, murmuring into her neck.

'I'll be coming to visit as soon as you're up and running. Until then, love, look after yourself. And Finn. Settle in and have a lovely time.'

Strangled, Aileen nodded vigorously. 'We'll try, Mam, we'll try!'

'Eh? You'll fly? But are you not driving –?'

'We *are*! You're the one who'll fly, with Joe, in a few weeks. Now, go on in and cook him a nice lunch.'

Nodding, grasping that maybe husband and wife wanted to say their adieux alone, Tessie trudged sadly into the house, and Joe squeezed Aileen's hand with a kind of desperation. For several anguished moments neither of them spoke; and then abruptly he released her with a violent peck on the cheek.

It was his way of telling her to be careful, to look after herself and their son, to call him if they urgently needed him. Some powerful emotion seized her, and suddenly she wondered what exactly he was going to do for the next eight weeks, where he would go in those spare moments not claimed by Dave Doherty. Tomorrow he was moving in with Tessie, she would look after him, but . . . ? She wasn't his babysitter, and he wasn't a child.

'I – I'll call you the minute we arrive and let you know how we're getting on.'

'Aye. Well. Right, so. Off you go – Finn, take care of your mother, d'you hear me?'

Throwing his eyes up to heaven, as if he and his mother were merely going to the end of the road, Finn nodded reluctantly. While he had done a terrific job of packing the car, he had said virtually nothing while doing it. Ignoring the procession of neighbours who trooped in with cards, gifts and good wishes, he busied himself with – almost buried himself in – the stacks of bags and boxes. Aileen was dreading the thousand kilometres of silence that lay between him, her and Le Mas. Or, more likely, the thousand kilometres of heavy metal. She'd have to concede something, if he was going to share the driving.

God, she thought suddenly, I wish Shona were here. I wish she didn't have to go to that meeting with her solicitor this morning, I want her here telling me I'm doing the right thing, that I'm not about to make the most huge and horrible mistake of my entire life.

I'm not, am I?

Tessie stood on the doorstep, smiling and waving a last brave wave. Aileen knew she would be sobbing all over Joe the minute the car was out of sight. Would Joe, in turn, be sobbing over her? Or shedding even a few tears, at the very least, manfully disguised as a bad cold?

Turning to her, Finn yawned and stretched. 'Come on, Ma. Let's get moving.'

Feeling as if some vital limb were being amputated, she got into the car.

Gruesome. That was how Aileen would later remember the long, long journey down to the southernmost reaches of France, so different to the first one with Shona, the one they had famously done twice. She and Shona had talked all the way, getting comfortable together, laughing, exploring, enjoying. Whereas Finn took a very different view: apparently his priorities were to conquer the French road system as fast as possible, and to divulge nothing, but nothing, to his mother. During the entire two days they spent exclusively in each other's company, zooming down autoroutes at breakneck speed, he volunteered only two opinions on anything: it was great to see so many burger joints, and this clapped-out car was a heap of junk. Her heart in her mouth, the dashboard needle rocketing, Aileen wondered whether maybe Finn had found his vocation: airline pilot.

But there seemed no point in saying anything, because his responses were as laconic as they were monosyllabic, the long gaps between filled with music which appeared to have one purpose and one only: volume so loud you couldn't even shout over it. Eyes front, he showed no sign of even seeing, much less appreciating, the landscape in which they were travelling; castles, rivers, flowers, forests, mountains all flew by like bullets, blurring in Aileen's vision until she felt so sick she had to surreptitiously palm an aspirin into her mouth. Any comment, she knew, and he would be quite capable of jamming on the brakes, jumping out, maybe abandoning her to continue alone while he hitched home in the righteous rage of a twenty-year-old male. It had been his birthday a few weeks earlier, he was no longer a teenager. What was he, exactly? Looking sidelong at him, Aileen wondered, and found herself feeling inexplicably sorry for him. Clearly, this breakneck drive was unconnected with any wish to actually arrive, to start living in the Languedoc.

And yet . . . somewhere in the midst of feeling sorry for him, she felt something else too. Something perilously close to irritation, if she would allow herself to feel such a thing. With every passing day, it was getting harder to respect a twenty-year-old man who did nothing for a living, who seemed to have given up so comprehensively so early, who said or did nothing to encourage his own mother on what was, after all, a very big adventure. And one undertaken partly for his benefit, at that! Here she was, swirling with hope, doubt, anticipation, dread, euphoria and curiosity: here he was, driving as briskly as might a paid chauffeur, indifferent to everything around him, either visible or invisible.

'But mothers aren't visible' her neighbour Marion had once asserted, 'they're just links in the food chain. And laundry chain. My young fellas wouldn't notice if I dropped down dead

– they'd only notice that their plates were missing off the table.'

Marion had surely been joking, couldn't possibly mean that for a minute, could she? After all, Dymps's son Damien, although only ten admittedly, wasn't like that. On the contrary, he was affectionate and outgoing and demonstrably loved his parents. Finn was just . . . just a bit reserved, was all. A late developer, still caught up in the trauma of adolescence. Some day – soon, hopefully – the chrysalis would emerge into a fully fledged butterfly.

I'm not fooling myself, am I, to believe that? To believe that my son is a basically good lad, whose development was damaged by events he hardly remembers?

I'm not wrong. I can't allow myself to believe for one moment that I'm wrong – because where would that leave him, and me? Where will we all be, if Finn never, ever emerges from under this blanket of all-consuming apathy?

'Jaysus' Finn said, so suddenly that Aileen jumped, 'it's getting very bright.' And then, as if objecting to that, he snapped down the sunshield, squinting at the road which was beginning to shimmer in the sun.

The sun! So lost in her thoughts had Aileen been that it had snuck up on her unnoticed, rising from misty fields, creeping over turreted castles and mountain-top villages, gradually reaching its zenith in a piercingly blue sky that would warm the heart of a stone. It was not a hot day, but it was brilliantly bright, slicing through Aileen's wintry thoughts. Suddenly, all memory of murky Irish cloud evaporated; it was impossible to resist the allure, the sheer joyousness of this gleaming, beautiful day.

'Look, Finn' she breathed, 'isn't it fabulous?'

Briefly, he glanced at a swathe of vines sweeping up to the foot of a hill, on which a creamy castle snugly reposed, embraced in a wisp of mist. Aileen thought the whole view had a kind of fairytale quality.

'Yeah' he sighed, 'it's okay.'

Had he swung round and hit her she could hardly have felt more deflated. It *was* fabulous, for God's sake, whether he liked it or not! It was new, too, all but singing with freshness, the closest he had ever come to seeing a fairytale spring to life. Or was ever likely to come. Did he have to do this? Did he have to burst her bubble immediately, before they even reached Le Mas des Cigales?

Why? Why, why?

Perhaps sensing her rising resentment, he turned to her more conversationally. 'So – nearly there, huh? Where do we go first, the house or the airport?'

They couldn't go straight to the house – not until tonight, when the papers were signed and Shona owned it – but somehow Aileen was glad of that. She wanted to get to the airport as fast as this car would carry her, seize Shona off her arriving plane and share all her mounting enthusiasm with someone – someone enthusiastic, someone positive! Once the two of them were together, she would slough off this growing desire to shake Finn – to hit him with a shovel, if the truth be known, because he was grating on her teeth like chalk on a blackboard.

'The airport is called Salvaza' she said neutrally, 'there should be signs coming up for it soon. If we're early, we'll just have a coffee and wait.'

Salvaza, when they got to it, turned out to be a cute, doll-size airport, and Aileen was delighted. So small, so handy, no fuss or milling crowds; just a handful of relaxed passengers with the casual aura of people who maybe owned houses in the area, commuted regularly. It was possible to take a table in a café overlooking the runway and watch for Shona's plane, which Aileen fervently did. Soon, she prayed, let it be here soon, soon, soon. Taking her first shot at speaking French, she ordered two coffees, and when they arrived she and Finn gazed into the minuscule cups, which seemed to match the size of the airport.

'I think you blew it, Ma' Finn said at length, 'these are espressos.'

'Oh, well. Does it matter?'

'I'd have preferred regular. With milk.'

Something snapped in her head. Some very thin little thread. 'All right, then' she said, 'call the waitress and explain what you want.'

'But – you know I can't!'

'Then drink your espresso.'

An expression of fleeting annoyance shot across his face. But he said nothing. Instead, he put his Walkman on his head, barricaded himself inside his music and left the coffee to go cold.

Shona, Aileen thought. Shona Shona Shona.

Saying nothing more, she drank her own coffee, got up, strolled round the airport, went outside for some air and then – whoosh! – heard the roar of a landing plane. Turning, she was just in time to see it flash down the runway, its Irish tricolour doing something unexpected to her when she saw it; some silly emotional thing that didn't make any sense.

The plane slowed, turned and trundled back towards where she stood, sets of stairs rolling out to meet it – no walkways here, apparently – and she craned her head when it stopped, virtually under her nose on the other side of a wire fence. Doors opened, a blue-uniformed steward waved cheerily to the ground staff, passengers began to decant and – yes! There was Shona! Racing in to the arrivals area, Aileen flew to meet her, her spirits soaring when Shona spotted her, waved and smiled a huge smile, a smile that said whoopee, here we are, isn't this great! Moments later, she was through passport control, and they were in each other's arms, half incoherent with joy.

'And this is Crys' Shona burbled, pushing forward the lovely, willowy girl Aileen had met in Heyden's a few months before, who looked somewhat . . . different . . . ? today. Aileen couldn't put her finger on the difference, but thought there was one. Crys was smiling, but didn't look quite so sparkly as she had that day.

'*Bonjour*, Crys! I've been here an hour, my French is practically fluent now!'

They all laughed, and wheeled luggage, and were almost at the exit when Shona stopped to look around, puzzled. 'Where's Finn?'

'Oh – I was nearly forgetting him! He's upstairs in the café, hold on while I run up and get him.'

Up she went, and down he came, and off everyone set for the car. 'It's going to be a tight squeeze, but – oh, Shona, it's so good to see you! Isn't it a gorgeous day, isn't this great, we nearly have our house at last – what time is our appointment with M Delatre?'

'Three o'clock. Just one more hour, Aileen, and we own Le Mas!'

'Yes! Well, I won't actually, you will—'

'We will. It will be ours. Wey *hey*!' Eyes sparkling, she punched the air, and Aileen thought how great she was looking today, rosy with anticipation, fit and fresh in jeans and a chunky white sweater. A uniform never really suited Shona, she thought; she looks much better in her own clothes, younger and way more relaxed.

It was indeed a tight squeeze in the overloaded little Ka, but they piled in and set off for Carcassonne, Finn driving, Aileen and Shona doing all the talking. 'My parents wanted to come with me' Shona said, 'but I said no, wait till things are sorted – they're a bit past the camping-on-floors stage. We'll have to go shopping tomorrow, girls, first thing! Beds, duvets, pillows, saucepans, crockery – yippee!'

A heavy sigh from Finn. Aileen ignored it. 'I've brought as much stuff as I can and Joe will bring as much as he can when he comes – but it's not nearly enough to furnish a place the size of Le Mas. Wait till you see it, Crys – it's something else, isn't it, Sho?'

Yes, enthused Shona, it certainly was. Crys and Finn would be knocked out. Crys and Finn smiled small, tight smiles, and said nothing. Now that Shona was here, Aileen could handle Finn's taciturnity . . . but why was Crys so quiet? What was the matter with her? 'Are you okay, Crys?'

Crys shifted in her seat. 'I'm fine. Just a bit tired. We were up at six to get to the airport.'

'Cup of tea' Aileen decreed firmly, 'that's what we all need.'

'My ass' Shona shot back. 'The minute we get out of M Delatre's office with everything signed, sealed and delivered, we are going to the nearest hostelry for champagne!'

The signing took for ever. For ever and ever, amen. And then some. Everyone sat solemnly around M Delatre's desk, staring astonished at the stacks of papers that Shona was signing in batches: '*une petite signature*' carolled M Delatre again and again, 'here and here and here . . .' But Shona never stopped smiling, unlike the owners who were selling Le Mas. A delightful Italian couple in their sixties, they were very friendly, but looked ready to weep, actually wringing their hands, clutching each other as if they could hardly bear it. They adored Le Mas, they asserted, and were only selling it because Signora's mama in Genoa was getting on in years, needing them nearby. Thinking that Mama must be at least ninety, Aileen tried to console them while Shona went on signing, for so long there almost came to be an air of permanence about it, as if it were her fulltime job. A French notary presided over the whole performance, handling the hassle-free sale for both parties and getting an awful lot of money, Aileen thought, for precious little work. Unless maybe he'd discovered some ghastly problem with the house, but was saying nothing, in league with M Delatre? Crikey. It was so hard to be sure of anything, in a foreign country with a foreign language.

Let it go right, Aileen prayed silently, let it go right. Let there be no problems. Let this be the best thing I've ever done and Shona has ever done. Let this house light up our whole lives.

And then, just as Shona must surely be getting cramp, it was over. Le Mas des Cigales was hers. 'Congratulations' chirped M Delatre, and surprised everyone by formally kissing her on first one cheek, then the other. For a fascinated moment Aileen wondered if the notary was going to kiss her too? Kiss everyone? But he gathered up his papers, shook hands and departed. And then Shona whirled round to Aileen.

'We've done it' she breathed, sweeping her into a hug, 'we've got it, Aileen, we're in business! We're partners!'

By the time a bottle of champagne was despatched in the brasserie next door, afternoon was melting into evening, a radiant mauve tinge blushing up the clear blue sky, the forti-fied *cité* fading into black silhouette on the horizon. They emerged into crisp clear cold, made a dive for a nearby shop that was selling bed linens, and came out staggering under a pile of duvets. The Languedoc, at night in February, was chillier than Aileen had imagined.

'And now' Shona promised Crys, who seemed to be flagging, 'you get to see the house. Finn, too – are you fed up yet, Finn, after ferrying us round all day?'

'No' he said shortly, 'not yet.'

'Great. Then let's hit a supermarket on the way. We'll get basics and – and eat out tonight! My treat!'

Aileen saw that Shona was completely euphoric, all but shouting in the street, yelling aloud that she was the new owner of Le Mas des Cigales. Flushed and visibly thrilled, she practically waltzed back to the car, only to discover that the duvets wouldn't fit.

'Never mind' she chirped, 'you two go on, Crys and I will follow in a taxi.'

So they did, and that was how Aileen chanced to arrive at Le Mas minutes before Shona did. Getting out of the car, she walked up to the house and stood on the gravel looking up at it, breathing in its serene silence, inhaling the garden's earthy, wintry scent. For just that brief interval, while Finn busied himself unpacking the car, it was her house, hers alone; just for those few fragrant minutes.

Oh, ecstasy! It's even lovelier than I remembered it . . . I love it, she thought, I love it to bits. I wish it were truly mine. But next year, if everything goes right, if we are all happy here, maybe it will be mine. Maybe I will have something, at last, to call my own. Not just a house, but a home, sheltering a family that loves it, and loves each other.

There was a whoosh of tyres on gravel, and Shona's taxi swept into the drive, its door opening before it stopped as Shona leaped out, stood for a split second with eyes alight, and then, running up to the house with arms outstretched, shouted at the top of her lungs: 'Oh, yes! Come to Mama, baby, come to Mama!'

Who? Me? For a bewildered moment Aileen thought Shona was shouting at her, but then she realised Shona was talking to the house, as if it were a living being – not only talking to it but hurling herself at it, throwing up her arms to hug its sturdy wall, beaming as if reunited with an old, beloved friend. Tottering out of the taxi behind her, heaped with duvets and pillows, Crys raised the one eyebrow that was visible, caught Aileen's eye, and they laughed in unison.

'Get a grip, Sho! It's a house, not a lover!'

Whirling around to face them, Shona beamed, her face flushed and her eyes dancing. 'But it's beautiful! I love it! I can't wait – look, Crys, didn't I tell you it's divine! C'mere, put down that stuff and have a proper look, tell me what you think!'

Passing the parcels to Aileen, Crys paid the driver and stood back a few paces, slowly, thoughtfully, drinking in the view. In the last violet wisps of dusk, under a silvery slice of new moon, Le Mas des Cigales did indeed look ethereally beautiful, perched on its tranquil little hill, its arched lavender shutters snugly keeping out the cold . . . and Shona looked beautiful too. Radiant, Crys thought, absolutely radiant. What was all this baloney about buying this house just for an investment? Clearly Shona was stone mad about it . . . and so was Aileen Hegarty, standing there enthralled, her face full of wonder.

H'mm. Impartially, Crys nodded. 'Not bad. It'll do for tonight, anyway.'

'Not *bad*! Are you mad, it's sensational, it's –' And then, realising Crys was teasing, Shona laughed, grabbed a pillow from her grasp and thumped her with it. 'This house is *fabulous*! My mas is *magnificent*! Say it, or I'll beat you to a pulp!'

Laughing, Crys skipped out of the way, fending off the pillow with her arms. 'All right, all right! It is, it is – on the outside anyway, when are you going to let us in?'

'Right now.' Extracting the hefty iron key from her pocket, Shona marched up to the front door, fitted it into the lock, took a deep breath and swung open the double doors into the hall, singing a fanfare as she went.

'Ta-*ra*!' Here we are, in you come – come on, Finn, come on, the lot of you! Look at this airy hall, look at these ancient tiles, they're called *tomettes* –' Poised on the steps behind her, everyone peered. It was pitch dark. And freezing cold, an icy blast sweeping out as if she'd opened a fridge. 'I think' Crys remarked, 'perhaps we'd better leave the architectural niceties until we find the lights and get a fire going.'

Laughing, Shona patted at the walls until her hand hit a switch, and flicked it on. The hall flooded with light . . . and what a hall it was, with its vaulted ceiling, thick walls and rusty-red, hexagonal old tiles. Crys's first thought was that, if she owned this space, she'd scarcely furnish it at all; perfectly bare, it was perfectly lovely. Her second thought was that you could throw a party right here, without going near any of the other rooms.

'Wow' she breathed. 'Wowww . . . I have to admit, Fitzpatrick, you have taste.'

Whoops. Something in Aileen's expression told Crys instantly that she'd said the wrong thing, should have included her in the compliment – after all, it was Aileen who'd originally set out to find the house. Was this week going to turn out to be tricky, or what? Blowing on her fingers, shuddering with cold, she changed tack.

'Where's the heating? Where's the fireplace? Are there any logs? I refuse to see another inch of this house until somebody gets some heat going . . . I'd no idea it would be so bloody freezing.'

'Even southern France' Shona announced as if she'd lived here for years, 'gets quite cold at night in winter. I think maybe we'll leave the gîte until tomorrow, all sleep here tonight –'

'On what?' Finn piped up so unexpectedly that everyone turned to look at him. 'Are there any beds?'

And that was when another thought hit Crys: Finn hadn't made any comment to his mother on the house. Hadn't congratulated her on it, or admired it, or wished her luck in it . . . or anything, at all.

'Not as such, but there should be inflatable mattresses somewhere, they were to be delivered . . . Finn, wouldja ever for God's sake see if you can find the boiler, there's a good lad?'

Shona looked at him imploringly, and he trudged off towards the back of the house while she flung open the doors of the sitting room – complete with a stack of logs beside the fireplace, and firelighters, and matches.

'Oh, brilliant! The Italians must have left them for us, aren't they dolls!'

In no time Shona had the fire going, and as they stood thawing around it a rumble of pipes indicated that Finn had got the heating going too: thank God, Crys thought, at least there's something that surly young fella can do. 'Now, show us the rest, Sho – and Aileen!'

Off they trooped to tour the house – Shona proprietorially leading the way – and it was, undeniably, a beautiful house, old, roomy, cosy as it warmed welcomingly up. In the kitchen, the Italian 'dolls' had thoughtfully left a box of first-night basics, and in one of the bedrooms there was a pile of rugs and throws with a note: 'Just in case!' As they toured the Mas Shona's smile got wider and wider, and Crys was impressed: this was indeed a wonderful house, a terrific 'investment' as Shona called it.

'Well' she said at length, 'you are – both – to be congratulated. This is going to make a gorgeous guesthouse. If we had any wine I'd drink a toast to it, and to you two.'

'There is wine' Shona grinned, 'but no glasses! No crockery

or cutlery either, we're going to have to eat out whether we like it or not – we can walk to the village, it's only ten minutes.'

So that, eventually, was what they did, trooping down to the little village of Mézalas twinkling at the end of the hill, settling themselves into its cute bistro, Shona translating the blackboard menu which defeated everyone else. Admiringly, thinking how very capable and comfortable Shona seemed to be in France, Crys raised her glass to her.

'Well done, Sho. And Aileen. You've found yourselves a treasure and I hope you are going to be very happy partners in it.'

Beaming, Shona threw her arm around Aileen's shoulders. 'You can bet your bottom dollar on that. We are going to have a magic time in Mézalas – aren't we, Mme 'Egarty?'

Turning to each other, they laughed and raised their glasses. Yes, they were. They were going to have a whale of a time, and make a roaring success of Le Mas, and even Finn, finally, was forced to clink his glass to that.

For the next few days, Shona went spinning round like a whirlwind, taking charge of her 'crew', assigning jobs to Aileen, Finn and Crys. Aileen was to buy furniture, decide on decor, get the kitchen, bedrooms and bathrooms up and running; Finn was issued with a list of plumbing and electrical jobs, anything to do with heating or hardware; Crys was to make non-stop pots of tea, do the shopping, cook meals and play cheerleader.

'Bossy bag, aren't you?' she challenged, and Shona grinned unashamedly.

'Well, I've got all the paperwork to do, I'm the only one who can deal with the *mairie*, the phone company, water company, electricity, bin service, get residents' permits for Aileen and Finn, then there's the tourism office to notify, Le Mas has to be registered as a B & B if we're to have any customers . . .

safety regulations to be studied . . . we're not here to have fun, y'know!'

Ruefully, Crys smiled. 'So it seems. You lied to me, Shona Fitzpatrick. Got me here under false pretences, to be your slave.'

'Yeah. Now get cracking, we'll be needing high-energy meals if we're to do all this work.'

So Crys wended her way back to base camp in the old timbered kitchen, and Shona stood looking at her disappearing back, wondering. As ever, Crys was being helpful and cheerful and the great friend she always was, but . . . what? Shona couldn't put her finger on what was missing – apart from the wild nail polish – all she could say was that Crys didn't quite seem herself. Although she joined in every conversation, threw her opinion into every decision, laughed at every joke, something about her seemed suspended in some way, as if her mind were not fully in France. Perhaps it wasn't – perhaps part of it was still in Ireland with Gavin, wistfully watching parents pushing babies in buggies? Wondering what to do, what would happen if they never became parents?

Something's bothering her, Shona decided, and as soon as I get a minute I'm going to sit her down and find out what it is. At least Crys is communicative by nature, whereas that Finn Hegarty . . . . well, okay, he's doing whatever he's asked, but is he ever going to *speak*? How Aileen puts up with him is beyond me. The only thing I can say in his favour is that he seems handy with a toolbox, can fix a few things. But I sure wouldn't want to be stuck in a lift with him.

'Shona!' Aileen's voice sang down the stairs. 'The delivery van is coming up the drive with the sofas and chairs, I can see it from the window – go out to them quick, and tell them where everything is to go!'

'You tell them! You've got to practise your French, Aileen!'

Flustered, Aileen came running downstairs, looking happy and apprehensive all at once. 'I can't, I'm not up to explaining things yet—'

'Then how are you going to manage when I'm back in Ireland?'

'God knows' Aileen admitted, 'I'm dreading the day you go. Where's Finn? He can help them carry in the stuff – were we right to get yellow sofas, do you think, or should we—'

'Aileen, would you ever keep the head. Yellow is what we decided and yellow will be lovely. Your B & B will be lovely. Life will be lovely, if you calm down and let it.'

'Yes, well – sorry. Am I panicking?'

'You are. No need. *Bonjour, messieurs.*' Airily, Shona twirled round to the delivery men, shaking their hands as one apparently did in France, and Aileen quailed: what if anyone started kissing anyone? Already M Delatre had kissed Shona yesterday when he brought the stored garden furniture she'd persuaded him to deliver, and people kissed each other in cafes, in shops, in the street . . . she'd faint, and Finn would expire entirely, if anyone did that to her, or to him.

What was Finn, in fact, feeling or thinking about France? Thus far he had offered no comment, but then he was at a disadvantage, outnumbered by three talkative women, which must be why he was spending so much time up a ladder, painting ceilings, checking gutters and roof tiles. Later, when Crys and Shona were gone, she'd have to sound him out . . . but first, let him see a bit more of the place. When Le Mas was organised, in another week or two, they'd have a chance to explore the area, find out what facilities might exist for his age group. At least he wasn't whining about wanting to go to bars at night – because, visibly, all this unaccustomed work was wearing him out. After a day of shunting furniture, painting walls, grouting tiles, fixing leaks and chopping logs, he was just like the rest of them, glad of a hot meal, glass of wine and early night. Exciting as this venture was, this first bit of it was also exhausting.

'Shattered' Aileen told Joe when the phone was working, 'we're all having a great time, but we're shattered, there's so much to do . . . Shona's a slavedriver. She wants us open for business by Easter. How are you?'

Fine, Joe said; he was fine, delighted to hear the move was going smoothly, Tessie was here beside him, would Aileen like a word with her? Faster than she could draw breath, she found herself talking to her mother. Anxiously, Tessie wanted reassurance that they were all eating good hot breakfasts.

'Yes' Aileen lied patiently, 'porridge every morning, Mam. Wait till you come over, the food is wonderful, the bakeries are beautiful—'

'And woollens' Tessie continued, 'I hear it's very cold over there at the moment.'

'Yes, but it's sunny, fresh and crisp.'

'Crisps? You want me to bring crisps? Cheese and onion, or salt and vinegar?'

Oh, sweet God. 'Cheese and onion, Mam! I'll call you again tomorrow – bye!'

Damn, Aileen thought as she hung up. It's not her fault, God love her, but I'm not going to get much information out of her about Joe. Or out of him, apparently, about himself. What's he doing? How's he getting on? Is he missing me, and Finn? Is he wishing he was here with us, or—

'Aileen! Come in here and tell me what you think – is this table better here, or over by the window?'

'Coming, Sho. Let me see – I'd put it over there, I think, in front of the fireplace.'

'Right' Agreeably, Shona nodded, and ten minutes later the table was firmly ensconced by the window.

A week shot by at the speed of light, and by the end of it Le Mas was, incredibly, starting to look comfortable, attractive and even, as Crys put it, 'seductive'.

'Would you want to stay in it' Aileen asked, 'for a holiday?'

Crys nodded eagerly. 'Yes, I would – if I ever got a holiday!'

Contritely, Shona patted her shoulder. 'Sorry, Crys. I didn't mean to make you work so hard, and now you're leaving tomorrow, you haven't even been anywhere, seen anything – tell you what. Your flight's not till late. Why don't we all take the day off tomorrow and go into Carcassonne, visit the *cité*, see the sights . . . ?'

Listening to this, Aileen considered. And then, tactfully, made another suggestion. 'Even better, why don't you two go in by yourselves, have a girls' day? You can take my car, I've got plenty to do here – so has Finn, haven't you, Finn?'

Yes, Finn asserted, he had. A girls' day out in some ancient old town wasn't his idea of – anyway, that big delivery of logs for the fire was coming, he'd need to spend the day chopping them.

'Well, if you're sure . . . ?' Shona said politely, relieved when everyone said they were. It would be great to get a few last hours alone with Crys.

And so she and Crys set off next morning in Aileen's little Ka, wending their way through miles of golden fields and gnarled black vines, snoozing villages and dusty streets, the whole place looking as if it only ever woke up occasionally, maybe once a century.

'Laid back, isn't it, this Languedoc?'

'Yes – do you like it, Crys? What do you think?'

Turning to Shona, Crys surveyed her a moment before answering. 'I think it's a whole other world, and it suits you down to the ground. I've never seen you looking so well.'

Briefly, Shona took her gaze off the road to look at her. 'Really?'

'Yes, really. You're happy and busy and full of energy, bossing people round, organising things, making decisions . . . it just fits you like a glove. I don't know how you're going to go back to work in your office.'

'No – neither do I! Assuming I have an office to go back to. From here, it seems so far away. But the case is coming up soon, my stomach's starting to clench just thinking about it. I should be out marketing hotels at this minute, not preparing to do battle with Terry bloody O'Hagan. Even if I win, I don't know how the hell I can get my promotion after such a scene – dammit, Crys, it's not fair!'

'No. It isn't. That sexist pig should have been sacked years ago.'

'Yes, he – no! I'm not going to talk about him, not let him ruin this last day with you. I don't want to talk about him, I want to talk about you.'

'Me?' Crys glanced sidelong at her, and she glanced back as they came into the outskirts of Carcassonne, wending their way past what appeared to be some kind of auction the entire length of the narrow street.

'Yes. You. I can't say exactly what it is, but you don't seem to be yourself at the moment. Not quite, not entirely.'

'Oh, I'm fine. Just a bit tired.'

'Tired? That's my fault, then. I'm sorry. I didn't mean for you to spend so much of this week working.'

'Ah, that wasn't work! It was fun. I'm just sorry we didn't get a start on the gîte as well.'

'I'm glad we didn't. You did more than enough. I'm going to take you shopping in the market this morning, and then for a long lazy lunch somewhere nice.'

Crys protested; but Shona was adamant. Ditching the car,

they made their way on foot into the depths of the town, where a huge awninged market all but engulfed them, reeking of sausages and garlic and vast simmering vats of paella. Sniffing, tasting, jostling, Crys had fun choosing goodies to bring back to Gavin, and two hours elapsed before they reclaimed the car to drive on up to the vast, thickly walled *cité*, which turned out to be amazing inside.

'Oh – shops! Restaurants! Boutiques! I thought it was going to be all museums and armour and stuff!' Crys stood back laughing, and Shona laughed with her. 'So did I, the first time I came here. But it's fun . . . come on, let's explore.'

Exploring took a long time, and for the first time Shona felt that Crys was, at last, getting a flavour of France. Although the *cité* was full of tourists there was nothing tacky about it, the windows full of enticing soaps, perfumes, dolls, pastries, wine and cheeses did not detract from the sense of strolling through history; at every turn the ramparts and drawbridges, turrets and arrow-windows bespoke the price France had paid over the centuries for today's peaceful prosperity. La Cité was a monument, but a living one, full of bustling vitality, and they enjoyed every moment of a visit that was bewitching, intriguing.

'But I need to sit down!' Crys pleaded eventually. 'This is bigger than I am!'

'Yes. Let's have lunch. Is it warm enough for outdoors, if we go to that place with the patio heater?'

'Yeah. I'm starving – will they still be serving, d'you think, at nearly three o'clock?'

'Can't see why not. The place is full of people, isn't it? We can't be the only hungry ones not eating to a timetable.'

But the waiter was 'desolate' when he came to serve them: lunch was finished. No chef, no hot food: only a sandwich if that would do? Crossly, Shona frowned. 'Oh, damn! I wanted to treat you to a delicious meal! If I were in charge of tourism round here, hot food would be available!'

'Well, you're not. Would a cheese *and* ham sandwich be asking too much, d'you think? I'll faint if I don't eat soon.'

On the point of going somewhere else, Shona suddenly noticed that Crys did look a bit shaky, reluctant to get up once she had sat down. Which was not like Crys, who would normally spring up like a gazelle and bound off indignantly.

'All right. If we beg him he might toast it for us.'

What Shona said to the waiter after that Crys didn't grasp, but it didn't sound like begging; it sounded like crisp precise instructions, decisively delivered. Within seconds, their drinks were brought; within minutes, two piping hot sandwiches arrived, packed with cheese, ham, onions and tomato. Eagerly, Crys seized hers.

'Oh, thank God. You don't take any prisoners, do you?'

'I just think a busy tourist restaurant should be able to serve hot food at any time it's open. They'd easily make enough to pay a chef. Anyway, we've got something, so *bon appetit* . . . and thanks for everything, Crys. You've helped so much and been so wonderful.'

Crys bit into her sandwich. 'Wonderful my ass. I've been – well, as you say, not myself. A little bit under the weather. Apologies if I drove anyone nuts.'

'What? Crys, don't be silly! It's great you could come to see the house, and cook those lovely meals for us and do everything else you did, I'm just sorry you didn't seem to enjoy it as much as I wanted you to . . . what's the matter? Should I have taken you out more, done more sightseeing, were you disappointed?'

Clasping her hands around her cup of hot tea, Crys shook her head. 'No. Not at all. On the contrary, I was delighted to be with you, to get away.'

'From Gavin, you mean? Is he still hassling you, Crys? Is this baby thing still seriously bothering you two?'

'Yes . . . and no. I mean, it is. But maybe it won't be for much longer.'

What? What did that mean? Anxiously, Shona stared at her. 'Why not? Are you giving up? Just leaving nature to take its course, whether he . . . ?'

Unexpectedly, Crys flinched, looking past Shona up into the boughs of a plane tree. 'No. Just the opposite, in fact. I think nature may already have taken its course. I – I think I might be pregnant.'

Electrified, Shona sat staring, sandwich stalled in her hand. 'Oh, Crys! Dear God, why didn't you tell me this before? I wouldn't have let you lift a finger, I'd have had you lying down sipping peppermint tea . . . oh, *Crys*!' Even as she spoke Shona felt a flood of protective emotion flowing through her – unlike Crys, whose expression was oddly impassive.

'I didn't tell you because I didn't know for sure – still don't. I just think I'd better do a test when I get home, because I – I *feel* as if I am.'

'What do you mean? How do you feel?'

'I feel tired and funny and – and kinda detached, or something. I can't describe it.'

'Well then, we'd better get you on your plane back to Gavin – if you are, he'll be delighted! And so will you – after all this time, your worries will be over!'

Crys's gaze was still somewhere in the depths of the tree. 'Mmm. Maybe they will. Or maybe they'll only just be starting.'

'What?' Bewildered, Shona couldn't make out her meaning.

'Shona . . .' Abruptly, Crys put down her sandwich, her hand shaking, her eyes faintly glistening. 'Shona . . . can I tell you something? I've got to tell someone . . .'

Seizing her hand, Shona gripped it. 'Yes, of course – Crys, what is it? What's the matter?'

A silence tightened; silence that seemed to rise and sharpen like a stalagmite between them. And then, as if she had been slapped hard on the back, Crys blurted out the truth. 'The – the matter is that I – I don't *want* to be pregnant. Don't think I want a baby, at all.'

Don't *want* a baby!? But – after a pause that seemed to go on for eternity, Shona heard herself stammering. 'But – what – Crys, I don't understand. Don't get this . . . I thought you were desperate for a baby!'

'No. *I* wasn't. Gavin was, but I . . . I wonder if that might be why I never conceived. Never before, in five years . . . because, subconsciously, I didn't want to? I didn't know it at first – didn't see it for years – but now, just when I suspect I might be pregnant, I've realised that maybe it isn't what I want, at all.'

'But – then – ?' Still holding her hand, Shona couldn't speak to her, couldn't find words for this.

'Then what do I want? I want *other people's* children, Sho! I love driving those funny little mites to school, I love my volunteer work, I love raising money for those little black kids – kids who are poor and sick and hungry, because they've had the misfortune to be born in Africa, while I, a little black kid myself, had the good fortune to be born in Ireland. I've got so much and they've got nothing and they – they're all my babies! I haven't time for one of my own, I don't want to be distracted by one, I – I don't want to be pregnant! But Gavin wants me to be – he – I just don't know what to do, it's tearing me apart!'

Crys's voice rose, on a note of anguish that tore at Shona as she sat there slowly absorbing the shock, unable for several minutes to say anything.

Oh, Jesus. What did you say, to this?

Horrified, she sat there wondering, watching Crys's eyes

216

filling with tears, feeling achingly sad for her, and apprehensive. What all this was going to do to Crys and Gavin's marriage, she couldn't even begin to imagine.

'Crys . . . don't cry . . . come on . . . maybe you're not pregnant at all.'

'I am. I know I am. Gavin will be thrilled, and I – I just feel like someone has put a gun to my head, is marching me away from where I want to go. If I tell him that, it – it'll destroy us, Sho. I love Gavin, I always thought I'd do anything in the world for him, but . . . but I don't want to do this. I do not want a child, a specific child, of my own. I thought I did, but . . . it was Gavin who did.'

Very slowly, Shona sat back, thinking. 'Are you sure, Crys? Maybe this is just a panic attack. Maybe you're simply pregnant and in shock.'

Vehemently, Crys shook her head. 'No. It's more like a . . . a feeling that has slowly been sneaking up on me, over a long time. I've tried to ignore it, tried to pretend it would go away, but it hasn't, and now it's at the point where I have to confront it and admit it exists. To myself – and now to you – but not to anyone else, because how do you say it, Sho? How does a woman tell anyone, much less her husband, that she doesn't want children? It sounds so – unnatural!'

'Not to me, Crys. I understand it. I've never been mad keen on the idea of kids either. I don't know why some people make motherhood sound mandatory – after all, look how Aileen's son has turned out! I'm sure there are joys in it if it's a real vocation, but should every woman be expected to have the same vocation? If you'd rather be driving a relief truck to Zambia or whatever, then that's what you should be doing.'

'That's exactly what I want to be doing. Recently I'd even been wondering how Gavin would take it if I told him . . . would it wreck our marriage? Or does he love me enough to let me go, let me do it? To give up *his* dream, of having children? To maybe even come with me to Zambia or wherever the next famine might be?'

Closing her eyes, Shona pictured the scene in her mind: Gavin hearing that, instead of nestling in the bosom of his nuclear family in Ireland, he was going to be scooping out powdered milk supplies to milling moppets in a field tent. Remembering his face that day they'd met for lunch at Moran's, she could see the curiously hardening expression in his eyes.

'Maybe you shouldn't say anything to him just yet, Crys. Not until—'

'Until I know for sure I am pregnant, that I am going to drop everything to mother his child? Until I can tell him he's getting what he wants without mentioning that it's at the expense of what I want? Oh, God, why didn't I face up to this sooner! Why didn't I admit to myself that I'm not maternal, not in the normal domestic sense anyway, why didn't I just tell him –?'

'Because you love him, Crys! Because you wanted to be a good wife, to make him happy . . . and, if you are pregnant, he will be happy. Deliriously happy. At least you'll have that comfort. Later, when the child is older, maybe—'

Crys seemed to slump, deflate as if someone were slowly letting the air out of her. 'When it's finished school and college, you mean, when it's twenty-two and I'm over fifty, I can go to Africa then? Assuming, of course, that Gavin doesn't want a brother or sister for the first one, in which case I might be nearer to sixty before I'm free? Oh, Jesus, Shona, what am I going to do?'

Reluctantly, sadly, Shona sighed. 'I don't know, Crys. I'm going to have to think some more about this before I can try to figure out any answer that might help. Meanwhile, it's getting late, you have to get to the airport. For God's sake do a pregnancy test when you get home and call me right away with the result, okay?'

Standing up, Crys slid into her jacket, not looking at all enthusiastic about leaving for the airport. Or doing the test. 'Yeah. Okay. I will. Tomorrow.'

Attempting comfort, Shona patted her shoulder as they moved off, walking in step, silently mulling over what would, in other circumstances, have been great news. Might yet be great news, if Gavin could somehow share his elation with Crys – perhaps his joy would simply be contagious?

She could only pray that it would. And yet she understood, too, how Crys was feeling, how torn, how ambivalent. For many women motherhood was the most thrilling thing on earth, but if she were brutally honest with herself – as perhaps Crys should have been – it did not appeal to her. Did not cry out irresistibly, did not pull her into its grasp; it was simply something other people did, and mostly enjoyed, in their other lives. What was right for them was not necessarily right for her, or for Crys. Crys, the one person who'd never thought she would be happy with Brendan Wright . . .

As they reached the car at the bottom of the hill, Crys gazed up at the fortress on top, concentrating on it wistfully, as if trying to print it on her memory. Resolutely, Shona smiled. 'It's only a two-hour flight, Crys. You're not going to Mars, you know.'

'No, but . . . oh, Shona, Have you any idea how lucky you are to be staying here, in this lovely place, doing what you want with nobody to account to? Nobody making your decisions for you, nobody trying to push you this way or that? Nobody trying to make you into anything you're not?'

Clang! At that moment it suddenly hit Shona, as loud and clear as the wedding bells that might have rung out: Crys was right, and so was Brendan. He and I were wrong for each other.

He wanted a family and I, eventually, would have gone mad. I adored him, but I would have been stifled, come to resent him in time . . . and he knew it. He didn't *dump* me, he saved me. From myself. From what might not, after all, be such an urgent need to get married. Certainly not to anyone who'd constrain my life the way Gavin is constraining Crys's. She tried to make me see that, last winter, but I was blind to it then, I didn't *want* to see it.

'Yes, I . . . I think maybe I do, Crys. It's magic to be in love, and I was in love with Brendan . . . but now I'm starting to wonder whether love would have lasted, been strong enough to let me put my life on the back burner for his.'

'It's not easy, Sho. I'm wondering whether I can do it for Gavin . . . I hope I can. I really hope I can, because I do love him. But there's a price for love.'

'Yes . . . for everything. Right now I have freedom instead . . . and maybe I'll pay the price for that, later on when I'm some sad old spinster all on her own.'

'You – ha! You'll never be that. You'll have me! And all the other people who love you, in all kinds of ways. Maybe you'll even meet some guy who'll let you do your own thing, share your life without trying to take it over.'

Yes. Maybe. And Brendan Wright would never have been that man. Today, at this moment so far away from him, Shona could see that with utter clarity. Thinking about him, and then about Crys's predicament, she fell silent for much of the short trip to the airport, Crys equally silent beside her, communicating as only close friends could, scarcely saying a word.

At the airport they hugged fiercely, and Shona punched Crys gently under the chin. 'Let me know, right away – and don't worry, Crys. Whether you're pregnant or not, you're at a crossroads, you're going to have to make some tough decisions . . . but I'll be with you all the way. I'll listen and I'll think and

I'll be honest with you – and I'll help you, whatever you want to do.'

Strangled, Crys said nothing, only squeezed her hard, swiped her sleeve across her eyes and ran to her plane. Immobilised, Shona stood watching her, feeling for her, horrified by the thought that came unbidden and unwanted: there but for the grace of God go I.

8

Finn was outside chopping logs with vigour, and Aileen ignored the suspicion that there might be emotion in his energy, subliminated rage in every blow of the axe. This was a transition time for both of them, and she felt unable to sound him out until she first got a fix on her own feelings.

Which, on this crisp sunny Saturday, were briskly positive. With Crys and Shona out of the house, a kind of mellow quiet was flowing in on the sunbeams, their light faintly washed with spring. Only February; yet Le Mas des Cigales seemed to be warming up in some tentative, intangible way. And, she thought, carrying a cup of tea into the living room, I'm warming with it. Warming to it, as well.

Who could not fall in love with such a lovely house? We've only been here a week, and it's been all go up to now, but this morning I have time to pause and look around me, take stock of how I feel about being here. And – apart from missing Joe – I feel good about being here. Feel that we've achieved enough that I can sit down, now, and savour this tea, enjoy this view. Shona was right about putting the table by the window . . . as she's so often right. Really I'm beginning to wonder what she's doing working for anyone else – someone as motivated and dynamic as her should be working for herself. Directing things, running things, she has such natural flair for being in charge, without annoying her 'crew', as she calls us. Far from resenting her organising skills, I'm grateful for them.

This first week would have been a nightmare without her.

But in another week she'll be going back to Ireland, and I'll have to start coping on my own. That being so, maybe I should take today off to do some thinking, and exploring. When I finish this tea, I could slip down to the village, see whether I can find my way around and do a bit of shopping without causing any kind of international incident? If I bring a dictionary I can't go too far wrong . . . though I must admit there's quite a difference between a crash course in Galway and real live French in France. I don't think I'm going to be fluent quite as fast as I thought.

Oh, well. Rome wasn't built in a day. As Shona says, I have a choice: either I can fight like blazes to get fluent, or I can just muddle along with the locals, and find other English-speaking foreigners to make friends with. Apparently 'ex-pats' tend to cosy up together for comfort, some of them never learn French properly even after years. Right now, I don't know which I'd rather do. I must say I miss Marion and my other neighbours . . . but that's what Shona would call 'thinking negative'. Which I can't afford to do, because I've made my bed here and now I am going to lie in it. Love it.

At least we have beds! And all this other stuff. Le Mas is already beginning to look a little bit like one of those delicious houses I used to see on TV and in the magazines . . . dreamy, almost unreal. But it's very real. All this initial expense is real, too. I'm going to have to work harder on Joe to release some of Finn's college fund, because this furniture, gorgeous as it is, does not come cheap. Splitting expenses with Shona is a great saving, but still – and all this paperwork, too! I cannot believe they're already looking for us to pay some bloody residential tax, do these blasted bureaucrats not even give anyone time to draw breath?

Oh, the hell with them. I'm all on my own today and I'm

going to enjoy it. I'm already enjoying sitting here relaxing. Even the simplest things look so pretty, even that little jug of flowers, this big bowl of fruit here on the table. Shona's idea, of course, but I will keep it filled when guests start coming, the colours look so warm and lively together. I'd never have thought of putting limes with tomatoes, but it really works. The decor is working, too, that buttery yellow is perfect with the old red floor – I must admit Finn did an amazingly good job of painting, way neater and faster than I expected. Especially since French paint is, as he says, 'crap'. I wonder if there's any kind of training course he could do, if he wanted to make a career out of painting? Dear God, I'd be so delighted if he'd consider it – but he'd probably say he wouldn't understand a course in French.

Still. I'll mention it. Anything would be better than seeing him sign on the dole, when we've only just arrived, as if France already owed him something. Anyway – where's my jacket? Let's leave him to his logs, and walk down to Mézalas – let's even take a wicker basket, like a proper little French housewife!

Mézalas was bustling when Aileen reached it, and as she wended her way through the market she was surprised by the number of foreign accents she heard, American, English, something that might be Canadian or Australian. More than once she was tempted to tap people on the arm and say 'Hello, I'm Irish, I've just arrived, can you tell me what you're doing here and how it's working out? Do you like living here, are the people friendly, does it cost the earth or are you making ends meet?' And a barrage of other questions. But maybe they were only on holidays? No . . . hardly, in February, in this tiny village, haggling confidently over the price of eggs and fish. Something about these particular foreigners said they were residents, and she had to admit it was comforting to see and hear them. Maybe there was some kind of club she could join?

It was a tempting thought. And other things were tempting too – huge steel buckets of exquisite flowers, juicy shellfish fanned out on beds of ice, bubbling pots of some delicious-smelling brew called *langue de boeuf*. Some kind of beef, presumably? Plus masses of clothes – not as good value as Dunne's Stores, though, ho ho – and shoes and linens, house-wares and cosmetics. But the thing that most caught her eye was not in the market, it was in the bakery windows that lined the street, and she thought Tessie would have to be strait-jacketed when she saw it. These were no mere bakeries, these were art galleries, displaying the tiniest, prettiest, most wicked cakes she had ever seen. 'Sinful' Tessie would cry, before plunging in up to her elbows, and Aileen was sorely tempted to do exactly that. Could these cakes possibly taste as good as they looked?

Just one, she decided. They look criminally addictive, but I've got to find out . . . chocolate, or marzipan, or raspberry, or that little one with those beautiful oranges and berries? Oh, God. This is like a drug store, in the most literal sense, if I taste one I might get addicted for life, balloon to twenty stone or whatever that is in kilos. But – one. Just one, and then I'll never ever do it again, I swear.

'*Bonjour, madame.*' The assistant seemed both friendly and helpful. Hovering, Aileen pointed, her finger oscillating like the needle of a compass, undecided which way to swing. Finally it came to rest over a celestial creation of dark chocolate, oozing pistachio cream, studded with tiny violets like twilight stars; bewitched, she watched as it was placed on its own tiny tray, lovingly wrapped, sealed, beribboned and handed to her. All this fuss, over one individual little cake?

And then a different kind of fuss, as she strove to under-stand the price, until the assistant wrote it down for her and she gasped: waahhh! Joe would kill her if he knew, and she was fleetingly, disloyally glad that he was not here at this scandalous moment. Flustered, mumbling thanks, she clutched the minuscule package, backing out of the shop as if it were a bomb, which in a way it kind of was. So the magazines warned, anyway, tut-tutting: 'a moment on the lips, a lifetime on the hips.'

But if that were the case, she might as well enjoy it, no? Write it off to 'cultural research', find a café and – would they let you bring it in with you, eat it in one place when you'd bought it in another? Well, there was only one way to find out. So she found a café, a crowded noisy one where she might pass unnoticed, and sat down trying to look nonchalant. After only a minor battle, she managed to convey that she wanted a milky coffee, and when it arrived she guiltily unwrapped the cake – whereupon the waitress came running back to her, beaming, with a plate and a fork, as if encouraging her in her delinquency.

Oh, that cake. Oh, that *café au lait* . . . if she lived to be a hundred, she thought, she would never forget them, her tastebuds tickling into ecstasy. So this was why people raved about French food! Well, no wonder! When cup and plate were empty, she felt like crying. And nearly did cry, when she recognised for sure that she could never do this again. Not unless she wanted a new career as a government health warning, a waddling example of what happened to people who couldn't stay away from France's magnetically alluring bakeries. How cruel, to come all this way only to have to immediately renounce such pleasure!

Well. At least she had done it. Just the once. Now all she had to do was make her way out, back down the street with its stalls full of . . . lychees? Were these pink fuzzy things real lychees? Were these walnuts as nature produced them, before they went into a plastic pack? 'You must try everything' Shona had said, hadn't she? Right, so. Let's try them. And – oh, what the hell – let's get some of that *langue de boeuf* too, after all we'll need something for dinner tonight. And maybe that cheese, pyramid-shaped, exotically dusted in ash? Might as well be hanged for a sheep as a lamb.

Before she knew it her basket was bursting with food, she had spent a fortune and she was facing the climb back up the hill, which appeared longer and steeper than it had on the way down. I'll never do this again, she promised herself, in future I'll go to the supermarket – Aldi or Lidl or the cheapest there is – and we will live on plain normal food. Affordable food. I'd better not say anything to Joe about this awful binge.

Still . . . this is lovely! And those tulips, there were always gorgeous glass bowls of them in those magazines . . . pink, or cream, or yellow, which would look best in my brand-new living room? Pale yellow, of course, it's such a big room I'll need a couple of dozen to make any impact – oh, look, pear liqueur, and cherry! I've never tasted such a thing before, I wonder if . . . maybe just one bottle? Such beautiful tall bottles, hand labelled. Yes. Let's try the pear. Only there isn't room in my basket for all this stuff. I'm going to have to buy another. That stall over there has heaps of them, a big one with a good strong leather handle would be great, after all I'll be using it all the time – plain wicker, or should I go mad and get that fuchsia one?

Get a grip, Aileen. Plain wicker, at your age. But the other's so pretty . . . oh, it is delightful shopping outdoors like this, I can feel the sun right between my shoulder blades. And the weight of all this shopping, it's getting heavier by the minute. I might have to get a taxi to take me home.

No. I will walk. That will be my punishment, for this spree. It'll be some slog, but it'll work off the cake. Besides, I don't know where the taxis are. There's the beauty salon though, the pharmacy, how *do* they all make their windows so attractive? As for the lingerie in that window – good grief, it's barely dental floss! Even the street itself is so romantic, this whole village now I'm seeing it properly. I love all those big shady trees, and that fountain, and these wrought-iron gates with little courtyards behind. Everything has such mystique, it's like being in a film – oh, damn!

Well, that's not so romantic, is it? My shoe is ruined. France might not have litter like Ireland's, but it has more dog-dirt than I've ever seen anywhere. And more dogs, all these floppy little creatures that look like miniature mops, but make such a mess. Just when you're thinking everything is so beautiful – ugh. Now I'm going to have to go into that pharmacy and buy a pack of wet-wipes, if I have enough money left. After that I'm going straight home, before I do any more damage.

But first, maybe I should just get my hair washed and cut while I'm here? It needs it, I'd have to get that done even in Ireland. Okay. Let's try this place, it doesn't look too ritzy. How do you explain what you want, what's the French for 'hair'?

Gathering her wits, rehearsing her speech, she sailed into the salon, and was courteously greeted; could they be of help? Yes, she stuttered, could they please wash and cut her *chevaux*?

The assistant convulsed. Literally clutched her desk, laughing out loud, repeating the phrase for all her colleagues to hear until the entire staff was falling round in stitches. Blushing furiously, entirely bewildered, Aileen panicked, grabbed her bags and fled. What on earth she had said she couldn't imagine, but one thing was clear: she'd made a total hash of her first attempt at communicating, and had better go while the going was good.

And so, sweltering in her winter jacket under a surprisingly warm sun, she set off up the hill, pausing after a few minutes to calm down and rest, gulping the air that tasted clean and cool as mineral water. All around her, even from this low elevation barely two hundred metres up, a stunning view billowed out across the fields of dark stumpy vines over to other low hills, each topped with its ancient church, from which bells began to toll noon one after another as she sat down on a wall, some resonant, some blithe, in a concert that was all but orchestrated. Wow. Visual impressions, it had to be admitted, were very powerful; France looked like a painting as she sat studying it, absorbing its tranquillty, its deep aura of pure serenity.

Enchanted, she lingered where she was for a long time, maybe fifteen or twenty minutes, wondering intermittently what Joe was doing at this moment – pointing a customer in the direction of the slug pellet shelf, or listening to a complaint about the weedkiller?

Whatever it was, it surely couldn't compare with what she was doing, here in this pastoral tableau. Even if her visit to the village had ended ignominiously, this view was compensation for her blushes, and would surely knock him sideways when he saw it. Which would be soon enough, now; only another seven weeks until he arrived with Tessie.

Tessie. And Dymps. Out of the blue, blue sky, Aileen felt a sudden stab. A piercing stab that took her breath away, agonising as a stitch in her side. Maybe she actually had a stitch, from hauling this stuff up this hill. Surely she couldn't, on this beautiful day in this beautiful place, with her baskets loaded with beautiful things, possibly be feeling anything so silly as homesick? Even for one fleeting instant, before she came to her senses and stood up, got moving, back to Le magnificent Mas?

No. After a mere week, during which she had talked to both her mother and sister on the phone, that was too ridiculous for words. Ludicrous, for a woman standing here in the middle of her own dream, in the midst of such warmth, such luxurious beauty. At home, it was probably lashing rain and freezing cold, the traffic in Eyre Square at a steaming, fuming standstill. Joe and Tessie were probably getting on each other's nerves and Dymps was probably dashing to drive one child to its music lesson, the other to its soccer, racing home to prepare lunch before racing back again to collect one and then the other, way too busy to even think of her stupid sister out here in the middle of nowhere. Her sister who was, after all, no pining teenager, no airhead adolescent, but a grown woman in her forties, for God's sake, who had made a decision, implemented it and had the good fortune to be getting on extremely well with it.

Aileen Hegarty, you are *not* homesick. You are doing exactly what you set out to do this morning: enjoying yourself. You are an absurd, ungrateful, pathetic nitwit to think for one moment otherwise, and I do not want to hear another cheep out of you. Get on up that hill, now, and be quick about it.

Work. Good hard work, that would do the trick, banish the guilt of profligate spending, the shame of whatever she'd said to the hairdresser and any nonsensical, nostalgic thoughts of home. This *is* home now, Aileen reminded herself, my son is here with me, Shona will be back this evening and she won't want to find me here languishing, nor running up massive phone bills. From now on I'll only call Joe, Tessie and Dymps once a week, and keep it short at that. No more gossip about who was on the telly or who got engaged or who won a grand on the lottery. Especially when I don't have any gossip at this end. Now, where's the hoover? Did we buy a hoover? Yes. How could I forget, when it cost what it did? Get moving, missus.

Three hours or more elapsed as she cleaned the house, pausing in each room to admire its evolution. Two of the guest bedrooms remained bare as yet, but two others were well under way, one dressed in apricot with checked accessories in lavender; the other in dusky pink with striped accessories in fresh blue, all set against plain walls painted chalky white. Although a few touches remained to be finished, they already looked so cosy and pretty, she thought, that she could curl up in either one and have a little snooze for just a few . . . no. No way, Madame 'Egarty, you are here to work, you have a house to run.

Outside, she could hear Finn still rhythmically chopping, as if he'd got into the swing of it, and was relieved. In fact he'd even made his own lunch, the evidence of crumbs and wrappers was strewn around the kitchen, but nonetheless, he hadn't waited for mum to hand it to him. Hunger, she thought with satisfaction, must have driven him demented. Now, apart from the distant thud of his axe, there was no sound or sign of life at all, and as she worked a thought dawned on her: where was everyone? From the upstairs windows she could see the neighbours' houses, three or four of them within a range of one kilometre, all encircled by tall cypresses like her own, but not a voice did she hear, not a car, not a footstep. Le Mas was infinitely quieter than ever her house in Galway had been, where the street was always lively, and when she thought of her neighbours there another thing struck her: did any neighbours actually exist here, or were these surrounding houses empty, holiday homes maybe? In Ireland, it was the friendly custom to drop in to welcome new arrivals, maybe with a plant or cake or some such little gift, but she'd been here a week now and had yet to clap eyes on anyone. Once or twice she'd seen people out working in the fields, but they'd scarcely looked up, certainly never waved or called a greeting. The genial France of the films, in which people convivially congregated around bottles of wine or pastis, sociably nattering about the harvest and the weather, seemed to be mythical. If things didn't liven up soon, she might well be reduced to going to mass to see if anyone lived in this rural wilderness at all.

Well, she thought, it's different. Different was what I wanted and different, clearly, is what I've got.

Driving back from the airport, feeling some inexplicable need of loud music, Shona tuned into the local radio station, on which she was surprised to find Freddie Mercury shrieking his tonsils out. 'I Want to Break Freeee . . .' yeah, that was just the job, maybe it would distract her from her churning thoughts of poor Crys, who'd looked so dismal when she left. Now, with the clarity of hindsight, she could see all too well what Crys had been trying to say last November, when she'd made those remarks about marriage and motherhood not being for everyone. What she had been doing, essentially, was warning Shona: don't do anything that isn't you, whether the world thinks you should or not. And – she had been right. Now, while she herself was possibly embarking on a pregnancy about which she did not seem remotely enthusiastic, here was her friend Shona, driving along through this bright vivid land-scape, free as a bird, her mood as sunny as the day itself. As Crys said, nobody was dictating to her, trying to direct her life, and there was a lot of liberation in that thought. Concern for Crys apart, she could not feel anything other than good as she made her way back to Le Mas, after a delicious day spent in the bustling market, the fascinating *cité*, seeing all kinds of new things . . . her whole life, almost, in a different perspective. Here, with no social circle to put any pressure on, no colleagues to compete with, it just didn't seem to matter what she did; nobody knew her, nobody could gossip or criticise or wonder why on earth she wasn't hitched at thirty-six years of age.

I needed this, she thought. I hadn't realised I needed to get away from it all, from routine, from winter, from the whirling carousel I'd been spinning on . . . but I did. I only bought Le Mas as an investment, but it – it's doing me good. I feel awake, fresh, full of healthy energy, as if I'd shaken off something heavy and cumbersome. Of course, Le Mas is a big project, but it's fun. I'm really enjoying organising it, getting the show on the road, and Aileen is so easy to work with, it doesn't feel like work at all. There's just the right amount of challenge in it, stimulating but not exhausting, and what a kick it will be when the first guests check in! When the gîte's fixed up and I have my own apartment! I just know it's going to work. I will see that it does.

And I can trust Aileen to see to it too, she's so reliable, so flexible, nothing seems to bother her. Does it? It doesn't seem to, she's simply working away, getting on with everything, no complaints, no rows over anything. She's not great on decor – well, Le Mas is much bigger than her previous premises – but she absorbs ideas in a flash, she gets the picture. We're talking the same language and, if only that gruesome son of hers would get his ass in gear, we'd have a great team. I hope her husband doesn't rock the boat when he arrives, doesn't start grumbling about all the money we've spent or anything else – you've got to speculate, Joe, to accumulate! Trust me, and it will all work out!

Meanwhile, I have one more week before I have to go back to Ireland, so let's make the most of it. There's still an awful lot to be done. I won't even think about this court case coming up, or the implications if I lose it – I'll only think about Ireland when I'm in Ireland, and France when I'm in France. I wouldn't mind being here in the summer, I must say, it must be absolutely divine. But summer's always so busy, peak period in the office, all those rampaging tourists to be accommodated

. . . I wonder how Emily's getting on? I'd love her to come here to see Le Mas, soon before it fills up with paying people. Which it will. I'll get that girl in the local tourist office on my side – bribe her, I suppose, France is probably as bad as everywhere else – and she'll send us more business than we can handle. I loathe the thought of bribing anyone, of not surviving on merit, but the reality is that you can't, not in your first season anyway. We're going to be depending on goodwill in the Mézalas area so I'd better start oiling local officials even if it strangles me. Probably the mayor and half the local council will be expecting crates of champagne in return for sign-posting and brochure listing . . . greasy palms, yuk! But I can do it if I have to – just don't ask me to sizzle up bacon, eggs and sausages for six every morning. The cooking and cleaning are the part of running a B & B I'd hate; it's the business end I can manage.

Crys must be nearly home by now. I hope she's cheered up a bit. Hope everything works out for her, too . . . maybe if she is pregnant she'll come round to it, change her mind, start feeling happy about it. I hope so. . . why didn't she admit to herself that she'd rather go work in Africa, and tell Gavin, ages ago?

Because she was afraid to, I suppose. Afraid of losing her man. But – I've lost mine, yet here I am, down but not out, not nearly as devastated as I was barely three months ago. At the time, I thought I'd die. Now, I'm beginning to wonder whether he was really right for me, just as Crys is beginning to wonder if pregnancy is right for her. If a baby really is on the way, and she wants to stay married to Gavin, then she's going to have to do a whole lot of adjusting. A whole, huge heap.

Can she do it, I wonder? It would be awful to have a baby she doesn't want, the poor little mite, totally unfair to resent it . . . maybe she'll swing round and turn into one of those obsessive mothers who bleat on about their baby's every burp, every beep. But I can't see her doing that. In all the time I've known her, Crys Sheehan has been many things, but never boring.

Polish your nails, Crys! Get back in the saddle, do them emerald with magenta stripes! If there is a baby, tuck it under your arm and get on with your life! It won't be ruined, not unless you let it . . . nor will mine be ruined, now that I think about it, by this court case, whatever the outcome. I won't let it be ruined.

I can choose whether to let it be or not. So can Crys. If you can't choose your battles, you can at least choose your tactics, and your attitude.

'Hi, anyone home, it's me, I'm back!' Swinging into the hall, rubbing her hands against the gathering chill of evening, Shona shouted into the depths of Le Mas, and was startled when a male voice rumbled out.

'Yeah, hi, I'm in the kitchen. Ma is upstairs, be down in a sec.'

Flummoxed, she gaped at Finn's back, visible way down in the kitchen where he appeared to be making a sandwich; was she hallucinating, or had he spoken? Actually uttered a whole sentence? Disbelieving, she made her way tentatively down the hall towards him.

'Er . . . hi, Finn. How was your day, did everything go okay?'

With a curt nod, he chomped into his sandwich. 'Yeah. Got the wood nearly done. Bloody starving. Ah well, back to the grindstone. See ya later.'

With that he decamped, taking his sandwich with him, and next thing a light clicked on at the back of the house, illuminating him as he picked up an axe and bent over a vast stack of logs, three-quarters of which appeared to have been reduced to manageable proportions. Well, she thought. Well, well.

He mustn't *be* well! There's no other explanation. You couldn't exactly accuse him of being chatty, but he sounded nearly halfway human. I'd got so used to his silence, it's as if a tree had spoken. As if a tree had made itself a sandwich.

'Hi!' Looking grimy but cheerful, Aileen came down the stairs, aproned, trundling the hoover and a hammer. 'How was Carcassonne, did you have a fun girls' day? Did Crys catch her plane?'

'Yes . . .' Impulsively, Shona decided to say nothing yet about Crys's putative pregnancy. If it was confirmed, she'd tell Aileen all about it then. 'She should be safely home by now. What did you get up to?'

'Well, Finn chopped logs all day. Without even being asked, never mind hassled. I suppose there must have been nothing else for him to do! I did lots of stuff around the house, this afternoon, but I took the morning off, went down to Mézalas to do . . . er . . . a bit of shopping.'

Shucking off her jacket, Shona sat down, thinking that the house looked lovely, was good to come home to with its lights on and a fire burning. 'Uh huh, so what did you buy? These flowers?'

'Yes – and way too much other stuff! I got totally carried away.'

'Hah! Seduced by *la belle France*, eh?'

'Yes. Everything looked so irresistible. And then I went to the hairdresser.'

Glancing at Aileen's hair, Shona was puzzled: unless grunge was her new style of choice, Aileen did not appear to have been 'done'. She looked the same as she'd looked this morning, only messy, as if after a lot of housework.

'Oh?' Cautiously, Shona tried to sound her way around this mystery.

'And the weirdest thing happened. I asked them to cut my

236

hair, and they all collapsed laughing. I couldn't make out where I went wrong.'

'What did you say to them?'

'I said could they please *laver* and *couper* my *chevaux*, that's all.'

Aileen looked baffled, and Shona snorted with laughter. 'Oh, Aileen – you asked them to wash and cut your horses!'

'Oh, no! Did I?'

'Yes. We're going to have to do a bit of French over dinner this evening, I'll teach you what to say next time. What is for dinner, anyway, d'you want me to start washing or chopping anything?'

'No thanks. I bought it all ready-made. Beef stew. In the market, it smelled delicious. We only have to heat it up with some rice. But first I need to take a bath.'

'Great. You do that while I set the table. You and Finn seem to have been working so hard, let's have a nice meal with wine and candles and all.' So saying, she located the box of cutlery as Aileen decamped, distributed the cutlery and went into the kitchen to open some wine to breathe. There, sitting on the worktop, was the plastic box of stew Aileen had bought, and she picked it up, curious to see what exactly . . . oh, God!

I'll say nothing, she thought quickly. I'll just eat it and tell her afterwards. She can't have known, can she?

Sweaty, vaguely spectral in the dusk, Finn came in, and she whipped the box out of sight, wondering what he'd say if – and what their future guests would say, when they caught sight of him. He did less than zero for the image she wanted to build of Le Mas as a chic yet friendly guesthouse, he was only short of rattling his chains as he loped around like a caged chimp . . . maybe he'd find some bar or cybercafé to hang out in, somewhere? Get fed up and go back to Ireland? Take a job in Toulouse or – or anything, God, please. Just beam him up, off my back, the mere scruffy sight of him is setting my teeth on edge.

Scratching his sides, shaking sawdust off his arms, he looked hopefully at her. 'Will we be eating soon?'

'Yes, you'll just have time for a quick shower.'

Taking the hint, he wandered off, and by the time he returned dinner was ready. Bracing herself, Shona poured wine for everyone – they would be needing it – and sat down while Aileen ladled out the stew.

It wasn't actually bad. The sauce had a tomatoey flavour and there were nice crunchy gherkins in it, the rice kind of mopped up the . . . shutting her eyes only briefly, Shona managed to swallow most of it, while Finn and Aileen cleared their plates, blissfully oblivious. And then Finn turned to his mother.

'That was great, Ma – new recipe?'

'No. I bought it in the market.'

'What was it?'

'Some kind of beef – *langue* – Shona, what is *langue*, anyway?'

Oh, God. Oh, well. 'It – er – it's – um – tongue.'

'*Tongue?*' As if electrified, Finn gripped his empty plate. 'You mean to say I have just eaten some animal's *tongue*?!?'

'Uh . . . yes . . . a cow's . . .'

'Oh, *gross!*' In one movement he was on his feet, flinging back his chair, out of the room and gone. Horrified, Aileen stared into the vortex where he had been.

'Oh, Shona . . . I had no idea . . . my French is hopeless! I'm making such a hash of everything.'

Yep. She surely was. Shona couldn't keep a straight face. 'Doesn't matter! You'll get better!'

With a kind of desperation, Aileen poured them each another glass of wine. 'I'd better get better! If Joe had been here, if I'd served him cow's tongue, he'd have gone berserk! I'll have to beg Finn not to tell him.'

Suddenly Shona thought of Crys, also so anxious to placate her man, to keep him happy as Aileen apparently yearned to keep her men happy. Were all these guys worth so much anxiety?

'Aileen, who cares. It was just an accident. You – you have a lot on your plate at the moment, that's all!'

Simultaneously they gazed down at their plates, and next thing they were clutching each other, howling with laughter as Finn's boots stomped furiously across the wooden floor overhead. A few minutes later he reappeared downstairs, dressed for outdoors.

'I'm going down to the village for a pint.'

With that he was gone, leaving Aileen biting her lip uncertainly. On the one hand, he deserved a break she supposed – in fact it was a miracle he hadn't gone looking for a pub before now. On the other, she didn't want him getting into any . . . but then, trouble would be harder to find in French, wouldn't it?

Reassuringly, as if reading her thoughts, Shona smiled. 'I don't think he'll be gone very long. Meanwhile, let's make some tea.'

Tea was made and slowly savoured in the new armchairs by the fire; Aileen found Shona stimulating company, while Shona felt relaxed around Aileen. Able to question her, too, without fear of offending.

'D'you enjoy being married, Aileen, having a family? Is it fun being a mum?'

Teacup in hand, Aileen laughed. 'Not these days! Finn was fun when he was small. But I wish now he'd find a job and a girlfriend and let go of my apron strings. Not that I don't appreciate having him here with me at the moment. But it can't go on for ever, can it?'

'Nooo . . . and what about Joe? D'you miss him?'

Thoughtfully, Aileen reflected. Did she? Yes. And no. On, and off. Today, she had missed him. 'Well, put it this way. We've been married a long time. I'm enjoying the break. But I wouldn't want it to be for ever, either.'

'Do you – uh – do you still love Joe the way you first did? Or does passion fade?'

Shona hesitated slightly, but curiously, and Aileen considered. 'Well, passion is . . . is one thing. Maybe it frays a bit . . . but love is different, Sho. I think maybe it even grows. In my case, anyway . . . I love Joe more now than I did when we first met. He was so solid when Hazel died, so supportive . . . it brought us closer. Fortunately, because otherwise it would have destroyed us. It would have been so easy for him to blame me, but he never did. He's a good, kind man and that's why I want him here with me – miles away from the pub and his boozing buddies. He doesn't want to come – for that very reason! – but he'll have to eventually.'

'Mmm. I suppose. I hope! But what if he hates it?'

Aileen frowned. 'He probably will hate it, in the beginnning anyway. But I'll cross that bridge when I come to it.'

Shona didn't say what she thought, which was that she couldn't for the life of her imagine Joe Hegarty ever fitting in here, in any shape or form whatsoever. He was intrinsically Irish and he would, in her view, absolutely loathe the Languedoc. If Aileen was saving him from cirrhosis, she was exposing herself to – well. Did people like the Hegartys ever get divorced? Or did they end up just quietly, permanently hating each other? Bored brainless down here, Joe might never forgive his wife for uprooting him, for 'wrecking his life', as he would see it.

'Well – I hope you know the risk you're running! You're a

brave woman, Aileen. And what about you? Do you like it, so far?'

Vigorously, Aileen nodded. 'Oh, yes! It's lovely . . . well, obviously the language is a bit of a problem at the moment, and people don't seem as neighbourly as they are at home, and – uh – it's easy to spend a lot of money very fast! But it's a beautiful place, isn't it?'

'It's gorgeous. And what about Finn? Does he like it yet, d'you think?'

Aileen frowned into her tea. Thus far, she had no idea what Finn thought. Even as she sat speculating, the front door slammed, and he was back, hurtling into the room between them, furiously tearing off his jacket. In unison, they looked enquiringly up at him. 'Back already?'

'Yeah – there's only two damn bars in the whole village, and they were closed! The whole place was dead as a doornail, not a cat stirring at nine o'clock in the bloody evening! Christ almighty, what kind of a dump is this?!'

Well, Shona thought, I guess that answers my question. It doesn't look as if we're going to have Finn on our hands much longer.

Next day, Crys rang Shona to confirm that yes, she was pregnant. Yes, Gavin was ecstatic. No, she hadn't told him how she felt.

'But – Jesus, Crys, you can't live a lie—'

'Shona, I'm pregnant now, okay? My life no longer belongs to me. It belongs to my – my family. I'm just going to have to get my head around that.'

Yes. Shona could see that that was exactly what Crys was going to have to do, and was glad that Crys could see it too. But, even as she hung up with all the words of encouragement she could muster, she thought of her friend with sympathy, and some sneaking sense of loss. As Crys said, she would, henceforth, belong to her family . . . maybe even start putting their friendship on some kind of back burner?

I couldn't do it, she thought. I couldn't rearrange my life around a child. I'd hate to be having a baby just to please its father. I'd hate to have to drop Le Mas or any other project, the way Crys is going to have to drop Africa. I would, now that I think about it, murder anyone who tried to drag me into anything I didn't want to do, or out of anything I did want to do.

Does that make me a horribly selfish person? Seriously unsuitable marriage material?

Maybe it does. Maybe, if I'm honest about it, I'm not cut out for the caring, sharing kind of relationship that most women want. Maybe it's better to be honest now than sorry later . . . God, I just hope Crys can cope. And adapt. And make a go of being a mum, as well as the wife of a man who – while handsome, likeable and hard working – seems to be a little bit of a tyrant behind the scenes? I'm starting to see that maybe there's more to Gavin Sheehan than meets the eye . . . apparently there's more to Joe Hegarty than meets the eye, too. I'd never look twice at him, but Aileen thinks he's great. Seems to genuinely love him, plodder and all as he is.

Well. Each to her own. I wonder what 'mine' is?

God knows. But at least now maybe I'm starting to see what it isn't.

During her remaining six days at Le Mas Shona worked on the gîte as well as the house, trying to get the tiny cottage livable because, by the time she returned, the main house would be full of guests. Already in sound condition, all it needed was a lick of paint, a table and chairs, a sofa-bed and basic household equipment; niceties such as curtains, wardrobes, bookshelves and the like could wait.

'Wendy house' Finn scoffed, 'hardly room to swing a cat.'

This was true. With just one bedroom, a kitchen, bathroom and small living room, the gîte was ideal for one person, or two 'close friends' at most, but Shona didn't mind that. On the contrary. Its small scale made her feel both snug and independent, as well as having the advantage of being cheaply and easily run. By comparison, the main house looked enormous.

'Are you sure' she asked Aileen on her last evening with a sudden surge of doubt, 'you can manage? On your own for six weeks, until Joe arrives?'

'Yes' Aileen insisted, 'I can and I will. Just so long as Finn doesn't storm off and desert me!'

A little anxiously, she laughed, and Shona decided against admitting her concern that Finn might well do that – which would be great in the long run, just so long as he didn't do it yet. Le Mas was way too big, and isolated, for Aileen to live in alone. Even now, they had not spoken to any neighbours, got to know anyone beyond the briefest of 'bonjour's. The French, it had to be admitted, were not exactly queueing up to form a welcoming committee.

'Well – okay, if you're sure. Call me if there are any problems. Meanwhile, the girl from the tourism office will be coming round to say hello—'

Aileen grinned. 'To inspect me, you mean, like you used to do! What's her name?'

'Aude. Aude Villandry. For God's sake be nice to her if you want—'

'Shona. Relax. I'm not a complete idiot. I've done this before, remember?'

'Yeah. I know. I'm fussing over nothing. I have every faith in you, Aileen, really!'

They both laughed, but both sensed the importance of the moment: Le Mas was about to become a business. Shona owned it, Shona had helped set it up, now everything depended on Aileen to make it work. Reassuringly, not letting Shona see how terrified she was of tackling it without her, Aileen gripped her shoulder. 'I'll get on with Aude just as I always got on with you. She'll make sure we're listed in the tourism office, and Finn is going to put up our sign tomorrow – you never know, a car might pass this way some day!'

'H'mm. We're a bit off the beaten track, for sure. We're going to be relying a lot on goodwill and word of mouth.'

'Yes. But let me worry about that. You have your court case to worry about.'

Yes. And Shona was worried about it. But this wasn't the moment to say so. Airily, she smiled and went off to pack her suitcase, feeling as if she were being marched to the guillotine.

Next morning Shona and Aileen stood together on the front lawn, looking admiringly at Le Mas basking in the woven, intermittent sunlight; although it was still mild the weather was also getting a little cloudy. Throwing her bag in Aileen's car, Shona grimaced. 'God, I love this place! I don't want to leave!'

'Tough. You have a career and a life to get back to. Now, I'll drive – at least that's one thing I've conquered in France!'

Off they set, leaving Finn in charge with unvoiced unease: should any crisis arise, he was unlikely to respond with much initiative. Thank God the airport was little more than an hour away. As they drove to it they discussed marketing strategy for Le Mas, whether it might be worth taking out advertising in some Irish magazines or newspapers, and they discussed financial outlay to be settled between them, and they discussed Joe whose phone call last night had been oddly curt: Tessie, he said, was 'having a go' at him and he was tired of not living in his own home. What he meant by 'having a go', apparently, was that Tessie had accused him of not supporting his wife – her daughter – enthusiastically enough, which was an entirely unfair thing to suggest.

'Then he should be glad to be coming over here to rejoin his wife!'

'M'mm. Mam will be coming too, but only for a week. Dymps too, I hope, and her husband and kids. I must say it'll be great to see them all.'

Aileen smiled wistfully, and Shona felt a frisson: she wasn't going to go and get homesick, was she? Oh no, oh please, not now. Not when Le Mas was going to need a cheerful, eternally smiling hostess, welcoming guests without a care in the world. Once the family visit was over, Aileen was not even to *think* any more about Ireland.

Yet she, Shona, couldn't help thinking about it as they made their way to the airport. What would happen, in court? At work, afterwards? She'd been so busy here she'd scarcely had time to speculate, but now her skin began to prickle with anxiety. Like Crys, she was about to return to Ireland holding her breath, not knowing what the future might hold or how anything would work out.

'Well . . . here we are' she said at length, getting reluctantly out of the car when Aileen parked it, feeling a sword of Damocles suddenly dangling over her head. But Aileen said nothing, shading her eyes with her hand to watch the incoming flight which was just landing, and as she stood there looking wistfully at it Shona felt another jolt – was it her imagination, or did Aileen really look nostalgic? Even this tiny little bit of Ireland, this plane carrying its flag, disembarking Irish passengers, seemed to be hypnotising her.

Well, she has only been here two weeks. But still – she's going to have to toughen up.

'Come on, what are you gawping at? Are you going to give me a hand with my luggage and wave me off, wish me luck?'

Aileen snapped out of her reverie. 'Yes, of course! You're not to worry about a thing, Sho. I'll get to grips with Le Mas and you will win your court case, bury Terry O'Hagan ten feet deep.'

In the airport they were soon surrounded by arriving passengers, and Aileen smiled: 'God, don't they sound so – so boisterous! I wonder if any of them are looking for somewhere to stay, I should be handing out cards for Le Mas – could even give a few guests a lift back with me!'

She wants to, Shona saw. That's exactly what she wants, company to replace me, people to talk to and have a laugh with, people from home. These next few weeks are going to be hard for her.

'No, Aileen, you can't tout for business yet, the house isn't ready!'

'I suppose not. Never mind – so, off you go now, and win your case, and ring me regularly and – and come back soon!' With a surge of emotion, Aileen grabbed Shona and hugged her to her, long and hard. Fighting a feeling of desertion, Shona hugged her back, sensing the tightening bond between them. And then, wrenching herself out of Aileen's embrace, she whirled away.

Clenching her fists, Aileen stood watching until she could see Shona no longer, until the rumbustious mob of Irish arrivals began to disperse around her, laughing and joking as they headed off to pick up their rental cars. As he left the building one of the men dropped a newspaper on the concourse floor, and she raced to pick it up, her throat tightening as she grasped it: today's *Irish Independent*. Never, in Ireland, would she have done anything so unhygienic as picking up someone else's newspaper. But here, in France, she gripped it like a winning lottery ticket, which no power on earth could prise from her fingers.

It's my reward, she told herself. I am dreading driving back to Le Mas on my own, especially that awful bit of the road that turns into a bridge, with no Shona to encourage me or help if anything goes wrong. So when I achieve it, when I get safely back to Mézalas, I will sit down with this *Indo* and a cup of Barry's tea, and read all about what Ireland is doing without me.

The drive back seemed to go on into eternity, not only because Aileen got lost, asked for directions and misunderstood them, but also because of the bridge. Shona had talked her over it en route to the airport, distracting her from its horrors, but now she had all the time in the world to contemplate the looming nightmare. A Roman viaduct built centuries ago, it spanned a foaming river with nothing but empty space in the – how many? – hundreds of feet between it and the churning water.

Don't look down. Over and over she repeated the mantra, slowing the car to a crawl, sick to her stomach as she edged onto it, as far away from the parapet as possible. A very low parapet, it did nothing to blinker the view, she was nauseously aware of the hideous height from which she could see for miles on either side, her face and hands beading in sweat as she gingerly nudged along in second gear.

Just as she reached the highest, halfway point a car came screaming up behind her, its driver hooting and waving furiously; in her mirror she could see him mouthing at her to move over and let him by. But that would mean moving closer to the edge . . . surely he could see her problem, that anyone driving so slowly must be frightened of ancient, soaring bridges? But if he did see he evidently didn't care, because he continued to hoot and wave all the way, deliberately intimidating, the front of his car all but touching the back of hers, so aggressively he seemed to be trying to push her over the edge. By the time she finally got across she was almost in tears, and had to pull in when she got there.

Fuck him, she thought as she sat shaking, fuck him for a bloody French frog. Okay, maybe that's irrational, maybe an Irish driver would do it too, but at this moment I hate *him*. I'm driving a foreign car, he could see its Irish plates, would it have killed him to give me a break?

Bastard. Bloody miserable, ignorant lout. And bloody gruesome, horrible bridge. At this moment I hate France, hate hate hate it . . . I'm going to ring Joe tonight. Ring him and have a long chat with him – God, why can't he be here when I need him? Why, why, why?

Eventually, after another wrong turn that took her spinning around a series of roundabouts, she found her frazzled way back to Mézalas, where the sight of shops reminded her that she'd better get some groceries . . . but it was lunchtime, and every last one of them was closed.

Oh, for chrissakes! What kind of ridiculous country was this, that you couldn't even buy a loaf of bread for two hours in the middle of the day?! Did they all have to go off to stuff their faces, could they not organise a roster the same as Irish shops, let people get on with their daily round? Now she'd have to go all the way to the hypermarket, which was miles away and the size of a football stadium, it would involve tracking down a loaf of bread and a pint of milk amidst lawnmowers, televisions, clothes, bicycles and acres of stuff. She'd never get back at this rate.

Oh, sod it. Let's just have a tomato salad for lunch, then, open a tin of soup. I couldn't be arsed with all this. Unless of course Finn has whipped up a lovely lunch to greet his mother with, walked down to the bakery for hot baguettes? Ha! Pigs might fly.

In a distinctly disgruntled mood she drove on up to the house, to find Finn sitting in the living room, doing absolutely nothing. Nothing at all, not even browsing a magazine or listening to his Walkman: just sitting, staring blankly at her, as if life had come to a standstill in her absence. Nettled, she surveyed him sharply.

'God almighty, Finn, have you nothing to be doing?'

'No' he drawled, 'I kind of ran out of things to work on, and . . . Ma, when are we ever going to get a telly? And a computer? This place is like a goddamn morgue.'

'Finn' she exploded, 'there are a dozen things need doing, all you need is eyes in your head to see them! As for televisions and computers, have you any idea what those luxuries cost, any idea how much I have been spending on *necessities*?!?'

'But a telly's a necessity. So's a computer.'

'Not to me. We can't afford cable yet and there's no point in having a television until it's in English. As for computers – why don't you go out and find a cybercafé? Huh? Just get off your ass and open your eyes, Finn, use your wits!'

She heard herself shouting, saw the wounded amazement in his face, and didn't care. Okay, so France was no picnic for him. Okay, so he had been wrenched away from home. But hey, guess what, Finn, I'm struggling here too, this is all new to me as well! And I am doing it for you, for you and your blessed father, I am trying to get this family out of its rut, on its feet! Stop thinking in straight lines, get out of this tunnel vision, do not expect instant perfection here! You are twenty years of age and I – I – oh, sweet Jesus!

Storming off to the kitchen, she slammed together an ad hoc lunch, and ate it fuming while he stared accusingly at her across the table, waiting for her to calm down and, she supposed, simply be his normal mother again. Good old Ma, who'd soon relent, head off to the hypermarket this very afternoon to buy a television and a satellite dish and . . . no. No, she thought, as in no way. I am not doing it, Finn, and that's that. If you want hardware, go out and get a job, earn the money for it and buy it yourself.

Or do anything else you like, only stop *looking* at me like that!

Arriving back to wild wet weather, with no hint of spring whatsoever in it, Shona was delighted to find Crys waiting for her at the airport. What was it about airports, that made you feel so alone, if nobody was waiting to claim you? Eagerly she sprang into Crys's waiting arms, feeling devoutly grateful for her friend, who was smiling and looking more like the Crys of old.

'Come on' Crys said firmly, 'let's go have a jar and a chat.'

So they did, and Shona felt much better for both, enjoying the warm atmosphere of the pub they chose, not wanting to go to her apartment which would be . . . well . . . empty. And cold, with nobody there to turn on the heating.

'So tell me all the news! What have I been missing?'

'Oh, the usual, more corruption scandal, a murder in Limerick, inflation's up three per cent . . .'

Sometimes, when Crys starting beating this drum, Shona wondered whether she might be a politician *manquée*, should be standing for election. But this was hardly the moment to say it. 'And you?' Gingerly, she scanned Crys for signs of pregnancy, but as yet there were none. 'How are you? And Gavin?'

Crys studied her nails, which, Shona noted, were painted again. Not brilliant gold or sparkling silver, just a demure shade of pink. 'We're fine' she said at length, her voice sounding carefully neutral. 'I've signed up for ante-natal classes, and we're talking about names – what do you think of Jeremy for a boy, Rose for a girl?'

'I think those are very – nice – traditional names! Wouldn't Zarathustra or Venus or something be more your style – Nelson Mandela or Che Guevara!?'

'Oh' Crys sighed, rather dreamily Shona thought, 'we couldn't do that to a child. He or she would get an awful time at school.'

I must be hearing things, Shona thought. Crys looks well, but never in my life have I heard her sound bourgeois before. What the hell is this about?

It's about Gavin. I bet my bottom dollar it's about Gavin. Now that he's going to be a father he's going to be a real old Victorian pater familias. He's going to brainwash her, before she knows it she'll be knee-deep in babies and nappies and homework and name tags and school runs. Politics will be out the window and she'll be talking about the price of Pampers. My lovely friend Crys Sheehan is being hijacked by her charming tyrant of a husband.

Am I going to go along with this?

Yes. I am. If it's what she wants. If I want to keep her friendship. If I can keep the embers of the old Crys glowing deep down there somewhere in the midst of sudden suburbia. I am not letting Gavin get her all to himself.

'Well, school is a way off yet! Do we have an ETA for this baby?'

'Yes. Early October. I'll have all summer to get ready for it.'

She smiled beguilingly, and Shona smiled back, not deceived. Get psychologically ready for it, that was what Crys meant. Convince herself she really wants it, it's all for the best, everything will be great.

And maybe it will be. I'm hardly in any position to argue, am I, en route to the Labour Court where my own future might well explode in smithereens? God, I can't believe the case actually starts on Monday. *Mon*day! Waaahh!!

'Crys' she said tentatively, 'are you busy on Monday?'

Crys nodded. 'Yes. Normal working day, driving the school bus – only I've swopped rosters, haven't I, with Jim?' Unexpectedly, she grinned, and reached over to pat Shona's hand. 'Because I'm going to court with you, aren't I? Surely you didn't think I'd let you go on your own, Sho?'

Shona didn't know what she'd thought. All she knew was that she was profoundly touched, and comforted, to know that Crys had thought of this, thought of her and would come with her through the ordeal.

This is what friends do, she thought, draining her drink. They get each other through their court cases, and their pregnancies, and their break-up with Brendan Wright, and their marriage to Gavin Sheehan. They get themselves into all sorts of messes, and they get each other out.

Quietly, calmly, Tessie sat sewing buttons onto a batch of her son-in-law's shirts. On the other side of the room, Joe sat reading a DIY manual. It had been at least twenty minutes since he last turned a page, and Tessie knew his mind was not on it. His mind, almost visibly, was on his wife. Saying nothing, she left him to his thoughts; if he wanted to disclose them, he would.

At length, apparently, he did. Letting the manual slide on his knees, he looked across the room at her, and sighed.

'Have you heard anything of this rumour that's going around?'

Serenely, she continued to sew. 'What rumour, Joe?'

'The one about me and Aileen. Dave Doherty says it's all over the pub and beyond.'

'Oh, pub talk. I wouldn't mind that.'

But – wasn't she interested? Didn't she want to know what people were saying about her own daughter?

'They're saying she's left me.'

Tessie bit off a length of thread and glanced at him. 'People are saying my daughter has left her husband?'

'Yes. That she's run off to France, that we're splitting up.'

'Well, you know that's nonsense and I know it and Aileen knows it, so why worry?'

Why worry?! 'Because it's outrageous, that's why! Aileen would never leave me, she has no reason to even consider such a thing.'

'No. But people will talk, I suppose, when a woman goes off without her husband. They have a way of putting two and two together and always getting five.'

Tessie threaded her needle anew, and Joe sat looking at her, thinking that she might be a bit more annoyed on his behalf – on Aileen's, too. This kind of gossip was extremely irritating, all the more so for being completely untrue. It was rasping at him like a hair shirt, making him feel scratchy and edgy. How dare anyone say such a thing! He would be going to join his wife as soon as possible, and in the meantime – in the meantime he was going to ring her, now this minute actually, because he had a sudden urge to talk to her.

Which is another thing! All these phone calls, the manager of Telecom will be throwing a small champagne celebration for five thousand close friends, flying them out to Hawaii on a fleet of private jets. It'd be cheaper to just *buy* Telecom, the rate these bills are running up. So much for all that guff she used to quote me out of those magazines, about people living in the sun on a few tomatoes and loaves of bread.

Is it worth it? Is this whole crazy adventure making her happy? If I thought it was . . . well. Maybe I'm not the greatest husband in the world, the richest or most glamorous, but I do want my wife to be happy. I want her to look the way she . . . the way she used to look, before Hazel. Long ago as that was, she never looked quite the same after that. If France can put some of the sparkle back in her face – that's all I ask. That's all I ask.

And a respite from Tessie, before I throttle her. Has she no idea what it's like going down to the pub when you think everyone is talking about you behind your back? Which is why I'm not in the pub, this evening. And what does she mean, I'm not 'supportive enough'? I let Aileen go off and do it, didn't I? Sent Finn with her? Will be going myself, as soon as I can? What more does she want?

Women. Impossible. You can't win. Where's Aileen's number? The eyes are going, I'm going to have to get specs.

'Joe! Oh, I'm so glad you've called!'

Well, that's something. She sounds pleased to hear from me. That doesn't mean there's anything wrong, does it? She's not missing me, or lonely or anything like that?

'Yeah, well, it's cheaper at night – how are you getting on?'

'So far, so good. Except that Shona left this morning, and then I had a row with Finn.'

'What's he done?'

'Oh, nothing, it'll blow over. We're just sort of – you know – adjusting.'

'Is he giving you guff? D'you want me to speak to him?'

'No, no – actually he hasn't been too bad, considering. I suppose it'll be easier for all of us when we get to know people and find our feet.'

'Have you not got to know anyone?'

'No, not yet. But we will.'

'H'mm. What's the weather like?'

'Turning a bit murky.'

The weather. Why do I always end up asking her about the

weather? Why can I not find anything more interesting to say to my own wife? Why can't I just spit out the truth, dammit? Admit that I – I miss her?

'Well, batten down the hatches, don't get caught in any storms.'

'No. We won't. The house is really solid, Joe, no leaks or anything.'

'Good, good. I'd better put you on to your mother so, let you have a word.'

Handing the phone to Tessie, Joe cursed silently. Why am I putting her on to her mother, when I still want to talk to her myself, still want to hear the sound of her voice?

Why can't a grown man of forty-five years of age communicate with the woman he's been married to for two decades? Simply tell her, for God's sakes, that he loves her, whether she's taken leave of her senses or not?

I don't know why. All I know is that I never was any good with words and never will be. That kind of conversation strangles me, is way out of my reach.

And now Aileen is way out of my reach, too. I want her here beside me tonight, not a thousand bloody miles away in bloody France. Where she might not be at all, if I'd only – Jesus! What if she meets some flaming Frog? Now that Shona's gone, she's on her own, she'll be needing all kinds of help, who knows where she might turn?

The sooner I get over there, the better. I don't want to go, but I don't want any smarmy Frog muscling in on my wife, either. Those lads are notorious for their way with women – but they needn't think they can look sideways at my woman.

Oh, no. Back off, lads. Maybe my wife has gone funny in her forties, maybe our relationship isn't quite all it could be these days – but it is still *ours*. Got that? Our messed-up, bogged-down, going-nowhere private property. So hands off Mrs

Hegarty, because Mr Hegarty, let me tell you, is not a pretty sight when he's provoked.

And as for you, Dave Doherty, you can drink on your own tonight, and wipe that smug grin right off your kisser. Just because your wife left you does not mean that mine has left *me*. She has done no such thing, and if you were any kind of a friend you'd be scotching that rumour. Because if I try, it'll only make it worse, won't it?

Damn! I could murder a pint. But I am not going down to that pub and have them all laughing at me – or worse, sympathising. I am not spending my entire night denying something that is a vicious, malicious *lie*.

9

It did not happen overnight. It took time for the storm to gather force, to coil into Shona's life and decimate everything it touched. But she could sense it coming, feel it, with each passing day.

Her first visit to the Labour Court, accompanied by Crys, her father and her union rep, was unremarkable. Apart from the loathsome sight of Terry O'Hagan, sitting across the room smirking amidst his cronies, nothing untoward happened; it was all about explaining background to the arbitrator, giving a straightforward account of her career to date and listening to her adversary give his. Then a lot of paper-shuffling, and abruptly that was that: proceedings would resume on Wednesday.

On Wednesday, Crys couldn't be with her, and her mother arrived instead of her father. But that was support enough, for another swift session that was curtailed after a mere hour, without either party getting a chance to don their boxing gloves. Another date was set for the following week, and she groaned – so maddeningly slow!

The following week, both of her parents were busy, but to her surprise Emily O'Brien showed up, simply appeared without warning on the steps of the courtroom. 'I know how these things can drag on' she said, 'and people can't get to every single session, so I thought I'd get to this one. And maybe a few others, if you like.'

Touched, Shona clasped her hand. 'I can't believe you've driven all the way from Connemara, Emily! You are so good and I can't thank you enough.'

Emily winked at her. 'I'm the one to be thanking you. I got my listing in the *Charming Country Houses* guide.'

'Oh, great! I'm delighted for you!'

But that was the only delightful feature of an otherwise slow, exasperating day, one on which Terry O'Hagan gained some small invisible advantage by bringing his pretty, well-dressed daughter with him; could the father of such a charming young lady possibly be a sexist lout with malice aforethought? The girl sat beside him, wide-eyed, touching his arm from time to time, making it clear that she certainly didn't believe a word of these lies about dear daddy.

'I should rent a kid, is that it?' Shona fumed. 'Some cute child to make me look respectable, instead of the wanton harlot he's trying to make me sound?'

'Well' Emily allowed dubiously, 'it always looks better in court if one is married, preferably with children. Single people can be . . . um . . . viewed with suspicion.'

'But why?! That's nonsense! Discrimination!'

'Yes, but that's the way these things go. What you need is a man to produce in court, some solid upstanding kind of guy – you don't by any chance have a brother, do you?'

'No – and I am not dragging any of my male friends into this, just to give me "respectability", thank you very much.'

Outraged, Shona sat through Terry's account of how she had 'always had an eye for the men . . . a history of unstable relationships . . . constantly convinced herself male colleagues were making passes at her when they were doing nothing of the kind'. Several times she wanted to jump up and protest, but was restrained, curtly informed that her turn would come.

Saying goodbye to Emily afterwards, she wanted to go home and weep, to kick the walls with impotent rage.

But, when she did get home, the phone was ringing, and she recoiled as if scalded when she heard the voice at the other end.

'Shona? Hi, it's me, Brendan. I hope you don't mind my calling you?'

'N-no' she stuttered, flailing wildly for her wits. After four months – Brendan – what on earth – ?

'I just thought – well, I've been talking to Emily. She's told me all about this court case of yours and I – well, it's outrageous. So I decided to give you a shout in case you might want any . . . er . . . moral support? I'd be more than willing to accompany you to the next session if you think it might help.'

She was flummoxed. Did he genuinely care? Or had Emily somehow recruited him, in that nonchalantly persuasive way of hers, clinging to her conviction that a man would 'look good' at Shona's side? Could Emily even be trying to steer the pair of them . . . back . . . together? So many things shot through her head, she heard herself gulping inelegantly, and had to steady herself, get a fix on this totally unexpected conversation. Just for one fleeting moment, she wanted to howl: 'Yes! Come over here right this minute, Bren, this whole thing is a nightmare, I need you! I want to lay my head on your chest and sob all over you!' For several suspended seconds, she wavered, feeling magnetically drawn to him, to his help. She could have it, if she chose.

Whereupon, of course, she would look like a feeble nitwit. One who couldn't manage without him. Plus, that would be playing along with the court's perception of her, as if she were not good enough as an individual in her own right. Okay – it would help her case. Brendan's presence would give her 'respectability'. But at what price?

Steeling herself, she drew a deep breath. 'No. Thank you very much for calling, Brendan, and for offering, but I – I'm managing fine on my own, thanks.'

'Are you sure?' He did sound concerned. Genuinely. After all, they had not parted bitterly; he had been sorry to break up with her, sorry that she felt unable to give him the priority he felt he needed in a serious relationship.

The kind of priority Crys was now giving Gavin. The priority that turned you into someone else, turned your whole life around.

'Yes. I am sure. It's very good of you to volunteer, but it's not necessary. I can cope.'

The very saying of it made her feel that maybe she could. She could get through this wretched case under her own steam, and win it.

'Well – okay, if you're sure. Best of luck, then, Sho, I hope it's all over soon, I know the kind of ordeal these things can be. You have my number if you change your mind.'

Grateful, but unwavering, she thanked him again and hung up, reeling. Even though she was getting over him, suspected now that they might not have been happy together, his voice, his concern and goodwill, still affected her powerfully. He was still a very nice man and, physically, she missed his embrace, would give almost anything to sink into it at this moment. Just slide, sink into his arms, let him take over, do whatever it took to get through this whole horrible ordeal.

But – no! She'd got this far without him, wasn't going to start back-pedalling the moment the going got tough. Wasn't going to start accumulating any kind of emotional debt. Wasn't going to let the weight of this case crush her – after all, Terry O'Hagan *had* assaulted her, which was why she had hit him, she was in the right here!

Is that enough, I wonder? Is being in the right and telling the truth enough to win a court case? I always assumed it was. But now I'm beginning to wonder if it's not all about something else entirely, about image and perception and manipulation.

In which case, I should have said 'Yes, Brendan, please do come along and make me look like a wronged little woman, take me into your protection, frighten off that nasty horrid Terry O'Hagan and show the arbitrator what a respectably escorted lady I am.'

In other words, live a lie. Suffocate. Oh, God, I wish I were back at Le Mas, painting walls and planting tomatoes, a million miles away from all this.

Losing concentration on the dishes she was washing – expensive dishwashers would have to wait – Aileen opened the kitchen window, folded her arms and leaned out on the sill that was deep enough to serve as a desk. In the distance, church spires pinpointed the crumbly, ancient old villages, in which she could visualise the tinkling fountains, the sunny squares shaded by huge plane and lime trees. Embraced by silvery olive groves, each village harboured quaint little shops, rambling alleyways and tantalising courtyards, the whole vista draped in warm, soft air under cottony skies. This is exactly what the magazines promised, she acknowledged, here I am where I wanted to be, practically on the front page. The only thing lacking is Joe; when he gets here, he'll see what this was all about. Only another month to go, now, surely I can survive that long on my own? Not even on my own, because Finn is here with me. I keep expecting him to crack, to say he hates it and go storming off home, but miraculously he hasn't.

Of course, there isn't any 'home' to go storming off to. 'Home' is rented out, so that's not an option. But still . . . has this anything to do with Joe, I wonder? Did he make Finn promise to stick it out until he arrives? Sometimes I suspect maybe he did.

And I'm glad, if he did. Gorgeous as it is, I'd go nuts here all by myself. It is so frustrating not being able to talk to people! Not understanding these notices that arrive in the post, not being able to explain myself in the shops, not even being able to talk as fluently as the five-year-olds I hear in the streets. I really must winkle out some other expats, as Shona calls them, and find out how they manage.

Meanwhile, at least the house is coming along. It feels too big for me, but when it fills up with guests, everything will be more normal, more fun. For Finn, too. If he'll just hang in a while longer, he might find his feet, make some friends, get something or other to occupy him. He'll have to start looking for some kind of work, because he can't be hanging around this house once there are guests in it.

Still – at least I've got him away from that computer of his, and those dodgy friends, and those shady activities I could never quite pinpoint. Was he mixed up in drugs, in some shape or form? I still don't know that he was, for sure. But I'm still glad I've dragged him down here, however much he hates it, his links have been broken. Does he hate *me*, I wonder, for doing it?

Oh, Finn. I wish I could talk to you. I wish you would talk to me. I wish Joe . . . I'm fooling myself if I think getting fluent in French is going to solve anything, really. Sometimes the Hegarty family's communication problems just seem insoluble in any language.

The warm, windy afternoon mutated into a wild, stormy evening, and Aileen was taken aback when a few spattering raindrops grew rapidly into a torrent; somehow rain made the Languedoc feel darkly different, unpredictable and vaguely hostile. Lighting the fire, she went round the house closing all the shutters, and was just settling down with a book when the lights flickered, and went out.

Uhhh! It was creepy in the firelight, and she called out for Finn, who materialised with a torch. Between them they found candles and lit several, but Aileen began to feel uneasy as the increasingly violent wind ripped through the trees outside, the rain hammered on the roof – good grief, such rain, never in her life had she heard the like. Was this a regular feature of life in the Languedoc? If so, they'd have to install a back-up generator, a guesthouse couldn't have its guests wandering round in the dark. Suddenly she felt very conscious of the distance that separated Le Mas from its neighbours, and of the lack of street lighting out here in the country. It was completely, absolutely pitch dark.

'Well' she sighed to Finn in the shadows, 'I suppose there's no choice but to go to bed and hope that this will blow over by tomorrow.'

'Yeah. Pity we can't get the weather forecast or ring someone to find out what usually happens.'

Yes. All right, Finn, you've made your point. Now, let's get some sleep.

But sleep was impossible. Within minutes of scrambling into bed Aileen was tossing and turning, clutching a pillow over her ears, but nothing could drown out the howling, the screeching of a gale now verging on a hurricane, nor the pummelling of rain that was becoming a deluge, gushing down from a mal-evolent sky slashed with lightning. Even from behind the shutters Aileen saw the first glaring flash, and shrieked: this was really getting frightening. Getting up, she groped for her dressing gown, and stumbled out onto the landing to find Finn also emerging from his room, fully dressed as if he hadn't gone to bed at all.

'Jaysus' he said, 'this is a horror movie.'

Weakly, Aileen laughed. It was horrible, and his sardonic voice was a comfort. Never in Ireland had either of them experienced a storm of such ferocity, never had— suddenly, there was a crash downstairs that made them both jump and Aileen scream aloud.

'Oh God, Finn, what was that – where's the torch?'

'Don't panic, Ma – here, let me go first, watch yourself on the stairs.' Amazingly, he sounded calm, and Aileen marvelled at how suddenly wonderful it was to have a strapping twenty-year-old son in the house.

Picking her way down the stairs behind him, shuddering as her feet touched the cold tiles in the hall, she followed him into the kitchen, where the noise was coming from, and there were the two shutters flying back and forth against the wall, wrenched loose because, she guessed, she hadn't attached them properly. There, also, was a diaspora of broken glass: several of the panes had shattered where the wind must have hurled some branch or gravel against them.

'Stop there, Ma, the place is full of splinters.' Authoritatively, Finn held up a hand, shining the torch into the debris. 'Uh, oh – there's water here too, getting in from somewhere.'

Aileen peered, and there was indeed water, trickling from – where? She couldn't make out where, but it was spreading even as she watched, forming a horribly fascinating puddle on the floor.

'My God, we'll be flooded – is the phone still working, who on earth do you call in this kind of emergency – ?' Even as she said it Aileen realised the futility of the thought; she had no idea what number you dialled or what you said when it was answered. All she could do was pray that the water wouldn't get any worse.

'Let's get some more candles going, Finn, try to fix those shutters and mop up this mess.'

'Yeah – wow. We're so high up here, at least water should drain away, but it must be something else down in the village. It'll be afloat if this continues.' Peering out of the broken window, he looked out and down towards Mézalas, which was invisible in the Stygian dark.

Aileen wasn't worried about the village, which presumably enjoyed the advantage of having heard and understood the weather forecast – and was used to this kind of weather, maybe? Could this sort of thing possibly happen often? There had been nothing about storms or floods or lightning in those sunny, flower-festooned magazines. What did worry her was the roaring noise, the combined force of wind and rain that sounded as if they were trying to kick the house down. In the dark, with this water pooling on the floor, the whole scenario was infernal.

Turning away from the window, Finn squinted at her through the gloom. 'Here, leave this to me. I'll light the candles and clear up the glass, you go upstairs and get dressed, there's no point in trying to sleep through this racket.'

That was for sure. Picking her way back out through the hall, she was groping for the staircase when suddenly a thundering bang froze her in her tracks, brought her hand flying petrified to her mouth. The noise was right beside her, so loud it made her heart skip a beat and her mouth drain dry, and then with a gasp she realised what it was – somebody thumping, at this ungodly hour, on the thick wooden front door.

Quivering, she was unable to open it; her hands were trembling and the key was invisible. 'Finn' she croaked, 'Finn, come here, quick.'

No response. He couldn't possibly hear her. But the banging persisted, and he must have heard that, because without warning he was standing beside her, torch in hand, reaching to open the lock. Horrified, she tried to stop him.

'No! Finn, it's the middle of the night, we don't know who it is—'

'Ma' he said laconically, 'get a grip. Burglars don't usually knock on front doors. It's probably just one of the neighbours has a problem or something.'

So saying, he turned the key, unbolted the door and swung it open, to reveal a hefty moustached man of about fifty, swathed in oilskins, carrying a big, industrial-strength torch.

For a moment, they all blinked at each other. And then the man launched into a flow of French, pointing repeatedly at Finn, then to himself, then down to the village. Baffled, but intrigued despite herself, Aileen hauled him into the hall, where he stood dripping, babbling and stabbing at Finn.

Well, she thought, isn't this a lovely way to meet the neighbours. Standing here in my dressing gown in the dark with the wind all but stripping me starkers – God, it'll take the roof off, at this rate! At least Finn is dressed, but what must the pair of us look like? What is this man trying to tell us?

'I think' Finn guessed finally, 'he's trying to tell us there's some problem in the village, and he wants me to go down there with him.'

'What? Is he mad? In these conditions? Finn, you're not to budge. You're not setting foot out in that storm.'

For a moment, he thought about it. And then he looked hard at her. 'Ma, you said you wanted us to integrate here, right? Settle in and get to know people? Well, this strikes me as a good way to get to know them. Clearly somebody needs a hand with something.'

'But – Finn – no –' Even as she grasped at him he pulled

away from her, nodded at the man with a gesture indicating he should wait, and vanished in search of waterproof gear. Left looking at the squelching man, Aileen floundered hopelessly, still uncertain who he was.

'*Là*' he barked suddenly, grabbing her arm and spinning her round to face sideways, until the penny dropped: he must live in the next house down the hill, the old limestone one with goats tethered in the field around it. Then, firmly, he started making come-hither signs, getting-dressed signs, until finally she understood that he wanted her to accompany him as well as Finn, for some completely incomprehensible reason – God, there wasn't going to be an earthquake, was there, some awful disaster everyone had been warned of on the news? Hastily, gathering her wits, she nodded and raced upstairs to get dressed.

Identifying clothes by touch, she threw on a random assortment and went back down to find Finn bundled into an equally bizarre ensemble, but one that looked sturdy at any rate, and the man grunted in satisfaction as they trooped out in file behind him, following his lead.

'Where is he taking us? What's happening? Finn, do you understand any— ?'

'Not a word' he conceded, 'we'd better just play along and see what happens.'

A broken leg is what will happen, she thought as she tripped along in the mud and the murk, grabbing at Finn as they scrambled away from Le Mas, tacking across the fields, climbing a drystone wall with the rain peppering them like bullets, fumbling through wildly flapping branches, clutching at each other until, eventually, they stumbled into sight of what appeared to be the man's house. Light glowed in its windows, confirming Aileen's suspicions: a back-up generator. So, power cuts are frequent, then, are they? Great.

When they reached the door the man shoved it open and they tumbled inside, spluttering and streaming, in a sodden heap. A dark woman appeared in the hall, about her own age but looking older in a faded overall, her hair pinned haphazardly up, her buttony eyes dark, bright and scrutinising.

Nodding at Aileen, she beckoned to her, while the man who was apparently her husband directed his attention to Finn, gesturing incomprehensibly in the direction of the village. The general idea seemed to be that he, and Finn, were going down to it.

'No' Aileen said to her son, 'it's far too dangerous, you don't know what he wants you to do—'

'I won't do anything stupid' he replied in a tone she'd never heard before, 'but meanwhile I think the idea is that you're to stay here with his wife.'

Stay here? Well, at least it was warm and bright – had these people seen the lights extinguished in Le Mas, and decided to offer shelter to their unknown new neighbours? No, Aileen thought, this has more to do with Finn, it's him they want, I've only been brought here because I could hardly be left alone in such a storm. Jesus, I wish Shona were here to tell us what's going on, why this man wants Finn to go out with him! I don't want him to go. But he looks as if he's going to go – is he off his head, what's come over him?

Yes. Even as she stood gazing imploringly at him, he nudged her towards the waiting woman, gave her a look that said 'don't worry', turned on his heel and followed the man back out into the storm. Clutching her throat, fighting an urge to haul him back, Aileen stood immobilised as the door banged behind him.

The woman beckoned again, leading the way into an untidy, all-purpose living room where a table stood strewn with the remnants of supper. Hustling a snoozing dog off a battered armchair, she gestured at her to sit in it, and nodded satisfied when she did. What now, Aileen wondered, how are we going to communicate? I suppose a pot of tea will be produced anyway, and we'll muddle along from there. Maybe she'll be able to explain where her husband has taken my son, and why.

Sure enough, the woman disappeared into the depths of the house, and Aileen sat waiting for a long time before it dawned on her that she had been mistaken. There would be no tea, no befuddled attempts at conversation, because the woman had simply gone back to bed for the night, leaving her to doze in the armchair as best she could.

All night the rain pummelled down, all night the wind screamed and thunder exploded in snarling bursts around the farmhouse; this storm, Aileen thought incredulous, is absolutely epic. Biblical. Did Finn manage to fix those shutters before he left, or are we going to find Le Mas awash in the morning, pulverised?

Not that the house matters, compared to my son. How dare these people just – just kidnap him, like this! Dragoon him into heaven knows what? I suppose I'd know what if he and I both had mobile phones . . . but there must be a phone somewhere in this house surely, why is nobody ringing with any news? Are the lines down? I wish I knew where he is, what's going on, is he all right. What made him agree to do this, whatever it is? I never saw such a look on his face before, so – so determined. Even his voice was determined, as if he'd made up his mind and there was no point in arguing. For all his faults, this is the first time I've ever known him to defy me outright, do anything foolhardy.

There's no point in trying to sleep. Even if this armchair were comfortable, which it certainly isn't, I'm too worried. How could that woman have simply gone off to bed and left me here? Is she not worried about her husband? Has she not a hospitable bone in her body, that she wouldn't even try to talk, or offer a drink, or anything? It's a wonder she even left the light on. But how about a towel to dry my hair, madame, or a rug to keep me warm, or even a bed for the night – all out of the question, huh?!

Well, wait till you come to my house some fine day, just you wait. You can whistle for your warm welcome, madame.

Oh, Finn! Be careful! You might not be the most perfect son in the world, but you're the only one I've got!

Aileen had no idea what time it was when the farmer's wife appeared at her elbow next morning, looking accusing as if she should have woken hours ago. Following her indicating finger, she turned to see a steaming pot on the table, bread and butter; evidently breakfast was grudgingly available. Or France's version of it at least, which did not include sizzling sausages, bacon, mushrooms or any of the other items for which she was suddenly ravenous.

Stiff, damp and instantly thinking of Finn, she cupped her hand telephone-shape to her ear, miming at the woman: any news?

Amazingly, the woman nodded. Somewhere, some invisible phone must have rung. 'C'est bon' she said, with a shrug that verged on approval. Just two words: but they made Aileen go weak at the knees, relief flooding through her as she muttered silent thanks to whatever deity had protected Finn, and even managed to smile at Madame.

After a bowl of hot chocolate and some buttered bread she felt better, enough to get up and go to the window for a weather update. At last it had stopped raining, and the wind had abated, but the sky was still pewtery. On the grass outside she could see strewn debris from the storm, garden furniture upturned, a watering can flung amidst the chickens, an enigmatic rubber boot being chewed by a goat, several slates torn off the roof of the shed.

'I should go home' she said to the woman, pointing to Le Mas, but the woman shook her head, saying something about '*électricité*' which made Aileen wonder how, if she needed an electrician, she would get hold of one. Even if she could decipher the Yellow Pages, which seemed to be listed in some kind of code, she was entirely incapable of conducting a phone call. Oh, well. At least Finn was safe, which was the only thing that really mattered this morning.

But where was he? For an hour or more Aileen had no choice but to potter about the house with her taciturn hostess, helping to wash dishes, sweep floors, peel vegetables for soup and do all the morning chores, which were dreary without any chat to liven them up. If there were any other members of the family there was no sign of them, maybe because Monsieur and Madame were old enough to have grown-up children who'd left home. Children of Finn's age, probably off doing something with software in Toulouse or Montpellier, sleeping soundly in comfy beds last night while Finn Hegarty was dragooned into some kind of territorial army.

It was nearly noon before – at last! – she heard male voices, looked out the window and saw him a hundred yards down the hill, coming up it on foot with Monsieur, both of them draped in khaki oilskin capes they hadn't had before. For God's sake, would nobody even give them a lift after they'd been out all night? But they didn't sound perturbed, or even tired: incredibly they sounded jovial, she could hear gruff laughter as if some kind of communication were in progress.

In they trudged, and she nearly fainted when she saw the state of Finn, filthy, caked in mud, with a massive bruise under his left eye, his clothes reduced to rags. If she hadn't known him, she'd have been afraid of him: he looked like some wild creature dragged from the jaws of a rottweiler. Not that Monsieur's condition was much better, but at least he didn't have a bruise like Finn's. Flying to her son, she scooped him into a hug, not caring how embarrassed he might be.

But he didn't recoil. Instead he hugged her back, grinned and said 'Howya, Ma' as the farmer's wife sprang into action, trundling in with piles of towels, indicating that he – unlike his mother – was invited to take a hot shower. Soon, she gestured, hot soup would be served; he was to make himself at home. Meanwhile, without even bothering to wash his pitch-black hands, her tattered husband delved into a cupboard to produce a bottle and two tiny glasses.

Aileen stared as the glasses were filled, slammed down on the table, lifted up, clinked and drained. Swallowing the contents in a gulp, Monsieur slapped Finn on the back, poured him another shot and beamed at Aileen, saying something unintelligible but clearly approving. At some stage of the last twelve hours, it would appear that Finn had made a friend.

'But Finn, where were you? What were you doing? I've been worried sick – how did you get that bruise – tell me what's been going on!'

For a moment he studied the murky liquid in his glass. Then, like the older man, he knocked it back in one gulp. Then he turned to her.

'I've been working' he said, 'with the fire brigade.'

'Fire brigade?'

'Yeah. The village was flooded last night – so were several others. They were really short-handed. Apparently this hill used to act as a sort of dam, but since it's been deforested the water runs down off it into Mézalas, which fills up like a bucket. Raoul here is an auxiliary fireman and the captain rang him to tell him he was needed, as well as his son who's also a volunteer. But the son – his name's Paul – is away at college in Toulouse, so Raoul thought of me. He'd seen me chopping logs at Le Mas and thought I might be able to give a bit of a hand. So I did.'

'What – what did you do, exactly?'

Madame intervened with her tureen of soup, and from the alacrity with which he took a steaming bowl, Aileen saw that her son was starving. Half the bowl and half a loaf of bread were despatched before he spoke again.

'At first I sandbagged houses with Raoul here. It wasn't much use though, the water was rising faster than we could work, people were getting trapped, some of them even climbed out windows and up on roofs . . . so the next job was to start rescuing them.'

'How?'

'Well, up on ladders, of course! You know those wind-up ones the fire engines have.'

Aileen closed her eyes. Those huge ladders that unfolded into infinity, forty foot high or more?

Finn grinned. 'We don't all suffer from vertigo, Ma! I didn't mind, I just went up with the other lads, there were dozens of us, and in the end we got half the village out. They're all down in the community centre, their houses are wrecked but at least they're safe, the town hall is organising food and clothes and stuff for everyone.'

Nonchalantly, he picked up his bowl and swallowed the rest of his soup while Raoul, with a kind of paternal pride, tried to communicate further details of what exactly had happened. Try as she did to follow, Aileen couldn't grasp what he was saying, but she did gather that Finn had acquitted himself honourably, and that Raoul was most impressed with his young neighbour.

'Well' she said, 'I'm very glad you're safe. Now let's get you home, you need to change and get some sleep.'

'Yeah. Okay. But I'll shower here in case there's no hot water at home.'

Standing up, helping himself to towels, off he went, escorted by Madame proffering an armload of clothes which, presumably, belonged to her absent son. Raoul delved into the cupboard, extracted a third glass, filled it from his unlabelled bottle and shoved it across the table at Aileen. Then, lifting his own, he proposed a toast – to her son, apparently. Incredulous, she made out the words '*courageux*' and '*exceptionnel*'.

Finn? Finn Hegarty? She could hardly believe her ears. The whole scene seemed surreal as she obediently raised her glass, clinked it against her newly genial neighbour's and sipped its enigmatic contents.

Uhhh! Spluttering, her eyes watering, she nearly choked, and Raoul laughed. A rough-and-ready man, who didn't look as if any amount of scrubbing would ever get him clean, he appeared to be seeing her properly for the first time, acknowledging her as the mother of the young lad who'd pitched in to help the village in its soggy plight.

'*Bienvenu*' he said suddenly, and she knew what that meant even though nobody had said it before. Welcome.

In a kind of hypnosis, Shona watched the waters of her career swirling down the drain. By the time the case ended, she knew she was going to lose: and yet the verdict, the clinical finality of it, hit her like a brick.

'I'm so sorry' Emily said as they emerged stunned from the courtroom, flanked by her outraged parents who were already talking 'appeal'. Shona could scarcely find words for any of them; all she could see looming before her was an endless vista of horror. Working with Terry O'Hagan – smirking this minute as he swept out on his tide of victory – was going to be unbearable. She would not be sacked, but neither would she ever be promoted. She would never market any hotels, never get a pay rise, never get one step further up the ladder of the tourism industry. She had been the wronged party, but Terry O'Hagan was the victor, and he would never, ever let her forget it.

'No' she said suddenly to her parents, 'I won't appeal. There's no point.'

'But why not? Shona, you have to –'

'No' she repeated flatly, in a tone that made her mother frown.

'But then what will you do? You can't possibly continue to work in that office with that man under these circumstances.'

'No. I can't. And I won't.'

Everyone looked at her, but something in her face forestalled them from asking her what, then, she would do instead.

'Tell you what' her father said with forced cheer, 'why don't I take us all to lunch. Let's talk this over and see what we can come up with.'

For his sake Shona agreed to lunch, but in the restaurant she steered the conversation adamantly away from the court case, which was over and done with, and from her future, which also seemed to be over and done with. Instead she chatted resolutely about anything and everything else, longing for the moment when she could go home, shut herself in the bathroom and throw up, purge herself of the nausea swirling all the way down from her head to her heart.

As suddenly as it had deteriorated, the weather improved again, with such promise of spring that Aileen would have thought she'd imagined the storm had it not been for the question it raised: where did you get a generator and how did you go about installing it?

'I'll ask Raoul' Finn volunteered, 'since he already has one.'

And, to her amazement, he did, setting off with all the vocabulary he would need, gleaned from a dictionary and scribbled on a scrap of paper. He was gone for over an hour, and Aileen was glad of it; even if she still knew nobody, at least Finn seemed to be getting a foot inside France's barely-open door. In his absence Le Mas was visited without warning by Aude Villandry, the inspector from the tourism office. Hastening out to meet her in the drive, Aileen wondered whether she was supposed to kiss the brisk and surprisingly young woman who emerged from a trendy VW Beetle. French etiquette was such a murky business, quicksand into which you could sink without trace.

But no. The dark, petite Aude shook hands in a crisp, eminently unkissable way, clasping a clipboard on which Aileen could see a long, long list of boxes to be ticked. On the point of offering tea, she decided against it: Aude looked like the kind of person who might construe it as attempted sabotage. Pretty as she was, with the diamond brightness of youth, her aura radiated steely purpose, her glossy hair shone like a warrior's helmet, her nut-brown eyes gleamed with zeal.

Grimly, Aileen gritted her teeth as she led the suited, shirted young woman inside, thinking already how different she was from Shona Fitzpatrick, who on the day they first met had sat down at the kitchen table and chatted for fully twenty minutes before asking, with a friendly smile, to be shown around the house. She'd made notes as she went, but she hadn't peppered her paper with bullet-points as Aude now began to do, frowning when she saw the shutter swinging off the kitchen window.

'The storm' Aileen explained, 'and me. I'm not used to shutters. My son is going to fix it this afternoon.'

At least that was what she hoped she was saying, groping frantically for the words, unable to tell whether the impassive

Aude understood or not. An X went into a check-box, and Aileen winced: Shona would kill her if she didn't pass this test. Shona who hadn't rung for a few days now, to update her on the progress of the court case which sounded as if it was going badly – so badly that she didn't dare enquire.

Aude tapped her pen on her clipboard and spoke in clipped English. 'Hair dryers? Trouser presses? Tea trays? You have all these facilities in each bedroom?'

'Yes' Aileen nodded, feeling like a schoolgirl producing homework, 'I mean, not yet, but I will have.'

Another X went into another box. Looking as if she expected Le Mas to be fully fitted and furnished, even though it wasn't due to open for another six weeks, Aude marched into the sitting room, and swept her gaze around it like a search-light.

'No television? You have no television, for your guests?'

Aileen bridled. 'No – not even for myself or my son, yet. But I will have the television before I have the guests, don't worry.'

Looking sceptical, Aude X'd yet another box, and suddenly Aileen wanted to punch this neat, petite little terrier, who at half her age clearly had no idea how much time it took to get started in a foreign country, set up a business and make a house a home. I hate this little witch, she thought, screwing her smile to her face as Shona had directed, leading the way to the bathrooms which no, sorry, didn't actually have any towels in them yet, or even soap for that matter.

'You're a little early' she said as apologetically as she could, 'I wasn't expecting you for another week or two.'

Aude did not look up from her checklist. 'It was lucky I could fit you in today. There are seven new guesthouses this season in the Mézalas area. I must inspect them all this week and again next month.'

Next month? Oh, God. 'Oh, everything will be well under

277

control by next month. Right down to the chocolates on the pillows!'

She laughed. Aude did not. 'Chocolates? But that is not a requirement. Chocolates are hotel standard. Four-star hotel.'

Yes. Yes, I know that, you prim little prat. It was only a tiny joke, to ascertain for sure that you are absolutely devoid of all sense of humour. Now that we've established that you are, why don't you take that clipboard of yours and—

'Hey, Ma. I've got all the info on the generator. Who's the bird?'

Whirling round, Aileen found Finn standing at the bottom of the staircase staring up at her, and Aude staring down at him, aghast.

'This is – this is your son?' Pointing to him with the end of her biro, she looked like an industrial buyer rejecting a particularly unpalatable consignment of produce.

Yes. Yes, Mlle Villandry, this is my son. I'm so used to him I don't even see the purple hair any more – what there is of it – nor the spotty skin nor the biker boots nor even that unfortunate T-shirt he's chosen to wear this morning, with that slogan on it. *Screw Saddam*, indeed. And screw you too, Mlle Villandry.

'Yes, this is my son, Finn. Finn, this is Aude Villandry from the tourism office. She speaks excellent English.' Which means, you clumsy oaf, she probably knows you've just called her a 'bird' and Le Mas's grading is out the window.

Laconically, Finn grinned up the stairs. 'Howya.'

Aude peered down at him. 'How are you.' But Finn, evidently uninterested in any health bulletin, was already vanishing into the kitchen, and Aude, visibly appalled, was turning saucer-eyed to his mother.

'He lives here?'

'Yes. Of course. He's my son. I'd be lost without him.'

278

Only as she said it did Aileen suddenly realise the truth of it, how very lost she would be here without Finn, no matter how distasteful he might look to strangers. Apparently Aude thought he would look extremely distasteful to them, because she was now jotting at speed on her notepad in tiny code-like script.

Well, Aileen sighed to herself, that's that, then, isn't it? There isn't even any point in showing her round the garden, where we're planning to put the jasmine or herb garden or organic veggies. She's writing off Le Mas, and Shona is going to go ballistic, and I'm going to be flown back to Ireland in a jamjar.

It was late evening, and Aileen was sitting at the kitchen table wrestling with figures on bits of paper, trying to work out some way of affording the generator that would, Finn said, be extremely expensive to buy and equally expensive to install. Even with Shona splitting the cost – assuming Aude Villandry did not simply close down Le Mas before it even opened – it was going to be a major, unforeseen investment. And Joe, she suspected, was going to be a major obstacle to getting it. He would explode when he heard these figures.

When the phone rang, she cowered. 'Finn, answer that, and if it's your father tell him I – I'll call him back later.'

Finn picked up the phone. 'Oh, hi. Yeah, she's here, hang on, I'll get her.'

It was Shona. Marginally less awful than Joe, but still, she wasn't going to like these figures either. Nor the news of that tourism office inspector's visit. Reluctantly, Aileen went to the phone.

'Sho, how are you? How's the court case going, is there any— ?'

Shona's voice cut through her sentence like a blade. 'It's over. Can you be at the airport at two tomorrow afternoon?'

'What?'

'Carcassonne airport. My flight gets in at two.'

'But—'

'Think of me as your first customer. A distraught, shattered customer who urgently needs a holiday and is booking into Le Mas.'

'Oh, Jesus. You've lost?'

'Yes. Lost the case, and everything that goes with losing. Please, Aileen – pick me up?'

Never before had Aileen heard Shona speak in such a tone, a tone trembling with tension – even tears? This was not her business partner speaking, this was her friend, the friend who'd been assaulted by her boss and now, apparently, raped by him as well. Rape did not have to be physical to do what it was doing to Shona's voice.

'I'll be there. Two o'clock. In the meantime – look, don't worry, get a grip and try to get some sleep—'

'Well, actually, sleep is not in my plans at all, Aileen. Crys has invited me round to her house, where I intend to spend the night face down on the floor with a hopefully enormous bottle of brandy. Or whiskey. Or both.'

Shona, until now, had always been the busiest, briskest woman Aileen knew, cheery and sensible, not at all the type to wear her heart on her sleeve. But one look at her, as she came off the plane, told Aileen how gutted she was by the loss of her court case. Hefting her holdall, she came forward with a taut, wan smile, and Aileen rushed forward to sweep her into a huge hug, full of sympathy that was laced with almost maternal concern. Although only six years separated them in age, Shona looked stripped, today, of confidence. Wearing no make-up, dressed in jeans and a jacket that any teenager could have worn, she looked almost childlike, her eyes radiating vulnerability.

'Come on. Let's get you home.'

Obediently Shona followed her out to the car and they set off, through the town of Carcassonne at which, today, she scarcely glanced. Unsure what to say, Aileen said little until they were well out into the luminous plains of Languedoc-Roussillon.

But eventually she had to ask. 'Have you been sacked? Is your job gone?'

'No. I haven't been sacked. I've resigned.'

'What?! But – oh, Shona – you should have gone straight back into your office with your head held high, toughed it out, your colleagues will have forgotten this whole episode in no time—'

'Yes. Probably they will. But I never will.'

Aileen eyed her. 'Was it that bad?'

'It was grotesque. There is no way on this planet I could ever – *ever* – work with that unspeakable ape again. He would have gloated from here to eternity.'

Yes. Well. Aileen supposed she could understand that. 'But how did he win? I mean, okay, you hit him, but he did assault you – ?'

'Yes. I admitted what I'd done and he denied what he'd done. Simple strategy, really. And successful.'

Aileen felt sickened. While she didn't personally know any people like Terry O'Hagan, she knew they existed; people on the make or take, people with no principles at all, no regard for who they hurt, what they cost, no interest in anything or anyone bar their own precious, lying, cheating, tainted selves. Without taking her eyes off the road, she touched Shona's shoulder.

'Oh, Sho. I'm so sorry. I'm angry for you, and disgusted.'

Wryly, Shona smiled. 'Thanks, Aileen. I appreciate that. But there's enough anger and disgust in me, right now, to fill Le

Mas to the rafters! I couldn't stay in my little flat, I felt as if I'd explode. I stayed all night with Crys, and then first thing this morning I rang the office, gave in my notice. The "human resources" manager, as he is ludicrously called, wanted it in writing. I told him I didn't give a fiddler's what he wanted, and got straight on the plane.'

'I'm glad you did. I – I am selfishly delighted to see you! Horrified by what's happened to you, but so happy to have you back.'

Shona frowned, a little anxiously. 'Why? Is everything not okay?'

'Oh – yes, it is. Nothing is wrong at all. It's just that . . . well, maybe I miss my friends a bit. And my husband and sister and mother. I didn't realise the first month or two in a foreign country could be so – so isolated.' Deliberately, she kept her tone light.

'H'mm. Everyone says that about France. The first ten years are the toughest.'

'Ten *years*?!?' Aileen gasped, and Shona smiled grimly.

'Yeah. The French are so reserved, it takes years to get to know them. You wouldn't want to be holding your breath to be asked round for a cup of tea or a bite of supper. Or even a chat – but you'll be able to chat them up once your French improves. The ice should melt a bit at that point. They actually quite like the Irish, if you were to hold a St Patrick's day party for instance you'd find them all on the doorstep like a shot.'

Aileen considered. 'Well, I would, if I knew anyone to invite! The only person we've got to know so far is Raoul, our neighbour. Or, to be accurate, Finn has got to know him. I'm glad one of us is getting somewhere with someone.'

'Finn? How did Finn get to know him?'

So Aileen told her, and Shona struggled to hide her surprise. 'Well, good lad Finn, that was a brave and decent thing to do! And what about this Raoul, does he maybe have a wife you could get pally with?'

'He has a wife, yes. One I could get pally with, no.'

'Oh. Okay. I get the picture. And what about the storm, did it do any damage to Le Mas?'

Aileen hesitated. She didn't want to start throwing problems at Shona in the state she was in today. But suddenly Shona grinned, as if flickering to life. 'Come on, spit it out! What happened?'

'Nothing serious – just a broken window and a bit of a flood in the kitchen, which receded back wherever it came from. But the power went off – Sho, that can't happen when we're open for business. We're going to have to buy a back-up generator, and they're fierce expensive.'

'As in?'

'As in a good few thousand. I really don't know where we're going to get it. Plus, some bills have come, for water I think, and bin collection, even though you've already paid the rates – I feel kind of fleeced in France, already! They seem to charge for everything bar the air we breathe.'

'Yeah. And they're probably working on that.'

'Probably. It kinda takes the fun out of things a bit. I'd no idea it would all be so expensive.'

Shona smiled. 'I hear that lots of foreigners leave France after a year or two, throw up their hands in disgust and move back home. Mostly because they didn't research it enough before they came.'

She didn't sound at all accusatory, nor did Aileen think she meant to be, but she did grasp the truth of that remark. All her visions of France had revolved around sunshine and meadows and wine and pretty houses, a lovely laid-back lifestyle that had nothing whatever to do with realities like bills or storms or frosty natives or mountainous paperwork.

'I suppose maybe I didn't do enough homework. Which reminds me – the inspector from the tourism office called.'

'Oh, yes, Aude. I hope she was helpful?'

'She was a wagon. A horrible little jobsworthy with a check-list and an attitude. Half my age and twice as cocky.'

Shona closed her eyes and groaned. 'Oh, no . . . Aileen, we have to get on with her, if we want her to send us any business.'

'I know. That's why I gritted my teeth and was icily polite. But you should have seen the way she looked at Finn – as if he were a dog with fleas. I wanted to punch her.'

'Jesus. Tell me you didn't?'

Suddenly Aileen laughed. 'No, I didn't – actually do it, I mean! But she's coming back next month.'

'Well, we'll just have to seduce her somehow then. But don't worry, I know this business, I can do it – her work was my work, until now!'

After a pause, Aileen bit her lip. 'But Sho . . . will you still be here next month? If you've quit your job, you'll have to find another, you can't hide out here in a sulk – not unless you've won the Lotto?'

'No. Right now I don't think I could win the first round of a TV gameshow. First Brendan dumps me, now my career's up in smoke . . . where am I going wrong, huh? If you know, Aileen, would you mind telling me – what the hell am I doing wrong?'

Not immediately answering, Aileen thought about it, but couldn't find any reply. Shona simply seemed to be having a wretchedly bad run of luck. She was talented, she was attractive, and she was getting nowhere. Which must be hugely frustrating for her, and miserably dispiriting. Not to mention a tragic waste of someone so bright and eager, with so much to offer.

'I don't honestly know, Sho. All I can offer is sympathy and support and – oh, God!'

Recoiling from the road ahead, she groaned as the car rounded a bend into sight of the bridge, the huge Roman viaduct she dreaded driving over. Every time she drove to or from the airport, she had nightmares the night before or the night after or both, sweating and writhing. Curiously, Shona surveyed her.

'Go on. Look at those other cars already on it. It's perfectly safe.'

'I know. But I hate it. I absolutely loathe and detest it and I can't help it and I can't explain it. Why – why don't we swop places and you drive over?'

'Because, Aileen, it is part of living in France. You have to conquer it. Now, just get into the inside lane and over we go.'

Grimacing, almost whimpering, Aileen nodded and nudged the car very, very slowly onto the bridge. Of course Shona was right, this bridge somehow had to be assimilated into her personal landscape, but still – oh, Jesus. Oh, sweet Jesus. Longing to shut her eyes, clutching the wheel, she tasted blood on her inner lip as the car tottered along like a terrified tortoise.

'Keep going . . . look straight ahead . . . think of something else.'

Dymps. That was what Aileen thought of, for no apparent reason: her sister Dymps who was coming to visit next month. Inexplicably gripped with sheer longing to see her, she kept her image fixed in her mind until – phewwww – they were finally over the viaduct, and she pulled immediately into a lay–by.

'Sorry. I always have to pull in here, to pull myself together.' She was actually sweating, and Shona could see that her vertigo was as real as it was acute. 'Well done' she said, 'and remember, it'll get easier every time.'

'No' Aileen replied firmly, 'it won't. It gets worse every time. Oh, what made me come here, why didn't I move to Holland!'

Deciding to make light of what was clearly a genuine problem in Aileen's mind, Shona laughed. 'Well, you're stuck with France now, and it's stuck with you!'

'Yeah. I don't know which of us is the winner there. Now, let's get home, I could murder a cup of tea.'

Tea. Well, Shona supposed, some people leave their native habits at home, and some bring them with them. Tea isn't very French, but it is very Aileen. And very good for this hammering hangover that is doing my head in.

Shona all but threw herself on Le Mas when they reached it, taking a key from her pocket as she ran to her little gîte, opened its door and hurled herself inside.

'Oh, *yes!* My lovely mas . . . it's so good to be back.' Coming in behind her, Aileen watched as she touched the walls, breathed in the air and then squealed as something caught her eye at the window. 'Look! Daffodils! Coming up already!'

Turning to look, Aileen saw that she was right. She hadn't noticed the daffs herself, which were only green furled shoots as yet, but they were definitely there, poking up impish noses through the red earth. A heartening sight, and a welcome for Shona right enough. But—

'You're not going to stay here, are you? I mean, sleep in the gîte?'

Shona thought for a moment. 'Yes. I think I am. I don't want to be in your way all the time, especially not in the mood I'm in at the moment. If thoughts could kill, Terry O'Hagan would be stone dead today.'

Aileen was conscious of some small disappointment. 'But

the house is much more comfy, you've hardly any furniture in here.'

'Oh, there's enough. What I need more than anything right now is space – just for a little while, until I calm down and start thinking what to do next. What to do with the rest of my accursed life, that keeps going wrong no matter what I do.'

'Oh, Shona! Don't start getting depressed. The darkest hour is always just before dawn. Things will buck up, you'll see.'

'Yeah. Or maybe I'll just shoot myself.'

She laughed archly as she said it, but Aileen saw that she really was upset, and could hardly blame her. 'You can't do that. You have to start figuring out how we're to afford our new generator. Come on up to the house now and let's put on the kettle.'

So they went up, and there was Finn, with the kettle already boiling. Aileen nearly fainted. 'Tea? For us?'

'Yeah. I heard the car. Knew you'd want a cup, you always do – hi Shona, what's all the news from mother Ireland?'

She had to laugh. 'Bog mother Ireland. Right now I am thrilled to be out of the whole bloody mess. Hey . . . this place is looking good!'

It was looking good, Aileen acknowledged; Finn had finished painting the walls and all the DIY jobs, while she had repositioned furniture, put up pictures, strewn cushions and throws that softened the look of the rooms, made them homey. With Finn standing here over the worktop, Barry's teabags in hand, the place even felt homey. Unbuttoning her jacket, she dropped it on the back of a chair and sat down.

'Well, I must say, it's lovely to come home to a cuppa – everything okay, Finn, while I was out?'

No answer. Instead, he shrugged awkwardly, and colour crept up his cheeks as he busied himself with the tea. Immediately, she sensed that something had happened. Which must be why he was making tea . . . to soften whatever blow was about to fall. Oh, God! He's twenty years of age, can I not even trust him on his own for one blessed afternoon?

Springing into mother mode, she eyeballed him. 'Come on – what is it? You may as well tell me and get it over with.'

Still he hesitated, laying out milk and mugs with slow, elaborate care. 'Well . . . okay' he sighed at length, 'it's a bit embarrassing, but I guess you'll find out anyway.' Pouring the tea, he put down the pot, went to a bench in the corner of the kitchen and, while Aileen waited full of dread, picked up a newspaper.

'The local rag' he muttered. 'Apparently it comes out once a week. Raoul brought it over while you were out.' Baffled, Aileen took it as if it contained something obscene – and there, in full colour on the front page, was a head-and-shoulders picture of himself. '*Finn Egarty*' said the misspelled caption, '*le jeune irlandais qui a sauvé la famille Louvel de leur maison inondée. Voir p.5.*'

Speechless, Aileen gazed at it. 'But – what are you doing – what does it mean – ?'

'Uh – I dunno – something to do with the floods – Shona here can probably translate it.' Scarlet, scratching at his forearm, he looked at her with a kind of bashful enquiry, and Aileen handed over the paper. Astonished, Shona read aloud. 'Finn Egarty, the young Irishman who saved the Louvel family from their flooded house. See page 5.' Turning to it, she found herself staring at another photo of Finn, standing this time with his arm around the shoulder of an older man, named as Raoul Lascaux, both of them muffled to the eyes in scarves, oilskins and boots, up to their knees in water in front of a huge ladder, grinning at the camera. For a moment they all gazed at it, and then Shona read on.

'In the absence of his son Paul, a regular volunteer with the fire brigade during the storms to which our region is increasingly prone, Captain Lascaux recruited the assistance of his new neighbour Finn Egarty during last Tuesday's emergency. The young Irishman (20) proved to be of invaluable help in rescuing all four members of the Louvel family, who were trapped on the roof of their house when the flood waters rose to a height of six metres. Despite violent winds and rain that almost obscured vision, M Egarty had no hesitation in permitting himself to be winched up to the roof, where he first secured Jean-Claude (4) and then his baby sister Isabelle (2) to a rope before carrying both infants down to safety. He then returned to the roof for their mother Françoise, and finally for their father Philippe, who later expressed his gratitude to, and admiration of, this courageous newcomer to Mézalas. The Louvel family was later housed overnight at the community centre along with the nine other families made homeless by the floods.

'While M Egarty speaks little French, he conveyed that he has no experience of rescue work but was very happy to assist the community in its emergency.'

Well. With a kind of awe, Shona fell silent, handing the newspaper back to Aileen, who sat looking first down at it and then up at her son, as if seeing some totally strange man who had materialised in her kitchen.

'You – you went up on a *roof* – you carried a full-grown man down a *ladder* – ?'

He waved a hand, looking genuinely mortified. 'Yeah, but it wasn't any big deal, the roof wasn't that high, the guy wasn't that heavy—'

'Finn. I have never seen this Mr Louvel, so I've no idea how heavy he might be, but I have seen the roofs in Mézalas and I know how high they are – oh, my God, if I'd known, I'd never have let you go out that night!'

'Ma, wouldja relax. I'm not a kid. Well able to cart a couple of snappers down a ladder, they were like a pair of dolls, I had them down in no time.'

'But you could have fallen – slipped – hurt yourself – !'

'Ma, I didn't, did I? So let's just forget this now, I only showed it to you so you wouldn't go ballistic if you saw it in the shops or round the place anywhere.'

She couldn't answer. Couldn't do anything only sit there holding the paper limply in her hand, tears rising in her eyes, thinking how horribly differently this might all have turned out. Thinking how she might have lost not one child, but two. And then, without a word, she got up, went around the table to Finn, took him in her arms and clasped him to her, holding him as if she would never let go.

Cringing, blushing, he gave her only two or three seconds before wriggling free, turning beseechingly to Shona as if she might rescue him. 'Ah, for God's sake, Ma, wouldja give over – Shona, tell her to knock it off.'

But Shona would do no such thing. Suffused with shame for all the awful things she had thought about Finn, about what a useless layabout he was, she looked at him and thought, there now, that's what you get for judging a book by its cover. I judged him when I was the one busy making a mess of my life, when he was the one who went out saving someone else's. Not just one life, but four, at huge risk to his own.

'Finn' she said, 'I owe you an abject apology. I haven't been very nice to you, and now all I can do is say how extremely sorry I am, and congratulate you and tell you that you are one hell of a guy. Your mother is so lucky to have a son she can be so proud of.'

'Oh, jaysus, wouldja all stop making such a fuss.' And then, spotting an escape route, he looked again at Shona. 'Uh – I know you've only just arrived, but if you wouldn't mind – I need a bit of help with something – ?'

'With anything. With pleasure. What is it?'

'It's Raoul. When he came over here with the paper he started on about something, but I couldn't make out what he was saying. D'you think you could come over with me to his house and ask him what it was?'

'Of course. I'll come right this minute. Have you any idea what it might be about?'

'Uh – well, I'm not sure – but I think maybe it was something about some kind of job.'

10

Who would have believed it? Aileen still hardly could, one morning three weeks later as she stood in the kitchen packing sandwiches for Finn's lunch. Like herself, he had yet to make the transition from sliced bread to baguettes, but he had made a far more important move: he had, against all the odds, got himself a job. Well, not official employment yet, as such, because first he had to do this training course, but even the training was turning out way better than anyone could have thought. Not only was it a sponsored scheme for youngsters like himself, which gave them pocket money while they were doing it, but somehow he seemed to be managing to communicate with the other lads on the course, and – most unbelievable of all – he was enjoying it. Joe, when he heard the news, had had to be practically stretchered off the phone.

Never in a million years would Finn have applied for such a course under his own steam, nor even known it existed. Raoul was the one who knew, who explained it all through Shona, who got the forms and signed him up for it. It was a course in roofing houses, a skill that made Aileen clutch her chest when she thought about its dangers, but Shona persuaded her that Finn must do it.

'Definitely! For lots of reasons! He'll be earning, he'll be learning, he'll be out of the house, meeting people his own age, picking up a bit of French – Aileen, this is a godsend, don't look a gift horse in the mouth!'

And so, seeing that she was right, Aileen didn't quibble. Suppressing her fear that Finn would fall off a roof and be killed, she slapped a smile on her face and said yes, isn't this great, isn't Raoul wonderful to think of it! As indeed Raoul was. Apparently, within hours of the newspaper appearing with the photo of Finn and himself in it, he had received a phone call from a man he knew, a builder called Gautier who was looking for roofing workers and reckoned that Finn Egarty could be exactly the kind of fellow he needed. And so a deal had been struck with this man: if Finn completed the month-long apprenticeship, he would be taken on by M Gautier, at a rate of pay that put the heart sideways in Aileen: it sounded literally like danger money. Nonchalantly, Finn asserted that heights didn't bother him at all, that the whole thing sounded pretty cool really, if only he had transport to get to it. Where-upon Raoul had offered the use of his absent son's motorbike, an offer Finn had seized with alacrity.

Now, two weeks into the course, he looked exactly the same, still wore his dayglo-Mohican hairstyle and aggressive clothes, but she could see something changing in him, something that gladdened her heart. Not only did he get up at seven each morning – a startling phenomenon – but he came back each evening in good form, with even a smile as he recounted his day's news. She couldn't make out how he was getting through the course in French, but he just shrugged and said it was more practice than theory, all you had to do was watch the instructor and the other guys. They worked in pairs, one throwing up the tiles to the roof and the other catching them, with a knack that was all in the wrist; a good roofing team could do a roof in two days flat. She prayed he was the one on the ground, but he preferred being the one on the roof, and she saw she was going to have to learn to live with that. The worry of it could hardly be any worse than the worry she'd endured for two years since he left school, about what he was going to do for a job: now he was finally on his way to getting one. On his way to getting a life, at last. Once or twice recently he'd even failed to show up for dinner, calling her to say he was staying out for a beer with 'the guys'. She hardly knew whether to laugh or cry, but decided she'd better go for the former.

'Ironic, isn't it?' Shona remarked wryly. 'A thirty-six-year-old experienced employee is out of work, while a twenty-year-old youth is snapped up. Sometimes I think John Cleese was right about the world being basically mad.'

But she said it without rancour, helping Finn with paper-work and the French he was now much keener to learn, and Aileen saw that Shona was relieved to be distracted from her own career hiatus. Having posted off her written resignation, she was lying low, licking her wounds and, Aileen noticed, spending very little money. Galvanised, Aileen whizzed round the house fixing all the things Aude Villandry wanted fixed, determined to get Le Mas into business and into profit as soon as possible. Soon, Joe would be arriving. Dymps and Tessie too, her first guinea pigs, who were instructed to bring over as much 'proper Irish bacon' as possible.

'Oh for heaven's sake' Shona exclaimed 'buy French bacon!' But Aileen wanted her breakfasts to be as Irish as possible, a feature that would entice custom, make people feel they were getting better value at Le Mas than at rival French establishments with their fecky little croissants. Meanwhile, whatever Shona might say, she was delighted to have her here; life became so much easier when someone understood what was going on, and so much cheerier with a friend working along-side. Within days of her arrival, Shona had shouldered all the administrative side of things, even been to see Aude Villandry 'just for a little chat'. What was discussed Aileen didn't dare ask, leaving Shona to handle something in which she had so much experience, feeling way better now that she had company. One evening they even went to a little concert down in Mézalas – just a local gig in the community centre, but it was enjoyable, it was 'out' as Tessie would say, and it held promise of some eventual social life. When Joe rang, she was conscious of sounding slightly less stressed over the phone – while he, in turn, sounded more enthusiastic now about coming over to join her. Why that should be she didn't know, but she was heartened by the newly firm note in his voice: 'Yes, I'll definitely be there on the third of April – rashers and all.'

Packing up Finn's sandwiches, now, she handed them to him with a smile, and he actually kissed her cheek as he dashed off, not noticing her following him out as he jumped onto Paul Lascaux's borrowed motorbike and zoomed away in a cloud of dust. Idiotically, she stood in the doorway waving at his vanishing back, watching him with renewed affection – there, see now, all my son needed was a chance! He may be no better than anyone else's, but he's no worse either, Raoul Lascaux seems to think the world of him at any rate. I must bring Raoul over a bottle of whiskey or something to thank him for his—

Oh, my God! What on earth – ? Clapping her hand to her mouth, stifling a scream, Aileen suddenly shot across to Shona's gîte as if jet-propelled and yelled up the stairs: 'Shona! Where are you – come quick – sweet Jesus, the garden – !'

Shona came running down, towelling her hair with one hand as she ran, tucking her shirt into her skirt with the other. 'What? What is it, what's wrong?'

Aileen grabbed her sleeve, looking as if someone had slapped her hard across the face. 'Come out here – look – *look*! The veggies, the herbs, the lawn, everything – they're every-where – oh my God, what is it?!?'

Swivelling her gaze around the land to either side of Le Mas, Shona stared: the entire two acres were decimated. Completely wrecked, spattered with hundreds of foot-high hills of earth, churned up as if by a JCB. In unison, struck speechless, they clutched at each other, ashen. Eventually, Shona found her voice.

'Moles. We've got fucking moles. Hundreds of them, by the looks of it.'

'Moles?' Aileen had heard of their existence, but never seen one in Ireland.

'Yeah. France is riddled with them. They do the same damage to gardens as termites do to houses . . . oh, Aileen, look at our lovely herb patch, our veggies we planted only last Sunday . . .'

She sounded ready to sob, and Aileen felt the same as she slowly surveyed the scene, absorbing the extent of the destruction, which was utterly comprehensive. These moles, which appeared to have arrived en masse overnight, had literally left no stone unturned; even the garden furniture that had been Shona's housewarming gift was tilting to starboard, the chair legs sunk into mounds of earth. The lovely landscape was, at a stroke, reduced to a lunar wasteland.

'But – but what are we going to *do*? Is there some kind of extermination service, or poison, or do we shoot them or what?'

Shona exhaled a long, grim sigh. 'Yeah. Some people do actually shoot them. In the château where I once worked as an au pair, they used to put down steel traps. Other people swear by pouring paraffin into the holes, or planting garlic, or millions of mothballs . . . but moles are such a scourge, I don't know if anything really works.'

'But Sho, we can't have the place looking like this, you'd think there'd been a rock festival or army manoeuvres – and our produce –'

'I know. I'll go over to Raoul to see what he suggests, and

then I'll go down to the garden centre – ring the Department of Agriculture – oh, bugger the little bastards!'

Looking outraged, she whirled away, leaving Aileen feeling immobilised and horribly deflated. Just when things had been going so much better, she thought, do we have to have this? Can we never take one step forward without having to take another step back? What possessed me to choose a country so endlessly peppered with bloody pitfalls?

Over the next couple of weeks they tried everything, but nothing worked; the moles were all but waving and jeering at them. 'It's heartbreaking' Aileen lamented, 'to see the house looking so lovely and the garden looking – looking as if tanks had been doing manoeuvres in it!'

Worse still, the grass began to grow with the advent of spring, but they were unable to mow it, couldn't get their expensive ride-on lawnmower in between the mounds of earth. When the garden centre recommended steel traps, the hideous job of emptying and re-arming them fell to Finn, who soon began to weary of having to do it every morning. On a long-term basis, this problem clearly could not go on.

'That's it' Shona stormed one day, 'I'm going to do what Raoul said and buy a gun. It's the only way.'

Aileen gasped at the prospect of having such a weapon in the house, but Shona was adamant. When it was acquired and licensed and Raoul showed her how to use it, she took to going out into the garden at dead of night, whereupon a series of explosions rang out, putting the heart across Aileen and littering the terrain with sleek, velvety black corpses, all of which had to be collected and incinerated. Uhhh! No longer in love with the view from the kitchen window, she decided that all the windows did, after all, need blinds. More expense.

'I feel' she confided one morning, 'as if we're living in

Afghanistan or the Amazon or somewhere – somewhere wild!'

'Well, I don't care if I've to sit out there with that gun every night for months' Shona retorted, 'I am going to win this battle and that's that.'

Her eyes gleamed with fiery resolve, and Aileen saw the extent of her tenacity: Shona could certainly not be accused of being a quitter. Which was odd, when she had quit her job, and was effectively hiding out here in France, with no hint of what she eventually intended to do. It must be hard, Aileen thought, to bounce back from losing both your man and your career. Shona needed time to think.

Meanwhile, Finn graduated from his training course into fulltime employment, and Aileen was intrigued when he came home on the evening he earned his first pay packet, toting a small black chunk of hardware.

'What's that?'

'It's called a digibox. When you plug it into your television, you can get free-to-air channels. BBC World, ITN, Sky and . . .' his grin widened, 'and RTE radio.'

She was electrified. 'RTE? Radio? You mean, Gerry Ryan, Marian Finucane, Joe Duffy, Pat Kenny – ?'

'Yeah. I got it cheap off one of the guys who's updating his gear. Now all we have to do is get a telly. The radio comes in through the telly.'

Feeling as if he had showered her with diamonds, she went out next day and, with reckless regard for yet further expense, bought a television. We needed one anyway, she reminded herself as her credit card slid through the slot. It's an investment. Joe will want this, he won't mind . . . will he? Oh, God. But I don't care. I'd sell my soul for RTE, I'll feel so much closer to home, to Mam and Tessie and everyone else who'll be listening to exactly the same programmes, now, at the same time. I'll be in touch with everything and everyone. Finn is just wonderful to find out about all this for me. And to buy that gizmo out of the very first money he's ever earned.

The first I know of, anyway, that's legal and clean and honest. Oh, it's such a relief that he's working! And settling in here, too, faster than I am myself if the truth be told . . . he's looking so much healthier and happier these days. Maybe it's the flexibility of youth. Maybe it's just taking me a bit longer, that's all, to rev up at my age. But then, I didn't come here just for me, did I? I came here primarily for my family, and I'm so much happier to see him so much happier. That part of the plan actually seems to be working, whatever about the other hassles.

Shona blew a fuse when she saw the digibox. 'RTE? For what? What's the point of coming to France to listen to Irish radio? You might as well have stayed in Galway.'

Digging in like the moles, Aileen held her ground. 'Well, we're all supposed to be living in the global village nowadays, aren't we? Which means we can have Irish radio, and Irish bacon for that matter, in France if we like – besides, if any Irish guests find their way to Le Mas, they'll be thrilled to hear RTE.'

'Then they might as well have stayed at home too.' Her tone was crusty, and Aileen put it down to her nocturnal vigil with the moles, which was wrecking her sleep pattern.

That, and maybe the fact that Finn was now contributing more to Le Mas's budget than she, who was sixteen years older and owned the house, was able to contribute herself?

Eventually the moles became less prolific, but the damage was done, the garden effectively rotovated, the young crops ruined. Arriving for her second visit in her zippy Beetle, Aude Villandry got out and stood gaping at the wasteland, awestruck.

Great, Aileen thought. That's Le Mas written off then, isn't it? She'll never send anyone to stay in this – this building site! Glumly, she trudged out to greet her. '*Bonjour*, Aude.'

'*Bon Dieu*' said Aude in return, scarcely able to wrench her gaze away from the destruction. 'Is this the work of *les taupes*?'

'Yes. We're at our wits' end. They've wrecked the lawn, the flowerbeds, vegetable and herb patches – everything. Just when I've got the house sorted, it's all perfect inside.'

Aude emitted a kind of whistle. 'I think perhaps you need my uncle . . . he has an extermination company.'

'Well, thank you for offering, but we've already investigated that. Professional help is way too expensive.'

'I see. But, Mme Hegarty, we cannot have this. I could not send anyone here in these conditions . . . I tell you what. Let me speak to my uncle, and see what I can arrange. He might be willing to . . . um . . . negotiate his fees a little, maybe even spread out payment over some months . . . at the end of the season . . . ?'

She raised an eyebrow, and Aileen raised one in return. Today's Aude sounded much more helpful than the Aude of last month. What had Shona said or done to her?

'Well – if you think he could – we'd certainly be happy to talk to him.'

'Then I will ask him. He will call you tonight. Now, may we go indoors?'

In they trooped, and once again Aude trotted round ticking her checklist, nodding like a little mandarin. 'Ah yes, this is much better. Le Mas is most attractive now. Once the moles are gone, the tourist office in Mézalas will be happy to send you guests. We will be grading your B & B as a three-star.'

She said it so calmly, it took a moment to sink in; Aileen all but clutched the wall until her wits returned, and she called out to Shona who was at a tactful remove, painting the shutters of her gîte. 'Sho! Come on up here, I'm opening a bottle of bubbly for Mlle Villandry!'

Only when they were gathered with glasses in hand, clinking and congratulating, did it dawn on Aileen that, for all the refinements that had been made to the house, perhaps the improvement that most impressed Aude was that Finn was no longer to be seen in it?

Aude despatched her uncle, a helpful and rather handsome man called Léo who, in turn, despatched the moles, agreeing to a staggered payment plan 'because I understand, *mesdames*, it is only your first season here. Everyone needs a little help in the beginning, *non*? But I warn you, the moles may come back, they are a permanent plague. Meanwhile, I think you must now have the garden repaired, landscaped . . .'

Even though she knew he was right, Aileen quailed. Joe had finally agreed to release some of Finn's college fund, but this was going to consume every penny that remained. Thank Christ Finn was working, now, and didn't need it! Much as she loved Le Mas, there were times when she wondered if she had created a monster.

On the plus side, she felt much more in touch with Ireland now she could hear Gerry Ryan and his colleagues, smiling to herself as she thought of the things she'd always taken for granted: radio, and rashers! And then, for no clear reason, she thought of Joe. Apart from his awful snoring, she was looking forward to having him here too . . . apparently absence actually did make the heart grow fonder. Down in the village, when she went shopping, she was further encouraged by her newly warm reception from the thawing shopkeepers. Everyone seemed to have heard what her son had done, she was recognised and saluted as his mother, and she also discovered that rescuing the Louvel family had been a far more difficult business than Finn had admitted. In the gale, an experienced fireman had tried first, and failed; the family had been in serious danger of being blown off their roof. Horrified as she was to hear the full extent of the episode, she felt a surge of pride when the grocer shook her hand and the baker gave her a beautiful cake 'to welcome you and your son to Mézalas, madame'.

Just before Easter, Shona suggested abandoning Le Mas one day to go for a picnic. 'Much as I'd love to lunch in some nice restaurant, we can't afford it. So let's take the car and the guidebook and find some field or river or something instead. This is your last chance of a break before your family arrive, hopefully followed by a steady stream of customers.'

In the end it was too warm to go very far, only down to the old Roman town of Elne, feeling summery as they embarked in light skirts and sandals. Near Elne they found a blossoming apricot grove in which to sit on a rug and spread a tablecloth, and as Aileen put on a straw sun hat she at last felt something of the romance that was, allegedly, France. It was a baby-blue spring day, their wicker basket was filled with delectable food, and she made up her mind to make the most of the foaming, fragrant drifts of petals, of the precious leisure, and of Shona's undivided attention.

Unpacking the basket, wallowing in the heady scent of apricot blossom, they talked little at first, lingering over cold asparagus they sucked in their fingers, chilled mineral water, some kind of plaited bread neither of them had tried before, spread with olive tapenade. It was very peaceful, they could hear no sound beyond the distant chug of a tractor, the faint drone of early bees amidst the trees.

'So' Shona ventured at length, 'what's the verdict so far, Aileen? Are you happy here? Is it everything you hoped for – or most of it, at least?'

Biting into a sweet cherry tomato, Aileen considered. She didn't actually want to talk about herself, she wanted to talk about Shona. But of course Shona had beaten her to it.

'Yeess . . . well . . . let's say, so far so good? It's been tougher than I thought, which makes me wonder what other surprises France might still have in store. It's cost a fortune, but hopefully we'll soon start earning some of that back. It's not friendly, yet Raoul Lascaux and Aude's uncle Léo have been so helpful . . . the weather's delicious, but when there is a storm it's horrendous . . . there's so much bureaucracy, yet the pace of life is beguiling . . . the countryside is gorgeous, yet there's been so little time to explore. Let's say that overall the balance is positive – particularly for Finn. It gives me such joy to see him looking happy, making friends, finding some purpose in life at last.'

'Mmm. He really does seem to be getting on his feet. It's you I sometimes wonder about.' Shona said it so idly, almost casually, that Aileen couldn't understand why the words made her feel a warm flush of – of what?

'Me? Oh, I'm fine. And will be even finer when Joe arrives with Dymps and Mam.'

Thoughtfully, Shona reached into the basket for a peach, found and bit into one, letting the juice trickle down her chin. 'Yes. You've been living for that, haven't you? You can't wait to see your family.'

What was that supposed to mean? 'Well – yes, of course I have! That's natural enough, surely?'

Shona smiled. 'Yes. Of course it is. No need to prickle. It just makes me wonder, is all . . . your mother and sister are only coming for a week, Aileen. They'll soon be back in Ireland again, which maybe means you'll be missing them more than ever?'

'But Joe will be staying. I'll have him. And my new customers. I'll be too busy to think about much else.'

Shona said nothing, wondering how true that might be, wondering also whether Joe would take to this alien country, unknown new life. If he didn't – what then? This coming summer was going to be crucial, in more ways than one.

As if reading her thoughts, and deflecting them, Aileen turned the conversation back on her. 'I know what I'll be doing for the foreseeable future, Sho. The question is, what will *you* be doing? H'mm? Tempting as it might be to hang out in your little gîte all summer, you can hardly afford to do that – or are you by any chance heiress to some vast fortune you've forgotten to mention?'

'Ha! If only! I'm mortgaged up to the hilt, as well you know – but, Aileen, I couldn't go back to that office. Not after what happened. I just couldn't. I'd be left there pen-pushing for the rest of my life, going nowhere – apart from raving mad. I don't know what the alternative is, but I am working on it, have been doing a lot of thinking . . . I'd love to stay here, if I could only find a way.'

Stay? Here? 'But Sho, surely that would be easy! You speak French, you'd get a job in a flash.' Aileen wasn't surprised by Shona's choice; she was so comfortable in France, it fitted her like a second skin.

'Yes. If I wanted a job, which I may yet find I do. But what I really want is a career. One that would let me pick up where I left off, something with real prospects – I know, that probably sounds picky for someone in my position. But I *need* something engaging, challenging, rewarding . . . something I can love, in a kind of way. You forget, I don't have a child or husband to love, nobody's waiting for me with open arms in the evenings. I have buckets of undivided attention to give my work, which is why I want it to be something worthwhile.'

Aileen thought that over. She could see, she supposed, what

Shona meant. Still . . . 'What about Aude? She might know of something in local tourism.'

'She's too young. I need to network at more senior level. I will – er – be forty in a few years, you know.'

Forty. H'mm. The sobering jolt of that silenced them both for a few minutes. Peeling an orange, Aileen remembered: it was when I turned forty that I started thinking about moving abroad. It was like an itch that had to be scratched. But Shona has always seemed so – so stable, so steady!

'Well. I hope you find what you need, Sho, I really do. Who knows – maybe some divine Frenchman will turn up to sweep you off your feet!'

'Do I look like the sweeping-off type? My feet are way too firmly planted on the ground.' Shona smiled, almost as if rueing her own nature, and Aileen had to smile back,

'If you say so. Still, don't count it out. Even if my own life isn't exactly fizzing with romance, somebody's has to be.'

Looking down into the grass, Shona plucked a blade, and played with it. 'Are you happy with Joe, Aileen? Are you really looking forward to seeing him?'

Yes. She could give an honest answer to that. 'I am. In fact I've been thinking a lot about him lately. He's no Lothario, life with him holds no surprises, but he's mine and I want him here, with me. I'm not like you, Sho. I couldn't live alone, don't want to be independent . . . I'm what they call a people type of person. Family and friends, the more the merrier. There are some things I'd like to change about Joe, but then maybe there are things he'd like to change about me, too.'

Out of the blue, Shona thought of Crys, and Gavin. 'Well, maybe. But don't change too much, Aileen. I think you're great as you are, and doing way better than you seem to think.'

A compliment? Aileen couldn't remember when she'd last had one, from anyone. Quietly thanking Shona, she tucked it away in her mind, like a flower pressed between the pages of a book, to remind her of this spring day in a French field full of apricot blossom, adrift on sunshine and friendship.

Now, Aileen thought. Now is the last chance I'll get, to talk alone with Finn before Joe and Mam and Dymps arrive. I am dreading this conversation, but we have to have it. I need to know, need to find out . . . we need to go back before we can go forward. The time is right; I'll sit him down tonight after dinner, share a bottle of wine with him, treat him like an adult and – and try to get the truth out of him.

Please, let him talk to me. He's been so much more open and approachable lately . . . yet he could still slam the door on me, vanish back into his shell, if I push him too hard. It's going to be tricky and I'm going to have to watch every word I say. Keep a firm grip on myself, too, not get emotional, the last thing we need is the whole thing collapsing in a puddle of tears. Being a parent is so difficult, sometimes. But this is part of my parental duties, one of my last and maybe the hardest. Oh, I hate doing this! It's as delicate as surgery . . . how do you take a scalpel to someone's soul without letting them feel any pain?

I don't know. All I know is that I have to try.

Steeling herself, she cooked Finn's favourite meal, lasagne, that evening, and invested in a bottle of good wine to go with it. At least you could do that here without breaking the bank. Then she had a word with Shona, who agreed not to eat with the Hegartys this one night.

'If you're sure . . . but it's so risky, Aileen, opening up old wounds.'

'I know. But I have to find out whether Finn's is festering or healing. Maybe he doesn't even remember, isn't scarred at all. But I can't stand not knowing any longer. He's my only child and if he is hurting in any way I want to help him.'

Tactfully, Shona nodded, and said no more. After she went off to her gîte Aileen sat down alone, waiting for Finn, preparing her words in her head, talking herself back sixteen years, to the day Hazel died. In her memory every detail was screamingly vivid; but then, she had been an adult. Finn had been only four.

By the time he came in she was so lost in thought she didn't hear him, and jumped when his voice rang out. 'Hiya, Ma! I'm starving, what's for dinner?'

'Lasagne.'

'Great. I'll just shower and be with you in five minutes.' As he raced up the stairs her heart raced too, and she had to steady herself, gripping a chair, slowing her breathing. Let him have forgotten, she thought. Let him look blank and not remember anything. Let me have been worrying all these years for nothing.

When he returned she was putting the hot dish on the table, and he glanced around. 'Where's Shona?'

'She – she's busy tonight. Sit down now and enjoy this, tell me about your day.'

Attacking his food, still eating elbows-out in his clumsy way, he told her about it. M Gautier, his new boss, had got the contract for a whole new housing estate, there would be buckets of work over the summer, he was going to buy Paul's motorbike outright if Paul would sell it, two of the guys were going camping at Easter and had asked him to go along . . .

'Will you?'

'Sure, why not? Time I saw a bit more of France. They're going to the coast, someplace down near Perpignan – hey Ma, this is great lasagne. If I ever get a girlfriend she'd better be able to cook like you!'

He grinned artlessly, and she refilled his glass, playing for time until she realised that right now was the time, the perfect moment when he was relaxed and at ease with her.

'Well, that's what mothers are for . . . and mothers always hope their sons will find nice girls. I – I like to think that if your sister had lived, she'd be the kind of girl who – who'd cook her boyfriend a hot meal now and again.'

Fork halfway to mouth, he paused, looking up at her with – with what? Mere curiosity, or something more?

'My sister? Hazel, you mean? God, Ma, that's a bolt from the blue. I've never heard you talk about Hazel before.'

Desperately, she tried to look nonchalant. 'No, well . . . maybe I should have. Sometimes I wonder whether it's right to – to let her slip away from us. She was only a baby, but she was one of us. Do you . . . remember her . . . at all?'

His face changing, he didn't answer, and she saw in his eyes that he did. Don't, she said to herself; don't rush in, don't hurry him or force him. Let him think, and talk to me when he's ready. If he wants to talk.

Taking up his fork he suddenly resumed eating, nodding with his mouth full. 'Yeah. I remember.'

Oh, Jesus. 'Do you, Finn? What do you remember?'

Slowly, he chewed his food, swallowing, head down, not looking at her. 'I remember that she smelled nice, and she had a – a kind of gurgly laugh. Her hair was sort of red, and she had green eyes and fat fists.'

'Yes. She was a pretty little thing.' Floundering, she groped for direction, and then without warning Finn did look up, directly at her.

'Ma – tell me something?'

'What?'

'Why – how come there were never any photos of her or anything, round the house? Like, no reminders? Were you and Dad so devastated you just wanted to forget she'd ever existed?'

She felt as if she were standing on the Roman viaduct, leaning down over the water as it surged around the black rocks far below.

'I – no – we – we didn't want to forget her, Finn. Of course we didn't. Nor will we, ever. But we thought that maybe it would be better if you did . . . you were so young . . . we didn't want you to pine for her . . .'

Every word felt plucked from her throat with hot pincers. Sitting back, abandoning his food, he picked up his wine glass but did not drink from it, staring into it with his face more focused, more intent, than she had ever seen it. Suddenly she glimpsed an adult, a man.

'You mean – you didn't want me to – remember that I killed her? That's what you're trying to say, isn't it?'

His voice was so low, she had to strain to hear it. But she had heard.

'Finn! No – that isn't – what I—'

'Yes. It is. It is what you meant, and it is what I did.'

The whole room seemed to freeze, to seize them in an icy grip. Staring at each other, bereft of words, she knew they sensed each other's anguish, and terror, as the lid slowly lifted off Pandora's box.

'Finn, it was an accident –'

'Right. I didn't mean to do it. I didn't know a sweet could choke my sister.'

Struggling to stay steady, somehow she managed it. 'Oh, Finn. Of course you didn't – we never for one moment blamed – you were only trying to be kind – I was the one who left you alone –'

'Yeah.' His voice was husky, his gaze still deep in the wine. 'I remember. You went to talk to someone at the door . . . maybe you think it was your fault, that's why there were no photographs . . . but I . . .'

Achingly, she yearned to reach out to him, to reach across the table and touch him. But she couldn't move. 'You what, Finn?'

Her voice was gentle, and she gasped as the wine glass flew across the room, hit the wall and splintered. As it smashed, he leaped to his feet.

'*I was the one who killed her! I did it! It was me!*'

She jumped up; by the time she got to him his face was fragmenting, dissolving in pain so acute it frightened her. 'Finn – no –'

'*Yes!*' As sobs wrenched from his throat she realised she had never seen him weep before, never once since Hazel's death: he had grown up a quiet, stoic little boy, singularly indifferent to punishment and reward alike. Now, he was weeping the tears of a lifetime, tears that she saw had been dammed up inside him for sixteen years. But it was not his fault, it was *not*.

His fists clenched, his whole body heaving, he stood in the middle of the room, bending forward as if agonisingly cramped, his face contorting, flooding. Aching for him, she stood with her hand soldered to his shoulder until, with a kind of spasm, he jerked free.

'Let me – let me –'

He couldn't get the words out, and so she waited. I've waited so long, she thought, so long for this. Too long? Should I have done it earlier . . . or not at all? He's in a kind of hell. All this time, my son has been imprisoned. Shackled with guilt, sealed into all this grief.

'Let me *say it*! Let it *out*, let *me out*!' Collapsing back onto his chair, he folded his arms on the table and buried his face in them, shaking, gasping as if he were drowning. Doing what so desperately needed to be done, leaving her to stand in silent witness, watching the dam break, the anguish pouring out in torrents. For many minutes he wept, and wept, and only when the dam was drained did he raise his streaming face to hers.

'I'm sorry – I've been sorry since I was four, every day of my life – I wanted to tell you but you never wanted to know – you locked her away and turned the key –'

'Yes. We did. We didn't know whether you realised, Finn, didn't dare ask – you were only a little boy, already traumatised by your sister's death, it would have been too cruel to ask if you understood what had happened, or even remembered. That's why we locked our memories of Hazel away, and never talked about her.'

Slowly, he raised his face a fraction further, letting it slide between his hands. 'And that's why Dad drinks.'

It was not a question. It was a flat statement. And it was true. Like his son, Joe too was a prisoner, shut into the eternal torment of never, ever daring to mention his dead daughter. That was why he went out every evening with Dave Doherty, that was why the Hegarty marriage had slowly shrivelled, their sex life stunted by repressed emotion – because you could not liberate emotions selectively, could you? Set one free, and they might all come tumbling out, pell-mell, uncontrollable. As clearly as she could see her son sitting before her, Aileen could suddenly see Joe too, see everything to which her own guilt, her own sorrow had blinded her for so long.

'Yes, Finn. I think that is why your father drinks. Why he goes to that pub practically every night of his life, without ever getting drunk.'

Gulping for air, struggling to compose himself, he brushed tears from his face: hers stung like needles in her eyes.

I wish it hadn't happened. I wish I'd never been born. That's what he's going to say.

'I wish you'd done this years ago. I can't tell you – how many times – I've wanted to talk about Hazel, to tell you I knew, to

accept the guilt and take it off you. But you and Dad were so
– so –'

So blind? So scared? So protective of you, Finn? Where did
we go wrong, she wondered; tell me where?

'So stupid! I can see why you did it, but I wish you hadn't.
Maybe when I was a kid I was too young to talk about it, but
once I got into my teens I could have handled it, it would have
set me free, I *wanted* the responsibility—'

In a flash, she saw something.

'Oh, God! That's why you did it, isn't it? That's why you
went up on that roof and rescued those children, that whole
family – ?'

Vehemently, he nodded. 'Yeah. I wasn't scared because
nothing worse could happen to me than already happened to
Hazel. All I saw was my chance to get two kids to safety, to
make up for her in some weird way . . . someone told me the
little one, Isabelle, was only two, the same age as Hazel. So I
went up, and I got them down, and – it felt so – like I could
breathe properly. Like I'd been holding my breath all my life
and suddenly I wasn't any more.'

'So that's why you've been so different since. That's why I
finally felt able to talk to you this evening . . . even without
consciously making the connection, I just somehow knew that
now was the moment to do it.'

Again, slowly drawing his breath, he nodded, his face still
flaming but no longer tortured. 'Yeah. Maybe it's true about
women having intuition, sensing things. Oh, Christ, I'm so
glad you had the guts, at last, to bring this whole thing out in
the open . . . now I can share the guilt, take my half off your
shoulders onto mine, where it belongs.'

Quietly, standing behind him, she stroked his prickly, purple
hair, so lightly she did not think he even felt her fingers. 'Finn,
I think whatever guilt you may have been feeling, which seems

to have been considerable, was absolved the day you went up on that ladder.'

Eagerly, he turned to look up at her. 'Do you? Do you, Ma? Have I done my penance, d'you reckon, can I get on with my life now?'

Another flash. *So that's why he failed his exams. Twice. Deliberately.*

Moving round the table, she sat down facing him, and took his hand. He did not snatch it away. 'Please, Finn. Please, get on with your life. You are my son and I love you and I want you to be happy. Hazel didn't get her chance so I want you to take it for her, I want you to forget all about a terrible accident that happened when you were only an innocent toddler. An accident for which we must stop blaming ourselves, because it's crippling us. We have to let go. We *must*.'

Sitting upright, he pulled his hand away then, and thought about what she was saying to him. Thought in silence, for as long as it took.

'All right. I will if you will. So long as it's clear now – so long as you know that I remember what happened. I know what I did, I accept it and I'll never forget. I don't want you to protect me any more, or pretend Hazel never existed. I want you to let her be part of us, let me be an adult and –'

He hesitated. 'And what, Finn?'

'And let me talk to Dad? I want him to know that we've had this conversation, that the taboo is broken, that he can try to move on now with his life, too.'

She hesitated in turn. 'You don't think maybe that's my job?'

Emphatically, he shook his head. 'No. It's mine. Let me do it. All I want you to do is to – is to for Christ's sake put up a picture of Hazel somewhere in this house, if you have one, like any normal mother would do.'

She didn't have one. She had dozens, in a shoebox under

her bed. 'All right. I will. After you've spoken to Joe. I know he's been a bit sharp, a bit impatient with you sometimes, but that – that's nothing to do with Hazel. I think it has more to do with himself.'

Speculatively, she looked at him, and he surprised her by smiling wryly. 'Yeah. You might say that Dad's been bottling things up.'

She had to smile back. 'Well, he didn't bottle much up when I told him about that family you saved. He was very proud of you – and he told you so, didn't he, on the phone?'

'Yeah. Well. Sort of. Joe Hegarty isn't exactly the world's greatest communicator, is he?'

No, she thought, he is not. But I'm profoundly glad I managed to communicate with you this evening, Finn Hegarty. It hurt like hell, we're both raw as hide, but it was worth it. You look so relieved, so liberated . . . would you answer just one more question, I wonder, if I put it to you? You look so drained, maybe you've had enough. But I'm going to give it one last shot, because I so badly need to know.

'No. Your father isn't a great communicator, Finn . . . but he has been worried about you. Worried, and watching you too.'

Looking more intrigued than surprised, he met her gaze without evasion. 'You mean, while you were away house-hunting a few months ago? I felt like he was tracking my every move, couldn't make out why he was acting like some kind of amateur detective. What was that all about?'

'I asked him to do it. Because – well, you were spending so much time shut away on your computer, and hanging out with people we never saw, never met. There was never any evidence, but we couldn't help wondering whether you might . . . be . . . mixed up in drugs in any way.'

She blurted out the final few words, and he looked at her with a kind of incomprehension, as if he had no idea how she could possibly have reached such a ludicrous conclusion.

'Why? What put drugs into your heads?'

'I don't know. Maybe it's something all parents worry about. Especially when their sons are so uncommunicative – I mean, what *were* you doing on that computer, who were you hanging out with in Galway?'

Stretching back in his chair, his streaked, ravaged face pale but composed, he reflected before answering.

'I was on the net, where you may be surprised to hear there are a lot of websites of interest to guys my age. Perfectly normal, legal stuff, which is as much as you need to know. As for my mates – I never brought them home because they were all losers like me, scruffy, tattooed, unemployed, the kind parents always hate. They weren't exactly model citizens – but they weren't criminals either. None of us ever did any drugs unless you count a few Red Bull cocktails.'

His face was frank; for all his faults, she had never known him to lie. All he was saying, basically, was that he was a normal youth, with interests and friends of his own which did not concern her. Her anxiety had arisen entirely from her own imagination, a mother's over-protectiveness of her only surviving child.

Stretching out her arms, the only thing she could think to do was invite him into a hug, and he accepted it, holding her to him briefly but tightly, in a way that changed the balance between them. At a stroke her boy was gone, and her adult son was indulging his sorely, long-misguided mother.

Somewhere in the back of her mind, instinct whispered to her: he needs a girlfriend. Have I set him free, now, will he claim the confidence to go out and find one?

Returning from a trip to the village market next morning, Shona surveyed Aileen's pallor, but did not enquire into it.

Whatever had happened between mother and son was between them; if Aileen chose to divulge details she would do so, whenever she was in the mood. Clearly she wasn't in it just now: she looked exhausted, and Shona was glad she could offer a bit of gossip that might revive her.

'It's a good thing Joe's arriving soon, because it seems you're getting a bit of a reputation down in Mézalas.'

Aileen spun round bewildered. 'I'm what?'

'M'mm. I heard it at the fishmonger's stall. Mme 'Egarty, the Irish lady, the talk of the town. Mother of the fabulous Finn – who by the way appears to be getting a reputation all of his own. Anyway, rumour has it that Mme 'Egarty, who has no visible sign of a husband, has become pally with Aude Villandry's uncle Léo. Which would all be very nice and sociable were it not for the unfortunate fact that Léo has a wife, who I gather is not amused by the news of this – uh – competition for Léo's charms.'

For a moment Aileen said nothing, looking merely puzzled. And then she surprised Shona by not laughing, but frowning irritably. 'What? What kind of baloney is this? Are they off their rockers?'

Shona grinned. 'Didn't you know? French women are incredibly possessive of their men. Anyone not attached to one of her own is seen as a threat.'

'But – oh, for chrissakes – I have a son, I wear a wedding ring –'

'They think you're a widow. An attractive one, I might add, who could upset the village apple cart if . . . if Joe Hegarty were not due to arrive next week and completely confuse the grapevine!'

Shona laughed aloud; Aileen marched indignantly around the kitchen, packing away groceries with a righteous air. 'I never heard such rubbish. They must all be paranoid, or live extremely sheltered lives. Or both. I barely spoke to that man Léo for twenty minutes, only about the garden at that, I was no more than civil to him.'

'Then that must be all it takes to become the new number one femme fatale.' Shona laughed again, and after a pause Aileen laughed reluctantly with her. 'They must have precious little to amuse them. A woman of my age –'

'Is considered by many Frenchmen to be in her prime.'

Aileen didn't answer, merely raised a sceptical eyebrow, but Shona saw this snippet slowly sinking into Aileen's consciousness, and wondered whether it might come in handy some day. Even Joe Hegarty, presumably, had his pride? At the very least she, Shona, would make sure it reached his ears.

But it was the phone that reached her ears at that moment. When she picked it up the call turned out to be for Aileen, her sister Dymps babbling at distracted speed, and Shona handed it to her.

After a minute of stricken silence, during which she was apparently unable to muster anything more than gasps and gestures, Aileen's face crumpled, her voice rang out like a shot.

'Oh, *no*! Oh, Dymps – you can't – I was looking forward so much – oh, this is terrible!'

Tensing, Shona sat wondering what news was unfolding; but it was another ten minutes or more before Aileen hung up, looking devastated as if some absolute catastrophe had happened. Anxiously, Shona waited.

'Jillian has chicken pox!'

Oh. Phew. Was that all? Shona had only once met Dympna's daughter, Aileen's niece Jillian, at Christmas last year. A nice kid, but . . . 'So?'

'So they can't come! She's in quarantine, there's no way Dymps says – oh, Shona! I've been dying to see them, I can't believe they're not coming!' Sinking down at the kitchen table, she propped her elbows on it and plunged her face into her hands. 'Oh, no! It's not fair! My sister, her family, I haven't seen them for months!'

Shona, not having a sister or a niece, could only try to look sympathetic. 'Oh, what a shame. But never mind, maybe they'll come in summer instead –'

Aileen stared at her as if she were thick as a brick. 'But they can't come then, Le Mas will be full! At least that's what we hope – we have to make some money this summer, Shona, you know we do, we can't have our families or friends taking up rooms! Which means – oh, I can't believe this! *When* am I ever going to get to see them?'

A fair question, Shona supposed, and one that was clearly very important to Aileen. The next thought that crept into her head made her feel so guilty that she decided, for now, to say nothing about it. Later, when Aileen had got over her disappointment . . . well, in a day or two, whenever she saw a chance, she would mention it then. Not now, because this wasn't the moment for disloyalty, or any kind of plotting. This was the moment when a friend was supposed to be sympathetic and supportive, and so that was what she had better be. Suppressing a sigh, and a small, camouflaged smile, she went to the cupboard and got out the Barry's teabags. Something about Aileen's distracted expression suggested that the household was plunged into mourning, and strength would be needed to get through this appalling tragedy.

Still . . . there was no point in letting three perfectly good beds go to waste, was there? The ones that had been awaiting Dymps, her husband and children might as well be put to use. My parents, Shona thought, would love to come over. Emily O'Brien would too, a holiday would be a tonic for her. And Crys would be here like a shot, if her doctor lets her fly . . . what a pity there just isn't any room for Gavin.

Waking early on the morning of Joe and Tessie's arrival, Aileen lay perfectly still, staring at the ceiling, wondering why her throat was dry and her heart was pounding. Then, slowly, the scene swam into place in her mind: Mam, at last, and Joe! The mere thought of seeing her mother made her feel wobbly, and as for Joe . . . would he really be on the plane, was he thinking of her at this minute as he, too, woke up? Some dreadful apprehension prickled under her skin, her stomach tightening against the silly, secret fear that Mam would arrive alone, bearing his excuses. *No. Sorry, love. Can't get away. Not yet. Be with you as soon as I can, I promise . . .*

Sitting up, hugging her arms around her knees, she pushed the thought away. Of course he would come, if anything were amiss he would have told her by now, all she had to do was get up and get ready to greet him. What she should do was take a long, scented bath – or a brief scented shower more accurately, since water was such an expensive luxury in France. Then she would have all morning to psyche herself up, while Shona went to the airport. That was the agreed plan, since she didn't want Finn tearing jet-propelled down the autoroute. Shona didn't mind driving over that bloody viaduct and someone had to stay here to prepare their welcoming meal. A knockout, luxurious French lunch . . . Shona could hardly do that, since she barely seemed able to tell a saucepan from an egg whisk. It needed to be a really good meal, one that would instantly convince both Joe and Tessie that this was a marvellous country.

It is marvellous. It's gorgeous and I love it. Well, maybe not as much as Shona seems to love it, not yet – but it has its charms. As I apparently have mine! I can still hardly believe that story of hers, about the local women being jealous, saying I'm attractive, thinking Aude's uncle took a shine to me . . . they must be mad. But, whatever about all that, it looks like a nice day outside. Nice enough to wear my pink linen dress?

Yes. I think so. Joe's never seen it, and maybe I can get away with it now I've lost a few pounds. God only knows how, with all this tempting food, it must be the worry of getting Le Mas on its feet, and Finn sorted . . . but both of those projects are well under way now. I can relax, can't I, for this one day?

I have to relax. I have to be here beaming when Mam and Joe arrive, and besides I *want* to be. It's so disappointing that Dymps and her crew aren't coming too. But Mam will be definitely be here, and Joe says he will for sure.

Of course he will! What on earth is wrong with you, Aileen Hegarty? Get up and get into the shower and stop worrying, you'll only spoil this wonderful day for everyone.

The morning's pearly sunshine evolved into a clear, hot day, delighting Shona as she set off for the airport. 'Joe and Tess will be thrilled when they see this. It's like midsummer. Sure you don't want to change your mind and come with me?'

'No. They'll have luggage, the car is small, there's that viaduct, lunch to cook—'

Hearing herself babbling, Aileen stopped abruptly. Shona was sharp enough to maybe guess the terror she was trying to conceal: her vision of Tessie coming off the plane alone, and the scene that would unravel. The beginning of the end of her marriage.

'Okay. Then I'll hit the road. Should have them back here about two, all going well.'

'Yes' Aileen gulped, smiling ferociously. 'All going well.'

Surprising her with a fleeting kiss – God, she was getting so French! – and a squeeze of her shoulder, Shona departed. Scarcely had she gone than Finn ambled into the kitchen, dishevelled in some ragged outfit that passed for pyjamas; he had taken today off to be here for his father, and had made the most of the morning, apparently, to sleep late. Feverishly, Aileen pounced on him.

'Finn, it's after ten! Get dressed!'

'Why' he drawled, scratching his ear, 'what's the hurry?'

'Your father and grandmother are coming!'

'Yeah, I know. So?' Lazily, he shook cornflakes from a box into a bowl, flapped barefoot to the fridge for milk. 'They won't be here for hours yet, will they?'

'No, but I – I need you to –'

'To what?'

She couldn't quite think what. 'To scrub the patio table' she finished lamely, 'and – and put up the parasol, we'll eat outdoors.'

He yawned. 'Right. Relax, Ma.'

But, try as she might, she couldn't. Her stomach felt the way it had felt before her first date with Joe, all those years ago, tight and tingling, gripped by scudding emotions. Pacing around Finn while he munched with maddening slowness, absently noting that he had not shaved his skull for some days, she wondered what he would say if she dared ask him the question that was fermenting in her mind: will your father like it here, do you think? Do *you* like it, Finn? Are you settling in now, are you happy enough to help Joe settle in too? I wish I could ask you – but I can't, because if you said no, if the truth were that you'd rather be in Ireland, I couldn't handle it. Not now, not with Joe already on the plane. I daren't ask; all I can do is hope.

Eventually she seized her lunch ingredients, washed, chopped and prepared them all in a flurry, and raced upstairs to change into her pink linen. In fact she might as well have another shower, after those onions – God, how could Finn be so *calm*, with his father arriving?!

After the second shower she stood staring at her reflection

in the bathroom mirror, wondering whether Joe would see her as she saw herself, or what or who he might see. I'm his wife, she reminded herself, I don't have to prove anything, perform in any way, it's not as if he's our first customer crossing the threshold of Le Mas. He's just Joe. My husband of twenty-two years. That's all.

Does this linen – ? Yes, thank God, it fits, and no, I don't think my arms look fat in it. Where are those silver earrings Dymps gave me last birthday? Am I too old for lilac eye-shadow, or – ? Oh, what the hell. Mascara, too, and lipstick, might as well be hanged for a sheep as a lamb. Not that I am any spring lamb! But I must say, I do feel better in this lot, it's ages since I dressed up. It's even kind of fun.

Jesus, Joe. Don't do it. Just don't spring any surprises on me, is all. Just get off that plane and get here and—

'Ma!' Finn's voice filtered up from the hall. 'There are two guys here at the door looking for you!'

The police. Joe was dead. Mam, too, and Shona, all massacred on the autoroute – her mind whirled into orbit, her feet scarcely touched the tiles as she flew downstairs, gasping with petrified anticipation: who else could possibly be looking for her, why?

'*Bonjour, madame*' said a laconic voice, and there stood Aude's uncle – Léo something-or-other, she had failed to grasp his surname the day they'd first met. He'd come then about the moles, and was now toting some other man she didn't recognise.

'*B - bonjour. Excusez-moi –*' Tucking back her hair, snapping on the bracelet she realised was still in her hand, she shook hands as was expected in France. Smiling, relaxed in clean jeans and a check shirt, Léo grasped her hand and, still holding it, introduced his companion.

Straining to understand, she gradually gathered that they

had come – hell's bells, now just when she didn't want to see anyone – about the garden. Léo wished to check the mole situation, and the other man, Jacques, was the landscaper he had promised to produce. Small, dark and dapper, Jacques was eagerly clutching some paperwork under his arm.

'Oh – *oui* –' Still breathless, knowing she looked flushed, she waved vaguely out at the garden, trying to convey that they should go ahead with whatever they needed to do. But, said Léo, miming in turn, they wanted her to accompany them. Jacques required information: what kind of flowers and shrubs, to be planted where exactly? If she would be good enough to point out sites, give him some idea of her taste and wishes, he would mark out everything on the graph paper he carried, and then afterwards they would all sit down while he drew up a plan for her approval?

Damn! Striving to conceal her impatience, she nodded acquiescence. After all, the garden did urgently need fixing, and it was good of him to bring this landscaper. Turning to Finn, hissing to him to get dressed, she went out into the sunshine with the two men, and Jacques produced an illustrated book, full of flowers for her to choose from. Peering into it, getting distracted despite herself, she left Léo to inspect his mole traps, of which there were still dozens around the perimeter of the lawn. What should be planted, when the flaming moles were conquered, what would resist heat and storms and whatever other menaces lurked in the Languedoc? Perhaps she had better discuss this properly, actually, give Jacques and Léo her full attention, because Shona would murder her if she got it wrong.

And that was how, two hours later, Joe Hegarty arrived to find his wife sitting on a blazingly hot terrace, radiant in the sun, made up and dressed to the nines, sipping an *apéritif* as she laughed and chatted with a Frenchman on either side of her, both of whom appeared to be hanging on every syllable she uttered. Giggling at her own mangled French, she did not immediately see him, nor Tessie and Shona as they stood drinking in the charming vision she presented.

Putting down his suitcase, drawing himself up, Joe cleared his throat, looked hard at her and waited for her to notice him.

I I

It was Finn who, without warning, clicked the camera, framing a memory of his parents that would last a lifetime. Joe, flanked by Tess and Shona, immobilised with shock as he gazed at his tanned, elegant wife, flanked by two laughing, admiring Frenchmen. Aileen, seated between Léo and Jacques, looking up at him with sudden enquiry in her eyes, wondering who was this stranger standing before her.

Joe? Joe Hegarty? No. There had been some incomprehensible mix-up. Joe Hegarty wore a moustache, saggy sweaters and baggy jeans, battered trainers and a drinker's paunch. His nose was red-veined, his hands were creased with grease after his day's work, his buttons gaped and his shoulders tended to a kind of resigned droop. This man, who was standing bolt upright, was wearing leather loafers, freshly ironed Chinos, a light sports jacket and a pale yellow polo neck. His face was clear and clean-shaven and he looked at least ten years younger than Joe Hegarty. Utterly bewildered, Aileen could only stare at him, waiting for some explanation.

And then, ignoring the Frenchmen as he pushed between them, the man leaned over her, grasped her by the shoulders and kissed her firmly, deliberately, full on the lips. Aghast, Aileen recoiled; and only then, forced to look into his eyes, did she recognise the man she'd been married to for more than twenty years.

'Aileen.' It was his smile that did it. 'Are you not even going to get up and say hello to your own husband?'

She tried. Tried twice, her legs crumpling under her, and finally managed to stand upright. But she couldn't say hello: her voice was padlocked with shock. Who – how – what had happened!? Where was the Joe she'd left behind in Galway safely installed with her mother, who had tampered with him and how? This Joe looked taller, and distinctly thinner, and furthermore he was surveying Léo and Jacques with a look that said 'Beat it, boys, her husband's here now so why don't you run along.' Never, in all her life, had Aileen seen Joe look like that before; not actually aggressive, but prickling with possessiveness.

Léo, swiftly getting the picture, hauled Jacques to his feet. Thrusting out his hand, he indicated the gardening book with a nonchalant grin. 'We have been planning the garden . . . but it is lunchtime, we will not delay further.'

Belatedly, Aileen thought to introduce everyone, but by the time she found her voice glasses had been drained, books packed up and goodbyes said. Skipping like a startled rabbit, Jacques followed Léo down the drive to their car, and Joe stood watching them, arms folded across his chest, as if ensuring their departure. As their car pulled away, it left a resounding vacuum in its wake.

For a long moment, everyone stood looking at everyone else. And then Finn, with a strangled snort, exploded in laughter. 'Way to go, Dad! That's what you call making an entrance!'

Ignoring him, Joe stared at his wife with the steely gaze of an inquisitor. 'Who the hell were those two?'

Aileen's first reaction was to stammer explanation; and then she surprised herself by staring back at him with a poise she'd never known she possessed. 'They were' she said with a kind of cool hauteur, 'friends.'

'Friends.' Sceptically, he looked as if the word was fizzing on his tongue. 'I see.'

Something in his tone needled her. *What* did he see, what was that insinuating tone meant to mean? Well, let him see whatever he liked. The nerve of him, bursting in here looking like a total stranger, interrupting a perfectly innocent, pleasant gathering in that challenging, accusatory way! Deliberately ignoring him, she marched around him to embrace her mother.

'Mam . . . oh, it's so good to see you!'

Their hug was long and affectionate, leaving Joe sidelined until he thought to embrace Finn, punching his shoulder with a kind of macho heartiness. 'Well, I must say lad, you're looking good!'

Finn was looking good, or much better at any rate than he'd looked before. Weeks of outdoor work and fresh food had darkened his formerly pasty skin, brightened his eyes and cleared up his spots. Lightened his step, too, in some way that Joe couldn't quite identify.

'So are you, Dad – what's with the threads? Where's the 'tash?'

Sitting down, Joe emitted a kind of rumble. 'Ah, I just lost a bit of weight. And your grandmother here bought me a few new bits and pieces, said I couldn't be going to France in me dungarees.'

Finn grinned. 'Dunno why not. They all wear 'em round here. Raoul Lascaux looks Neanderthal.'

Suspiciously, Joe squinted at him. 'Who?'

'Our neighbour. And his wife is positively prehistoric.'

Wife. So at least some of these fellas had them. Looking at his own, Joe bristled. Enough with the mother, now. Was Aileen never going to give him one kiss, one hug, one iota of the attention she was giving Tess? Had she completely lost interest in him, now she had these flaming Frogs dancing attendance round her?

Turning at last to look at him, she surveyed him in a way that was still somehow cool. 'So who's been messing with you?'

Feeling a fool, he grunted. Tess had got carried away, completely overdone the makeover. 'Your mother, is who. New clothes she said, new look, new everything.'

'H'mm. New figure, too?'

'Ah . . .' He could feel himself flushing. 'I just decided to give up the drink. For a while. For Lent.'

Faintly, Aileen gripped the back of a chair. Joe Hegarty had given up *drinking*? Catching her eye, hearing her unvoiced shock, he nodded defensively in her direction. 'You've changed a bit yourself.'

Yes, she thought, I have. I've weathered two months here without you. I've got our new B & B up and ready to rock. I've lanced the boil that was bubbling in your son for sixteen years. And I put on this dress, this make-up, this jewellery for *you* this morning, you stupid man, not for Léo and his chum who were here uninvited and entirely by chance!

'Yes' she said composedly, 'well, why don't we all sit down and have a little *apéro* before lunch?'

Joe eyed her. 'A what?'

Sweetly, she eyed him back. 'A drink, dear. What we were just starting when you arrived. I'm sure Mam would love a sherry – and what'll you have, mineral water?'

Catching the tinge in her tone, he flinched inwardly. He'd thought she'd be thrilled to see him. Evidently, she was not. On the contrary. She was put out that her little chat with her French chums had been disrupted. With sudden longing, he thought he could murder a beer. Only he wasn't going to fall into the trap she was so nastily setting for him.

'Yes, cold water would be great . . . thanks.'

Standing a little apart, Shona surveyed the scenario, catching Finn's eye, and they raised a mutual eyebrow. Somehow this happy-family reunion didn't seem to be quite going according to plan, there was an edge to it, as if Joe and Aileen were fencing in some way. But one thing was crystal clear: both looked rejuvenated. Shona had never seen Aileen so dressed up before, never suspected she could emerge so soignée. As for Joe – well. Miracles would never cease.

'I'll sort the drinks' Finn said, and vanished indoors. Gazing after him, Joe thought he must be hearing things. Finn was volunteering to help with something?

'Well' Tessie piped up in the chatty tone of someone missing all the vibes, 'this looks lovely, dear. I can't wait to see inside the house . . . only it's so warm out here, I hardly want to move! Is the weather always so gorgeous?' As she said it she removed her 'good' cream cardi, and sat back like a cat stretching contentedly on the hearth.

Aileen laughed ruefully. 'Not always – there was a storm that nearly blew us away. Your grandson was the hero of the hour . . . I didn't want to worry you with it at the time, but he'll tell you all about it now you're here.'

'He looks well' Tessie said, happily.

'He is well' Aileen said, firmly.

There was an impasse. And then Finn arrived with a tray of fresh bottles and glasses, Shona sat down and joined them, and a round of celebratory drinks was poured.

'Cheers' said Joe, valiantly raising his glass of Perrier.

'Cheers' said Aileen equably, 'and *vive la France*.'

Oh, yes, he thought. *Vive la* flaming *France*. So maybe Dave Doherty was right, and my wife has left me, after all?

We'll see about that. We will just bloody well see about that.

After her sherry in the sun, and lunch, and a tour of Le Mas, Tessie admitted with a kind of wilting smile to being 'just a little tired, dear. Maybe a nap would be a good idea?'

Thinking it would be a very good idea, Aileen sent Finn to take Tessie's bags to her room, and with a final speculative glance at Joe Shona also melted away; his aura was all but shouting that he wanted to be alone with his wife.

But when he was alone with her, Joe found that he couldn't for the life of him think what to say next. Aileen seemed to be having the same difficulty, and for a little while they sat facing each other amidst the lunch leftovers on the patio, uncomfortably picking at scraps, murmuring inanities like two strangers thrown together on a blind date. What did you say when someone turned out to be so very different to what you were expecting? Eventually, for want of purpose, Aileen stood up.

'Maybe you'd like to go for a walk, have a look around the village?'

Relieved, Joe stood up in turn. Anything would be better than this. 'Aye, why not. Lead the way.'

And so they set off, slowly in the heat, touring the ravaged garden, down the drive out into the somnolent laneway which gradually widened into the road to Mézalas. For some obscure reason Joe urgently wanted to take his wife's hand, and for some even fuzzier reason he did not take it. She was pointing out neighbours' houses along the way, talking about Raoul Lascaux and Finn's exploit with the fire brigade.

'I only discovered afterwards that he'd rescued the entire family . . . it was so dangerous, I'd never have let him go if I'd known at the time.'

'Well' Joe commented, pleased to find they still had some subject in common, 'it seems to have made a man of him. He's not the same young fella he was at all.'

'No. He isn't. I think he's growing up, at last. Coming out of his shell, making friends . . .' She wanted to tell him about the talk she'd had with Finn, but somehow couldn't: it was too weighty a subject to embark on at this moment, when she was feeling so inexplicably awkward with Joe. Besides, Finn wanted to be the one to broach it. Raising her hand, she swept it in an arc out to the horizon.

'Isn't this the most wonderful view?'

'Yes. Are we going down to that village?' Mopping his brow, Joe paused; if it was this warm in April, what on earth would it be like by July?

'If you like – that's Mézalas, it's nearer than it looks, only about ten minutes.'

Right, he thought: ten on the way down, twenty on the way back. Or thirty. I should have changed into something cooler. She looks so cool, in that sleeveless dress . . . I suppose she can wear things in this climate she never wore at home. Next thing I'll have to buy a pair of ruddy shorts. And sandals.

Slowly they ambled down to Mézalas, which was shimmering in the heat haze, just emerging from its afternoon siesta as they wandered into it. Spotting a trickling fountain in the middle of the square, mercifully shaded by trees, Joe sank down on its cool, mossy rim.

'Phew. Dusty little place, isn't it?'

'Well, yes, I suppose – but isn't it sweet, too? That's the bakery where they sell cakes from paradise, that's the hairdresser's where I made a fool of myself, there's a market here in the square every Saturday morning . . . we could have a cold drink in that café if you like.'

Gratefully he followed her to it, taking a table under a big white parasol, lowering himself into a wicker chair with the suspicion that he might have to be winched back out of it. His feet, in leather shoes and socks, were throbbing. Even if he could think what to say, it would be difficult to summon the energy. When the waiter arrived, he pantomimed iced water with an eagerness that made her smile.

'So you really have given up beer?'

He thought about it. 'Not beer, as such. What I've given up is going to the pub with Dave Doherty.'

Clasping her hands, she rested her forearms on the table, looking curious. 'Why?'

'Because – because it was bad for me health. Your mother said.' He didn't add that Tessie had meant his physical health, whereas it was his mental health he'd started to worry about. Was everyone in that pub really talking about his rocky marriage?

'Well, you look the better for it.'

'Do I?'

'Yes. Much. I had to do a double take when I saw you.'

And I had to do one when I saw you, too. 'What about the moustache? I can grow it back, if you think—'

'No. Don't. You look years younger without it.'

'Okay. If you think so.'

Their drinks arrived and, feeling the conversation faltering ominously, Aileen began to tell him all that had happened, all the snippets of her daily life, the mountain of minutiae to be caught up on. After only a few months, he'd missed a lot. Sipping his iced Evian, he listened in silence, nodding at intervals, yearning to interrupt with the only question he really wanted her to answer.

What's the story with that Léo guy, who scarpered so fast when I arrived?

'. . . So the plumber fixed the leak, and Finn replaced the broken glass and . . . Shona has quit her job . . . Le Mas is getting three stars . . .'

You look lovely. Do you know that, Aileen Hegarty? You look beautiful sitting there babbling like a brook, with those new freckles on your nose, the sun bouncing off your bracelet . . . have your eyes got darker or were they always that colour?

'. . . Spent so much, but I couldn't help it, there have been so many . . .'

*What? Why do you sound so apologetic? You have nothing to apologise for, **that I know of**. I wish I had the strength to carry you up that hill and . . . I wish we could talk about us. Why can we never talk about us?*

'Better be getting back, Mam will be wondering . . .'

His glass was empty, but he couldn't seem to move; he felt etched into the early evening, part of the street furniture. If someone had told him he was to stay where he was for the rest of his days, well – so be it.

'Joe? Are you feeling all right?'

Somehow he heaved himself up, nodding nonchalantly. 'Yes. Fine. Thanks.'

'Should I get some tomatoes so we can have a light salad for supper?'

I don't know! I don't care! The only thing I want is you!

'I'll get a few anyway, in case anyone is hungry.'

And so he stood on the pavement, watching her select tomatoes from the grocer's stall, all but screaming aloud with frustration. *I've got to say something. Got to do something, before I explode. I haven't come a thousand miles to talk about tomatoes.*

Giving him the paper bag to carry, and rather an odd look to go with it, she set off at a clip that was, in his estimation, far too brisk for such weather, facing that climb back up that infernal hill. Such was her pace that he found himself lagging behind, trudging and panting; even after losing ten pounds, he was evidently going to have to lose more. Why was she walking so fast, as if she didn't want him to catch her up, didn't want him alongside her?

'Aileen' he gasped eventually, when they were a couple of hundred yards up the hill and the plains were beginning to roll into view down below, 'stop. Wait a minute, for God's sake.'

Looking back over her shoulder, she raised her sunglasses to peer at him. 'Why? What's wrong?'

'Nothing.' Puffing, he caught up with her, stood for a moment steadying himself, inhaling deep breaths. And then, reaching out, he hurled himself over the edge.

'I just wanted to take your hand, that's all.'

As he said it he seized it, amazing her with not only the gesture, but the tightness of his grip. Jesus. Was he going to have a heart attack, or what? He was very red in the face. Indulgently, she waited until his breathing slowed, and then they walked on, in silence, in step.

It was new. It was nice. It might even have been vaguely romantic, stirring memories of the way they'd walked as teenagers so long ago, had not a quenching reality suddenly hit her: oh God, he's huffing and puffing so much, I hope he isn't going to snore tonight.

Joe did not snore that night. But he did keep Aileen awake. Or was it some other man who shucked off his jacket when they reached Le Mas, looking at her as if for the first time? Some man she'd never met – or long forgotten – who took a step towards her, shut his eyes, clenched his fists, looked at her again and then, without warning, lifted her clear off her feet, scooped her up into his arms? As she was carried up the stairs she had a feeling of being kidnapped, might almost have shouted for help if her brain had been working, if her limbs had not inexplicably been melting, her mouth opening and shutting like a puppet's. It must be the heat, she thought, it must be the heat. It's fried his brain *and . . . sweet God, is this happening?*

But the night was even hotter. Sweltering, incandescent.

Coming downstairs for a glass of water in the middle of it, drowsy after the 'nap' that had lasted halfway through to dawn, Tessie was befuddled to find a heap of tomatoes strewn all over the hall.

'Don't ask, Gran' Finn said when she queried him next morning, 'just ask them no questions, and they'll tell you no lies.'

Amiably, he winked at her, leaving her baffled: what was that supposed to mean? Since when could tomatoes tell lies, for heaven's sake? France must be sending Finn soft in the head.

Coming up to the main house from her gîte later that shimmering morning, Shona paused to survey the scene that met her gaze. Out on the terrace, Joe was sprawling in a deckchair, coffee in hand, looking like a man remarkably revived from yesterday's long journey. Nearby, Aileen sat at the table, coffee untouched under her nose, with a distant, dreamy smile on her face.

Ah. Ah ha. So. This looks like it could be a good moment. Seize it, Shona.

Approaching the terrace, she waved cheerily. '*Bonjour!*'

Aileen flapped a few fingers in her direction. 'Hi . . . how are you?'

'Fine, thanks.' And there's no need to ask how you are, is there? I can see exactly how you are, Mrs Hegarty, this fine morning.

'There's some juice here if you'd like . . . I think Mam is scrambling eggs . . .'

Shona stifled a grin. Ah no, thanks, I'll just have whatever you're having . . . or I would if I could. Joe Hegarty, huh? Well, who'd have thought it. You look like a woman who barely remembers her own name.

Sitting down, Shona nodded at Joe, and he smiled back – as

335

smug as all that, huh? I see. And there was me thinking it could go either way.

Idly, she poured some juice, almost reluctant to disturb the atmosphere that hung like honey in the air. But it was the perfect moment.

'Aileen, I've been thinking.'

'Mmm?'

She's hardly listening, Shona saw. I could ask her if she'd mind lending me a million this morning, and she'd simply say yes, sure, here you are . . . 'Well, the thing is, since your sister and her family aren't able to join us . . . how would you feel about me inviting a few other people instead?'

Lifting her coffee, Aileen looked up. 'Like who?'

'My parents. And my friends Crys and Emily – you know them both? I'd love Crys to have a break before her baby is born, plus Emily is around the same age as your mother, they'd be company for each other.'

Aileen gave it no further consideration whatsoever. 'So they would. Good idea. Ask them all. After all, you own Le Mas!'

'True. But you run it. I wouldn't want to impose—'

'Oh, nonsense. They'll be no trouble. Why don't you ring them now, this morning?'

'I will, then, if you're sure.' Pleased by Aileen's easy agreement, Shona sipped her juice, and then raised her glass to Joe as he sauntered over to the table. '*Bonjour*, Joe! Enjoying France so far, are you?'

He was about to assert that he was when Shona and Aileen caught each other's eyes, and both suddenly erupted in laughter, doubling with it, explaining nothing, only spluttering and giggling in that maddeningly silly way women had.

Oh ho, he thought, glowering at them, ho ho. Very funny, ladies, have a good laugh now, at my expense. See if I care. At least I've got my wife here with me this morning, in body and soul, which is more than can be said for you and your late lamented boyfriend, Miss Shona Fitzpatrick.

Pouring himself a hot coffee, he smirked at her, bent to blatantly kiss Aileen, and floated back to his deckchair.

For a long time after Shona left her, Aileen remained where she was, absently holding her cup in her hands, gazing out across the valley. This heat was so immobilising . . . . but it hadn't slowed down Joe Hegarty in the least, last night. On the contrary.

I can't remember when, she thought. I actually cannot remember the last time we made love like that. It's so long ago, I'd forgotten it was possible, forgotten all those reserves of passion as if they were oases dried up in a desert. We used to have nights like those, once, long ago when we were first married . . . where did they go, how did we lose them?

When we grew up, I suppose. When we became steady sensible adults, with work to do, responsibilities, commitments, demands on our time. We had a child to rear – two children, for a while – Joe had his job and I had my B & B. It's so hard to run wild all night in bed when you have to be up at six to cook breakfast for people who stay in your house, cramping your privacy, cramping your style. I don't think I even realised how inhibiting it was. But that's not a problem here, the walls are two feet thick . . . not that we were thinking about the walls, last night! After such an unpromising start, we certainly made up for lost time.

What possessed Joe? It was more than just the fact of not having seen me for a few months. It was something – something to do with Léo. The situation couldn't have been more innocent, yet Joe reacted almost as if he suspected the man of having an affair with me, or aspiring to have one. It must be true what they say, about every man being jealous of French men. Well . . . if it brings out the beast in him like that, then maybe I should invite Léo to visit more often! Our sex life is suddenly revitalised, and it would be wonderful if we could sustain it the way it went last night. Is it possible, I wonder? Or will the novelty wear off, will Joe start rolling over and snoring again the way he used to? He didn't snore last night – not that he got much sleep – had it something to do with the weight he's lost? It must have.

Oh, hallelujah! No more pub, no more Dave Doherty, no more rivers of beer, and no more snoring?! I thought it would take ages to break him of all those habits, yet here he is already broken of them all – and of his own free will. I don't know what Mam said or did to him, but she seems to have worked miracles. Now, if I can just get him settled in here, ease him somehow into France, French life . . . well. That's going to be another day's work. I'm not exactly what you'd call integrated myself, by a long shot. But maybe now Joe's here we can work at it together. And work at our marriage, since he won't be going off to work at anything else. He'll be free to help me, we'll see much more of each other . . . our marriage might not have been broken, but it was certainly damaged. Now, who knows? Maybe it's not too late, maybe we can take another shot at it, fix it so we can't even see the cracks? Some day I might even get him to open up to me about Hazel, find out what he really thinks or feels. I got Finn to talk to me, and it did him so much good, it's worth trying for Joe too.

Why have we hardly ever talked about Hazel? Because he thinks the subject might upset me? Because he's still doing his macho protective thing, being 'manly', steering his family through a crisis that happened sixteen years ago? He's a good guy, and I know he's always meant well, but he's kept so much bottled up. He doesn't realise that you have to let go, finally . . . let go, and move on, if you can.

Anyway. It's so tempting to simply sit here dreaming all day, leave him to snooze and catch up on his sleep, but he'll burn in this sun. Besides, I'd like him to see a little of the Languedoc, have a day on my own with him before all these people of Shona's start arriving. Would Mam mind, I wonder, if I left her here today with Shona? Why don't I go and ask her.

'Mam! What are you doing – still scrambling eggs?' Wending her way into the kitchen, Aileen peered, her vision blurring in the move from light to shade.

Tessie looked annoyed. 'I'm trying to, but they won't scramble properly, there's something wrong with the milk.'

'Oh. It's not the same as at home, Mam. It's UHT – they do something to it to make it last longer.'

'Well, I don't like it.' Tessie frowned, looking as if her heart were hardening against France, or the milkman at any rate. Aileen smiled. 'Mam, it's very hot today, I was wondering if you might—'

'I'll stay here. Indoors, in the shade. It's far too hot for me outside. You have the house done up so lovely, I'll be perfectly comfortable here with a book or a few magazines.'

'You wouldn't mind if – if I go off with Joe for a while? I can make us a picnic and leave you a cold lunch, Shona's around if you want company—'

'I'll be fine. You go off with Joe, now, after all he is your husband and you haven't seen him for a long time.'

Calmly, she seemed to dismiss the subject, and it was only then that Aileen noticed a ceramic bowl in the middle of the table, neatly stacked with the tomatoes that . . . oh.

Oh. Uh. Thanks, Mam. You're really being very – what? What did you say?

'Mam, did you hear everything I just said?'

Drily, Tessie looked at her. 'Yes, dear. I did. I treated myself to a new hearing aid. It's worked wonders.'

Joe and Aileen went off to the fishing village of Collioure, where the day evolved in a way that neither of them expected. Insisting on driving, Joe not only mastered the French autoroute but pronounced it 'great', and although the heat was sweltering he merely said he'd prefer to roast than freeze, which he'd been doing all winter in Ireland. When they parked in Collioure, he took Aileen's hand, squeezing it complicitly, and then further surprised her by buying a guidebook.

'Well, I'd better find out where exactly I am, hadn't I?'

So they sat on the beach, reading the guide, discovering that pretty little Collioure had been a bit of a flirt, a favourite haunt of painters over the years including Matisse and 'some bunch of lads called Fauves, it says here. What the hell are Fauves when they're at home?'

Aileen didn't know, but she was pleased to see Joe interested, and relaxed, wearing the faintly proprietorial air of a man having recently reclaimed his wife. Far from criticising France, or setting his mind against it, he seemed happy to simply mingle amidst all the other tourists, exploring with no agenda at all.

'Nice little place, isn't it?'

Aileen had the oddest flash of *déja-vu*, of having been on honeymoon with this same man years and years ago, holding hands in the sun. 'Mmm . . . let's get some ice-cream? Raspberry, honey – oh, lavender, let's try that?'

Gamely Joe tried it, and nodded. 'Uh – unusual. Not bad. I hear the French eat the most peculiar things.' But he said it with a smile, as if he were prepared to indulge the nation in its folly. And then, while she licked the melting ice-cream, he looked candidly at her.

'So – do you like it, Aileen? France, I mean? You wanted so badly to come here . . . are you happy, now that you have?'

She knew what he meant; it wasn't the kind of question he could have asked her over the phone. They had badly needed this day, this time together. In his eyes, she could see that he wanted her to be happy. See that maybe he'd been worrying about her, thinking unvoiced thoughts, the kind of thoughts that strangled so many men like Joe Hegarty.

'Yes . . . I'm happy, Joe, now that you're here and Mam's here and Shona seems to be staying on. I missed you . . . I even wondered, once or twice, whether you . . . whether you really wanted to join me, or whether in the end you might rather stay in Galway with your work and your pals.'

What? What on earth had made her say that, where had such sudden candour come from? Surprisingly, he didn't challenge or even query her meaning, seeming to accept the blurted question as if it were natural. Instead he inclined his head, tacitly acknowledging what had lain dormant between them for months now, or maybe for even longer: the unspoken fear that their marriage might be in danger, not of breaking up, but of simply petering out. That was what had been so hard for so long: the lack of anything definite to get a grip on. At least when you had a blazing row you knew where you stood. But the Hegartys hadn't had a blazing row, a blazing anything, for years. Not until last night.

'Yeah. Well. I did do a bit of thinking about that. About you and me and Finn and . . . I may as well admit it, Aileen. I did wonder where we were all going, why you seemed to want to run away . . . I thought maybe it was me you wanted to get away from.'

There was an uncertainty, a tentative humility in his tone that tripped something in her heart. Was that really what he had been thinking, even dreading? That moving to France was her way of leaving him? Was that why he'd hesitated about coming over, delayed for so long? Suddenly, as she searched his face, something clicked between them, and she knew she was right. He had thought she'd left him. Left him without even having had the courage to tell him.

'Oh, Joe . . .' Reaching out, she touched her hand to his face. 'I think . . . I think we're going to have to try an awful lot harder. We've lost sight of each other, let everything slip and slide so far away . . . this must be what people mean, when they talk about drifting apart. If we have drifted, then . . . well, there are two of us in it. Half of it must be my fault.'

Averting his face, he plunged his hands in his pockets, looking out to sea, over the blue, blue horizon. Thinking.

'What do you mean? You haven't done anything.'

'No. Maybe that's the problem. Maybe I've been distracted, worrying about Finn, about money, about anything and everything except you. Not noticing you enough, paying attention . . . you haven't been happy, have you?'

'I – I haven't been happy that you haven't been. I thought maybe it was just . . . uh . . . the age you're at. Or the baby, that you never got over.'

Hazel?! Joe was talking about *Hazel*? For the first time almost since her death, he had voluntarily mentioned her? And now, she was the one finding it hard to do the same, to meet him halfway? Involuntarily, she put her hand to her throat.

'What makes you say that, Joe? I thought I did a pretty good job of – of getting over her.'

'You did. Too good. I knew things couldn't be right, the way you just packed that child away in your mind, as if she'd never existed. But since that was your way of dealing with it, I thought the best thing was to go along with it, just leave you in peace.'

Astonished, her mind whirling, she gazed at him, seeing things she had never seen before. Seeing a whole slew of things to be talked about, at last, from his point of view, and then from hers, and then from theirs. Big things and small things, that would add up to the sum of their marriage, and decide where it would go from here. Only now, when they were alone together in this new country, new context, communicating properly albeit unexpectedly, did she realise how very close they had edged to the brink of disaster. The Roman viaduct swam into her mind, and she had her worst vision yet of its sickening, dizzying dangers.

Yesterday, he had taken her hand. Now, she took his, slipping her fingers into his pocket, touching his warm, callused skin. 'Joe, I'm sorry. If you haven't been talking, maybe it's because I haven't been asking. All of a sudden there are a hundred questions I want to ask you.'

For a moment he hesitated; then he slowly turned to look at her, fully, frankly. 'Well, there's only one I want to ask you.'

'What is it?' She heard her own voice, hoarse, raw.

'Do you still love me?'

It wasn't automatic. She didn't grab at him and assure him that yes, of course she loved him. Instead, she stood in silence, recognising the huge effort it had cost him to ask, to venture this question that made him so vulnerable. Taking what time she needed, letting him know that she had to think about it, she weighed her answer slowly, and very carefully. His honesty, his courage, deserved respect; and her response would commit them both irrevocably.

'Yes' she whispered at length, 'I do love you, Joe. I love you enough to want to go on, to work at it, if you want to go on with me, and work with me?'

He did not reply. He simply stood beside her, absorbing it, pondering the vista. And then, removing her hand from his pocket, he laced his fingers into hers, mooring her to him while still looking out over the ocean.

'It's nice here, Aileen. I think maybe I'm going to like it.'

Sliding her arm around his waist, she nodded, and leaned into his chest.

No more was said, that hot afternoon in Collioure, but as they wended their way back to Le Mas in the evening they knew that it would be. Tonight, or tomorrow, next week, next month . . . sooner or later, now, they would talk. Talk themselves down from the lethal ledge on which they had been perched. Neither of them knew how they had got up there, nor which of them had thrown the lifeline to the other; all they knew was that they were both clinging to it. In the car on the way home, they scarcely spoke; Aileen simply sat with her hand lightly resting on his leg, and he kept his eyes on the road.

Slicing into their reverie, Shona came bounding out to meet them. 'Well, I've been on the phone to everyone in Ireland! My parents can't come, because their own season is just starting – the boutique, the boats – but Crys and Emily are going to fly over on Tuesday.'

'Lovely' said Aileen, smiling distantly, wondering how long it might take to get politely through supper *en famille*, so that she could leave them all and take her husband to bed, where she would say and do things that would leave him in no doubt about her feelings for him.

I never knew, she thought. I never knew he was hurting so much. Not about *me*?

It's a good thing, Shona reflected as she embarked yet again for that fixture of expat life, the airport, that Crys and Emily are coming over. I don't know what exactly is going on in the Hegarty family, but it's something that doesn't include me. They're like American pioneers, circling the wagons, huddling together so nobody can get at them. I wouldn't dare ask, but it looks like some kind of regrouping . . . even Tessie seems a bit out on the fringes at the moment. With any luck she and Emily will hit it off, and they'll enjoy each other.

As for me – well, it looks like crunch time. I can't hang out here like this for ever, I have to take some decisions. Will take them, after I've had a good chat with Crys and find out how things are going with Gavin. Funny . . . I always thought Gavin was so gorgeous, and always thought Joe was such a plodder, yet if anyone asked me to choose which one I'd prefer for a husband, I'm not sure any more which one I'd pick. Not that anyone is asking! But Joe seems to be coming out of himself in some way, whereas Gavin – well, I suppose Crys will tell me more when she arrives. I mean, not that there's anything wrong with Gavin, exactly . . . it's just that I didn't realise he's so demanding, takes so much humouring. I couldn't humour anyone the way she seems to be humouring him; we'd be divorced within days, probably in casualty too.

More importantly, just now, what on earth am I going to live on? I don't want to worry Aileen – not that she looks as if she would be worried at the moment – but there is no way I can survive the whole summer until Le Mas starts making some kind of profit. Not that there's even any guarantee it will. I don't have a job any more, I don't have any income and I am going to have to seriously figure this out.

Maybe Crys might have some ideas? God, I am so looking forward to seeing her!

But several days elapsed before Shona got a chance to talk alone with Crys. Suddenly Le Mas seemed full of people, seven of them, settling in, milling round, getting acquainted, starting conversations that constantly got diverted. For the first time Shona and Aileen began to glimpse the way the place would look when it was fully functioning, buzzing with life, filled with people who needed all kinds of attention.

Although everyone was helpful and considerate, there were still endless meals to be cooked, laundry to be done, shopping, driving, entertaining. Naturally, everyone wanted to explore, which meant a lot of outings to places of interest, and everyone was on differing timetables: Finn who was working, Joe who wasn't, Emily who wanted to pack a lot into her visit, Crys who in mid-pregnancy preferred to rest in the shade and needed a lot of sleep. With a kind of serene detachment, Tessie set about replanting the vegetable patch, and Aileen watched with affectionate amusement as her mother knelt on the warm dry earth with a trowel, wearing a battered sun hat askew, getting dug into French country life at her own pace in her own way.

And then there were visitors, too. Raoul Lascaux dropped in, Finn brought two friends back from work for supper, Aude Villandry unexpectedly arrived to ask whether anyone had found a scarf she'd lost on her previous visit. Nobody had, but since everyone was gathered on the terrace ready to eat, Aileen politely invited her to join them, which Aude did, darting intermittent glances down the table at Finn, who was chatting at the other end of it with his new pals.

Oh, Aileen thought, looking at her, lay off, Aude! All right, so he looks weird, but he's not weird, he's my son and underneath all that tacky clobber he's a nice lad. In fact I can't see why you're so dressed up yourself, in this heat, in that jacket and skirt and tights and striped cravat. You'd look much prettier in a little cotton dress and sandals – anyway, my son is not some kind of freak and if you don't stop staring at him I may well say or do something we'll both regret.

'Pretty young one' Joe remarked, spreading Brie on bread; French cheese seemed to taste better in France than it did in Ireland. 'Who is she?'

'She's my cross' Aileen sighed, 'from the tourism office. I

have to be nice to her. But I hate the way she looks at Finn, as if he were something the cat dragged in.'

Thoughtfully, Joe surveyed his son. 'Well, he's not exactly Pierce Brosnan, is he?'

No. With his hair growing out, a sprouting mixture of sandy tufts and Mohican mauve, Finn was barely presentable this evening in a slashed T-shirt, combat trousers and a horribly aggressive pair of steel-tipped boots. But Aileen warmed to him as she watched him gesturing and laughing with his friends, relaxing, settling so amiably into this new country which, after all, he did not appear to hate. His French was coming on way better than hers, and she thought how much easier it must be to pick up new things at twenty than it was at her age. New people, too: she had yet to make any friends as he was doing.

Speculatively, she wondered whether he had yet talked to Joe, whether father and son had had a chance for a conversation she did not want to enquire into, sensing it was man-to-man. As likely as not, Finn would say nothing to her, but she hoped Joe would – if not immediately, then whenever the time was right. As yet, Joe had said nothing more about their marriage, either its past or its future; it was as if, lacking words, he was letting his body language do the talking. Suddenly, sex had become the medium through which they were communicating, and for now that was more than enough. Once, they'd even sneaked off for 'a nap' after lunch, which would have been out of the question at home when he was working all day in the hardware store.

So, she thought with some satisfaction, there's that much to be said for moving abroad at least. It breaks old patterns. It changes the way people communicate. It gives you new chances, and sometimes it even restores old memories.

I remember, now, the man I married. I remember the night

we made Finn, and the night we made Hazel . . . I remember being young, and looking the way Crys looks now, with that dreamy, expectant smile on her face.

On a morning mellow as warm milk, Joe shepherded his mother-in-law, her new chum Emily O'Brien, and his wife into the car. Despite not speaking a word of French, he had somehow gleaned from Raoul Lascaux that there was a vineyard in some nearby valley that made excellent wine, which the proprietor sold loose to anyone who sought it out, and Aileen had expressed interest in acquiring some. She would be needing supplies for her B & B, which through Aude now had its first bookings for early May.

So off they set, Joe looking comical Shona thought, in shorts; his legs were snow white. But his face was eager, and she was grateful to him for looking after Emily, who confessed to always having wanted to visit a vineyard. Apparently there were quite a number of things, in fact, that Emily had long wanted to do; 'You know, Shona, this is my first holiday in years and I must say I'm enjoying every moment of it.'

Waving them off, Shona turned and strolled barefoot across the reseeded grass to Crys, who was stretched in a deckchair with her hands rather majestically folded on her little bump. Iridescent blue nails, this morning, to match the sky; and long loose black curls, and some kind of drifting apple-green dress. Pleased to have time together at last, Shona sat down beside her.

'Well, I guess I'm the châtelaine for today! Can I get you anything?'

Crys lifted one queenly arm a fraction. 'Oh, no, thanks, I'm perfectly happy.'

Was she? Could she be, after all she had said about not wanting this baby? Or was her newly vague, drifting smile a

348

mere mask, hiding torment? I have to know, Shona thought. I have to take this chance while I have it.

Inclining her head, she looked closely at her, frankly curious. 'Are you, Crys? Are you . . . and Gavin . . . okay?'

Pushing back the brim of her hat, Crys sat up a fraction, letting Shona see her face without dissembling. Such a lovely face, and so serene, this peaceful morning. At first she didn't answer; and then, gradually, she seemed to accept the moment for what it was. Shona had the right to ask this question.

'Yeah . . . we are, Sho. We're okay.'

Okay? Was that enough? Would 'okay' get you through a resisted pregnancy and resisted motherhood? Closely, Shona looked into the brown, long-lashed eyes she knew so well.

'Tell me more, Crys. Tell me what's changed between you, that you can be here like this, so – so calm?'

Frowning, Crys seemed to briefly tense. And then she wasn't tense, she was flopping back in her deckchair with a smile spreading across her face like melting chocolate.

'I have.'

She said it so casually that for one fleeting moment Shona was almost disarmed – just one moment, that flashed down her spine like lightning.

'You've changed?'

'Yes.'

'Or been changed?'

'Oh, Sho, come on!' Lazily, Crys turned to reach for a glass of milk, held it cradled in her hand without drinking. 'I'm going to be a mother. It does things to people.'

'The last thing it did to you, as I recall, was send you screaming into orbit. You didn't want it, Crys, you know you didn't! You wanted to drive a relief truck to Africa and you were furious at the mere prospect of being pregnant.'

'Yes, well . . . I've been thinking. Thinking that maybe charity begins at home.'

What? Was this Crys talking, or Gavin? 'Maybe you'd better explain that.'

Somehow, Crys's expression seemed to convey that explanation was superfluous. But then, catching Shona's eye, she faced her defiantly. 'Look, Sho. I've done a hell of a lot of work for the Red Cross, at home in my own house, and that's what I plan to continue doing, okay? There's no way anyone can go off anywhere in Africa with a baby, all the drought-stricken countries are roasting hot for chrissakes not to mention riddled with disease. I'm nearly thirty, I have to have a bit of sense. Besides, who knows? Maybe this baby of mine will turn out to be the blueprint for a whole new world. A better world.'

'But – but you wanted to help those countries! That was why you didn't want a baby!'

'Well, I've decided I want one now. Later, when it's safely reared, we'll maybe review the situation then. For now, I am having my first child, starting a family which I intend to love unreservedly. I am going to give it priority over—'

'Over your own life? Your own vocation, which you know damn well is—'

'Shona!' Abruptly, Crys sat up and slammed down her glass. 'Stop it! Just *stop*, d'you hear? Don't say another word which – which might cause any trouble between us.'

For a few moments Shona did stop, letting this sink in, wondering how far you could push a friend without losing sight of her. Did Crys really not want to talk about this crucially important subject? She seemed almost unrecognisable, her voice rimmed with a hard edge Shona had never heard before.

And then, in the sharp silence, she heard the whisper of

truth, saw it rise and fall in Crys's eyes. Reaching out to her, she touched her arm.

'It's Gavin, isn't it? Gavin has talked you—'

Under her hand, Crys's skin was cool. Astonishingly cool, in the clammy heat. And her look was cool too. 'Shona, Gavin is my baby's father. Plus, my husband. Maybe some day when you have a husband you'll understand what that means, you'll find out how a marriage evolves, how people have to expand, to accommodate other people's wishes besides their own.'

As if she had been slapped, Shona recoiled, each word stinging her skin. At first she was almost numb with pain, her eyes stinging, scarcely able to believe that Crys could speak to her like that; and then as the shock wore off she saw that this was no longer Crys speaking, at all. It was Gavin. Gavin, the husband who took priority over a friend.

Was that as it should be? Maybe it actually was? Whatever had happened between them, he had won the battle for Crys. Like Joe Hegarty, he was apparently much more important to his wife than she, Shona, could ever have imagined. Which was why Brendan Wright had decided against marrying Shona Fitzpatrick, the maverick woman who could not put any man first in her wilfully selfish, and therefore solitary, life.

Letting her hands fall into her lap, she thought about it. Thought, and thought, trying to work her way at least halfway round to where Crys was coming from. How important, she asked herself, is Crys to me? How much do I mean to her? Can we ever go back to where we were before she said that, and do we want to?

I'm stunned. I'm horrified. I feel as if she's been kidnapped and doesn't want to be rescued . . . she's like that heiress Patty Hearst who was kidnapped years ago by revolutionaries and ended up joining their army. Should I leave Crys to simply march, now, to Gavin's drum? Move on, find other friends?

351

Maybe I should. We can't go on as we were. We can only go on if I'm prepared to take her as she is now. Mrs Gavin Sheehan . . . Jesus, I wouldn't be surprised if she actually christens this child in church and decks it out in white frills. Uhhh! All this for gorgeous Gavin, who adores her, so long as she plays by his rules?

Well. Guess what, Gavin. You're not getting her that easily. Some day Crys might just wake up, snap out of this hypnosis of yours and get herself back. If and when she does, she'll need her friends, because you won't be sticking around then, will you? You probably can't even imagine anyone sticking around, when someone fails to behave the way they're supposed to behave.

Crys, at this point in her life, is suddenly not behaving the way I thought she'd behave, at all. But I'm going to stick around, if she wants me to, because she's been my friend for years, and I love her, and yes, I am prepared to let her change, if change is what she needs or wants. Maybe it won't work, maybe we'll lose each other in the end, but hey, let's try. Let's see if Crys and Shona can weather a storm in their friendship. I couldn't do what she's doing in a million years, but does that mean we can only be friends if she does things my way?

If that were so, I'd be as bad as Gavin. I'd be manipulating her too, when she's vulnerable. If everyone pulls at her, in different directions, she might end up in bits.

As if in slow motion, Shona stood up, went to Crys, bent over her and, speechlessly, hugged her. At first Crys did not respond . . . and then Shona felt something shifting, loosening, somewhere in her depths. Without a word, Crys lifted her arms, draped them over Shona's shoulders, and touched her cheek to hers. Thus they remained, mute, until Crys found her voice, murmured almost inaudibly.

'Sho – I'm sorry – but I—'

Shona put a finger to her lips. 'Ssh. It's okay. I know. You're under pressure . . . you're having a baby. People are allowed to act weird when they're pregnant.'

Crys dipped her head, too late to hide the single tear that rolled down her face. And then, brushing it covertly away, she looked up again.

'Thanks, Sho. Thanks for seeing this from where I'm looking at it, and sticking with me.'

Like his vines, the vigneron was ruddy and stubby, wearing a navy beret with a stem that made him look, Aileen thought, like a flat-cap mushroom. Tessie and Emily, who had sampled no fewer than five of his wines, were giggling together like school-girls, finding their French hilariously fluent, encouraging Joe to fill up not one but half a dozen demi-johns with wine for Le Mas. Which Joe was doing, despite having barely tasted anything, because he had to drive the fifty kilometres home. Lugging the jars, he held them while first white and then red wine was pumped into them from huge vats in a pungent barn, grinning at the novelty of it all.

'Exactly like a petrol station! Pity Guinness wouldn't think to simplify life like this, eh?' With which he took a handle of each jar while the vigneron obligingly took another, and between them they hefted them one by one to the boot of the car.

'So' he said when all the jars were safely stored, 'what do we owe for all this, are we going to be ruined?'

Starting to pull notes from his wallet, he looked enquiringly at the vigneron, who gaped startled. 'Oh no, way too much, m'sieu, let's see . . .' fishing a notebook from a cluttered makeshift desk, he licked a pencil, jotted figures and thrust the result under Joe's nose.

'Good God. Is that all?'

Emphatically the vigneron nodded, and then without a word he walked enigmatically away. Two minutes later he was back, clutching a bottle under either arm, striding up to Joe, presenting them to him. Bewildered, Joe blinked, but the man mimed and made himself clear: this was good wine, more than mere table quality, and it was his gift to his new customers, whom it would be his pleasure to see again in the future.

Cautiously, Joe eyed him; and then he exploded in laughter. Loud, hearty laughter that Aileen had not heard for years. 'Well, isn't this the way to do business! Thank you very much, sir!' With that, he thrust out his hand, which the bereted vigneron vigorously shook, and each man slapped each other on the back.

As they made their way back to the car, he started to whistle, whereupon Emily smiled at him and Tess smiled enigmatically at Aileen. Looking around them all, Aileen saw them as if in a tableau, spotlit in the sun, and suddenly she found herself getting the picture. A whole new picture, seen in new light from a new angle, as if she had stepped sideways in an art gallery for a better view.

They're loving it here. They're all having a ball, taking to France like ducks to water, and I'm the one on the outside, looking in.

12

Emily was having a wonderful time. Simply wonderful. For the first time since Séan died a year ago, she felt sunlight stealing into her soul, the sensation of emerging from hibernation, waking up to find the world welcoming. It's been too long, she thought, since I was last in France. I'd forgotten the simple pleasure of eating warm fresh bread, strolling down a cobbled street, listening to the drip of a fountain, sitting perfectly still under a plane tree with the sun caressing my shoulders. Even those children playing in the alleyways . . . they sound like cicadas, chirping away, so bright and lively. There are no children in my corner of Connemara – none that their parents would dare let out anyway, for fear they'd be abducted or worse. In France, children still seem to have a childhood.

It's only a brief trip, but it's been a joy. It was so good of Shona to invite me, and I want to invite her out before I go home. Take her to a nice restaurant, the kind she doesn't seem to frequent any more. She's not saying anything, but I know things are tight since she quit her job. I'll ask her if she knows somewhere good, and hopefully we can go by ourselves. Much as I'd like to invite everyone, there are so many of them. Including Aileen's mother, who's been such good company. The more I get to know Tessie, the more I like her . . . but I do want Shona to myself, just for one evening.

'Somewhere really *French*, Shona! Not fussy, not trendy, not even in the guidebooks. Just some local bistro with great food and big white tablecloths and wine from the owner's own vine-yard, d'you know anywhere like that?'

Shona laughed. 'Yes. I think so. I've never been in the place, but I've seen it, heard the food is fabulous. Can't remember the name, but it's on the far side of the village, about a mile down a dusty little road in the middle of nowhere.'

'Right. Doll yourself up so, and we'll have a girls' night out.'

Doll they did, both aware that obscure bistros in remote corners sometimes turned out to be surprisingly dressy. Slipping into high heels, short dress, jewellery and lipstick, Shona stared at herself in the mirror: well, madame, it's been a while since you last turned up the voltage, hasn't it? But dressing up feels good tonight, if only for a change, it would be too easy to live in shorts all day every day, lose sight altogether of the Shona who used to have such a busy social life.

In true French fashion, the restaurant was almost full when they reached it just after seven, and the maitre d' frowned into his bookings. 'You're sure? O'Brien, table for two?'

'Yes. Quite sure.'

Tugging at his earring, he thought it over, and finally led them to a small table tucked into a dark niche between the fire-place and the kitchens. Emily and Shona smiled at each other: this was where two women always ended up, out of sight in case they might ruin the meals of proper couples. As the maitre d' was seating her, Shona looked up at him.

'If a table comes free anywhere by the windows, please let us know? We'll move after our starters.'

Uh. Uh, yes, of course. He glided away, and, glancing at each other, they resigned themselves to their assigned location. Window tables were for male-female couples. Opening their menus, they took comfort in its handwritten appeal, which included some beckoning dishes involving asparagus, aubergines, duck, tomatoes and anchovies.

'And a glass of champagne, I think, to start' Emily said enthusiastically.

'Champagne? Oh, no—'

'Oh, yes. I've had a lovely holiday, Shona, and I want to thank you for it.'

'Emily, I want to thank *you*, for standing by me through that awful court case.'

Raising one eyebrow and one finger a fraction, Emily attracted the waiter's attention and ordered a half bottle of Veuve Clicquot. Looking faintly surprised, he scampered away to fetch it. When it arrived and was poured, Shona laughed. 'Well, here's to our merry widow! It's a joy to see you looking so well, Emily.'

Appreciatively, Emily studied her rising bubbles, and sipped. 'Indeed. I won't pretend it hasn't been a hard year, Shona, but I must say I'm feeling much better now. Thanks to you.'

'Pfft! You like France, don't you? You've been here before, too, judging by your French.'

Emily smiled. 'Yes. A thousand years ago, before I married Séan, before . . . this and that. I spent a year at the Sorbonne when I was nineteen.'

'No! Did you really? Doing what?'

'Studying French and having a blazing romance with a lad called Gustave. As they say, memories are made of this.'

Hearing the song in her head, Shona nodded. 'So they are. Everyone should have a romance, before reality bites. What happened to Gustave?'

'Oh, he went off to be a scientist in Lyon, and marry some count's daughter. Then I met Séan and forgot all about him . . . but I never forgot France. It is just so lovely, isn't it?'

'Yes. I adore it. Which is why I'm going to let you into a little secret, Emily.'

Their first food arrived, and Emily smiled at her buttered asparagus as if meeting an old friend. 'Let me guess. You're going to stay here. You're going to sell your apartment in Galway and use the money to pay off Le Mas?'

Stunned, Shona gasped, salmon poised on her fork. 'How did you guess?'

'Oh, Shona – anyone can see that you belong here. It's simply in your blood. You think French, you breathe French . . . you belong. My only question is – what are you going to do? You'll own Le Mas outright but you'll hardly have much to live on after that, will you?'

'Enough for maybe six months. Breathing space. I know it's a drastic step, but it's the only option. I love it here so much, I want to stay, I know there's a price to be paid and I've decided it's worth it. Tell me, Emily . . . do you think Le Mas will do well?'

Her tone was anxious, and Emily reflected. 'Yes. I think it could do extremely well. If Aileen goes about it the right way.'

'What do you mean?'

'I mean that – well, she certainly knows how to run a B & B. She cooks well, keeps house well, she's a "people person" who loves having lots of life and buzz around her. My only worry is . . . whether . . . she's happy here?'

'Don't you think she is?'

Pausing, Emily dabbed her napkin to her lips, taking stock. 'No. If you want my frank opinion, Shona, I don't. Oh – she's not *unhappy,* now she has her mother and husband around her! But Tessie will be going back to Ireland . . . Aileen admits to having made no new friends here, she misses her sister, her neighbours, has scarcely learned a word of French, isn't really adapting very well if you want my opinion. She had her own reasons for leaving Ireland . . . but it's my guess that sooner or later she might want to go "home", as she significantly calls it.'

'Oh, God. Don't say that, Emily. I need her here! I couldn't run Le Mas to save my life.'

'No, I don't believe you could! But you must find some work, Shona – you're uncertain and unfocused and I've never seen you look so lost before. I wish things had worked out with Brendan . . . I realise now that you weren't suited to each other, but still, it's such a shame. I introduced you and I feel so bad about—'

'Don't be silly! You did your best, it wasn't your fault that two grown adults couldn't make a go of things after that.'

'And then your job—'

'Yes, well, I certainly have been having lousy luck. But look at you, surviving without Séan, all on your own out in the wilds of Connemara – is it difficult, Emily? Do you hate it, without him?'

'No. I don't exactly hate it. But I don't love it any more. Being alone at my age is not easy, especially not now that the Irish countryside has got so dangerous and everyone bolts their doors . . . it's not the Ireland I knew and loved. But Shona, don't try to divert the question, which is, what are we going to do with *you*? H'mm?'

'I don't know! I told Aileen I don't want a nine-to-five job, but I may have to settle for one yet – be grateful for one, even. My career prospects have hit what you might call a wall.'

Emily eyed her over a platter of arriving duck. 'Are you sorry you went to court, Sho? Sorry you didn't just ignore Terry O'Hagan and go on working with him?'

'Christ, no! I'd rather starve in a hovel.' Defiantly, she spooned some orange sauce onto her plate, grinning as the irony hit her, and looked around the room, away from a conversation which was heading dangerously close to the bone. A thirty-six-year-old woman with no career, no husband – even if she was glad she hadn't compromised, hadn't played

359

anyone else's game by anyone else's rules, she'd paid a hefty price for her independence. Maybe Emily – and who else? – thought her a prize idiot. That's what I must look like, she thought, to lots of people.

I could have had Brendan if I'd humoured him, could have kept my career by humouring Terry O'Hagan. Only then I wouldn't be here tonight, would I, enjoying this lovely meal in the Languedoc? I'd be in Galway, silently sick to my stomach.

'Are you enjoying your meal, Emily? Do you like this restaurant?'

'Yes, I am and I do! What do you think of it?'

'I think the food is absolutely fantastic. I just wish the service was a bit friendlier and they'd give us a decent table. Plus, if I were the manager I wouldn't be closing at nine o'clock, I'd stay open until eleven at this time of year. The French don't understand that tourists want to party and have fun!'

'Mmm. It must be admitted that rural France isn't exactly wild. But it suits me, at my age, I've had a marvellous time and you'd better invite me again!'

'Of course I will. In the autumn, when there's room – maybe by then I'll have a whole new career. Shona Fitzpatrick, champion shelf-stacker in the local Spar!'

'Oh, now, Shona. Don't get discouraged. You'll find something . . . suited to your bossy nature! Something managerial.'

'Like what?'

'Let me think about it.'

'All right.' This was one of the things Shona loved about Emily, that she did think, and try to help, could sometimes be quite insightful. At sixty, she supposed, you had to have learned something.

And so they continued their meal, savouring cheeses with a soft, nutty red wine, followed by a crème brûlée made by some angel temping as a chef. Then coffee, and finally, reluctantly,

Emily requested the bill while Shona went to check out the loo. God, French loos! A lick of paint wouldn't hurt this one, a few more towels, lighting that didn't snap off after two minutes. Plus, fresh little flowers would soften its utilitarian look. That's what I'd do anyway, she thought, if I ran this place.

When she returned, Emily was looking perturbed, embroiled in battle. The manager had informed her that the establishment did not accept credit cards and, flustered, she was rummaging so anxiously in her bag that Shona was outraged. Marching up to the desk, she collared the manager.

'If you don't take cards, why isn't there a notice in the door to warn people before they come in?'

With a sigh, he threw up his hands. Because, apparently, nobody had thought of it.

'Why don't you take cards, anyway?'

Because the bank . . . surely madame understands?

'No' she said, 'I don't understand. This is no way to run a business. Other restaurants take them, so what's your problem?'

Looking anguished, he signalled to her to lower her voice; heads were turning. But, feeling for Emily, she was incensed. 'My friend is offering you a perfectly good card. If you won't take it, then I'm afraid that's your problem, not hers.'

Everyone was listening now, the manager's look turning from confrontational to conciliatory. 'But if she does not have enough cash, madame, surely you could . . . between you . . . ?'

'No. I'm her guest. And she is yours. She's a tourist and tourists should feel welcome in restaurants. So I tell you what. She'll write you a cheque. An Irish cheque. How's that?'

'But – but –' He couldn't say what he was clearly thinking: bloody hell, my bank will charge me to cash a foreign cheque. Rooted, Shona stood her ground, waiting for an answer, unconscious of the diners also waiting agog at other tables.

Finally, after a very long pained think about it, he caved in, looking hugely resentful. 'Very well. If your friend will give me some identification. I will accept her Irish cheque. Just this once.'

'You'd better, if you want your money. You know, it's really too bad you don't run this restaurant a bit better, because the food and wine are great. I'd recommend it to everyone if it weren't for your attitude.'

So saying, smiling sweetly, she returned to Emily to soothe her ruffled feathers. Honestly! No credit cards, in this day and age?! 'Don't worry. It's all sorted. You can just write him a cheque.'

'Oh, Lord . . . what a fuss. I'm so sorry, Shona.'

'Why? About what? This is not your fault, all you did was treat me to a delicious meal.'

At speed, their coats arrived and they were hustled into them. Finn, who had obligingly delivered them to the restaurant, was coming to pick them up in Aileen's car. Frostily, Shona looked at the muttering manager, who was studying the cheque as if it were a blueprint for nuclear holocaust. 'Do you mind if we wait here until our lift arrives?'

Two chairs were grudgingly furnished, and Shona was still trying to calm Emily's blushes when, from a distant corner table, she noticed a middle-aged, curly-haired, bespectacled man putting down his napkin, standing up and making his way with a resolute air in her direction.

Oh ho. The owner, dining in his own restaurant, coming to sort her out? Well, he needn't think – stopping dead in front of her, the man made a small bow to them both, smiled politely, and took a business card from his pocket.

'*Bonsoir, mesdames*. Please excuse me. My name is Olivier Dessanges. I couldn't help overhearing your – er –'

'My row with the manager? Oh, it's a small restaurant, I

suppose everyone heard it! Sorry if I disturbed your dinner, but I was just so mad –' Shona laughed, and the man smiled. 'Well, yes, you did disturb us, but we were amused. And interested. It is rare for a customer to be so outspoken.'

'I used to work in the tourism industry' Shona replied drily. 'Challenging standards, trying to raise them, used to be what I did for a living. Why are you giving me this card?'

She glanced at it speculatively, and he raised a hand, as if to say this was not the time or place to explain why. 'Because, if you would be so good, I would like you to telephone the number on it whenever you get a chance.'

With that he bowed again, and was gone.

The card lay in Shona's bag for quite some time after that. Curiosity wouldn't let her throw it out, but neither could she bring herself to ring the number on it. That man, she thought, was trying to pick me up. I'm old enough to know a come-on when I see one, and I'm old enough to have learned from all the other men littering the path to where I am now. I'm just no good with men. Hopeless. Everything always goes pear-shaped, so I might as well admit I'm doomed to be single for the rest of my days. There's been a lot of pain, for all concerned, and I'm not risking any more. So there we are, Mr Dessanges, sorry, but *voilà*. Besides, I'm busy. I have to organise some advertising for Le Mas and get some cards of my own printed, I have a little alp of paperwork to plough through, all sorts of distractions.

Meanwhile, Emily, Tessie and Crys were all leaving, on three different flights on different days, which meant three more treks to the airport. 'Shona, you take Crys' Joe proposed, 'I'll take Emily and Aileen will take Tessie.'

That suited everyone. Shona wanted a last few hours to talk to Crys, hoping that maybe between them they might be able to see some window in her future, some hope that she might yet get another chance. For now, Shona saw, she has to compromise. But maybe she won't always have to. She's barely thirty; who knows what way things might turn out later? After all, if anyone had told me a year ago that I'd be selling my apartment in Galway to invest my whole future in France, I'd have said they were nuts. Now, it's probably me who's nuts. If anyone had told Aileen she was going to get her wish, that her dream of living abroad was going to come true, she wouldn't have believed it. Yet here she is. I just hope she's going to enjoy it, after all, hope Emily's wrong about her being homesick. Or that if she is homesick, she'll get over it. You can't keep changing your mind all your life about what you want, can you? Sooner or later you have to decide, and go for it, and stick with it. Christ, I hope Aileen sticks with Le Mas, for long enough to make a success of it at least. She's happier since Joe arrived . . . but she hates letting go of Tessie.

Such was Aileen's desperation to cling to her mother until the last moment that she even steeled herself to drive over the dreaded viaduct, and was very quiet on the day before Tessie's departure.

'Cheer up, Ma' Finn said laconically, 'Granma's room will soon be full of paying guests and you'll be a rich capitalist.'

'Shona' Aileen retorted, 'is the capitalist, since she owns Le Mas, and if anyone gets rich it'll be her. So why don't you go on down to the handball alley now, and hang out with your pals, h'mm?'

Finn had discovered not only a handball alley but a swimming pool too, a skating rink, tennis courts, a cinema, all kinds of local amenities that nobody had known existed. 'France' he enthused, 'has great facilities. I'm definitely getting to like it here.'

The same went for Joe, tanning as he pottered round doing

odd jobs, ambling down to the village to watch games of *boules*, somehow communicating with people much better than Aileen could. Isn't that rich, she thought; the man who has such difficulty in talking to his wife has no difficulty in talking to everyone else. In pidgin French, or sign language, or whatever is getting him by. My son and husband, who I was so afraid would hate France, are settling happily into it, while I . . . oh, God. I'm really going to have to do better than this. I *have* to stop listening to RTE and ringing Dymps and scrounging all the news from home. I'll think of it as a diet. Ireland is a box of chocolates that I simply must stop dipping into every day. It's not fair to Shona. Once our guests start arriving I have to give Le Mas my full attention and that's all about it. I have to learn French properly and make this bloody project work.

I just wish Mam weren't going home, that's all. I hate having to take her to the airport and put her on that plane. She's loved being here and I've loved having her, she's been such company and so helpful too, with the cooking and housework . . . I don't feel nearly so rushed or flustered when she's around. Emily says she has a 'soothing presence' and that just about sums it up.

Dammit, Mam, don't go. I wish you could stay. I'll have nobody to natter to, because Shona's not the same, she thinks I'm daft to take an interest in what she calls 'trivia'. But I am interested, I like talking about people's lives – okay, call it gossip if you like, but that's just the way I am. Now Mam will be gone and there'll be no gossip any more, because the only other woman I know here is Aude Villandry, and hell will freeze over before she starts gossiping. Or doing anything that might make me warm to her. Joe thinks she's pretty, of course, I suppose all the men do, but she's so cold.

In fact a lot of French women seem cold, now I think about it. Their prim little mouths look so disapproving, it's impossible to imagine them ever eating one crisp too many, or sinking a beer or laughing too loud, letting their hair down far enough to have any fun. They seem so – so distant, so disciplined. Unlike my sister and my mother, who are a pair of whoopee cushions.

I miss you, Dymps. And now I'm going to miss Mam too, more than ever. Not to mention feeling guilty about her missing me.

And then in an inexorable flurry of tears Tess was gone, Crys hugged Shona goodbye with glistening eyes, and Emily boarded her plane with a last nostalgic glance at France. Joe was very slow getting back to Le Mas after taking Emily to the airport, so long in fact that Aileen began to worry, wondering what had become of him.

'Well' she said when he finally arrived, tension making her tart, 'what kept you?'

'Ah' he said airily, 'I just decided to have a look round Carcassonne while I had the chance. Spent the afternoon browsing round.'

'Browsing what?' She couldn't imagine him doing art galleries, or shops, unless he'd found someplace that sold drills and hammers.

Shooting her the oddest look, halfway between wicked and defiant, he produced a plastic bag. 'I found a place' he said, 'selling nothing but these. They're in French, but that hardly matters.'

Handing her the bag, he waited while she opened it, took out the contents and gazed aghast. Videos. Five shrinkwrapped, scandalous, blue movies, each one featuring couples in lewd poses on the cover?! 'Joe Hegarty' she gasped, 'have you lost your marbles? What on earth's got into you? I'm the one supposed to be having the mid-life crisis, not you!'

'Ah' he said sheepishly, 'I just thought . . . a harmless bit of fun . . . we might learn something . . .'

We? We are supposed to watch these, together? Is that it? Spice up the sex life another notch – or are these emergency rations in case we start getting complacent again? Well. I – he – oh, honestly!

Fighting laughter, packing them primly back in their bag, she handed it to him. 'If your son finds these, they're yours, you can explain them.'

Leaning against the door, he seemed to think about it. 'Actually' he mused at length, 'I'd say Finn might be wanting to borrow them.'

'What?'

'Well, for God's sake, Aileen, you must have noticed! He won't want to be looking like a completely innocent idiot, will he, when it comes to the crunch?'

'What crunch? You mean – a girlfriend? Well, I hope he'll find one, but I also hope she won't be the kind of girl who—'

'Aileen' he sighed, patiently, 'you can't seriously mean to say you haven't noticed? Because if even I can see it, then it must be screamingly obvious.'

'What must? I have no idea what you're talking about.'

'I'm talking about our son Finn, and that young one who's planning to have him for breakfast!'

Absolutely bewildered, she stared at him. 'Young one? I haven't seen any young one, as you put it, all the friends he's brought home have been guys—'

Looking upwards, Joe addressed his next remark to the ceiling. 'She says she hasn't seen any young one. So, she's in denial then, is that it? My wife doesn't want to admit that her son is in imminent danger of being savaged by a scheming little French rip, because then he wouldn't be her little boy any more, would he?'

Utterly baffled, she heard herself repeating like a parrot. 'French rip? Who, where, what rip?'

'Under your nose! That little one with the shiny hair and eyes like conkers, who's always hanging round, dropping in at meal times when Finn gets home from work! What's her name – Ode?'

For a moment it still didn't sink in. And then, slowly, it did. 'Aude Villandry? But – you must be mad – Aude despises Finn! She looks at him as if he—'

'Aileen' Joe continued in the carefully rational tone of one addressing the village idiot, 'she's in love with him – or lust, at least. Any fool can see it. She never takes her eyes off him! Why else do you think she hangs out here so much? It's hardly for your bright eyes, is it?'

'No, but –' Scrambling to explain, Aileen found she couldn't. Somehow Aude had simply insinuated herself into the fabric of Le Mas, to the point where her visits now went virtually unnoticed. 'But Joe, she – she'd buy and sell Finn! She's way too sophisticated for him, far more mature, she—'

'She fancies the arse off him. And she's biding her time, waiting to pounce the minute she gets him on his own. I'm telling you, Aileen, he's a marked man.'

Well. Sinking down at the table, the shock of the blue movies fading into this much bigger shock, she sat trying to absorb it. Aude *Villandry*, that cool little miss in her neat suits, ticking her clipboard, looking like butter wouldn't melt in her pouting little mouth? But this was ludicrous – so ludicrous, suddenly, that she crumpled with laughter.

'Oh, Joe! Are you serious? Are you sure?'

'Absolutely. It's plain as the nose on my face. If our son doesn't watch himself, he will soon find himself ravished beyond repair.'

Shaking with laughter, Aileen found the whole picture

absurd. 'Oh, Joe. Finn is so scruffy, such a mess, a girl like Aude couldn't possibly have the remotest interest in him! I mean, how would she produce him at the kind of parties she surely goes to? How would she explain him to her parents, what would she – what would she *do* with him?'

'Well, I can't say for sure, but my guess is that she'd chew him up and spit out the bones. Whether it'll last is another matter, but I'd say it'll certainly get started – she's not the kind of girl to let go, is she, once she sets her mind to something?'

No. No, she was not. Aude had an aura of total tenacity, right enough. Indeed her icy single-mindedness was one of the many things Aileen didn't like about her. She couldn't imagine anyone less appealing as a – a daughter-in-law?! Sweet God!

'Oh, Joe. I hope this is all a mistake. It must be. I don't like that girl and I don't want Finn to get—'

'H'mm. Well, I can't say I find her warm, myself, or sweet or cute or anything of that nature. But, Aileen . . . maybe she's exactly the kind of girl Finn needs? Whether he knows it or not? She'd smarten him up, get his game together, point him in the direction of success with her stopwatch ticking.'

'I'm sure she would. Only I thought he'd been doing a pretty good job of getting his own game together, lately. He has a job, he's making friends, he's respected locally, in fact I hear the village kids think he's a real cool hero . . . what more does he need?'

'He needs a woman who'd take charge of him and make sure he – he never falls off his ladder, so to speak! They're both young, probably there'd be no question of marriage, but it's my view that a stint with that young one would do Finn no harm at all. Regardless of whether or not we like her, she'd be good for him.'

Would she? Well . . . yes. Even as Joe spoke, Aileen could see that he was right. A glossy girl like Aude would indeed put a shine on Finn. Her mere presence would enhance him, his crude manners and raw clumsiness would be buffed up into something much more presentable . . . and who knew? Maybe he, in turn, would even liven up the ice maiden, melt her chilly little heart. Maybe this unlikely pair would, in fact, suit each other very well. Provided Joe Hegarty was not imagining the whole scenario – after all, a man who drove his mother-in-law to the airport and came back with five porn videos had to have a vivid imagination. More vivid than she'd realised.

'Then . . . then d'you think maybe I should bite the bullet, and give Finn a little nudge in Aude's direction?'

'I do. Why not invite her round some evening, and then after dinner you and I can sort of . . . you know . . . slip away?'

Lewdly, he grinned at her, and she stared at the bag of videos, and then at him, and then she envisaged Finn, left alone with the purposeful, predatory Aude.

Well, she thought, I must be thick as a plank. I never even suspected Finn was being stalked by a drooling tiger. But then, neither did I suspect I was married to a sex maniac. It seems I've been so deep in the woods, I never saw the trees. When did I wander into the woods?

Could it have been when Hazel died? If that's the case, then we've all travelled a very long way to get back to where we should have been in the first place. We've wasted so much time, let our family fray so badly . . . if we hadn't come here, we might have fallen apart altogether. Whether I like France or not, at least it has given us all another chance.

Without telling Aileen, Shona contacted an estate agency in Galway to put her apartment up for sale. The thought was a terrible wrench but, as Emily said when she heard the news, 'you can't make an omelette without breaking eggs, can you?'

Next, she rang Crys, who had keys to the apartment. Would Crys mind giving them to the estate agent?

'Oh, Shona, no! You can't be serious – we'll never see each other again!'

'Crys, France is not Australia. Of course we will.'

'But I won't be able to visit you any more, not with a baby ...'

'Crys, it's only a baby, not a bomb!'

'It is a bomb. A bomb that's going to blow my whole life sky-high.'

'Crys, people survive babies. As friends survive separations. We'll struggle on somehow, you'll see.'

Reluctantly, Crys agreed to help with the sale, which would eat money before it even made any, because next Shona had to find both Irish and French accountants to lead her through the financial labyrinth the deal would create. Plus a tax expert to advise her about Le Mas, before it turned a penny either ... suddenly hands seemed to be plucking at her from all directions, rifling her pockets, she was spending hours at her makeshift desk in her gîte, so engulfed in paperwork that Aileen got suspicious.

'But Sho, what can be so important? It's such a lovely day, why not come out for a breath of air?'

'Because I have business to do, in two countries, two languages, everything's in duplicate and each contradicts the other!' Startled, Aileen backed off; Shona had never barked at her like that before. Could the French 'system' really turn nice people into shrieking savages? Apparently it could.

And yet Joe was adapting so surprisingly well. In the evenings he got into the habit of watching the village *boules* game from a bench on the square, until one evening one of the players sat down beside him, offered him a glass of pastis and asked whether he'd like to have a go. Yes, said Joe, why not ... by the end of that same week he had joined the

Mézalas *boules* team, again managing to communicate without words, and was getting to know all sorts of people. His days, which had hitherto involved a bit of gardening and handyman work, began to expand as word spread that he could put up shelves and fix leaks and repair lawnmowers . . . 'Well' he said modestly, 'if my son can find work here there's no reason why I can't too.' With which he emptied his pockets one evening, letting grubby notes float onto the kitchen table while Aileen watched hypnotised; it had never entered her head that Joe might earn anything, much less before she did herself.

But then, at last, her first guests arrived, one pearly evening at the end of April. She was kneeling in the mole-fortified vegetable patch when she heard a car coming up the drive, and stood up covered in earth to see a startlingly blond, well-groomed couple getting out of a shiny Volvo. Wiping her hands on her apron, she went to greet them, and they retreated from her grubby handshake in alarm. 'Sorry' she said in English, 'I was just seeing to my lettuces. Can I help you?'

In unison, their gaze travelled from her to the house, inspecting it with considerably more approval. 'Yes' said the woman in clipped English, 'we were wondering if you might have a double room for tonight?'

Yes! Oh, yes, come this way, let me show it to you. As they followed her indoors the couple explained that they had seen one of the ads Shona had put up locally, and thought Le Mas looked lovely in the photo. 'It is lovely' Aileen said proudly, 'we only bought it last winter, but it's a very old, comfortable house, and you are our first guests – where are you from?'

Austria, chorused the couple, inspecting the room thoroughly before nodding at each other, and then at her. 'This is very nice. Do you have anyone to help with our bags?'

Like, a gold-liveried porter? This is only a B & B, you know, not the Ritz! 'Yes, certainly, my son will be here soon, I'll send him up with them.'

And so, to her surprise, it snowballed; Shona's marketing was so successful that within a few weeks Le Mas began to fill up; and then as April blossomed into May it was full almost every night, one weekend Aileen even had to turn some people away. 'I sent them to Aude in the tourism office' she grinned at Shona, 'it was either that or build an annexe.'

'Over my dead body! Annexes are horrible and everyone hates them. You can't tack new onto old. Besides, the trick is not to over-expand. Stay small and not bite off more than we can chew. Speaking of which, how are the Irish breakfasts going?'

'Fantastic. In fact they're becoming our trademark. Word seems to somehow be going round that this is the only place you can get hot sausages and bacon and proper tea – I'll have to buy a bigger freezer and send Joe to Ireland for more supplies.'

'Actually, I'll go myself. I have business to do in Ireland.' Scarcely had Shona said it than she was doing it, beating a track to the airport yet again, glad of the chance to kiss her apartment a last goodbye. It had served her well and she was fond of it, but now it was time to turn it into money. After all, she reminded herself, it's only four walls, it has none of the character of Le Mas, it'll sell in a flash and I'll have forgotten it in a week. Meanwhile, I'll see Crys and my parents and Emily, there won't be time to mope.

I'm doing the right thing, she muttered like a mantra as she boarded the plane, I am putting all my eggs in a French wicker basket and everything will work out great.

For a change?

*

'No, sorry, Aude' Aileen said into the phone, 'I don't have a twin room for this weekend, everything's full. But while you're on, I've been meaning to ask you . . . would you like to come to dinner some night? I mean, to thank you for all this business you've been sending us?'

At the other end of the line, Aude all but purred. Oh, yes, thank you Haileen, that would be lovely. Fixing Friday night, they hung up, and Aileen smiled grimly. She'd better have a word with Finn, make sure he didn't have any plans for Friday.

'But I'm going canoeing' he said when he heard, 'on the lake, me and Henri and Romain.'

'Can you not go on Saturday?'

'Well, yeah, I suppose . . . but why? What's the big deal on Friday?'

'I'm giving a little dinner party to thank all the people who've helped us to get on our feet. Raoul Lascaux and Aude Villandry and her uncle Léo – I'd like you to be at it, Finn. We owe them all thanks, as a family.'

Once, he would have said 'no way, stuff that, Ma.' Now, he simply sighed. 'Yeah. Okay. If I can bring a friend?'

'Well, why not? Henri, or Romain?'

'No – neither, actually. A girl. Her name's Martine. She's in the handball club and she's kinda – y'know, cool.'

Oh, damn! In Ireland, Finn had never brought friends home – and now, he wanted to bring one here on the very night she didn't want him to? A girl, to compete with Aude? Racking her brains, she couldn't think of any way to deflect this Martine . . . oh, well. Aude would just have to take her chances, then.

'All right. Does she speak any English?'

'No.' And suddenly he was spluttering with laughter. 'She doesn't need to!'

Huh? What was that supposed to mean? Deciding not to think about it, Aileen directed him to sort a mountain of laundry, which he uncomplainingly did while she embarked on the ironing. For a while they chatted companionably, until night fell and Joe returned from his game of *boules*. Look at him, Aileen thought with pleasure; home at nine o'clock, without even a thought of going on to the pub. Whoever said miracles happen at Lourdes wasn't far off the mark. Not that there's a pub open anywhere, of course, at this outrageous hour in rural France.

Making himself a sandwich, Joe ate it standing up, half listening to a soccer match some of their guests were watching in the television room. And then, almost idly, he looked up at a photo Aileen had, tentatively and without comment, put on a shelf.

'How old was Hazel when that was taken? She's got a good few teeth, so she must have been – what? About two?'

'Yes' Aileen said without looking up from her ironing, 'it was just before her second birthday.'

In the resounding silence that followed, she wondered if the entire family might implode. Never in sixteen years had Hazel been mentioned like this before, openly amongst all three of them.

'She's got your eyes, Ma' Finn remarked casually, and Joe concurred with affable ease.

'Aye, she certainly has. Now, I wonder would those people mind if I just sat down with them to watch the second half of that match?'

With that, he wandered out, but not before Aileen glimpsed him exchanging the briefest of glances with Finn. And then she realised that yes, father and son must have talked, after all, somewhere along the line. What they had used for words she could hardly imagine, but . . . as Finn said, maybe words didn't always matter?

*

'Léo? What do you mean, he's coming to dinner?'

'Oh, Joe, grow up! I couldn't invite just Aude, it would look too obvious. So Léo is coming – with his wife, for your information.'

'H'mph.'

'And Raoul Lascaux, minus his wife, who I don't think has seen daylight for decades.'

'Aileen – it's not going to be – you know, like, formal, is it?'

'Joe, let me remind you that this was all your idea. For Finn and Aude, remember? Only it turns out that Finn wants to bring some other girl, so Aude will have to slug it out with her. But no, it won't be formal, just supper on the terrace, despite the language thing I suppose we'll all muddle along somehow.'

Entertaining in France, according to Aileen's guide for beginners, was easy. Especially in summer. All you had to do was buy the simplest, best-quality food available, and serve it with a smile. Simple as that. Nobody even expected to change plates, they'd simply mop with bread between courses . . . so long as the wine was nice and the cheese was ripe, you could hardly go wrong.

So. Down to the market, for Bayonne ham, and pink prawns, and curly lettuce and five smelly, squishy cheeses. Buckets of bread, and a box of tiny, exquisite little desserts. Fresh flowers for the table, and there we are. No point in fussing any further. All I want to do this evening is give my son a chance to get himself a girlfriend – if he hasn't got one already! Whoever this Martine is, I hope Aude doesn't crush her like a walnut.

It was a drippingly warm evening, and Aileen was lighting little votive candles along the table on the terrace when her guests all arrived within five minutes of each other; unlike the Irish, the French seemed to think that seven o'clock actually meant seven. First Raoul Lascaux, bashfully carrying a bouquet, looking as if he'd been fumigated; minus all the mud and dust, he was quite a handsome man. Then Léo the mole-exterminator, toting a tiny wife and a bottle of brandy; then Aude, glossily immaculate in a short shift dress, her hair slicked back, a pashmina pinned on her shoulder just *so*. It must be admitted, Aileen conceded, that she is an attractive young woman.

'Haileen!' Aude gushed, proffering some gorgeously wrapped gift. 'How are you, m'wah . . .' Air-kissing Aileen, she spun around beaming at everyone. '*Bonsoir* M 'Egarty . . .' Extending one manicured hand in Joe's direction, she simpered in a way that convulsed Aileen with silent laughter: it looked as if Aude expected the hand to be not shaken but kissed.

'*Bonsoir*' said Joe, rising stalwartly and unexpectedly to the occasion; Aileen nearly fainted to see him take the hand, lift it and – sweet God! – kiss its pearly little knuckles. For one startling second, Aileen saw Joe Hegarty metamorphosed into Sean Connery.

Cool as a cucumber, Aude let her gaze travel lightly over the assembled group but did not ask where Finn was, and Aileen had to give her marks for that, because if Joe was right then she must be dying to know. In fact Finn had gone down to the village on his motorbike to pick up Martine – who was certainly going to have her work cut out against this perfumed Exocet.

Léo's wife, Clémentine, wanted to see the house, so leaving Joe on the terrace with the others, Aileen took her inside, and was halfway through the guided tour – 'oh, exquisite!' – when she heard the motorbike sputtering up the gravel. Hastening Clémentine through the other rooms, she led her back out as fast as she could, propelled by curiosity. Could Martine possibly hold a candle to Aude?

No. Oh, dear God, no. Lifting off her helmet to reveal

tousled, spiky black hair, Martine jumped off the back of the bike, dropped the helmet with a clunk and came clomping across the gravel in black biker's boots, dungarees and a tattered T-shirt. Closer inspection revealed a tattoo on either arm, a nose stud, an eyebrow stud and – when she opened her mouth to say hello – a tongue stud. Nailed to the spot, Aileen had to take a deep breath before stretching her lips into what she hoped was a warm, entirely unfazed smile.

'Hi!' said Martine, in French, marching up to Joe, thrusting out her hand and shaking his heartily. 'You must be Finn's papa?'

Um – uh – yeah. Aileen was seized next, to be kissed like an old friend, and then everyone else got firm handshakes, including Aude who was looking at her as if at a scarecrow sprung to life. Well, Aileen thought, composing herself with an effort, at least she's not shy, this Martine . . . in fact she seems friendly, and those almond-green eyes are actually attractive. If someone gave her a makeover, she could look like a kind of roughed-up little Audrey Hepburn. But, dear God – dungarees, to dinner, with Finn's parents? Clearly she's not out to make any kind of impression on us. It looks as if she is just what Finn calls 'a friend' . . . so maybe she won't clash with Aude after all.

Where am I going to seat the pair of them? Aude facing Finn, with Martine beside him, or the other way round? H'mm . . . other way round I think, with Aude beside Finn, facing Joe? Yes. Let's do that, with Raoul beside me, facing Clémentine, and I'll face Léo.

'Well' Joe said, raising an unprompted glass, 'you're all very welcome. Why don't you all sit down, now, and we'll sample my wife's fabulous French cooking!'

Everyone laughed, breaking the ice, Finn whispering some kind of translation into Martine's ear. She giggled in a way that emphasised her youth – eighteen, nineteen? – and like a flash Aude was on her case. 'Don't you speak any English?' she drawled, and Martine giggled again.

'*Non*! Nuzzing!' Whereupon Finn gave Aude a somewhat frosty look.

'Martine' he said in a tone of some hauteur, a tone Aileen had never heard before, 'is a sculptor. You don't really need English to make statues.'

A sculptor? Everyone blinked, turning to look at this wispy urchin who scarcely looked strong enough to lift a suitcase, never mind a sculpture, and in rapid French Martine explained without apparently caring who understood and who didn't. Yes, a sculptor, training with a master near Toulouse, just finishing her first year's apprenticeship and loving every moment of it.

'But how' Joe enquired baffled when this was explained to him, 'would a little scrap of a thing like you heft a bloody great statue? I mean, does it not involve hammers and chisels and – ?'

Aude was the only one who could translate this, which she did, directly to Finn as if Martine were invisible. But Martine, her eyes sparkling, nodded eagerly. Oh yes, it did involve mallets and chisels, and weights and pulleys and . . . as her face glowed, Aude's darkened, and Aileen saw why: expecting to be the star of the show, she was finding herself relegated to the role of interpreter, talking not about herself but about this ragamuffin. What was more, Finn was reflecting Martine's animated aura as he looked into her twinkling eyes, all but sparking in the gathering dusk.

Jesus, Aileen thought, I've blown it. I should have put Aude facing him. Grasping a platter of shellfish, she stood up and passed it down the table with a sudden feeling of quiet, inexorable desperation: 'I hope you all like prawns?'

Oh yes, everybody chorused, they did. They all loved prawns . . . except Finn, who didn't appear to have heard her. And Joe, who didn't appear to have heard her either. As she looked down the table at her son and her husband, Aileen saw both their faces illuminated in the light from the candles, and realised with scorching, shocking certainty that Finn was completely under Martine's spell, gazing besotted into her eyes while Joe, no less hypnotised, was gazing into Aude's.

'Don't lie to me, you bastard!'

'Aileen, for chrissakes lower your voice, the guests will hear . . .'

'Bog the guests! Admit it! You were all over Aude Villandry all night! All over her like a creeping *rash*!'

Pale with fury, Aileen stood with clenched fists beside the bedroom chest of drawers, restraining herself with difficulty from grabbing the vase of flowers on it and hurling it at Joe, who was sitting on the edge of the bed looking – looking *inno-cent*, as if this outburst were all part of her midlife mania.

'I was trying to be nice to her, that's all, because it was so embarrassingly obvious that Finn wasn't interested in her. The poor girl looked . . . well, I just thought I should try to cheer her up.'

'Cheer her up? You were halfway down her cleavage, you disgusting little rat, you were smarming and schmoozing and – and – I don't know what's wrong with you, Joe Hegarty! All you ever seem to think about these days is sex, sex, sex—'

'So' he said mildly, 'maybe I do. Maybe it's the heat or some-thing, maybe it's all these lovely French lassies . . . but Aileen, thinking about sex is not a crime. Is it?'

'It is when you're a married man! Married to *me*, leching all over a girl young enough to be your daughter! My God, I nearly threw up tonight! What's *wrong* with you?'

Taking a deep breath, he seemed actually to think this over, roll it round in his mind before answering. And then, quite candidly, he answered her.

'Nothing is wrong with me. On the contrary, I've never felt more right. I am forty-five years old and, for the first time in my entire adult life, I am off the treadmill. I no longer have to get up at the crack of dawn and slave all day every day for somebody else. I am deliriously happy to be here helping you to run this lovely house in this lovely place, getting some sun for a change, making new friends, enjoying a game of boules out in the open of an evening instead of crying into my river of beer with Dave Dreary Doherty. I see my son working, I see him getting himself a lovely girlfriend, enjoying himself with his friends, and I say to myself – hey, Joe, it's not too late for you to enjoy yourself, too! France is fun, make the most of it! France is, after all, where your wife wants you to be! And hey, if she can flirt a little with her pal Léo, surely I can flirt a little with my pal Aude? It's only a bit of harmless fun, and what the hell is wrong with that, huh?'

What was wrong with it? He made it sound almost reasonable. Which made Aileen twice as furious. 'Harmless fun?! You made a complete spectacle of yourself—'

'Did I? D'you think so? Or would you by any chance be *jealous*, Mrs Hegarty?'

'Jealous? What? Me? Oh, don't be bloody ridiculous!'

'Well, I can't think of any other reason why you'd make such a mountain out of a molehill. I mean, we've been married over twenty years, I've always thought that if we could survive losing Hazel we could survive anything else, because if ever there was a long dark tunnel . . . Aileen, have you any idea what you've been like to live with all these years?'

He said it so quietly, how could it explode so loudly, like a bullet zinging into her face? The blood seemed to drain from her veins, she was clutching the wall behind her.

'I – I – what do you mean?'

She felt faint, could barely articulate; but he didn't move, didn't budge to support or console her. He simply sat on the bed, looking implacably at her. 'I mean . . . I know it wasn't your fault, but Jesus Christ, it was like walking on eggshells. You were so consumed with grief, I hardly dared breathe for fear of upsetting you.'

'But – I – Joe, it was *you* – you were the one who—'

'Bottled it up? Of course I bottled it up. I had no choice. That's a man's role, to be strong for his wife. Where would we all have been, if I'd done what I wanted to do, which was lie down on the floor and howl? Where would that have got you, or Finn? So yes, I bottled it up, I couldn't reach you, I watched you withering up and it nearly killed me . . . then you said you wanted to go to France and I thought, that's it, we've lost each other, she's leaving me. And then, I arrive here to find you're not leaving me, after all. To find you've put pictures of Hazel up like any normal mother would, to hear Finn telling me you're finally able to talk about her—'

'*I'm* able?! But *he* was the one who couldn't!'

'No. He was the one who *didn't*, Aileen, because you were the one who *couldn't*. He told me. In fact we had a very long talk about it. At the end of which we agreed that France has affected you in some way, cleared your mind, opened doors in your head, it's almost as if . . . well . . . anyway, he feels invigorated and I feel rejuvenated. Which is why, if I did flirt with Aude tonight, I make no apologies for it. Sex is healthy and sex is fun and – and I want another chance! A chance to shake off all the grief, a chance to live and laugh and – and be let love you properly, after all this time. It wasn't deliberate, but maybe

382

that's why I homed in on Aude tonight. To see how you'd react? See how she'd react? See whether I'm still attractive, to my wife or to anyone else?'

Staring at him, she couldn't remember when Joe had last spoken at such length, or so forcefully. All she knew was the confusing sensation of being picked up, shifted around on a chessboard, moved to somewhere she didn't want to be at all, wasn't meant to be. Angrily, she struggled in his grasp.

'Don't give me that, don't try to make excuses! And don't try to make out that it was me who was fragile, not Finn! Finn has been tortured, tormented by the memory of Hazel ever since he was four years old – it was *him*, and you, not me! You were the ones who couldn't cope!'

If only he'd contradicted her then. If only he'd said anything at all, anything she could get her teeth into, argue with, fight back with. But he didn't. Instead he let her words hang on the air like raindrops caught in a cobweb, trembling on the air between them. She could almost see each one, winking at her, mocking her.

For what seemed like aeons, there was silence between them. Until, very quietly, he lifted his face and his voice. 'Aileen . . . has it ever occurred to you . . . that you might just be looking down the wrong end of the telescope?'

Even as he said it, she saw it. Saw him wresting sixteen years of pretence, of defence, from her grasp; all those years of careful self-delusion. Delusion grafted on like a second skin, delusion that had, apparently, fooled nobody but herself. She hadn't been fine, she hadn't got over Hazel, she hadn't been the one holding everyone else together, at all. She had been every bit as hurt, as damaged, as Joe and Finn, throbbing with pain, and they had known this, sensed it . . . all this time?

She couldn't speak. Couldn't do anything, only slide slowly down the wall until she was sitting on the floor, her fist going to her mouth to stifle sobs that could not be stifled, her other hand clutching at Joe as he slid into focus through a veil of tears. Sitting down beside her, he put his arm around her shoulder and pulled her to him, letting her bury her face in his chest, rocking her like a child.

'That's it' he crooned, 'let it out. Let it all out, every drop of it . . . cry as much as you want, love, for as long as you want . . . and then maybe we can stop looking back at last, and start living again. Hazel can never come alive again, but I can, and you can. We can have one more chance.'

13

The freedom of it, the euphoria! For weeks afterwards Aileen felt light-headed, floating on the kind of cloud that France itself must have floated on nearly sixty years before, when liberated from oppression. In retrospect it seemed incredible that she had never realised how she had let the trauma of Hazel's death invade her mind, colonise her heart; incredible that she had convinced herself that Joe and Finn were the ones who were suffering. Of course they were – but they were not the only ones. It was a huge relief to admit her own pain, let it out and let it go, to the point where she could almost physically see Hazel's ghost receding, gliding away into the misty past. Not that she would ever forget her infant daughter; but now she could shake off the sorrow, even learn to smile at the memory of a little girl who had so briefly flitted in and out of their family, bringing joy that had been beautiful while it lasted. For the first time in years, Aileen slept deeply night after night, so deeply that she neither knew nor even cared whether Joe was snoring beside her; all she knew for sure was the warm strength of his arms, cocooning her in both freedom and security.

France, she conceded one iridescent summer morning, is very lovely. But it's not France I'm falling in love with. It's my husband I'm falling in love with, in a way I never knew was possible when I met him, nor even when I married him. He wasn't then the man he is today, nor am I the woman I was then . . . we were so young, there was so little to go on. Now, we have something solid, something so much stronger – something well worth saving, and working to save. We had to stay together, for Finn's sake, after Hazel died; but now we have a choice, and now I want us to stay together.

God, I had no idea there was so much going on in his head, nor in his heart! Did he never say, or did I never hear? Had we really grown that far apart? We must have . . . quietly, invisibly, another inch every year. One more inch, and we'd have fallen into the abyss. Now I know how that family must have felt when Finn plucked them to safety – dizzy, almost incoherent with relief. The Louvel family is not the only one that has been rescued.

And now, while Joe and I haul ourselves back onto firm terrain, Finn is finding his feet, too. I can hardly believe it – a girlfriend, no less! Thank God it's not Aude, after all – even if she still has her sights on him, for some totally inexplicable reason, she's never going to get anywhere, because he's mad about Martine. Little Martine, who doesn't even realise it yet . . . she'll never do anything for him, in the way Aude would have, but she can give him one great gift: she can make him happy. Is making him happy already, every time she smiles that pixie smile of hers . . . he's still a long way from catching her I think, but she's what he wants. He has a goal. She doesn't love him yet, but she likes him. For the first time in his life, he's fitting in, he has the kind of friends he can bring home, and he feels free to bring them. Against all the odds, France is working for Finn.

Working for Joe, too. Those two men of mine are blossoming here, loving it. I'm the only one who misses Ireland, misses Mam and Dymps and friends and all the silly little things that mean so much when you don't have them any more. But I'm not going to say anything about that, because I'm so much happier in every other way. In my marriage, in my work . . . Le Mas is taking off and no mistake about it. Shona will be thrilled, if and when she ever comes back – well, of course she'll come back, but what on earth is keeping her? I need my bacon and sausages, Sho, get a move on!

But Shona did not return until summer was simmering, until the days were at their hottest and longest and Le Mas was bubbling with life, with languages Aileen had never heard before around her breakfast table. Breakfast had moved outdoors, now, onto the terrace from which Dutch, Danish, Russian, Croatian and all kinds of people sat gazing dreamily down into the valley, hypnotised by sound of the church bell floating up from Mézalas. Sometimes they even let their maps and guidebooks slide to the ground, forgetting their plans to visit Toulouse or Montpellier or wherever had seemed enticing, staring off into space instead, hijacked by the heat and a pervasive sense of indolence. If only Le Mas had a pool, they sometimes said, they could stay there all day . . . Thankful that it didn't have one, Aileen made up picnic hampers and sent them off on long walks into the hills, from which they often returned half comatose with exhaustion. In their absence, she and Joe learned to do what the locals did in the afternoons, which was open the windows, close the shutters and have a deliciously refreshing nap, scented by the lavender which was now abundant everywhere.

Which was what they were doing when, one incandescent afternoon, Shona finally turned up. Hearing her opening the door of her gîte, Aileen sat up, clutching a sheet around her. 'Joe! Shona's here!'

'Is that so?' he murmured, reaching to pull her back beside him. 'Well, she'll probably be needing a little nap herself. I must say, this beats mixing paints and weighing out nails any day.'

Laughing, she flopped back into the pillows, where he was

laughing himself, and they decided that Shona's news would probably keep till evening.

'Oh, no! You can't have!'

'I can and I have' Shona confirmed, 'I didn't want to tell you until it was done, in case you tried to talk me out of it.'

'But – but selling your home is so drastic!'

'Excuse me – that's exactly what you wanted to do with yours only last year! Anyway, it's done. Found a buyer within a week. It was the only way to make money in a hurry. Now I am the proud and outright owner of Le Mas. My bridges are well and truly burnt, there's no going back to Ireland any more. Not for me, anyway.'

Appalled, Aileen sat down opposite Shona in her tiny gîte, wine in hand, absorbing this news with the sinking realisation that she could never in a million years have taken such a definitive step herself. On the contrary, it was a profound comfort to think of her house in Galway, waiting to be reclaimed whenever she should want it. Which, despite the beauty of Le Mas, was not entirely beyond the bounds of possibility.

Only how can I ever go home now, she thought wildly, with Shona investing everything in me, in this, in us? Oh God, I'm trapped! Everyone loves it here, soon they'll all have forgotten Ireland completely, except me! I'll never get to see Mam or Dymps or Galway again!

Suddenly she felt stifled in the sultry heat, the sweet scent of lavender making her head spin slightly as she realised that it had not rained, now, for nearly ten weeks. The whole countryside was bone-dry, desiccated, flattened with dizzying heat, and it came to her that she wanted rain. Badly, badly wanted the cool, fresh feel of rain on her skin.

'So' she asked, clearing her throat, trying to camouflage a rising sense of panic, 'Le Mas isn't just for fun, then, or an experiment, any more? You – you're going to put down *roots* here?'

'Yes. I hope so. I want to leave all the mess and the failures behind, Aileen, and try to create a happier future.'

Well – fair enough. Joe and Finn and I are not the only ones, I suppose, entitled to do that. 'I see . . . well, the good news is that business has been booming. I haven't done any paperwork, but I can tell you we've been full every night for the last six weeks, there's lots of money waiting for you to bank—'

'Oh, Aileen, well done! And thank you! You're making a great go of this place!'

Uncomfortably, Aileen knocked back a shot of wine. 'Oh no, it's not me – it's your marketing that's done the trick! You put up the ads, you got us onto the lists, you brought the business—'

'Which you then looked after. It takes two to tango, Aileen, don't try to do yourself out of your full share of the credit. You're obviously running a great show here, our guests are comfortable, word's going round . . . I am so grateful to you.'

Shona looked at her with such admiration, such gratitude, Aileen felt almost guilty. How, in the face of such success, could anyone possibly admit to anything so absurd, so pathetic as homesickness? It would sound childish, and if there was one thing Shona was unlikely to indulge, it was childishness. Even Joe and Finn, she was sure, would be unimpressed.

In a way, she thought, I've almost achieved what I wanted to achieve. I am healing, my family is knitting back together, business is much better than it was in Ireland, everything is turning out so well. But now, the awful thing is, I feel nearly ready to go back where I belong, which is in Ireland. I'll never fit in here the way Shona will. Never get used to the heat or the language or stiff French society, never put down deep roots or feel I truly belong. But – but what am I going to do? Joe and Finn are happy, I can't dig them up again when I'm the one

389

who transplanted them. I can't walk away from this thriving business; even if things are picking up in Ireland, Shona needs me here. She's great at the paperwork, but she hasn't a clue about running a—'

'Shona!'

'Mmm?'

'I've got it! I know what you should do!'

'Let me guess. Run for president?' Wryly, she laughed, but Aileen scarcely heard her as words tumbled out in an avalanche. 'You should set up a – a settling-in service! There must be hundreds of people moving to France every week, people who'd pay anything for someone like you! Someone who knows France, speaks French, can haggle with estate agents, get a phone, a plumber, an electrician, open a bank account, all that stuff! People who need a minder, someone to hold their hand here! You'd be brilliant at it!'

Thoughtfully, Shona raised an eyebrow. Focused as she had been on Le Mas, such an idea had never occurred to her – and it was not, now that she thought about it, a bad idea at all. She would enjoy such work, she would be her own boss, meet lots of people . . . what Aileen was suggesting could, actually, have a lot to recommend it.

'D'you know, Aileen, that could actually be a runner! I'm sure there must be some British people who do that stuff for all the Brits who move here, but nobody Irish is doing it for the Irish, that I know of at any rate . . . and an awful lot of Irish people are buying houses in France now they know what great value is available. Whether they're holiday houses or permanent residences, there's a lot of administration involved – and I've already done ours, bought Le Mas, got it sorted, so I surely could do it for other people too. I think you might be onto a winner!'

Aileen was almost levitating with enthusiasm. 'Yes! I know

you wanted to work in tourism, the hotel sector, but this would get you going for the moment, you could put ads in some Irish newspapers, distribute flyers locally in English—'

'And watch out for arriving removals lorries! This is a great idea, Aileen, I'll sleep on it and if it still looks good in the morning, I – I'll jump right in and do it. How did you think of it?'

How did she? Frowning, Aileen tried to remember. It had just come to her out of the blue when she'd been thinking of . . . of her own future, actually, not Shona's at all. Which was maybe why it was such a great idea – she hadn't been searching for it, it had simply smashed through of its own accord, pushing everything else out of the way.

'I don't know' she admitted, 'but you've helped me so much, Sho, I'll be delighted if it turns out that I've helped you. I can see that you really want to stay here.'

'Yes. Funny, isn't it? You were the one who wanted to come, and now I'm the one who wants to stay.'

Shona smiled, and Aileen quailed. Oh, God, she knows. She can see right through me. She knows I'm thinking of leaving . . . her in the lurch?

Rallying, Aude Villandry redoubled her campaign to seduce Finn Hegarty. Far from relinquishing him to Martine, she took to visiting Le Mas more frequently than ever, inviting Finn to all kinds of social events, plotting and manoeuvring like a little Napoleon, and Aileen had to laugh. Six months ago Finn had had no life at all; now he had a job, and two girls to choose between, and parents he actually talked to, even appeared to like. His appearance had mutated from serial-killer to work-in-progress, and often in the evenings he could be heard laughing somewhere in the grounds of Le Mas as Martine attempted to teach him to play a guitar, fey as a fairy, still apparently unaware of his burning lust for her. Either she'll break his heart, Aileen thought, or the pair of them will burst into flames some day, have the kind of blazing romance that Joe and I never had.

But Joe and I are catching up on a lot of things we never had. Joe and I will never be twenty again, we'd look ridiculous snogging and cavorting, but I feel ten years younger and he certainly looks it. We've rekindled a flame that was nearly extinct, we're in our forties but we still have years ahead of us . . . the only question is, where are we going to spend them? I can't haul him home, not when he's so happy here – reconstructed, as Finn says. Christ, I've created a monster!

A monster, and now I'm going to have to try to wrestle with it somehow. But maybe I should wait until autumn, when things cool down a bit. When Shona might have a new career under way? I know her heart is still in tourism, she yearns to market hotels, but for now I think she should just go with what she's got. A good idea is what she's got, and she's great at turning ideas into reality.

As I know, don't I? She's the one who turned my great idea into reality. In a way, she's the one who saved my son and handed me back my husband. Yet here she is, with nobody at all of her own.

Sometimes I look at her and I think, what a waste. Here's this lovely talented, bubbly girl and I just can't understand why nobody seems to want her.

In fact, all she's got here in France is me. Me and Le Mas. She never says anything, but that can't possibly be enough for a healthy young woman of thirty-six, can it?

I won't look back, Shona told herself one introspective evening; I won't think any more about my old career or my old home or my old flame. What's done is done, what's lost is gone for ever. I'm not Mrs Wright, I'm not head of marketing, but on the other hand I'm not top of the queue for a triple bypass either. I'm not on the dole, I'm not incapacitated or bankrupt or bereaved. If Emily O'Brien can survive, all on her own at sixty, I can survive. In fact I am going to call Emily right now and ask her what she thinks about my new relocation service. Or should I call it a settlement service? Let's see what she has to say.

'I think it's a great idea' Emily enthused firmly, 'why don't you call it The Great Escape? Or Red Tape in the Sunset?'

Shona laughed into the phone. 'There's plenty of that all right! But if I can untangle mine then I can untangle other people's – it's not tourism, Emily, but it'll earn me a crust. Beggars can't be choosers, huh?'

'Let's just say you ordered steak and the waiter has brought you sole instead. Which reminds me, Shona, did you ever call that man?'

'What man?'

'The one we met in the restaurant? Who gave you his card?'

'No, I didn't. I've washed my hands of men, Emily. The whole thing is a minefield and I'm tired of getting bits of me blown away.'

'Shona. Do me a favour? Call him, will you?'

'Why? What do you care? He was just some passing ship in the night, Emily!'

'You don't know what he was. All I know is that you have nothing to lose.'

'Except my time and self respect and—'

'Shona. Just do it, okay?'

So where was the bloody card, what had she done with it? Cursing Emily's eternal attempts to 'fix her up', Shona rifled numerous drawers, boxes, pockets and handbags before finally digging out the crumpled, wretched thing. Olivier Dessanges, it said, with a Toulouse phone number. Olivier Dessanges, who probably had a wife and three children and was looking for a game away from home. Toulouse, indeed. I'm not driving all the way over there for a Coke and a bag of crisps.

Emily's bonkers. I don't know why I – 'Hello? M Dessanges?'

'Oui?'

'My name is Shona Fitzpatrick, you gave me your card one night about six weeks ago in a restaurant near Mézalas—'

'*Ah, oui!* The lady who gave the manager a piece of her mind! I'm sorry, I didn't quite catch your second name?'

'Fitzpatrick. Shona Fitzpatrick.'

'Well, Mme Fitzpatrick, I don't know what took you so long to call me, but I am delighted you have. I was wondering . . . it's a little complicated to explain over the phone . . . would you be free for coffee some day this week?'

Would she? Not if he wanted to play footsie with her. Not if he aimed to be yet another notch on her bedpost. Sorry, pal. Closed for business. 'That depends, M Dessanges, on the nature of the coffee. Business or pleasure?'

There was a sharp intake of breath, a startled silence. When he spoke again, he sounded aghast. 'But Mme Fitzpatrick, I don't think you can have read my card properly?'

Huh? Curiously, she squinted at it, and there under his name was a line in tiny type: 'Gestion de la Groupe Entrime'.

Oh, Jesus. The Groupe Entrime meant nothing to her, but clearly he was some kind of businessman. And she'd just made herself sound like some kind of hooker. Tongues of fire shot up her face as she grappled to retrieve the hideous mistake. 'Oh – um – I just meant, what is the Groupe Entrime? What kind of management do you do exactly – ?' Oh horror horror horror.

'We are what you might call a rescue service. Financial troubleshooters. We turn around businesses which have got

394

into difficulty. Which means identifying their mistakes. Right now, we are trying to identify the mistakes of a hotel group which is er – tottering. The reason I gave you my card is that you sounded like a lady who knew something about the tourism industry – indeed you said you worked in it – and you were not afraid to speak your mind. We are looking for just such a person to assess this group of small country hotels. To draw up a frank, outspoken report that we can work from.'

Oh, no! Was he kidding? She would love such a project! But it was weeks since he'd given her the card. 'I see. And, uh, have you engaged anyone?'

'We have been interviewing, and are thinking of engaging someone. Unless you would be interested?'

Briefly, she thought of her new settling-in service. And then she realised she could juggle both. Like Finn, she seemed to be suddenly zooming from no choice to an abundance of it.

'Yes, M Dessanges. I would be interested. How about coffee tomorrow morning at ten in Carcassonne?'

'Actually, I'll be in Pézanas. How about the Cafe Molière?'

Yes! Even better, only half an hour away – what'll I wear, what'll I say, how will I convince him that he *must* give me this gig? Oh, God, assessing hotels, I'd do it for free! He says they're on the point of hiring someone else – but that's not going to happen, because tomorrow morning Shona Fitzpatrick is going to market Shona Fitzpatrick!

If, that is, she can look Olivier Dessanges in the eye. The man she thought was trying to pick her up, when the only thing he wanted to pick was her brains. I'd better not tell Emily that bit, when I ring her tomorrow to tell her about my lovely, lovely new job.

'Of course' Olivier Dessanges explained, sitting at a cautious distance from Shona, 'it's not exactly a job. It's just a one-off commission. There are eight hotels, scattered around the Languedoc, it should take about six weeks to visit them all and turn in your report.'

Six weeks. One-off. And she'd have to get a car. Still, it was a start. A foothold in the hotel business, that might lead to who knew where? Eagerly, Shona nodded. 'Six weeks will be plenty. I'll do you up a full assessment of each one, everything from cutlery to courtesy.'

'Everything. Location, access, facilities, food, hygiene, decor, staff . . . your previous experience speaks for itself, so I'll leave it all in your capable hands.'

With a courteous nod, he packed up his briefcase and departed, leaving Shona gazing after him, thinking that maybe her career wasn't entirely up in smoke after all. If this unexpected project went well, she might manage to turn it into some kind of consultancy, freelance as the chance arose . . . at least it was a chance. Not the kind of chance Emily had had in mind, perhaps, but she would be pleased nonetheless to hear about the unexpected nature of this encounter with Olivier Dessanges.

Making her way back to Aileen's borrowed Ka, Shona got in, drove to a second-hand car dealer on the outskirts of Pézanas and promptly invested in a three-year-old, nippy little Clio, to be delivered to Le Mas first thing tomorrow. It cost almost exactly as much as M Dessange's proposed fee, but as her father was fond of saying, you had to speculate to accumulate. Over the next year or so, the car would hopefully pay for itself.

Aileen, when she heard the news, was delighted. 'Great! Now you'll have two strings to your bow! Between this and the other project, you'll surely earn something, get a new career under way – and you'll be your own boss! No more Terry O'Hagans!'

No. Whatever other challenges might arise, at least there would be no more office politics, or sexism or harassment or any of the other things that drove people out of their jobs and half out of their minds. With a rising sense of refreshment, Shona spent the rest of the day sorting her wardrobe, assembling crisp little outfits from the jackets and skirts that had not been worn for months.

There was something therapeutic about it, something that made her feel rehabilitated, like an invalid responding to a miracle drug. Olivier Dessanges, she thought, you are going to be absolutely knocked out when you see my work, you are going to tell everyone how great it is and lots more is going to come from this!

Knee-deep in guests, and almost flattened by the scorching heat, Aileen wondered how she had ever run a B & B single-handed before. It made a huge difference that Joe was here to help her with this one, not only available but willing to share the housework, gardening, repair jobs: the heftier or messier they were the more he seemed to enjoy them. Whistling, he went about all his tasks with a cheerful nonchalance which not only lightened her load but lightened her heart; far from being under her feet, he was a chirpy, comforting presence, and in some invisible way the shared work was a bond, pulling them closer together, yielding a sense of joint satisfaction when, late in the evenings, they finally collapsed in unison over cold drinks and featherlight suppers. With the temperature touching forty degrees, nobody could eat much more than salads, and they were both losing weight. Weight that was no loss at all; Aileen nearly wept with joy the day she found herself slipping into a favourite dress that had been too tight for years.

'That looks good' Joe remarked, and she beamed, not only because it fitted but because he'd noticed.

'Thanks' she said, and they smiled at each other; little things, these days, seemed to yield so much simple pleasure. Things that had been neglected, forgotten, swept away somewhere at the back of their marriage . . . things which, she thought, had badly needed airing, things they would not neglect again. When her birthday came round, and he asked her what she'd like, she considered before answering.

'Perfume. I'd love some delicious, extravagant, romantic French perfume.'

Grinning, he tickled a finger behind her ear. 'Well, that's a change, Mrs 'Egarty! You used to want practical things – I seem to remember a hedge trimmer one year, a set of saucepans—'

'I must have been mad' she answered, 'a perfect idiot, a drudge who'd lost all sight of – well, anyway, I want perfume this year. Sexy. Expensive. Glamorous. Got that?'

He did get it, eventually producing not only a bottle of Bvlgari but a gorgeous bouquet of arum lilies as well, and a kiss.

'Happy birthday, love.'

In fairness, he'd always said that much. But this year he sounded as if he meant it, the 'love' had a new resonance . . . and Finn, to her surprise, gave her a beautiful present too.

'Got it in the market' he shrugged bashfully, blushing as she exclaimed over a soft chestnut leather handbag, 'Martine thought you might like it.'

Ah, Martine . . . so Martine was choosing Mum's birthday present this year, was she? Smiling to herself, Aileen realised that Finn must be gradually winning his battle for her, while Aude was losing hers for him. But she could do no more for Aude; Finn was striking out independently now, moving further every day from under his parents' influence. Besides, while Aude might have put a gloss on Finn, she would never have put a smile on his face, not the kind of smile Martine put without even trying.

'Will you thank her for me? And bring her to dinner on Saturday, if you'd like?'

'Can't do that' he said off-handedly, 'we're going camping for the weekend.'

Camping? Together? In a tent? With a pang, Aileen glanced at Joe, and saw that he, too, was struggling to stifle laughter, mixed with curiosity and a certain recognition: their boy was a boy no longer. Of course, parents were supposed to be cool about these things, display no emotion even when they were fizzing with it. But Joe couldn't entirely restrain himself.

'How many of you are going?' he asked with studied languor.

'Oh, just the two of us' Finn said airily, 'Martine and me, and maybe a bottle of champagne.'

With that he was gone, leaving the room almost throbbing with testosterone and a palpable sense of purpose.

'Beyond hope' Shona scribbled in her notebook. 'Scruffy, dingy, badly maintained and overgrown, possibly because the couple who run this awful hotel appear to put all their energy into hating each other. A rescue package would require major investment including new, enthusiastic management.'

That was the first one, in Béziers. The second one, near Nîmes, was slightly better. 'Poorly lit, poorly ventilated, poorly signposted. Excruciatingly slow service, but a lovely location plus an excellent chef. Revamping plus staff retraining could yield dividends.'

Each hotel was taking about four days to fully assess, and she was enjoying it hugely, even when the venue itself was grim as death, making her wonder why so many French hoteliers seemed to loathe their work. Would a smile really cost as much as all that? A new lightbulb? Fresh flowers, fresh vegetables, both of which could be grown on the premises? Did nobody ever consult any decor books? Was the waitress really having root canal work, or was that her normal expression? What was the point of a great view if the dusty window wouldn't open? Did anybody realise that those bedsprings squeaked and that tap leaked?

Every so often she returned to Le Mas to review and compile her reports, amusing Aileen and Joe with her tales of Fawlty Towers, sometimes complete with Basil. 'You should have seen the manager of the one in Lodève. When I told him the wine was corked, he picked it up, marched to the window and poured the whole bottle into the garden.'

'Ha! And did he bring another one?'

'Yes. Slammed it down with a thump. And then put both bottles on the bill.'

'Lovely. I hope you didn't pay for both?'

'I did not. I told him he was as crooked as his corkscrew.'

'How many more to go?'

'Only three. Why?'

'Because we have an Irish couple staying here at the moment, house-hunting. I told them I knew someone who could help if they'd like. They said they'd gladly pay five grand to anyone who could lead them through the maze of French paperwork.'

'Five grand? Really? Tell them I'll do it, if they can just wait two weeks!'

Well, this was turning out to be a busy summer. Busy and interesting, leaving no time at all for the languid life everyone thought she must be living, swinging in a hammock, glass in hand, reading novels as she sunned herself . . . but Shona was enjoying what she was doing, recapturing her lost sense of achievement. Meeting some nice people, too – until the awful day she drove her Clio up the drive of the last hotel on her list, and gasped in horror.

The Auberge Rose, as it was prettily named, was hideous. Rough and pitted, the driveway bounced and rattled the car as she drove up, to find herself facing a tatty, run-down farm-house swathed in briars that must once have been roses. The lawn looked as if it had not been mown for weeks; the shutters were missing slats, and when she went inside there was nobody at reception. Not unless you counted a snoozing dog, which leapt to life and began to bark demonically.

Backing off, she collided with a dark, lanky, distracted-looking man who, ignoring her, addressed the dog. 'Rupert! Cut it out!'

Growling, Rupert subsided, and the man looked at her apologetically. 'Don't mind him. He's harmless. Now, what can I do for you?' Rummaging amidst the mess on the desk, he located a pair of spectacles, put them on and inspected her as if waiting to be sold a set of encyclopaedias.

'I was wondering' she said, steeling herself, 'whether you have a room with bathroom for three nights?' Or whether this can actually be a hotel at all. If it is, it's on its last legs. I'd run a mile if I were a normal tourist.

'Oh . . . yes . . . I suppose so.'

'You suppose? Is that a yes or a no?'

'Well . . .' With a sigh, the man removed his glasses, pushed his hand through his mahogany-glossy hair and looked at her frankly. 'There's plenty of room all right. It's just that . . . er . . . I'm a bit short-handed at the moment. The room won't be ready for an hour or two.'

'Okay. I'll go explore the village and come back later.' Boy, I'm going to earn my keep in this one, aren't I?

Curiously, the man surveyed her, evidently surprised by her determination. 'All right, then. Come back at six and it'll be ready for you.'

With a kind of weary sigh, he smiled sadly as if to say 'Sorry, but as you can see, I'm in completely the wrong job here, haven't a clue how to run a hotel.' Although he looked little older than herself, there was a chaotic aura about him, something frazzled that made her wonder what could have happened to turn his hotel into such a disaster.

The building itself, if its bricks were sandblasted and repointed, had potential, a certain nostalgic charm. Probably, when it finally went out of business, someone would buy it for a song, fix it up, put in a pool and have themselves a lovely rural retreat.

'All right. See you later, then.'

With a little wave, she left him, and he waved forlornly in turn as she got into her car, looking resigned to never seeing her again.

Two hours later, returning to the Auberge Rose, Shona sat in her car for a moment, surveying the low, broad building, noticing an overgrown pond that badly needed clearing, a pile of garden implements rusting up against a wall, a terrace begging to be weeded and washed. When the place went up for sale, an optimistic buyer who didn't mind risking spinal surgery could, after a back-breaking year or two, have the home of his or her dreams. Feeling sympathy for whatever hero might undertake it, she got out and went in.

The dog was gone. In its place a little bell sat on the unmanned desk, the kind that went 'ping' to summon attention. Why hadn't that been there in the first place? Whacking it, she waited, and in due course the dark, harassed-looking man reappeared, mustering a smile as he arrived.

'So, did you enjoy your trip to the village?' Clearly he was trying to sound hospitable, rise to a task he found gargantuan.

'Yes' she said, smiling encouragingly back, 'it's a pretty village, isn't it?' God love him, she thought: what on earth would he do if a whole coachload of visitors arrived?

'It is. My mother was born in the house beside the *mairie*.'

'Oh? You're local, then? You grew up here?'

Sadly, he nodded. 'Yes. My parents owned this hotel. I inherited it five years ago.' Sounding as if he'd inherited an enormous, untractable white elephant, he took a key from a rack behind him, raising an eyebrow in the direction of her small suitcase. 'May I help you with that?'

It wasn't heavy, but she let him take it, following him out of the cool, shady lobby down a corridor, up a curving oak staircase which could have been lovely if anyone had cleaned it . . . was there anyone to clean anything? There was no sign of any staff.

'Are there many people staying at the moment?' Hoping to flush out some information, she got a shake of his head.

'Just an elderly British couple . . . there was a Swiss lady here last night but she left this morning.'

I'll bet, Shona thought. She went screaming off at top speed to the nearest Mercure, gasping for a squeaky-clean, properly manicured, efficiently run hotel, where she wrote a letter of outraged complaint to the group that owns this one. Look at the state of this wallpaper, and paint! The Auberge Rose will be closing down at the end of the season, that's for sure.

Reaching her designated room, the man put down her bag, unlocked the door and ushered her in to what, once, must have been a lovely room. The arched window was large, light streamed in, highlighting the frayed carpet, faded rose-patterned curtains, candlewick bedspread and huge, ancient wardrobe. To her left there was a white tiled bathroom with a deep old tub, and the whole place was redolent of recent scrubbing, a hasty mixture of detergent and furniture wax wafting almost visibly on the air. She could only hope the bed wouldn't be damp, in this humid weather.

'Thank you. Is there a hairdryer by any chance, or a television?' According to the guidebook listing, there should be both. Looking uncertain, the man opened the wardrobe door, and they both blinked in surprise as a small television was revealed.

'Ah – I'm not sure how many channels it gets, but . . . let me see . . .' Groping for a non-existent zapper, he shrugged apologetically before turning it on manually. Amazingly, a picture appeared. 'Well, there's TFI, anyway! And . . . a hairdryer . . . ?'

Eventually he located one in a drawer, such an antique model that Shona wondered whether it had last been used by Marie Antoinette. 'Voilà!' he said with a kind of pathetic pride, a sad grin as if to say, 'There we are, things aren't quite as bad as they seem, are they now?'

He was about to leave her when a thought struck them both. 'Will you be wanting dinner?'

She was ravenous. She would love, absolutely adore to go out and find some yummy, buzzy bistro that would cheer and enliven her after a long, busy day. But work was only starting. 'Yes please. D'you have a good chef?'

'I'm the chef.' Bleakly, as if informing her that he was the boot-boy, he edged towards the door, the evening sun gilding the hairs on his forearms, above which his shirt sleeves were rolled up. At least the shirt, Shona noted, was fresh. 'What would you like to eat?'

'I don't know! What's on the menu?'

'Whatever you like. There's only you tonight. I could do you a steak or some chicken . . .' Glancing at his watch, he raised an enquiring eyebrow, and she realised he was going to dash out to buy whatever food she ordered before the shops closed. Oh, well. At least it wouldn't be frozen.

'Chicken, then? With maybe a salad and some cheese?'

'Right. It'll be ready in about an hour.'

Off he went, and she sat down on the bed, which was the soft, old-fashioned kind, sneezing amidst the particles of furniture polish hanging on the air. I'm sorry, she thought, because you seem like a nice man, but honestly, you'll be way better off when the company closes you down and you can get a nine-to-five job in some office somewhere. Your mother would turn in her grave if she could see what you've let happen to her hotel, which must once have been such a sweet little place.

'Good grief.' Astonished, Shona stopped stone dead in the restaurant when she entered it an hour later. A low-ceilinged, timbered room, it was deserted, devoid of even the British couple she'd hoped to see eating in solitary splendour. Each empty, circular table was forlornly draped in a pale yellow cloth, but hers was freshly, fully dressed, weighted with glasses, cutlery and a bowl of pink flowers which must, she realised, have been swiftly purchased from the village florist. What was more, it was snugly set beside a huge stone fireplace, and the fire was burning, a pile of logs glowing gently as if to keep her company. As she stood staring, the manager appeared, this time wearing a striped apron knotted round his midriff.

'Please – sit down.' As he invited her to do so, he pulled out a chair and held it for her, and she realised he was to be waiter as well as cook. From the direction whence he had come, she could smell food cooking. Delicious hot, garlicky food, and fresh bread and . . . ?

'I've made you some soup to start with' he said almost apologetically, 'I hope you like tomato?'

Yes, she liked tomato. Sitting, she waited while a vast old

silver tureen was wheeled out, steaming, with a ladle and a white, deep soup bowl. Picking up her table napkin, the manager-chef-waiter unfolded it to reveal a full yard of damask, and set it on her lap before ladling out the soup, in which she could see chunks of fresh tomato and little green lengths of chive. In a basket, warm bread rolls were melting the tiny pats of butter beside them.

'*Bon appétit*' said the man, and left her gazing after him, astonished. Soup had never crossed her mind, much less this full-blown production, so thoughtfully prepared that she felt somehow guilty to be alone. A huge tureen, home-made, all for moi!?

It was delicious, and she was savouring its delicate flavour when the man reappeared, carrying a chiller bucket of wine. 'If you like Chablis, I thought it would be best with your meal . . . though I think there's some Sancerre if you'd rather . . . ?'

'Oh, no, Chablis would be lovely. But – where are the English couple? Aren't they eating here tonight?' She wished they were, wished anyone was.

'They did last night. But I think they're dining with friends locally tonight.'

Damn. Even if she hadn't got talking to them, she still wished they were simply here, that she didn't feel so horribly conspicuous. Maybe some other guests would wander in off the street? Except that the Auberge Rose wasn't on any street, it was a kilometre outside the village. Like Le Mas des Cigales, nobody would ever find it by chance.

The man poured some wine, and she sampled it: cool, flinty, perfect. The glass was twinkly-clean, too, contrary to expectation she could see no dust or streaks at all.

'Thank you' she said, 'that's lovely.' Nodding, he left her again, and as she ate she gazed around the room. Beamed and panelled, it would be at its best in winter she thought; she could imagine it cosily filled with truffle hunters quaffing claret after their day in the hills, tucking their big linen napkins into their collars as they set about four hearty courses, or maybe five or even six, laughing and arguing as they slipped bones to the dogs at their feet. In fact . . . why . . . ?

'With a mushroom sauce' the man was saying, back at her elbow; she realised she'd slipped into reverie. 'Is that all right?'

Why did he still sound so apologetic? The breast of chicken he was setting before her looked plump and juicy, its little pool of sauce contained fresh, finely-sliced mushrooms, and a separate dish contained wild rice wafting the most enticing aroma. Food-wise, everything was wonderful. 'Yes' she nodded, and he melted away, as if his mere presence might somehow blunt her appetite.

But nothing could blunt it. The simple meal was hot, fresh, home-made by an excellent cook doubling as a discreetly attentive waiter, and she could fault no aspect of it. On the contrary, it saddened her to think of him cooking all this just for her – and maybe for himself, too, to eat alone later? Food like this was meant to be shared, this room should be full of people enjoying it, someone should be playing that piano in the corner, where had things gone so horribly wrong? Was there a wife tucked away in an attic somewhere, or was this man as solitary as he seemed?

Mulling on it, she reached a decision as she ate, and looked frankly up at the man when he returned to refill her glass. 'Would you mind' she began, 'answering a question?'

'Certainly, madame.' Stoically, he waited.

'Would you mind telling me – where is everyone? Why is nobody else here eating your excellent food? Where are the staff? Are you eating your own dinner alone, out in the kitchen?'

'I will eat it later' he said simply, 'when I have finished

serving yours. As for the staff, the other guests . . . that's a long story. I won't bore you with it.'

'Actually, I wish you would. I'd like to know why this potentially lovely hotel is empty and you're here on your own . . . plus, the company I work for would like to know too. The Groupe Entrime. I'm here on their business – assessing this auberge to see whether it's worth salvaging, or should be sold off.'

Expecting surprise or maybe even a hostile reaction, she merely got a shrug. ' Ah, yes. My esteemed proprietors. So, you work for them?'

'Yes. At the moment, I do. Why don't you bring your meal out here, sit down, join me and tell me the background to this' – vaguely, she swept her arm around the ghostly room – 'this disaster?'

Gravely, he considered her request for what felt like quite a while before replying. 'If that is what you would like, then I will. But I will not attempt to make any excuses for my situation, nor plead for mercy. If the company wishes to close down the Auberge Rose, then – well, that is their decision.'

She warmed to him for that. Other hoteliers would gasp in horror, grab the brandy, go to any lengths to try to secure a reprieve for their tottering, badly run business. At least this guy was realistic enough to read the writing on the wall.

Disappearing, he left her alone for the few minutes it took him to assemble a main course identical to her own, which he wheeled out on the quaint trolley with a cheese platter for her – four or five full, ripe cheeses, and she smiled when she saw grapes and crackers alongside them. Apparently he thought she was English. There was an open bottle of Médoc, too, which he must have been warming in the kitchen.

Courteously, he poured her some, and handed her the cheese platter before sitting down opposite her and taking up his cutlery. No soup, she noted, for him, as if he did not want to delay the meal when she was so far ahead of him. Sitting back, she waited, helping herself to Cantal and chèvre while he made inroads on his chicken.

'Well' he said at length, looking at her with candid, navy-blue eyes, 'as you say, my auberge is indeed a disaster.'

'So' Shona continued some days later in Aileen's kitchen, nibbling olives as she told the sad story of Edouard Savary, 'his mother left the hotel to him, but he turned out to be hopeless at running it. He's a terrific cook but just no use, he says, at business. After a year, his wife persuaded him that it would be better to sell the place to the chain that wanted to buy it, so he could concentrate on the cooking while she ran it for the company, which wanted to maintain the 'family-run' image. So that worked out pretty well for another couple of years . . . until the wife, whose name was Ghislaine, met someone else. Whereupon she not only left poor Edouard, but left him holding the baby as well.'

'The baby? She abandoned her child!?'

'No, I mean the auberge! They didn't have children – for which she blamed him, apparently, his family has a history of sparse offspring or none at all.'

'So what happened then?'

'He went to pieces. Felt she was right, that he was a failure on every count, didn't contest the divorce. He's been on his own ever since, for nearly two years, battling to keep the place open because, if it goes under, that'll be yet another failure . . . the poor guy is under awful pressure, knows the company is bound to shut him down soon. Which he sees as an insult to his mother's memory, because the auberge flourished when she was alive. But he can't see any alternative. He did do a business management course, but says it was all beyond him. He's just not cut out for paperwork or any kind of administration.'

Shovelling sliced fruit into a bowl, Aileen paused to consider. 'Sounds like a square peg in a round hole to me. He'll be better off getting a job as a chef somewhere. Is that what you'll recommend in your report?'

'Well . . .' thoughtfully, Shona sucked on an olive, as if it might contain a kernel of wisdom. 'I should recommend it, obviously, cutting of losses and instant closure. In a way, I think Edouard might actually be grateful to have the decision taken out of his hands. But . . . Aileen, you're going to say I'm mad.'

'Oh, God. Am I? Why?'

'Because I think . . . I'd like to see . . . the place belonged to his mother, it was her pride and joy, it's a gorgeous old place and I'm wondering if there might not just be a way to . . . uh . . . salvage it?'

'Shona! Are you nuts?' Astonished, Aileen wiped her hands on her apron, hardly believing her ears; never before had Shona Fitzpatrick indicated the presence of one sentimental bone in her businesslike body. 'Why would you, or he, or anyone want to? Clearly this man – Edouard? – doesn't have what it takes to run a successful hotel. He sounds like a menace to himself and everybody else. Even his wife got away while the going was good. You say yourself the place is on its last legs – and that's what you're being paid for. Frank, honest assessment.'

'Yes, but . . . Aileen, you should see this poor man. He looks so lost. Looks like his life has been going so wrong for so long – yet he simply told the truth, didn't moan, there's something – something dignified about him. I got the feeling that maybe a helping hand could work wonders. Might even salvage his sanity, because I wouldn't say there's a million miles right now between himself and a nervous breakdown. At the very least, he's discouraged and depressed.'

'What?' Horrified, Aileen recoiled. 'Shona, get a grip! You do not need to go getting mixed up with – with some lame duck who couldn't run a booze-up in a brewery! What on earth has got into you, what is this nonsense?'

Popping another olive, reflecting on it, Shona entirely agreed. As Aileen said, she didn't need this mess on her hands, was not taking a properly objective attitude at all. Was, in fact, finding it difficult to sound or even look remotely detached . . . because, for some completely obscure reason, she had warmed to Edouard Savary. Respected him, for his candour, and liked him, for his valiant effort, the memory of those flowers on her table lingering in her mind. Yes, he was a mess, but at least he had the courage to admit it. Apart from her father, he was the first man she'd ever met who did not automatically assume himself to be the best thing since buttered popcorn. Edouard Savary was about as far as it was possible to get from Terry O'Hagan, or Gavin Sheehan – or even Brendan Wright for that matter, whose life had been so efficiently under control.

What would he make of a helping hand, if he got it? Whatever he might do, she did not think he would bite it off, at any rate. He was going through a difficult phase, and she knew, now, how that felt. Knew how it could happen to anyone – and, when it did happen, anyone deserved one more chance. Just one, provided they had the wit to accept it, and make the most of it.

Would Edouard Savary rise to that? Or was he beyond all rescue, should she wash her hands of this whole thing? It dawned on her that this was an important decision, one she would be held responsible for if she got it wrong. If she recommended to the company that owned the Auberge that a reprieve was justified, then she would have to make very, very sure that it was. Slowly, carefully, she thought about it, wondering, feeling Aileen watching her.

'Aileen. Can I ask you something personal?'

Cautiously, Aileen hesitated. 'Well – yes, but I won't promise to answer!'

'Are you glad you took the plunge, came to France? Glad we bought Le Mas? Happier in your – your marriage?'

Jesus. That was personal. But Aileen knew Shona well enough to understand that she wouldn't ask unless, for whatever peculiar reason, she needed to know. Looking at her, she could see that Shona was following some convoluted train of thought.

'Yes. Yes I am. While I can't say I've fallen unreservedly in love with France, or it with me, I can honestly say the move did me good. Did us all good. It was a wrench and I still miss home, but as a family we needed it. I have no regrets, if that's what you're asking – on the contrary, I'm very grateful to you for helping and encouraging me, and I'm delighted that Le Mas is working so well. We won't make a profit this season, but we'll pay off our debts, break even and – and make one next season.'

Next season. So far, nobody had even mentioned that. Now, suddenly, the question hovered . . . but this was not the moment to delve into it. First, there was a different decision to be made. Slowly, Shona smiled.

'Yes. Le Mas was a challenge, but I think we've risen pretty well to it so far, haven't we?'

'Yes. We have.'

'So. Should I see whether Edouard Savary can rise to one too, then? Or should I just drop him like a hot potato?'

Drop him! Run a mile! That was what Aileen urgently wanted to say, to shout. But, even as the words came rushing to her lips, she saw that they were not what Shona wanted to hear. Nor what she needed to hear, either? Aileen couldn't be sure; all she could see was some look on Shona's face that made her realise just in time that perhaps this man Edouard was not the only one who might, against all evidence to the contrary, rally to fight another day.

Divorced? Childless? In a ghastly muddle, but honest and likeable?

'Well' she offered guardedly, 'why don't you tell me what you have in mind?'

'So' Shona concluded at the end of a very long phone conversation that night, 'that's the picture, Emily. Not pretty, but there you have it. Now, I'm going to leave you to sleep on it. I have to file my report by Friday, so will you get back to me before then?'

'Yes. I will, Shona, and – and thank you. Whatever my decision, it's very good of you to think of me.'

'It makes a change' Shona said simply, 'from you always thinking about me! I would love it if your answer is yes, but I'll understand if it's no. I'm just floating the idea, is all.'

They hung up, and Shona sat where she was, chin cupped in palm, thinking. It was a big question, and a big decision. But one thing was certain: if Emily were by any miracle interested in coming to France to get the Auberge Rose on its feet, she would be the perfect person to do it. If Edouard Savary wanted her to do it. Which was another matter entirely; the poor man had as yet no idea that any of this was being discussed. When he heard, he might well say 'How dare you, the nerve, butt out of my business and let me go to hell in my own sweet way, thanks very much.'

If he did, then she would. But hey, nothing ventured, nothing gained. Smiling, Shona savoured the glow of satisfaction she had so long missed, that delicious buzz of sussing a project, shaking out a puzzle and fitting the pieces together. If Emily and Edouard did by any miracle manage to click, they could make a great team . . . and I, she thought with relish, could make a great job of marketing that little hotel.

I could make it *the* place to stay in the Languedoc, if you want more than B & B at the Mas des Cigales. Which is the next question . . . but let's tackle this one first.

'So' Dymps concluded dolefully, 'what with one thing and another, it'll be Christmas before we can get over to visit you . . . why don't you come here before that, Aileen? Just for a short break, even, on your own? I'm dying to see you.'

'I'm dying to see you too' Aileen replied, 'you and Mam and Marion and everyone . . . things will be quieter in the autumn, I could go then, but I – I'm afraid that if I go to Ireland I might never come back!'

'Oh, Aileen – are you that homesick? Really?'

'Really and truly. Only I don't dare tell anyone, because Joe and Finn love it here. Oh, Dymps, what am I going to *do*? They're both working now, Finn has a girlfriend, Joe is blooming, Shona is so pleased with the way business is going . . . I can't just walk away from it all! I – I've painted myself into a corner!'

Ruefully, Dymps laughed down the phone. 'Ha! Be careful what you wish for, eh? You wished for it and now you've got it. Mam says it's lovely, too. She's been talking about nothing but Le Mas since she got back.'

'Mmm. She had a great time, soaked up the sun, was no end of help with everything, quite honestly I was amazed how well she fitted in.'

'Actually, Aileen, you know her birthday's coming up in a few weeks?'

'Oh, Christ, so it is! I swore I'd be there for that, didn't I?' Fleetingly, guiltily, a white stretch limo flashed through her mind, the one in which Tessie was still waiting to ride.

'You did. But – well, if it would be easier, maybe I could send her there to you instead? Buy her a plane ticket for her present? How would you feel about that?'

'I – I'd feel great! She'd be thrilled and so would I, we could have a little party for her here, Emily O'Brien might be coming over too and the pair of them get on well – '

'So I hear. Apparently they've been in regular contact lately.'

'Then let's do it, Dymps. You send Mam over to me and I'll see that she has a lovely birthday at Le Mas with us.'

'Okay. It's funny, isn't it? Now she's the one who wants to be in France and you're the one who wants to be back here. Honestly, sometimes I wonder whether there's any pleasing anyone.'

You could be right, Aileen thought as she put down the phone. You could just be right about that, Dymps. Whoever coined the phrase 'having it all' hadn't a clue what they were talking about. If there's one thing I've learned lately, it's that nobody can have it all. We're lucky if we can have half, and blessed if we can have three-quarters. Wanting any more is just plain silly. Childish and greedy.

So which quarters do I want, and which does Joe want, and which does Finn want?

14

The good news was that Emily was on her way. The bad news was that she couldn't come for another few weeks yet, until her own summer season tapered off and she could spare the time. Humming with impatience, Shona turned in her report to Olivier Dessanges, recommending closure of four hotels, revamping of three and 'the Auberge Rose is restructuring, Olivier, could we possibly give it a bit more time before any decision is made?'

Dubiously, Olivier said he would ask his client. 'Do you think it's worth waiting for, Shona?'

'Definitely' she said without a blink. 'Three weeks, max, okay?'

'Okay. Max. Time is money, you know.'

It certainly was. So, pocketing her fee with a feeling of a job well done, she turned her attention to the Irish couple who were house-hunting in the area, using Le Mas as a base. A friendly pair called Des and Ciara Baker, they were trying to find 'an old house with lots of character, but in good condition, if that's not mutually exclusive!' He was an antiques dealer and she was a weaver and 'frankly some of these estate agents are sharks, they'd sell you any old shack . . . as for trying to open a bank account . . . import antiques . . . we had no idea it could all be so complicated. We speak a bit of French, but not enough for this kind of thing.'

Right, said Shona: she would find them an honest estate

agent, a reputable solicitor, set up their bank account, fill in all their paperwork and nurse them through the whole process, no matter how long it might take or what complications might arise, for a flat fee, half now and half six months hence, how did that sound?

Ciara Baker looked as if she might weep with relief. 'Oh, that sounds wonderful! You'll take the whole thing off our hands, set us up, deal with everyone and everything, all this nightmare form-filling and . . . ?'

'Everything. When you find your house I'll check that the land isn't zoned for development, get your water pumping, electricity working, phone installed, cable tv if you want it, supervise your furniture lorry, find workmen for any jobs you want done – even have flowers waiting when you move in, with wine and a corkscrew!'

Marvellous, chorused the Bakers, absolutely bloody marvellous. That night, Shona arrived for supper at Le Mas waving a bottle of champagne. 'Aileen, I'm in business! The Bakers have hired me to be their minder!'

'Whoopee! Here's to the first of many!'

It was a lively supper, with Joe, Finn and Martine, plus Tessie fresh off her plane from Ireland, looking remarkably lively for a lady turning sixty-five. 'I'm thrilled to be back' she said, 'and on my best behaviour, so maybe they'll let me stay longer this time!'

Wistfully, Aileen smiled. 'We'd love you to stay, Mam, now things aren't quite so busy . . . Emily O'Brien will be arriving soon and you'll have fun with her. Only – all our other rooms are still booked up, Shona, where are we going to put Emily?'

'In the Auberge Rose. That's the whole point, the reason she's coming—'

Interested, Tessie leaned forward. 'What point, what reason for what?'

417

So Shona told her, and Tessie nodded at intervals, looking fascinated. 'But that's a great idea! Emily could spend the whole winter here, running that hotel for that poor man – how big is it?'

'Not big. Just ten bedrooms.'

'Perfect. She already has six in Galway. She's so experienced . . . and she loves France she says . . . I wish I could do something like that.'

Around the table, there was an astonished silence. Defiantly, Tessie looked at Finn, who was visibly trying not to grin. 'Well, I would. It would be lovely to spend the winter here.'

'Grandma' he pointed out, 'there was a wild storm last winter. Massive floods. The weather isn't always as good as it is now.'

'I know that. But this house is up high, it doesn't get flooded, does it? Besides, there'd always be a few people staying, now Le Mas is getting established, it'd be far more fun than winter in Ireland, that everlasting grey sky . . . the food's so delicious, and I love that little village down the hill. We even have RTE on the radio. I think it's great here and if I were Emily – but Shona, does this man *want* her? I mean, he doesn't even know her, does he?'

'No. Not yet. But if Edouard knows what's good for him – I'm going to see him this weekend, to tell him his new manager is on her way. If he has any sense he will fall at my feet with gratitude.'

'Either that' Joe intervened, 'or he'll think you and Emily are a right pair of interfering biddies and send you packing.'

'Maybe' Shona conceded with a determined smile, 'in which case I will abandon him to his fate, his mother's hotel will be shut down and that will be the end of him.'

'God' said Joe with feeling, 'I don't envy the poor bloke, with

418

Miss Shona Fitzpatrick snapping at his heels. Personally I'd sooner have a Dobermann.'

'So' said Shona, leaning conspiratorially over the table on which she was jotting notes, 'this friend of mine will be arriving on Monday, Edouard. She has her own beautiful, very successful B & B in Ireland, years of experience, speaks French ... if you get on with her, and she with you, then I will persuade the company that owns this auberge to give you six months to get your game together. Emily will run the place, I will market it and you will cook your socks off. When you're not painting corridors that is, or clearing the pond or fixing shutters or doing any of the hundred things that need doing. How does that sound?'

Incredulously, Edouard Savary stared at this woman, this whirlwind who had blown into his life from nowhere and now seemed to be sweeping all in her path, hustling him along as if he were a fallen leaf.

'It sounds' he exhaled, 'miraculous. But – what if we don't get on? Or what if we do, but then she goes back to her own place?'

With a small sigh, Shona twirled her pen. 'Why don't we cross that bridge when we come to it? I mean, frankly, you've nothing to lose here, have you? So let's give it a shot and see what happens, hmm?'

Well, she was right about that. He did not have a lot left to lose. Never in his life, he thought, had he met anyone so forceful, so invigorating as this woman, whose smile was glinting like stainless steel. 'But why me, Shona? Why are you taking such an interest in me?'

'Because, Edouard, you are a challenge. I want to see your hotel not only back in business but turning into a perfect little bijou, which I will promote in all the right places . . . then other owners will ask me to market theirs, and . . . and I'll be doing what I've long wanted to do. All by myself, without so much as a by-your-leave from Mr Terry O'Hagan, or anyone else for that matter. I will be my own boss.'

'Terry O'Hagan? Who is he?'

'He is the slimiest creature that ever crawled out from under a rock. It was once my misfortune to work for him. Until the night he tried to assault me.'

'What!?' Stunned, Edouard sat bolt upright; the idea of anyone daring to do such a thing to this lady seemed as fool-hardy as it was disgusting. 'But – surely – Shona, he did not hurt you, did he, or – ?'

'He hurt my career. Which I am now trying to rebuild. Which is where the Auberge Rose comes into the picture. If I help you, Edouard, you'll be helping me, too.'

Suddenly her smile was softer, warmer, and in that instant Edouard Savary saw something in Shona he had not seen before: an appeal of some kind, as if she were silently holding out her hand so that he could take it, lift her to her feet. The idea of not being exclusively on the receiving end of help was a balm to his pride; for the first time in years maybe he could offer something in turn, to someone? It was so long since he felt he had anything to offer. So long since anyone had cared about him, or given him reason to care about them. With an unexpected surge of energy, he wanted to seize Shona, pick her up, clasp her to him and kiss her resoundingly on her resolute little face – which was not actually little now that he looked at it, but oval in shape, opal in texture, illuminated by eyes the colour of wistaria.

I like this woman, he thought. I like her and respect her and – and admire her. If I weren't so damn broke, I would like to whirl her off somewhere and thank her for – for having faith in me. Faith that I'm going to have to justify, because for all her charm I'd say she's the kind of woman who'd flay me alive if I let her down.

Has anyone ever let her down, I wonder? Dropped her from a height, the way Ghislaine dropped me? She's Irish, what on earth is she doing here in the Languedoc, marching into my life and taking over? I wish I knew her well enough to ask—

'Now, Edouard, I want you to set your mind to getting on with Emily when she arrives. Okay?'

'Okay.'

'And then, if she takes you on, I am going to lend the two of you a pair of hands.'

'Oh, no, Shona, you are doing enough already, I would not dream of—'

'Not my hands, Edouard. I have a friend, whose name is Aileen, and she has a husband, whose name is Joe. Joe is a handyman, used to work in a hardware store, can do all sorts of DIY stuff. I will sweet-talk him into coming over here for three days, no more, to get you started. All right?'

All *right*? But this woman, he thought wildly, is incredible. Fabulous. A life-raft in a churning ocean. I just wish there were something I could do for her, in turn, something more than just let her use my hotel as a kind of springboard to wherever she wants to go.

But what? She looks like the kind of woman who doesn't need a thing. She's not wearing a wedding ring, but there has to be some lucky guy somewhere in her life, someone who adores her and would smash my nose if I so much as offered her a drink.

Hasn't there? Wouldn't he? And what's a broken nose anyway, to a man whose whole life was, until this minute, about to be pulped?

'Shona?'

Standing up, he looked down at her, and she looked up in turn, dimpling the end of her pen into her cheek. 'Yes, Edouard?'

'Would you like a – a martini?'

She considered it. 'With three olives, and a twist of lemon?'

'If you wish' he said gravely, 'you can have an entire olive grove, and a lemon tree, and I will send a boy to Baccarat for the crystal.'

Her face detonated with laughter, and he laughed with her, and suddenly the auberge was leaping to life around them, resonating with the simple sound of people having fun.

Emily arrived carrying so much luggage that Shona eyed it askance. 'What's in that lot?'

'Hope!' Emily informed her. 'I'm hoping to spend the whole winter here, helping this man Edouard get his little hotel back on its feet. It'll be such fun, such a change – what's he like, where is he?'

'We're going straight to meet him at his auberge. He's nice, Emily . . . different from any man I ever met before, but nice. He's broke and divorced and in a fix – but he's charming too, unpretentious, doesn't take himself too seriously or blame anyone for anything. I like him.'

'Well, if you like him, that's half the battle for me.'

So saying, Emily let herself be driven to the Auberge Rose, where she gaped and peered through the windscreen as they drove up to it. 'Good heavens. This place is falling apart.'

'Not structurally . . . it just needs a facelift. Joe says he'll help. I'm working on Finn, too. Inside, it just needs redecoration and – and cheering up! I think it's an ideal winter hotel, should have lots of visitors in the truffle and shooting seasons. We just have to start attracting them, that's all – you know, log fires, cosy decor, hearty food. Edouard's a great cook.'

Intrigued, Emily followed Shona into the apologetic-looking auberge, where a black-haired, Mediterranean-looking man with denim-blue eyes came rushing forward, stretching out an eager hand. 'Hello! Mme O'Brien! Let me take these – I am Edouard Savary –'

Apart from the deep inky colour of his eyes there was nothing exceptional about him; his tan corduroys and white shirt could have been anyone's. His smile and voice were warm, his handshake was welcoming, but . . . but it wasn't until his gaze swooped to Shona that Emily saw, in a flash, what Shona apparently did not see at all.

Rapt adoration, bordering on worship, the look of a man not merely smitten but slain, his whole face glowing with hope and the kind of shyness that must come of having nothing to offer, nothing but his own self and soul. Was that why Shona seemed so blithely unaware of him as she permitted her cheek to be kissed, her arm to be touched? Good God, Emily thought, she scarcely sees this man, *as* a man. He has nothing, in material terms, and so she simply sees him as a project, whereas he sees her as – as Joan of Arc! Not just as a saviour, but as a woman, he is absolutely *exuding* desire for her. Desire he doesn't dare voice, in case it all goes wrong . . . if only he knew how often it's all gone wrong before, he'd be wearing a suit of armour. The poor fellow is an absolutely sitting duck.

'Mme O'Brien' Edouard beamed, 'allow me to show you around, and then we will talk over coffee in the lounge.'

'Put her luggage in room seven, Edouard' Shona said in her best director-of-operations tone, 'and make sure everything's plugged in, switched on.'

'Yes, of course, Shona.' His smile widened as if she couldn't give him enough orders, and then Emily followed him up the stairs, all but coughing in the wake of his billowing rapture, which floated down to mantle Shona like a kind of invisible fleece. A fleece, Emily wondered, that might warm her heart at last?

Cringing, Aileen recognised that it was time to call a family conference. No choice, no way out: she was going to have to ask her husband and son whether they wanted to stay on at Le Mas, and the answer was going to be a resounding 'yes', and she was going to be stuck in this beautiful, delicious, charming prison for the rest of her days. I'll never get back to Galway, she thought wildly, my friends will forget me and Dymps will say 'who are you?' and – oh, I am so homesick I could scream! I want gossip and rain and a packet of Tayto and Dunnes Stores and . . . and what'll they say, when they hear all that? They'll say I'm nuts. But I have to go home. I have to. I feel like a fool, and now I'm going to look like one too. As for Shona – how am I going to break it to her? Who's going to run Le Mas, if I leave?

Maybe Aude might know someone? Or maybe Joe will say 'no way, we're staying put'? Where would we live, if we did go home? We haven't even got a home, it's rented out.

I don't know. All I know is, I've got to tell them. Admit I bit off more than I can chew. France has been wonderful, but now it has served its purpose and I . . . oh, God. Let's just get it over with, see what they say. They're going to hate me for it, they'll say I don't know when I'm well off, don't know my own mind, am messing everyone around and causing endless disruption.

But nothing they can say will make me stay. I need my country, my friends, my language, my roots. My *home*.

Yes, Emily conceded after thorough, thoughtful inspection, the Auberge Rose was badly run down. But yes, it did have potential. Yes, she would find it a stimulating challenge to spend the winter here, helping Shona and Edouard to get it back on its feet. But only for six months: in April she would return to Ireland, where after all she had her own very successful B & B. Meanwhile, Edouard had better get busy doing all the things he was fervently promising to do, and Shona had better start attracting a few customers. France's food might be fabulous, but it was far from free, 'and we will need to eat occasionally.'

'We will' Shona airily asserted, 'I'll have a bit of money from the Bakers soon, we'll survive – even have fun!'

Emily saw that she was having fun already, bossing Edouard around, mapping out a rosy future for the auberge, juggling it with Le Mas as well as her 'settlement service'. Some people might be overwhelmed by so many activities, but the busier Shona got the happier she looked, her face glowing with pleasure as she sent Edouard out in waders to clear the pond, instructed Joe to remove and repair the tattered shutters, which she then persuaded Finn to paint 'pink. The palest, creamiest pink you can find for less than a tenner a tin.' She sweetly put every command as a request, and everyone jumped to obey; she was a very pretty, entirely charming tyrant. Smiling behind the scenes, no slouch herself, Emily got busy with furnishings, laundry, cleaning, organising 'and maybe we could get a girl on some kind of training scheme, Shona, to help out a bit?'

A girl was got. All kinds of grants, subsidies and enterprise-aid were sought as Shona began to storm the French system, ploughing her way through stacks of forms, visiting mayors, tourism offices, town halls, hauling help out of anyone who might be able to provide it. Breathless, Edouard spun around the auberge as if sucked into a cyclone, and Emily watched him closely, studying him, getting to know him, wondering whether he might rebel if Shona gave him just one more order. But if anything he looked more dazzled every day, unable to believe the upturn in events, the gleaming ray of hope that was Shona Fitzpatrick.

He's so different, Emily thought. Exactly the opposite of all the other men in her life, who were so assertive, so established, so gainfully employed, so *suitable*. Except that I never saw any of them, not even Brendan Wright, look at her the way this man Edouard looks at her. Not one of them ever gave her the freedom he's giving her, to do things her way, to be herself. They couldn't handle her confidence: Edouard looks as if he loves it.

Does she even notice? I don't think she does. But I won't say anything, not yet . . . I'll see how things develop, see if he can attract her attention without any help from me. I'd love this to work out, love her to be happy at last – but I pushed her into a man's arms before, and look what happened. Maybe Emily O'Brien should just mind her own business for once, settle in for a nice sunny winter and enjoy the change of scenery. What a lovely luxury, to spend six months in France!

Edouard's a nice man. Very nice. The more I get to know him, the more I like him. As Shona says, he's a mess, but he's a decent, honest mess. Candid, not at all bitter, hopelessly disorganised but ready to work hard – and devoid of the arrogance that ruins so many men. Brendan was a good guy too, but at the end of the day he did want Shona to have his children, run his family, do things his way. He wanted to be the boss. It never would have worked, not with a woman like her. Unlikely as Edouard seems, I think maybe he stands a better chance.

If she'll only give him one!

Stop it, Emily. You're here, you're keeping an eye on her, helping out – that's enough. Don't interfere. Don't even think about buying a big hat, or having the reception here at the auberge.

426

I wonder will they be engaged by Christmas? Then we could have an Easter wedding . . . out on the lawn . . . in a marquee . . . a string quartet . . . a blue hat . . .

Oh, for heaven's sake, Edouard, hurry *up*! I'm sixty, I can't hang around for ever while you get your ass in gear!

September, drifting into October, and the wine harvest . . . hundreds of vignerons out in the rust-red fields, harvesting their grapes, tractors chugging through the narrow streets . . . stuck behind one in first gear, Shona realised with surprise that she didn't care. Didn't mind one little delay, this mellow morning, because everything else was moving along, going so smoothly, so amazingly better than it ever had before. For the first time ever, she had the heady feeling of running her own life, of being in control with nobody messing her around.

The sun was lower than it had been, the air just barely tinged with the crispness of autumn, the first hint of year's end. The year in which, she thought, I lost my job and my man and thought I'd lose my mind.

But I didn't lose it. Instead, I came to France with Aileen Hegarty, and bought a house, and went into business, and made new friends and – and was happy. I can hardly believe how happy I am, how free I feel, how lovely this year has turned out to be. I didn't get what I wanted, but what I got is turning out to be so much better. I'm enjoying every minute of it, I'm liberated and stimulated and I'm staying here where I belong – unlike Aileen, who sadly isn't where she belongs at all.

She belongs in Ireland, is pining for home. When will she ever get the courage to admit it? I know she wants to go, I can sense it, see it, yet she still hasn't said it. I wish she would. She thinks I'll eat her, but I won't. I'll be sorry to see her go, but I'll find someone else to run Le Mas, now I know how to find people. I'll miss her, but there's no point in trying to keep her when she's so clearly, badly homesick. If she doesn't own up soon, I'll have to tackle her, talk to – oh, damn, why do mobiles always ring when you're changing gear!

'Hello?'

'Shona! Shona, it's me, Crys!'

'Crys?! Oh, I was going to ring you this very day – how are you – ?'

'Shona, it's a boy! A beautiful, beautiful boy!'

Even over the mobile, all the way from Ireland, across all the distance that separated them, Shona heard it: the trembling, exultant emotion in Crys's voice, the near-to-tears quiver that told her immediately what she'd been praying to hear. Crys was a mother, and thrilled to be.

'Oh, Jesus, wait, let me pull in – oh, Crys! Oh, I can't believe it – when – ?'

'Last night. Just before midnight. Ten days early. Seven pounds five ounces – oh, Shona, you've got to come, you've got to see him, he's *gorgeous*!'

'I will, I will! Is he okay, are you – is Gavin – ?'

'Gavin is in heaven and – oh, Sho, so am I! I had no idea, not until the very moment he was born, not until I saw him, held him, I never knew he would be so . . . beautiful . . . I can hardly . . .'

Even as Crys's voice halted Shona's did too, shuddering on the brink of tears, absorbing how hugely everything had changed, literally overnight: Crys was a mother now, there was no going back, nothing would ever be the same again. For the rest of her life, she would put herself second to her son, to his needs, she would never be carefree, crusading Crys again.

And the miracle was, she didn't sound as if she wanted to be. Against all the odds, she sounded ecstatic, choking with happiness that was as moving as it was astonishing. Their long friendship was going to need flexing and expanding, because this wasn't Crys any more, this was the mother of –

'What's his name? What are you going to call him?'

'Ha! Brace yourself, Bridget!'

'Oh, Crys! You're not going to do anything he'll hate you for, are you?!'

Half laughing, half crying, Shona held her breath, but the answer when it came wasn't as awful as it might have been.

'Luther. As in Martin Luther King. "I have a dream . . . " I'm going to see to it, Shona, that my son has lots of dreams. I will raise him to be an activist and a visionary.'

'I'll bet you will! And I love his name! Luther Sheehan won't have to divorce his parents after all – oh, Crys, I can't wait to see him, and you!'

Suddenly Shona's throat was clenching, clogging with tears, she was flooded with sudden longing, the pang that would always be part of living so far away from friends and family . . . Crys has a family now, she suddenly realised. Maybe not a perfect family, with Gavin to contend with, but a family nonetheless. A husband, and a son, people to care for, care about; a unit. Her bonds are tightening; from now on we'll have to fight for our friendship, work harder to stay in touch, stay close. I want to hug her, but she's not here – I mean, I'm not there. But we will stay close. We can do it and we will do it.

'Sho? Are you there?'

'Yes, I'm here, right opposite a florist's, I'm going to send you a *truckload* of flowers – and I'm going to come see Luther on Saturday.'

'What? You mean, *this* Saturday?'

'Yes. Day after tomorrow. I have to see you, Crys, and see your child. Being in France is no excuse. I'm on my way to visit my best friend and her new baby.'

A long silence; one in which Shona could almost hear the significance of the promise sinking in. And then Crys's voice, swirling with delight. 'Oh, yes! Oh, great! I'll be home by then, Gavin will pick you up at the airport – '

Shona smiled as she visualised him strutting up to her, swaggering with pride – but what matter? Crys was happy, and that was all that counted. 'Is Luther on solids yet? Should I bring a few frogs' legs for him to sample?'

'Don't you dare! Bring them for *me* to sample!' Crys's laugh was euphoric, bringing her so vividly close that Shona felt she could almost see her, touch her.

'Crys? Tell me – have you managed to paint your nails since producing Luther?'

'Oh yes. First thing this morning. Blue, for a boy.'

They both laughed aloud, and both burst into tears when they hung up, overwhelmed by thoughts and feelings that were unique to them, and would never make sense to anyone else. It was a long time before Shona could get out of the car and go to the florist, and when she did her legs were almost buckling with what she recognised as engulfing relief. Far from fighting her fate, Crys was embracing it, loving it.

For no imaginable reason, as she reached to choose a rose, Shona thought of Edouard.

Somewhat startled by the speed of Shona's departure – 'I have to see Crys, Emily, I have to!' – Emily waved her off, watching with interest as Edouard seized the chance to kiss her not once but four times. The French were big into kissing, but still, four was as far as it could decently go, and it dawned on Emily that here was just the chance she needed. With Shona away for several days, she would have Edouard all to herself, to interrogate at length and at leisure. She could find out whether those four kisses went more than skin deep.

And so they spent a busy, satisfying day working alongside each other, discussing menus, reupholstering a sofa, speculating what kind of guests Shona might inveigle into staying at the Auberge Rose; she had already placed advertising in several hunting-shooting-fishing magazines and there were five bookings for the long October weekend. But Emily held her fire: she would wait until after dinner, this evening, to delve into Edouard's personal dossier – family, friends, ex-wife, interests and activities, everything she could winkle out of him.

It was a warm, cloudy evening, tangy with wood smoke, and although there were only the two of them Edouard cooked a proper four-course meal, with such care that Emily wondered whether he was trying to impress her: could he possibly intuit that she was on to him, guessing how he felt about Shona and hoping she might put in a good word for him? Or was she getting her wires all crossed, was he simply incapable of cooking a bad meal, not romantically interested in Shona at all?

Be careful, she warned herself. Let him do all the talking. Just a handful of questions, casually phrased in a way that won't frighten him off. Honestly, I wish I wasn't such a meddler! But I have to find out whether he's the kind of man who really might suit Shona. Since she so wants to stay in France, I'd like it to be with someone who'll look after her – even if she thinks she's looking after him.

Settling down over their meal, they talked widely at first, and Emily drew from Edouard much information about himself: his passion for abseiling, his left-of-centre politics, his 'far more successful' brother, his unexpected taste for the American writers Bill Bryson, Anne Tyler, Michael Moore; the music of Nina Simone, Michel Sardou, Giuseppe Verdi. But it was Edouard who narrowed down the conversation in turn over dessert, steering it round to Shona, wanting to know about Crys and her other Irish friends, her interests and activities in Ireland, the career that had, he gathered, somehow got skewed by some man called Terry O'Hagan?

Yes, Emily confirmed, that was true, but maybe it had been for the best in the end, because now Shona was free to work for herself, develop herself, make the most of her good sharp business brain.

'She is sharp, isn't she?' Edouard grinned. 'She just arrived here one day out of the blue, informed me I was a disaster and took over. I feel as if I've been drafted into the army.'

Emily considered over a slice of creamy, sinful millefeuille. 'She does have that effect sometimes. In fact that may well be why Terry O'Hagan wanted her out of the way – she showed him up for the layabout he was. Personally I've always admired her for her drive – but maybe some people might find it a bit scary?'

'Ha – like me, you mean?' Edouard smiled genially, but suddenly Emily saw that, while his attempts at hotel management might be disastrous, he was not thick. Far from it: he saw exactly what she was getting at.

'Yes' she said candidly, 'like you. Like lots of people who could resent being organised, bossed around, sorted out, whatever you want to call it. Shona's a sweet girl, but many men might find her a handful, a bit too strong-willed?'

Reflectively, Edouard refilled Emily's coffee cup. 'And have they?'

Taken aback, Emily sat up straight. She hadn't expected quite such a direct question. And Shona would kill her for disclosing any personal information – if she found out. But Shona wasn't here, was she? Something about Edouard's candid look suggested that he could be trusted with a confidence, and so she decided to tell the truth.

'Yes. They have. Dozens, as a matter of fact. Her life is littered with the wreckage of men who found her physically attractive, bright and beautiful, but – but not marriage material! She's not maternal, she can be demanding, she doesn't take any prisoners . . . any man who expected his three children and his hot meals and his clean shirts would be sadly disappointed. As, indeed, several have been.'

H'mm. Mulling it over, Edouard surprised Emily by getting up, strolling over to the mantelpiece, taking down a box of small cigars and offering it to her. Laughing, never having smoked a cigar in her life, she refused, 'but you go ahead. I love the aroma.'

Lighting one, he inspected it, turning it slowly in his hand as he was apparently turning thoughts in his mind, before speaking again. 'I see. It sounds as if Shona has been hurt, then?'

Grimacing, Emily nodded. 'Yes. She has – as have some of the men. There has been a litany of disaster, and I'm coming to the conclusion that Shona will never have a normal, conventional relationship with any man. She – she's hard work!'

There now. That's your cards marked for you, Mr Savary. Don't say nobody warned you. Will you run a mile, now, or is there some strength under that gentle aura of yours? Am I entirely wrong in my belief that your current difficulties do not indicate stupidity, or lack of character, or anything much worse than bad luck? You've had the wits to accept help when it came your way, at any rate, which suggests that you might be smarter than circumstances indicate.

'H'mm. Hard work is exactly what Shona seems to thrive on.'

'It is. She has an energising effect on everyone . . . only some men would prefer the women in their lives to have a restful effect.'

'Indeed. But Emily, a demanding person can also be a very rewarding person, non?'

'Yes. I don't think anyone would ever feel short-changed by Shona. She asks a lot, but she gives a lot, to people she likes or

433

respects . . . she's helped me a lot and she's helped Aileen Hegarty and—'

'And now she is helping me. Do you think, Emily, that might mean she likes me? Do I dare imagine she even respects me, despite my – my problems?'

Looking suddenly, intently, at her, Edouard pulled on his cigar, and Emily sat back, weighing her words thoughtfully. It wasn't her business to disclose Shona's opinions, but . . . 'Yes. She does like you, Edouard. She told me so. Whether she respects you is another question, one I can't answer – but I will tell you this. Shona is the kind of woman whose respect you have to earn.'

'Yes. That's what I thought. And that is what I am trying to do, by working as hard as possible, admitting that she's better qualified than me, accepting the help that she has seen fit to honour me with. She – she's amazing.'

'Yes! Do you like her, Edouard, or do you find her – too much?'

Getting up again, he fetched a decanter and two small glasses, brought them to the table and raised a laconically humorous eyebrow. '*Un petit Cointreau, madame?*'

'My favourite. Thank you. *Vive la France.*'

Solemnly, sardonically, he nodded and raised his glass. '*Vive la France. Vive* Shona Fitzpatrick, who has fallen into my wretched life like manna from the sky. I like her very much, Emily, and . . . and I only wish I were not in such terrible difficulties just now. Difficulties that preclude me from – from telling her how much I like her.'

'But Edouard, it's catch-22. If you weren't in difficulty she wouldn't be here.'

'Well, that's true. I know I'm not the reason she's here, the reason is the Auberge, which she seems to see as the launchpad of her new career. So, if I can be of help to her in turn, that salvages my pride a little. But it does not resolve my problem.'

'What problem?' Oh God, Emily thought, don't let him say he has some awful illness or huge alimony or a prison record or—

'The problem of money! Don't misunderstand me, Emily, I like Shona enormously and I think you probably suspect how – how attracted to her I am. But she is a material girl, *non*? My kind of poverty would not amuse her for very long, if at all.'

No. You're right there, Emily acknowledged, thinking of Shona's often-voiced aspiration to 'a lovely detached house and three holidays a year'. In the long run, she was sure that Shona would get everything she wanted, with or without Edouard Savary. But . . . 'For the moment, Edouard, I think what Shona needs more than money is – is a little affection in her life. Warmth, companionship, someone to share things and accept her for what she is. Money might come later, but she's well capable of earning that for herself. If you're asking my opinion, I think the most constructive thing a man could offer her would be – support. Support and encouragement and the freedom to fulfil her potential. So far, nobody has ever offered that.'

'Do you think she would accept it, if it were offered? She seems so very independent.'

'She is. But no man, or woman, is an island, are they? Everyone needs love, everyone needs a hug, a smile, someone special waiting at the end of the day – someone who makes them feel special too! Until now, nobody has ever made Shona feel special. They've only ever made her feel that she doesn't fit their mould.'

A long silence. Making no attempt to fill it, Emily sat twirling her glass in front of the flickering flames, letting Edouard think, watching his face move and change as he digested what she was saying. It was a contradictory face, etched with a humility that admitted he might be down, overlaid with resolve that said he was not out. A failed marriage, a failed business – but an upheld chin that proclaimed faith in the future, no self-pity at all. Even a trace of a laugh, curling round the ends of his lips, enlivening his eyes, drawing her to him, confirming her belief that he could rise to the challenge of Shona. If encouraged, if given grounds for hope.

When eventually he looked up, his face was very frank. 'Do I understand you correctly, Emily? Are you suggesting that, if I work extremely hard and get the auberge back upright, Shona might respect me?'

'I'm sure of it.'

'And if I – if I confessed to Shona that I'm not exactly a conventional man, nor looking for a conventional woman, she might accept that?'

Eh? 'What do you mean, exactly?'

'I mean . . . oh, God, this will sound all wrong! But the fact is that the only thing I really want to do in life is cook. I love it, I'm blissfully happy at it, I can think of nothing more wonderful than a woman who could understand that and not expect me to – to run the whole show! I don't want to run it, that's why Ghislaine left me, she wanted much more than a house-husband. But maybe a house-husband might . . . suit . . . Shona?'

'I'd venture to say, Edouard, that there's nothing she'd love more. A man doing his own thing, not interfering with hers . . . if you're smart and go about it the right way, I think perhaps you could make each other very happy.'

His eyes lit up, in a flash he suddenly looked ten years younger, as if the burden of all his worries was lifting. 'Really? I ask you, Emily, because you know her so well . . . perhaps you might even consider . . . ?'

'Putting in a good word for you?! Yes, Edouard, I would –

on the understanding that you think long and hard first about everything I'm saying to you. Shona might be fun, but she's no picnic when the chips are down, forgive my muddled metaphor but – well, you'd earn your stripes with her. You'd have to live up to her high expectations. Have to bite your tongue sometimes. Have to let her get on with managing while you get on with cooking – and not blame her if she ever makes a bad decision, because she'll blame herself enough. Socially, some people might say "oh, she wears the trousers" – but it's my view that it takes a strong man to let a woman wear them if she wants, and not care what anyone says. Have you that much strength, do you think?'

It was a very personal, quite impolite question, but Emily didn't hesitate to ask it, because she wanted things clear – and isn't it great, she thought, to be sixty, age gives you such impunity, nobody takes offence! He didn't answer, but she saw that he was thinking, not sulking.

'Yes' he said finally, slowly, and she found his thoughtful tone reassuring. 'I think I have. I hope I have. But I will, as you say, think about it before I – do anything rash! If Shona has been hurt before, I would hate for her to be hurt again. I won't embark on anything I don't feel I can carry through.'

Trying hard to mask her delight, Emily nodded with what she hoped was dignity. 'Good. That's such a sensible answer, it only leaves me one more question.'

'Which is?'

'Are you – have you – do you – do you actually love her, Edouard?'

After all, he had not known Shona very long. But, looking astonished, he stared at Emily as if she had suddenly lost every last marble. '*Love* her? But Emily, is it not obvious? I *adore* her. I *worship* the proverbial ground she walks on. She has hit me like a *thunderbolt*! Should she ever deign to hear how I feel about her, I will pilgrimage barefoot to Lourdes in thanksgiving and throw myself flat at the feet of the miracle-working madonna.'

His expression was comical, but his tone was vehement, and Emily smiled archly. 'Is that a yes?'

'*Oui, madame*, that is a yes. I am a lamb to the slaughter. A sacrifice on the altar of Shona Fitzpatrick.'

'Fair enough, so. You have my permission, Edouard, to proceed with your tragically masochistic case.'

They laughed, but she saw resolve in his face, a squaring of his shoulders that left her satisfied, and hopeful. This man, she thought, is none of the things Shona ever wanted, and in my view that's exactly what makes him perfect for her. There's no way I'm going back to Ireland until I get that hat and that string quartet.

15

Leaning back in his chair, Joe folded his hands on his stomach with the contented look of a man who had just enjoyed a thoroughly delicious dinner cooked by his thoroughly delicious wife. And what treat might she produce next, for dessert? Speculatively, he eyed her as she cleared the table, handing plates to Finn who – would miracles never cease? – was whistling as he stacked them in the dishwasher. That boy, Joe thought, has changed out of all recognition. France, and Martine, and the status he acquired by rescuing those people from that flood, have worked wonders for him. I can actually look at him these days with pride, talk to him as a man, stop worrying about him at last. He knows what happened to Hazel, but he can handle it. He's going to be fine . . . and I have Aileen to thank for that. Bringing him here, bringing us all, was the best thing she ever did. She's brought our family back together.

Beaming, he looked at her, and at that moment she handed the last plate to Finn, sat down at the table, gazed around it at her mother and son and husband. Something in her face produced an expectant hush; she looked as if she had some kind of announcement to make.

'Well' she said at length, 'here we are, heading into winter.'

Yes. Indeed. Nobody could disagree with that.

'And so . . . it's time to talk.'

'Walk?' Despite her new hearing aid, Tessie looked perplexed: sometimes she still missed the odd word.

'No, Mam – *talk*. About us. About Le Mas. About France.'

'Well, I think it's marvellous.' Happily, Tessie looked around her for confirmation, and Joe nodded vigorously.

'So do I.'

'Me too' said Finn, 'I'm only sorry we didn't move here years ago.'

Everyone smiled; nobody saw the bombshell coming. Not until the very last moment, when with a sharp intake of breath Joe suddenly thought he glimpsed – what? Oh, God – Aileen – oh, no!

'Well' she said slowly, 'I'm glad you're all happy. But – there's something – I've got to tell you. I'm not happy. I'm unsettled and a – a fish out of water and I – I – want to go home.'

Had she produced a hand grenade, ripped out the pin with her teeth and lobbed it over the table, the horror could not have been greater. Stunned, everyone froze, staring at her in baffled, total silence.

Flushing, she stared at them defiantly. 'I'm sorry' she said, 'but I do. I'm homesick and it's getting worse every day . . . France has been fun, but I can't stay here for the rest of my days. I want Dymps and I want Galway and I want my *home*.'

No response. Just more horror, rippling round the table, everyone looking at her aghast. Fists clenching defiantly, she frowned back at them with the determined air of a dentist wielding a drill.

'But – but – ' Flummoxed, Joe groped for words. 'But Aileen – love – why – what *is* this? Why didn't you tell me? I thought – we all thought – '

'I know' she said wretchedly, 'everyone thought I was perfectly happy. And I was . . . at first . . . but the longer it goes on the worse it gets. I know you all love it here, but I miss home as if it were an amputated limb. I can't explain it, it's not logical, it just *is*.'

Sitting upright, retrieving his wits, wondering if there was no end to the whims of his endlessly capricious wife, Joe suddenly intuited that, behind the bravado, she was on the verge of tears. She was, to his amazement, genuinely aching for home, almost radiating a silent plea to him. Why hadn't she told him any of this before now? Confided in him, trusted him . . . reaching across the table, he took her hand and squeezed it firmly.

'Then we'll go home. That's all there is to it. I'll book tickets first thing tomorrow and take you back to Galway for – what? A couple of weeks? A whole month, if we can manage it – Aileen, you should have told me sooner, I had no idea!'

'No' she said, shaking her head, 'you don't understand, Joe. I don't just need a break or a holiday, I need . . . to go . . . for good.'

And there it was, out in the open, confirmation of what they all thought she meant, but hoped she didn't. Round-eyed, Tessie gazed at her daughter. 'But – but Aileen, you have Le Mas to run, your house in Galway is rented out, there's Shona to think of, your family . . . I mean, you're the one who brought them here! Now Finn has a job and a girlfriend, Joe is working, playing on the local *boules* team . . . you can't just keep dragging everyone back and forth like this, it – it's not fair! Not responsible!'

No. It wasn't fair, wasn't responsible. Aileen didn't voice the thought that came to mind, which was that she had given this family the chance it needed, and now she wished with all her heart that it would give her what she needed: the chance to go home, without recrimination, without complaint. Without the argument she could see brewing in their minds, the perplexed rebellion in all three faces. Even in Joe's, try to disguise it as he might.

'Well . . .' Straddling a chair, Finn thought for a moment,

441

looking over her head as if unable to meet her eyes. 'I have to say, Ma, this is a bit of a bolt from the blue. I mean, your business is doing great, Shona's delighted, Gran's enjoying herself, Dad and I have lots of work, there's Martine . . . I have to frankly tell you, I want to stay.'

Yes. She could well understand that. 'But' he continued, 'where? I can't stay at Le Mas, if you're not going to be running it any more. Maybe I could get a flat, maybe Martine and I could move in together – start living in sin?!'

His face brightened; Joe's settled into a kind of murky gloom. Oh, of course he would leave, if that was what Aileen really, badly wanted . . . but what about all his new customers, his burgeoning career as chief handyman and fixer to all of Mézalas? He was actually earning more than before, with the bonus of being his own boss, and Shona was starting to put even more work his way through all these contacts of hers.

What about his new pals, the *boules* team to which he was now committed? What about the great weather, great food? The peaceful rural environment which, now that he'd adjusted to it, suited him down to the ground? All this was to be abandoned, because Aileen Hegarty had taken yet another notion into her whirling head? Ah, no. Ah, here now. I don't mind taking her home for a break, he thought, but I'm not having this, not if there's any possible way out of it. I love her dearly, but . . . is there any way out? Anything I could possibly do or say, to change her mind?

'But, Aileen, we have no home to go to – our tenants have our house until February.'

She nodded. 'I know. But Joe, I'll never last until then. I want to go *now*. Soon. Just as soon as I can find someone to take over Le Mas. Shona's going to murder me, but – well, I can only hope she'll understand, that's all. We knew something like

442

this might happen, she said she'd manage if it did – maybe even bring over someone from Ireland.'

'Like Emily O'Brien' Tessie piped up, unexpectedly. 'If she weren't already busy with the Auberge Rose! I must say, I envy her, staying for the winter – '

There was a sudden, crackling kind of static in the air, as if an electric current were running between them all. And then Finn looked intently, speculatively, at his grandmother.

'Yes . . . Emily is staying, isn't she, Gran?'

In unison, their heads swivelled to him. What had Emily O'Brien got to do with this?

'And you like her, don't you?'

'Yes' Tessie confirmed, nonplussed but adamant, 'I do. We get on like a house on fire.'

Not immediately replying, Finn sat pondering, hammering out the situation in his head, unaware of his father watching him, pinning sudden hope on him, seeing in him not a problem son but a young man who could maybe – incredibly – save his bacon? Once Finn might have shouted, sulked, ranted or raved at his mother for disrupting his life; now he had the adult aura of someone weighing things up from everyone's point of view before voicing his own.

'So . . . if you like her, Gran, how would you feel about joining her?'

Peering at him, Tessie tried hard to pretend she was following this. 'What – where – at the Auberge Rose, do you mean?'

'No. I mean here. At Le Mas. If Mam really wants to go home, then maybe you could take over here – for the winter, for a few months? The Auberge Rose is only twenty miles away, you'd have Emily for company. And me, 'cos if you stayed here then I could too. Then Ma and Dad could stay in

your house in Galway until their own comes free in February
. . . that'd give Mam four months in Ireland.' Swinging round,
he turned to Aileen. 'D'you think four months might be
enough, Ma? A good big fix of your pals and your sister, that
would set you up to come back here next summer?'

Would it? Aileen had no idea. But it was a thought. Could
four months of Ireland satisfy all her physical and spiritual
cravings, pep her up, leave her fighting fit to . . . come back
here, run Le Mas again next year? It would, at the very least,
give her breathing space. Enough time to think, to decide, to
discuss it all with Joe, whose expression was already telling her
that he was clutching at Finn's tentative plan like a drowning
man thrown a rope.

Everything in his body language was begging her to
examine this compromise, accept it if she possibly could – and
he was, after all, her husband. His happiness mattered too.
Looking round the table, she realised that everyone was
holding their breath, willing her to say yes.

Turning to her mother, she searched her face for doubt, but
Tessie looked far more certain than she felt herself. 'Well . . .
it's an idea. I have to admit, Finn, it's a very good idea. But
Mam, what about you? Would you be able to run Le Mas over
the winter, do you think?'

Almost indignantly, Tessie squared her shoulders. 'Of
course I would! Do you think I'm too old, is that what you
mean? Honestly, Aileen! Sixty-five is nothing these days, I'm
fit as a fiddle. I've watched the way you do it – and besides,
things won't be as busy in winter. I'd be well able for it,
especially with Finn here beside me, Emily only down the
road, Shona in her gîte – it'd be brilliant! I'd love it!'

And then Aileen saw something she hadn't seen before: her
mother blossoming, her face opening up, looking as if she'd
been offered something she really wanted. She wanted France,

444

wanted winter sun, and above all wanted a chance to prove that she wasn't old, wasn't 'past it'. Her eager face, abruptly rejuvenated, proclaimed a woman seizing new purpose in life, grasping at new interest and stimulus. With Finn, Shona and Emily around her, she would be safe, Aileen recognised, and might very well be happy. Touched by the thought, Aileen felt her face relaxing into a smile; why should Tessie, so long widowed, not get another chance like the rest of them?

'You're sure? It wouldn't be too much?'

'Aileen, love, it's only dusting and grilling sausages and changing sheets! Not that I mean to belittle your work in any way, but I did raise a family you know, how different can that be to looking after guests? The only difference I can see is that the guests might be grateful once in a while and not squabble like spoilt children.'

Her tone was both arch and vehement, making everyone laugh, easing the tension. 'Well' Aileen conceded, 'I suppose we could give you a trial run! But I have to warn you, Mam, Shona's a slavedriver, sets high standards—'

'High standards' Tessie interrupted primly, 'are exactly what she'll get from me.'

Joe grinned. 'I can vouch for that! You looked after me really well last winter, hot meals, clean shirts, comfy bed . . . Aileen, love, I think your mother would do a great job of running Le Mas.'

She studied his face, and her mother's. 'Yes. I think we can all agree on that, at any rate. Which only leaves you – I'm really sorry, Joe, I know you'd rather stay here and I'm throwing a spanner in the works, but . . . would you absolutely hate spending the winter in Ireland with me?'

She was hugely, almost dizzily relieved when he didn't instantly say he would. Instead, like Finn, he took a moment to think. 'Hate it? Well, I can't honestly say it has me on my feet cheering. But I'm your husband, and I'm informed it's a husband's job to make his wife happy? Admittedly nobody ever mentioned, the day we married, the bit about having to traipse around the world with her . . . but yes, if that's what you want, then that's what we'll do. Ireland it is.'

'What about your job?' Her face and voice were apprehensive. 'Do you think you could go back to the hardware store?'

'No. I'll tell them I'm not coming back, apply for the redundancy scheme and get a bit of money. And then – well, there's not a lot of difference between making shelves for Madame in Mézalas and Missus in Galway, that I can see? Handymen are in demand everywhere.'

Gratefully, sensing his support, she shot him a look that made it all worthwhile: a look that told him she understood that he was making a sacrifice for her. Making it cheerfully, willingly, compromising in the way spouses did when they loved each other. Almost imperceptibly, her hand touched his, her fingers brushed his knuckles, and he felt his chest expand with something that had not been there a year ago. Or maybe it had been there, but it had been dormant: now it was rampant.

Around the table, there was a contemplative silence, in which Aileen surveyed her family, realising with satisfaction that everyone was getting a slice of the invisible cake waiting to be shared between them.

And Ireland! She was going to get a huge slice of it, four whole months, maybe even more, without a fight, without tears or pleas or wrecking anyone's life! She could go home without guilt, talk to Dymps non-stop for weeks and weeks, catch up on all the neighbours, all the craic – and not even have to work! If they lived in Tessie's house, continued to rent out their own, if Joe got a redundancy deal . . . suddenly she was overwhelmed. She had been working so hard, for so long, not only at her B & B but at her wretched, muddled family, which was wretched and muddled no longer. Amidst all four of them, stretching from one corner of their square to the next, she sensed contentment, a united warmth such as she had never felt before.

And they had Finn to thank for it. Hopeless, hapless Finn, sitting here beaming now as if he had just come up with the solution to a United Nations stand-off. Sitting here using his brain like an *adult*. Something caught in her throat.

'Finn' she whispered, 'thank you.'

Had she pinned a medal to his chest, he could hardly have looked more pleased. And then Joe kicked in too, looking at his son with gratitude, and respect, and so many emotions that had never been there before.

'Yes. That goes for me, too, Finn – you've saved my skin! You've found a way to make your mother happy, to let me hope that we'll be back here soon, to stay where you want to be yourself, and you – you've even got your granny off the dole!'

Everyone laughed; and then a thought occurred to Aileen. 'Now let's just hope Shona agrees to all this! We'll have to talk to her, see what she thinks – if we ever see her again, where in God's name has she got to?'

As she spoke their heads swivelled towards the window, four pairs of eyes gazed out at the little gîte, in which Shona seemed to spend less and less time as her life got fuller and fuller. It must be nearly a week, Aileen thought, since I last saw or heard from her. Has she forgotten us altogether, is the Auberge Rose her new baby, just as Luther is Crys Sheehan's new baby?

Maybe it is. Maybe I'd better call Emily and find out what exactly is going on over at that auberge.

And then I'll call the airline!

All the way back to France, Shona sat looking out the window of the plane, running in her mind the video of her visit to Crys. How very beautiful Crys had looked, a newly minted madonna, how rosy and chubby baby Luther had been, how satisfied Gavin had been; theirs was a perfect picture of a happy family.

And yet . . . and yet there had been something very faintly claustrophobic, slightly stifling, in the atmosphere. Perhaps it had just been the heating, raised to botanic temperature because of the baby, or perhaps it had something to do with the bonding that was clearly under way, the evolution of a new, almost hermetically sealed unit? Sitting together on a sofa with the baby between them, Crys and Gavin had exuded an aura of completion, and Shona had sensed that, while her visit had been very welcome, it had not been *necessary*. The three Sheehans were sufficient unto themselves, leaving Shona somehow on the outside, redundant.

Most women, she thought, would give anything to be on the inside. To be the one giving life to a lovely child like Luther . . . but it didn't stir any maternal urge in me. I'm sure the lad will be fun as he grows up, but at the moment it's all a little bit cloying, too sweet for my taste. Especially when I think of all the mental somersaults Crys has had to do to get to where she is now, the adapting and adjusting to a role she started out resisting. Anyone can see that she'll make a great mother – but I know what other great things she might have done too, I know the price she's paid for that child. He's adorable, but I simply couldn't pay that price myself. Which forces me to the conclusion that I don't – definitely do not – want children. There, I've said it, admitted it. In a way it's a relief. Thank God I didn't marry Brendan, who would certainly have wanted at least two if not three. But I love working, love being busy – I'd have made a careless, hopeless mother. Those few days with Crys have shown me for sure that I'm just not cut out for maternity. I recognise the truth, and I don't regret it. The human race will just have to stagger along somehow, without me.

I wonder how Emily and Edouard are staggering along? And Aileen? I'd better go straight to Le Mas, it's been ages since I saw her, the auberge has been eating up so much attention. But it'll be worth it when we have a smashing little hotel full all winter, getting rave reviews – I hope Emily has Edouard under control, isn't letting him near the bookings or money or computer or anything else he might mess up. Honestly, what a man, was ever anyone so unworldly! I'm sure he drove his poor wife half mad, is it any wonder she ran off with someone else, you'd need nerves of steel to live with the likes of that. It would almost be like having a child, a kid who'd get into all sorts of scrapes if you didn't keep him under firm supervision.

'So' Aileen concluded, half adamant, half petrified, 'that's the plan Finn has come up with. He and Mam stay, Joe and I go home . . . for long enough to have a good hard think, anyway. I'm really sorry, Sho. If you're not happy about Tessie running Le Mas, I'll try to help you find someone else.'

She was relieved when Shona shook her head, and failed to reach for the carving knife. 'No. Don't worry, Aileen. I knew you might leave, it was a calculated risk and I wouldn't want you staying on if you weren't happy. I'll have a chat with Tessie and if she can run Le Mas half as well as you've run it, I'd be delighted to have her. Emily will be delighted too, the pair of them can get up to lots of mischief together over the winter. But – what about Joe? How does he feel about going home?'

She was surprised when Aileen beamed, looking gratified almost to the point of smug. 'He feels – well, ambivalent. I think he's plotting for us to come back and spend six months here every year. He doesn't really want to leave, but . . . you know what he said to me, last night, in bed?'

Shona shuddered. 'I hardly dare ask.'

'Well, I asked him if he minded going, and he said yes he did, but he'd go because – you know, like Andie McDowell says in the L'Oréal ad ? – because I'm worth it!'

Aileen's eyes sparkled almost as if she were the actress in question, and Shona spluttered with laughter, thinking that the only one who could outstrip Aileen in self-congratulation at this moment was Crys. Really, what a pair of preening, basking! . . . but they were happy. They were her friends, and she was happy for them, even if their choices would not be her choices. Aileen was looking so radiant, she was moved as she looked at her, realising how soon she would be gone.

'I'm going to miss you, Aileen Hegarty.'

'And I you, Shona Fitzpatrick. You'd better take good care of my mother for me, I'll kill you if you break her or drop her or damage her in any way.'

They both smiled, the sad smile of friends diverging down different paths, and Shona promised to take excellent care of Tessie. Finn, too, and Martine – and who, Aileen wondered silently, is going to take care of you, Sho? H'mm? You might think you don't need caring for, but we all do, in one way or another. I'm going to ring Emily and try to find out whether there's any hope at all for Edouard.

Awestruck, Shona stopped dead when she got out of her car, gaping at the Auberge Rose which, in the mere week of her absence, seemed to have been done over by the festive hand of some flitting fairy. Gone were the heaps of rusty scrap, the broken shutters, the weeds and – above all – the dusty mantle of neglect. Vanished, as if they'd never been; in their place were orderly flowerbeds, matt pink shutters, a velvety lawn and a pond so clear she could see herself in it, gazing fascinated like Narcissus. My God, she thought, Joe and Finn – and Edouard? – must have worked like demons to do all this.

It's like one of those television makeovers with Diarmuid Gavin or Laurence Whatsit . . . except that I thought Joe and Finn and Edouard were all layabouts, not magicians. Wrong, Shona! They must have worked round the clock to do this lot.

Inside, more surprises: Joe Hegarty up on a ladder, doing something to a light fitting; Edouard, kneeling at the top of the stairs he was industriously waxing, and Emily on the phone at the reception desk, taking a dinner booking by the sound of it. She was astonished.

'Crikey, lads, you've been busy!'

Joe grinned down at her. 'Hiya Shona, you're back at last! Good trip?'

'Yes – and this makes my day! I can't believe you've done so much.'

Joe nodded. 'Aye, well, the pressure's on . . . did Aileen tell you . . . ?'

'Yes. She did. You're leaving. I must say, Joe, I'll be very sorry to see you go.'

'Ah, well – never say never. I'm hoping we'll be back in the spring.'

Putting down the phone, Emily bestowed a brief, regal smile on Shona and called up the stairs to Edouard. 'Four for dinner tonight, at eight!' Whereupon Edouard, turning round, catching sight of Shona, leaped to his feet. Racing down the stairs, seizing her by the shoulders, he kissed her repeatedly, with such warmth she felt welcomed home, such speed she was flummoxed. And then he was gone, muttering something about turbot and vegetables. Almost maternally, Emily smiled after him.

'He's leading a double life, these days – handyman by day, chef by night. Working himself to the bone.'

Shona laughed. 'As well he might, high time too! You seem to have galvanised him, Emily.'

'Let's just say that he and I have been hitting it off.' With another, rather enigmatic smile, she jotted something in her notebook, and Shona looked at her curiously, wondering at her complicit aura, as if she had forged some invisible new link with Edouard.

'I see. Got yourself a toyboy, huh?'

Removing her reading glasses, letting them dangle on their cord, Emily surveyed Shona as if she might be not quite the sharpest blade in the box. 'Don't be silly. Edouard will be snapped up by some attractive, appreciative woman of his own age. I'm sure eligible men don't languish any longer in France than they do in Ireland.'

What? Taken aback, Shona stared at her; the idea of Edouard being 'snapped up' by anyone had never crossed her mind. Honestly! Emily should lay off the magazines and get a bit of sense. Who in her right mind would want Edouard Savary, a divorced, distracted disaster?

'By the way' Emily added rather tartly, 'that was your pal Ciara Baker on the phone. Booking a table for herself and her husband, their estate agent and their solicitor. She says their new kitchen isn't fit to cook in yet.'

Bestirring herself – had her mind been wandering there, for a moment? – Shona nodded. 'Too right. The workmen are in, repointing the brickwork . . . it's good of Ciara to give us her business. What's more, her kitchen won't be ready for another six weeks, so I'd better tell Edouard to cook up a storm tonight! If they enjoy their meal, the Bakers could bring us a lot more business.'

'Shona' Emily replied with an air of thinly stretched patience, 'I'm sure Edouard can figure that out for himself. I'm also sure he puts his heart into every meal he cooks. There's no need to go fussing over him as if he were a remedial child.'

*

Looking unusually dismal, not her perky self at all, Aude Villandry sat on the other side of the table from Aileen, toying with a glass of virtually untouched pineau. For a long moment both were silent, and then Aude sighed in a way that said she was starting to recognise defeat.

'It's no good, Haileen, is it? It's just not working. Finn doesn't even see me. He only has eyes for – for that Martine.'

Suppressing a smile, Aileen grimaced sympathetically. It must be galling, when you were as young and pretty and chic and efficient as Aude, to lose your chap to a scruffy urchin like Martine. For just a fleeting moment, something almost like vulnerability whisked across the girl's face, making Aileen feel briefly responsible for her deflated mood.

'I think' she said as gently as she could, 'you might be better off, Aude, looking around for somebody else. I'm sure there are lots of—'

'Others! Hah, that's what I should do, find myself some other guy and flaunt him! Make Finn jealous!'

Her tone was slightly savage, and again Aileen checked a smile. She still had no idea what attracted Aude to Finn; all she knew was that her scarecrow of a son seemed unaccountably popular, with guys and girls alike. But he was mesmerised by Martine. Aude could dance a tango stark naked on this table with Brad Pitt and still not make him jealous.

'So what are you going to do with the tickets?' Aude had come to Le Mas waving tickets for a soccer match, Toulouse v Montpellier, hoping that Finn would be thrilled to take her to it. But he'd simply said sorry, he was busy next Friday night.

Another tragic sigh. 'Tear them up, and then slash my wrists.'

'Oh, don't do that!' They both looked up as Shona arrived, grinning at the tail end of the conversation she'd apparently caught. 'What's wrong, Aude?'

Glumly, Aude pushed the tickets around the table. 'Look,

Shona. Two tickets for the Toulouse–Montpellier match. Most guys would kill for them. But Finn doesn't want to go with me.'

'Really? Well, if that's the case, I'd love to go! I mean, if you don't want to waste them . . . I know I'm not Finn, but I love soccer. Haven't been to a match in ages. And hey, who knows, we might find you some other guy when we get there! God knows, there should be enough of them at a football match.'

Relieved, Aileen nodded. 'That's just what I was trying to tell Aude. Find yourself some other boyfriend. Forget Finn, go out and have a good time with someone else.'

Wavering, looking unconvinced and unenthusiastic, Aude considered. 'Well . . . if you like soccer, Shona, then I suppose we may as well go. I hate it, but who knows – maybe I will find another man, and make Finn sorry.'

Raising her glass, Aileen beamed. 'That's the spirit! Ruin his life! Cheers!'

But the soccer match faded from Shona's mind in the flurry that followed. All too soon now, Aileen would be gone, and Shona stalked her round Le Mas as she emptied wardrobes, packing bags, stripping the house of all her personal effects and Joe's, leaving horribly blank spaces where she had been. Surprised by the extent of the effect Aileen's departure was having on her, Shona leaned against a chest of drawers, plunging her hands glumly into her pockets as she watched a pink linen dress being folded away.

'God, Aileen, this is awful . . . I feel like I'm being abandoned!'

Pausing, Aileen looked up from her overflowing suitcase. 'Now, Sho, don't start going all weepy on me. You'll have Tessie and Emily and Finn and—'

'And Edouard' she almost said, but something stopped her. Shona still didn't seem to see Edouard as a man or even as a friend, only as a part of a project, a pawn on the chessboard of her new career. It was a shame, Emily reported, but so far there had been no progress at all. Indeed it was Emily's view that Shona was annoyingly obtuse, blind to the gem under her nose. A good smack would not go amiss. Nor for Edouard either, now that she thought about it, because since confessing how very keen he was on Shona he had done absolutely nothing further about it.

'I suppose he's shy by nature' Emily conceded, 'and wary after his divorce, and worried that he's not the successful kind of man Shona always went for – but still, Aileen, he's going to have to do *something*. Give her flowers, ask her out somewhere, whatever it is men do these days. I mean, she won't bite him, will she?'

'No' Aileen laughed, 'but if she turned him down, he might be kind of crushed. I mean, he's had so many other failures . . . it could be the last straw.'

'Rubbish' Emily retorted briskly. 'If he's any kind of real man, then it's time he acted like one. I'm sixty years of age and I've had enough of this nonsense, I want Shona settled before I shuffle off this mortal coil . . . and I want a string quartet at the wedding, too, at which I plan to wear a very large blue hat.'

Grinning, Aileen had advised Emily not to hold her breath. It might well be that Shona was wary herself, after all her own disasters, or it might simply be that she was destined to stay single. As Crys Sheehan had once said, maybe she was 'not marriage material'.

Looking at Shona, now, Aileen wondered. There were any number of reasons why Shona and Edouard might remain 'just good friends', if even that. So far, there hadn't been a spark of chemistry between the pair that she knew of. No sparkling eyes, no dewy glow . . . Shona usually just came home whacked from her day's work on the auberge, or with the Bakers, ate dinner at Le Mas and then collapsed asleep in her gîte. Or sometimes Aileen saw a light burning there late at night, signalling that Shona was at her desk, concocting advertising and marketing strategies for both Le Mas and l'Auberge, resolutely burning midnight oil.

It's not right, she thought. It's not balanced. Shona's all work and no play. When I leave she'll have even less fun. It's reaching the point where I'm glad she's even going to that soccer match next week, if only with Aude Villandry.

Oh, for God's sake, Sho, wake up, smell the roses!

And then, inexorably, they were en route to Carcassonne airport: Aileen, Joe, Finn and Shona, who was driving in very thoughtful, almost total silence. A silence that made Aileen feel guilty to be leaving, as well as anxious: Shona would be in charge of everything and everyone now, all on her own. Of course she was well able to run the show – but. Still. Tessie would team up with Emily, Finn would pursue Martine, everyone would have someone except her. Which would make this encroaching winter rather a bleak, barren place. Aileen had a sudden horrific vision of Shona playing solitaire alone in her little gîte, icy rain pouring down outside in the stygian dark.

The airport was busy as Joe and Finn steered the mountain of luggage into it, planting themselves manfully in the check-in queue 'while you girls go have a cup of coffee'. Obediently they went, but when they reached the upstairs restaurant Aileen didn't even try to order the *café crème* that had been such a challenge so long ago; instead she simply said 'champagne' in firm, fluent English.

'I've mastered many things, Sho, but French just wasn't one of them! Now, raise your glass and drink a toast.'

Speculatively, Shona raised it. 'To what – your speedy return to the Languedoc?'

'No. I think that will happen, but it won't be speedy. Not

before next Easter, at least. What I want to drink to is your *happiness* in the Languedoc, Sho. I want you to have a wonderful winter and I want you to be happier than you've ever been before in your whole life.'

'But I am happy. I'm busy, I'm working, I'm earning, I'm run off my feet!'

God, Aileen sighed inwardly, how can someone so bright be so thick? When it comes to herself, she just hasn't a clue. She thinks she's happy, when she's merely – merely marching in step, like I was with Joe, this time last year. I don't want her to feel like that, as if mere survival were enough. I want her to feel like I feel now – alive, Sho, *alive!*

'Look, just drink, okay? Here's to you, Sho – not to your work or any of the many marvellous things you have achieved, but simply to you. I want you to have a wonderful winter and emerge like a chrysalis next spring, butterfly-beautiful.'

Chrysalis? What? Aileen sounded as if she was flying high already, euphoric to be moving home. Dubiously, Shona lifted her glass aloft, clinked it to hers, and drank. '*Vive la France*, and all who sail in her!'

They both laughed, and they both prayed for Joe and Finn to arrive before the tears washed them away on a tide of barely contained emotion. Aileen had to dab discreetly at her eyes, but Shona remained stalwart until, twenty minutes later, she stood waiting with Finn, stoically watching the plane take off. And then it hit her.

Agog, Finn gazed at her as she uttered a kind of strangled sob, flicking her hand across her face so fast he wondered if he'd actually seen the wet gleam on it. Steely Shona, sobbing? Surely not. 'Hey' he said, surprising them both by slipping an arm around her shoulder, 'take it easy, Sho. Ma's not going to the moon. She said she'll ring us tonight. You can still talk to her whenever you want.'

Nodding vaguely, Shona tried to compose herself, and failed entirely. Instead she leaned into Finn's slogan-spattered chest, and appalled herself by weeping all over it, until he ludicrously found himself embracing her, comforting her as if she were the lost child that he himself had been until . . . until Martine.

The soccer match was mobbed, and Aude was appalled to discover that the tickets were standing-room only, not an attractive prospect for someone wearing two-inch heels. Plus, her greige linen jacket would be ruined in this crush – dubiously, she eyed Shona, who was cosily kitted out in an apricot-coloured sweater, cropped trousers and a rosy woollen scarf. Comfy flat shoes, too. Not a chic outfit, perhaps, but undeniably suited to the occasion. You could, Aude supposed with a shrug, get away with gear like that when you were thirty-six, beyond all hope of attracting male attention.

Whereas, at twenty-three, your purpose was to seduce, ensnare . . . and show Finn Hegarty just how many more fish there were in the sea.

'So' she said, turning to Shona, 'which team is which?'

Startled, Shona laughed. 'Oh, Aude! Toulouse is in mauve, Montpellier in orange, what kind of Frenchwoman are you? Which one are you cheering for?'

'Whichever wins' Aude replied without a blink, and Shona saw something in her at that moment, a steeliness that suggested the players would not be the only ones aiming to score. Personally she was far more interested in the match, it was ages since she had been to one and already the rooting, tooting atmosphere was infectious. Taking her mind off work, off Aileen's departure, lifting her spirits with their good-natured, boisterous chanting, the French supporters showed no inclination to violence or hooliganism.

A coin was flipped, the match kicked off and a cheer went

up. Keenly, leaning forward in unison with all the fans, she began to follow the action, interested at first and then absorbed, enjoying the fast clean play, the verve of players as balletic as they were skilful, remarkably graceful given their muscle . . . forgetting Aude, she got thoroughly immersed, supporting Toulouse just for the fun of taking sides. Alternatively clapping, laughing, shouting, she got more and more into the game, leaving Aude to study the male supporters, covertly check them over for looks, style and wedding rings.

'Wey hey!' she grinned at half time, flushed with excitement. 'This is fun!'

'Yes' conceded Aude, having scarcely even glimpsed the ball, 'and now, Shona, let us go to the bar for some beer.'

'Beer?' Shona couldn't hide her amusement. 'Wouldn't a cocktail be more your style, or designer water?' But even as she said it she saw Aude's motive: she wanted to meet men.

'Yes, well' said Aude defensively, 'I want to sit down for a minute, my feet are killing me.' So they made their way to the drinks area, where being French the barmen were also char-grilling merguez sausages in an enticing aromatic haze, and despite her heels Aude dived in amongst the milling supporters, smiling sweetly as she carved her path to the bar. Fascinated, Shona thought it was like watching the Red Sea parting, the men gallantly making room for the pretty little thing. Securing two seats, she sat down to wait.

And then Aude was weaving her way back, carefully carry-ing two plastic goblets of beer, intently not spilling a drop on her jacket or dress. Which made it such a shame when, just as she reached Shona, she collided with a tall exuberant man, and the beer went flying in all directions.

'Oh! Oh, mademoiselle, my apologies, I am so sorry – let me –' Reaching for a paper napkin, the man began to swipe and dab at her, and Shona suddenly frowned. Amongst the throng the man was almost invisible, she could only see the top of his head and one flailing hand, but – but didn't she recognise that voice ?

Yes. She did. It was Edouard, and he was patting at Aude as if at a fluffy little Peke, mopping in a flurry of apology, and a bit of a rush too, as if he didn't want to miss the rest of the match. Beside him, some other man was glancing at his watch, plucking urgently at him. And then Edouard, possibly following Aude's line of vision, turned round and saw Shona, his face detonating with delight.

'*Mais* – Shona! I didn't know you were a football fan!'

'I love it' she said, standing up, wondering whether he knew Aude, had the two ever actually met? Not that she knew of, so she'd better introduce them. 'Aude, this is Edouard Savary – Edouard, Aude Villandry.'

Hands were shaken, and in turn Edouard introduced his companion, a darker, shorter lookalike who turned out to be his brother Frédéric, and then they all gazed at Aude's beer-stained ensemble.

'I am so sorry' Edouard said in consternation, 'perhaps after the match you would let me buy you more drinks to apologise?'

Shona lifted a hand, as if to say it didn't matter, and the hand froze in mid-air as Aude, looking up at him, smiled her widest, sweetest, most utterly charming smile. 'That' she cooed, 'would be lovely.'

Eh? Astonished, Shona found herself somehow propelled back to the pitch by the brother, while Edouard steered Aude solicitously, his hand protectively on her shoulder, lest any of these big rough fans should hustle the fragile, fragrant little lady. Well, she thought as they regained their places, the Savary brothers still at their sides, play me for a piano. Aude Villandry is making *eyes* at Edouard Savary – and he, thirteen years older than her, is tucking her under his wing as if she were the prettiest little poodle? Honestly – *men*!

But then, men are what she wants, *n'est-ce pas?* That's the only reason she's here. To meet a man. For God's sake, could she not go for the brother? This Frédéric guy? No, of course she couldn't, because she's already seen what I'm only seeing now, his wedding ring. Frédéric is *hors de combat*, whereas Edouard is . . . single. Available. Eligible, as Emily says. And looking entirely enchanted by Aude Flirty-Cutesy Villandry.

A whistle blew, the match resumed and, as abruptly as if a light had been snapped off, Shona's interest in it vanished. All she could see, in her peripheral line of vision, was Edouard cheering on his team, beaming down at Aude when Toulouse scored, and Aude sort of snuggling up to him, as if to convey how agreeable it was to be enjoying the match alongside this new-found companion. While she, Shona Fitzpatrick, was left in possession of the runner's-up prize, the married brother.

Well, she fumed, see if I care! I'm not here to pick up men, I'm here to watch football! Drawing herself up, taking a deep breath, she emitted a loud yell of encouragement as Toulouse gained possession of the ball again, and was conscious of Edouard glancing curiously at her.

Yes, Edouard, that's right – football! I've been a fan for years, I even played for a women's team in Ireland, so there! Whereas Aude Villandry wouldn't know a football from a flapjack . . . she's way too young for you, and if you're twit enough to fall for her you'll tire of her in no time. Assuming you could possibly be interested in her in the first place – it's all pack- aging, you know, surely you're not shallow enough to be seduced by a silly outfit and a whiff of Chanel? Really, I'd have given you credit for better taste. Even Finn Hegarty wasn't fooled by a wisp of chiffon and a glossy lipstick.

Toulouse scored, and the crowd roared, and Shona roared

with it, her face flaming, fists clenching, eyes firmly fixed on the pitch.

They went to a bar afterwards, where Edouard did indeed buy drinks for everyone, and Shona was horrified by the slowly welling wave of rage that rose in her as Aude flirted shamelessly with him. Not that it had anything to do with her, of course, she simply couldn't believe that Aude could so speedily latch on to such a considerably older man, that was all. Nor could she believe the way Edouard was responding, touching her hand as he put a glass into it, sitting wedged beside her, actually laughing at some feeble joke she was telling – hah! Aude had about three jokes in her entire repertoire, Shona knew, and told the same three all the time. As you may find to your cost, Edouard, humour is not Mlle Villandry's strong suit. Don't say I didn't warn you.

What? Frédéric was saying something to her, and she had to force herself to listen, relying on her old welcome-to-Galway smile to carry her through while her mind ricocheted round in all directions, seething with curiosity – could Edouard really fancy that little stalagmite? – and some sensation she absolutely refused to recognise as pique. Plain, old-fashioned, pig's-eye pique. Which practically rocketed off the scale when, at the end of an apparently most enjoyable evening, Edouard stood up, put a hand on Aude's shoulder and kissed her cheek. Not four times, not twice . . . just once, gently, delicately.

'I hope, mademoiselle' he purred in a voice Shona scarcely recognised, 'we will have the pleasure of meeting again.'

Demurely Aude nodded, and then Edouard turned politely to Shona, took her hand and – and shook it, as if concluding a business meeting. 'Good night, Shona. It was nice to meet you, I'm glad you enjoyed the match.'

With which, grasping Frédéric, he was gone, Toulouse supporter's scarf flying behind him. Stupefied, Shona followed his departing back out of the bar, speechless.

It was nice to meet her, he said? *Nice?!?*

'Well' Aude smirked with huge satisfaction, 'I must say, Shona, I've had a lovely time. Haven't you?'

With frosty dignity, and enormous difficulty, Shona muttered that she had. Only one thing could possibly complete her joy, and that would be to kick Aude Villandry's racehorse little shins until they were black and bloody blue.

Tessie, on hearing the tale, was neither sympathetic nor optimistic. 'But Shona, I had no idea you were interested in this man.'

'I'm not remotely interested' Shona growled, 'I'm just outraged, that's all . . . you should have seen the carry-on of the pair of them. All over each other like a rash.'

'Well' said Tessie sagely, 'what's wrong with that? They're both free, aren't they? No impediments, as dear old Father McDonagh used to say, to this union of souls? I can't see what you're so fussed about.'

Huh. A fat lot of good Tessie was turning out to be. And how to suss Emily's opinion, without going over to the Auberge Rose, which was now to be avoided like the plague? Next day, Shona telephoned her, telling the details as if in passing, in the detached tone of one who couldn't care less about anything other than Edouard's shocking lapse of taste.

'I see' Emily murmured conspiratorially, lest Edouard be within earshot, 'you've blown it, then, have you?'

'Blown *what*?' Shona erupted, exasperated by both old biddies, who seemed to think she had some kind of personal stake in all this.

'Oh, nothing' Emily said soothingly, 'just the chance of a

messed-up, divorced, financially muddled man who drives a crocked old Citroën and doesn't, to my knowledge, even own an Armani suit. The kind of man you wouldn't touch with a bargepole.'

'Emily' Shona retorted shortly, 'I have an appointment with the Bakers' builder. I have to go now. Why don't you go back to your Prozac or Pernod or whatever it is you're on.'

All night, for several nights, Shona tossed and turned, unable to sleep, abandoning the attempt, getting up to work at her desk, abandoning that in turn, sitting at her desk in her pyjamas at three in the morning, staring at the memo-peppered wall. Floating in and out amongst the memos she kept seeing a blurred image of Edouard, smiling at Aude, kissing Aude's cheek – what in God's name was wrong with her? Why should she care? What did it matter who Edouard kissed?

Tessie was nuts. Completely daffy, always had been. As for Emily – she was losing it altogether. Alzheimer's, both of them, or whatever it was that afflicted people in their sixties with nonsensical delusions. She, Shona Fitzpatrick, was not remotely attracted to Edouard Savary, had given neither of them any basis whatsoever for such bizarre comments.

Had she? Was she? No. Okay – so he had been lively and animated at the match, carefree and quite different to her tragic 'project', no longer looking like a man in need of rescue. So, she had been peeved by his attention to Aude. So, he could turn on the Gallic charm. So, the cold night had caused his face to flush and his eyes to shine. So what?

So you'd better get your ass in gear, Shona Fitzpatrick, before Aude mops the floor with you.

He hasn't a bean. He works hard, he's a wonderful cook, he's a warm, friendly man. Those blue eyes of his are admittedly kind of sexy. And anyone who can laugh at Aude's pathetic little jokes has to have a sense of humour, as well as a kind heart. But he just isn't my kind of guy.

So who is, then? Are you waiting for Matt Damon to go down on his knees and beg?

The others were my kind of guy. Brendan Wright, and his dozen predecessors. They all had proper jobs, steady incomes, social status, nice cars, good suits and good prospects. They were all perfect, and it's not my fault that—

Shona, for a smart lady, you are being dense as a fog. Edouard Savary is a lovely guy and suddenly there's competition for him and, if you do not want to miss this last bus, you are going to have to chase after it. As fast as your legs can carry you.

But I chased before, didn't I? Without being obvious, I did my best, and all I ever got was hurt. I don't want to get hurt again, I can't take any more pain, or disappointment, or rejection.

Fine, so. You can watch Aude Villandry waltzing off with Edouard Savary and feel no pain at all. Watch from the sidelines, while she scores.

Shona. Listen up. You are thirty-six years old and you are pitted against a very attractive, very determined youngster of twenty-three. She will hypnotise him, and invite you to their wedding. Which you will attend all on your own.

Is that what you want? Or is Edouard Savary what you want?

The evenings were shortening rapidly now, cooling and crisping, the air wafting the first earthy scents of truffles and wood fires. Sweaters knotted around their shoulders, a dozen guests were at the *digestif* stage of tonight's meal, lifting aloft glasses of cognac the better to admire its amber tones in the firelight. They had, Edouard thought, the happily replete look of gourmands thoroughly savouring the afterglow of the meal he had cooked them, a rich winter menu featuring foie gras, mushrooms and pork with pungent onions. Catching Emily's eye, he smiled and nodded, sensing her pleasure, her satisfaction in his performance. Business was definitely, dramatically, looking up. Suffused with a sudden glow of achievement, he finished his rounds of the tables, removed his toque and apron, and surprised himself by sitting down at the piano in the corner, idly tinkling a few keys.

'Can you play?' Ciara Baker enquired from her table – the one at which she ate at least twice a week now, sometimes with her husband, sometimes with their new French friends.

'Yes. I like to play. But only for those who wish to hear me?' He didn't want to disturb their evening. But everyone looked round eagerly, apparently in favour. Including Aude Villandry, seated at a corner table with a girlfriend.

'D'you know anything jolly?' a hearty British voice asked, "My Old Man's a Dustman" or "Singing in the Rain" or anything like that?'

'No' Edouard admitted laughing, 'but I know Crocodile Rock?'

'That'll do!'

And so he started to play, diffidently at first, until he discovered that everyone knew the song, even the party of four game hunters from Pézanas joining in the chorus, fudging the words and laughing at their own gruff voices. Gaining confidence, he began to play louder, more energetically, and Emily sneaked in from reception to enjoy the fun as one song led to another, everyone clapping and stamping, having an impromptu, terrific time. Including Aude, she noted, whose admiring eyes never left Edouard's face, in profile not five yards from her own.

Well, Emily thought, to the victor the spoils. Aude is prepared to fight for Edouard, and it looks as if she might well get him. It's a crying shame, but it will serve Shona right. She hasn't made the slightest effort, none at all.

They were raising the rafters, halfway through Neil Diamond's Sweet Caroline when the auberge's front door suddenly flew open, and Emily jumped to her feet; she hadn't been expecting anyone else to arrive this late. But before she could reach her desk a lone body bolted past her, into the hall and through the restaurant at whirlwind speed, heading for Edouard at his piano. Such was its flurry she could scarcely be sure, but the blur looked very like Shona, was wearing Shona's rose-red scarf at any rate, Shona's chestnut hair flying in its wake.

Astonished, Emily watched as it shot up to Edouard and clamped its hand on his shoulder, whereupon he whirled round to stare up at the abrupt, panting vision.

'Shona!'

'Sorry' she said, sweeping her other hand around the room to encompass general apology, 'to interrupt your party. But – Edouard – I must speak to you.'

'Aw' groaned a voice, 'leave him alone, lady. We're having fun here.'

'I can see that' she conceded, 'but it's urgent. It – Edouard – I – '

Suddenly she was lost for words, unnerved by the accusing gaze of far more people than she'd bargained for, in this unexpectedly lively mood. As Edouard stood up, it struck her that she'd never heard him play the piano like this, never heard him sing either, in such an energetic tenor, hugely enjoying himself by the look of his flushed face and broad smile. As Aude Villandry was apparently enjoying herself, too.

'What is it, Shona? What is wrong?'

His tone was full of concern, naturally he assumed something must be wrong. Normally you'd scarcely catch a mouse abroad after eleven o'clock at night in France, never mind women bursting into restaurants to hijack the chef at gale

467

force. Flushing furiously, she registered fourteen pairs of eyes on her, waiting for explanation.

'Nothing is wrong' she hissed at him, ignoring Aude as if she were invisible, 'only – it's just that – oh, Edouard! I have to talk to you – now, in private! It's *important*!'

Briefly, as if sizing her up, he surveyed her. And then he held up both hands, in surrender and in apology. '*Mesdames, messieurs*, please excuse me. It seems I have a damsel in distress here, I must attend to her!'

Muttering, they all watched crestfallen as he followed Shona, weaving through their tables, out of the room. But not fast enough, apparently, because she turned back to seize his hand, and drag him after her so fast his feet scarcely touched the floor.

Only Emily saw the expression on Aude's face, and the expression on Edouard's too. One filling with dismay, one glowing with delight, the delight of a strategist whose plans were working like magic.

EPILOGUE

Six months later, just before Easter, Emily and Tessie met for lunch in a smart new Galway bistro. Very trendy, it was aimed at a young crowd, but that didn't deter them in the least, since they both felt so very rejuvenated.

'Well' Emily breathed as the waiter handed her a menu marginally smaller than the table, 'I must say, Tess, it's a great relief. I was afraid I was never going to get my string quartet, nor to wear my big blue hat either.'

'No, it was looking dodgy, for a while! But what is it they say these days? Never say never? I didn't think I was going to get my limousine ride either. But I did. Just last Sunday. Aileen hired a huge white one before she left for France, to drive herself and myself to Ashford Castle for a beauty treatment. Just the two of us – she wanted to thank me for running Le Mas all winter for her. As if it took much effort! I don't know when I last enjoyed anything so much. And now we have this wedding to look forward to next. A big traditional white one too – who'd have believed it?'

Emily paused to study the wine list. Oh, nostalgia! It almost brought tears to her eyes to propose a Languedoc red, and Tessie came over all misty too when she saw its name: Domaine du Mariage. She knew the very vineyard, had been to it one scorching day last summer with Joe and Aileen. When the bottle arrived they raised their glasses, and solemnly chinked them.

'*Sláinte*' said Emily.

'And health to the happy couple' added Tessie, and they savoured the first mouthful in blissful silence before getting down to important things. Like the bride and groom.

'What's she going to wear?' Tessie wondered aloud.

'I hear it's slinky' Emily confided, 'slashed right down the back, down one leg too, very daring. But then of course she has the figure for it. And it has long sleeves. She'll want those in autumn. No veil, apparently, just a silver comb in her hair, and no bouquet either, only one tall, dramatic fresh flower.'

Dreamily, they pondered this vision for a moment, before all the other details crowded into their minds. A honeymoon in Italy, a six-course champagne meal for almost a hundred guests . . . 'But then, of course, her parents are very wealthy' Tessie acknowledged, 'can you imagine giving them all that, *and* an apartment, to start them off?'

'I believe it's only a little apartment' Emily confided, 'just two-bedroom, on the top floor of an old house in Pézanas. But still, that should be enough, since there won't be any children to think about. Not for years yet, anyway.'

'I should hope not' said Tessie, firmly, 'Martine will barely be twenty by the time she gets married, and Finn won't even be twenty-two. I'm sure they wouldn't be marrying yet at all if she weren't an only daughter, and her parents didn't so much want to give her this wonderful wedding. But I must say I'm glad, because I didn't much care for the idea of Finn living in sin. He is my grandson, after all.'

Yes, Emily conceded, Finn was, and how amazingly he was turning out! He had had no idea that Martine's family was so extraordinarily well upholstered, and had laughed his socks off when he found out, hilarity had been unconfined. But, he'd said when he sobered up, that didn't mean that he'd be packing in his roofing job, which he loved, nor would Martine be giving up her sculpting to have any babies.

'Not for years, Grandma. We'd be happy to just live together only Martine's parents are so eager to throw this wedding for us, it seems kinda churlish to refuse – plus, I need a wedding ring. A big thick solid one, to keep Aude Villandry at bay!' Tessie smiled fondly as she recalled Finn's sheepish explanation for 'getting mixed up', as he put it, in this classic, luxurious, oh-so-bourgeois wedding. But Maman and Papa wanted their Martine to marry her 'lovely, sooo promising' boyfriend, and Martine wanted to make them happy, and Finn wanted to make Martine happy, and so the priest, the florist, the caterer and the musicians were all on red alert. Not to mention Joe and Aileen, who were in shock, Joe's jaw all but scraping the floor. Aileen said she was starting to adjust, but Joe was still speechless at the idea of their son becoming a scion of French plutocracy.

'It's just a shame' Emily lamented over her turbot – which wasn't a patch on Edouard's – 'that Shona Fitzpatrick wouldn't take a leaf out of Finn Hegarty's book, and get married as well. They could have a double ceremony.'

'Ah, no' Emily shook her head, 'I don't think there's any hope of that, Tess. No wedding, she says, no way.'

'No. Funny, isn't it? I don't understand these young women these days at all. It's a miracle Finn has managed to get one of the few reasonable ones left – one who's happy to marry the man she loves, anyway. Whereas Shona . . . I mean . . . . *shacked up*? What kind of carry-on is that?'

Emily pondered. Really the chef here had a few things to learn. If it weren't for the wine . . . sipping it, she reflected. 'Well . . . at first I was so put out. They don't want children and he's already been divorced, so they can't see any point in marriage.

But now I have to admit, Tess, they are having a lovely time living in sin! They look so happy, so in tune that anyone can see they're already married in all the ways that matter, in body and in soul. She's absolutely blooming and he looks as if he's won the lottery.'

Thoughtfully, Tessie mulled on that. 'Mmm. It has to be admitted, Emily, he played things very cleverly. When she rang me that time in a panic about Aude Villandry, I assumed Edouard actually had taken a shine to her. After all, Aude's so young and pretty – Shona was distraught!'

'I was too' Emily admitted. 'It never entered my head that making Shona jealous would be Edouard's way of courting her. It was so astute of him, it leads me to think that he reads her very well, understands her in a way that is likely to endure. Ever since they've been together he's let her take centre stage, take all credit too – as you know, the auberge was doing great business by the time I left, and is now absolutely flourishing with her at the helm. He just smiles and gets on with his cooking, takes her to football matches and sometimes plays his piano, while she does all the administration. And bossing-around, of course, which keeps him on his toes. I don't think the Auberge Rose will ever go into another decline, nor Edouard either.'

'Still' Tessie smiled wistfully, 'it's a pity she wouldn't give us a day out. Even if it were only a small wedding, just a little one for form's sake?'

'Tessie' Emily admonished, 'she's delirious with joy. Edouard is ecstatic. Should we not just be happy for them? I mean, nobody can have it all, can they?'

Tessie thought about it. And then beamed at Emily, conspiratorially. 'You're right, Emily. Wanting it all would be greedy. Every one of us got another chance, and that should be enough for us. Apart from Aude, who I suspect will live to fight another day! You, me, Finn, Shona, Edouard, Aileen and Joe . . . I hear that even Crys Sheehan is loving being a mother. We've been so lucky, and should be so grateful.'

Fleetingly, Emily had a vision of Edouard's twinkling eyes as Shona dragged him off to his 'doom', as she'd later called it, doubled with laughter. 'Yes. You're so right, Tess. Let's be very grateful – and let's have another glass of wine?'

'*Oui*' said Tessie without hesitation. 'That nice man who makes it says it's marvellous for the heart.'